MA[...]

Liz Young started wri[...]cluded being part of an ai[...]for TV commercials in Cyprus and working for the [...]s Armed Forces in Oman. She lives in Surrey. *Making Mischief* is her fourth novel.

Liz Young welcomes visitors to her website
www.liz-young.com

Praise for Liz Young

'Perfect comic timing and wickedly funny moments'
Cosmopolitan

'Feel-good romance' *Marie Claire*

'A lively Lisa Jewell-esque novel with a bit more bite
than you might imagine' *Daily Mirror*

'A jolly read' *Woman's Own*

'Offers plenty of funny moments – so enjoy it, with
a furry friend at your side' *Red*

'A warm, sunny read that is as astute as it is humorous'
Good Housekeeping

MAKING MISCHIEF

Liz Young

arrow books

Published by Arrow Books in 2004

1 3 5 7 9 10 8 6 4 2

Copyright © Liz Young 2004

First published in the United Kingdom in 2004 by Arrow Books

Arrow Books
The Random House Group Limited,
20 Vauxhall Bridge Road, London SW1V 2SA

Random House Australia (Pty) Limited
20 Alfred Street, Milsons Point, Sydney,
New South Wales 2061, Australia

Random House New Zealand Limited
18 Poland Road, Glenfield,
Auckland 10, New Zealand

Random House (Pty) Limited
Endulini, 5a Jubilee Road, Parktown 2193, South Africa

The Random House Group Limited Reg. No. 954009

www.randomhouse.co.uk

A CIP catalogue record for this book is available from the British Library

Papers used by The Random House Group are natural, recyclable
products made from wood grown in sustainable forests; the manufacturing
processes conform to the environmental regulations of the country of origin

ISBN 0 09 946036 X

Typeset in AGaramond by Palimpsest Book Production Limited,
Polmont, Stirlingshire
Printed and bound in Great Britain by
Cox & Wyman Ltd, Reading, Berkshire

For the Tree Frog Singers and their backing group, Wavelets On The Sand. I wish I had a CD of them, too.

But mostly for Andrew, with love.

With many thanks to Sarah at A M Heath,
and Georgina and Susan at Arrow.

One

Given what it sparked off later, that day should have come with a health warning. I could have done with one of those wizened crones they had back in the olden days, peering at entrails and muttering, 'Take care, dearie. August be a wicked month. I see water. I see goings-on, and hot gossip. 'Twill all turn into a proper dog's breakfast one day, just when you be a-falling in love.'

But all I got by way of portents was Rachel's zits.

Sixteen and a half at the time, during a late summer heatwave, I was spending a few days at my cousins' house, near Brighton. The beach would have been enough of a draw but the main reason I'd come was my cousin Rachel's sixteenth birthday. Her folks were not only providing a big party, they were also clearing off for the entire night. You'd think Rachel might be buzzing about this, but no. Early on the day before she was crying that she might as well be dead, would I just *look* at these spots?

'Two more!' she said tearfully, peering at them in the bedroom mirror. 'And I haven't touched any chips or chocolate for weeks!'

'You'd hardly notice them,' I soothed, which wasn't precisely true, but what could you say? I felt bad for having only one minute zit I could cover with my fringe, especially when I devoured junk like a gannet.

1

'They're *huge*,' she despaired. 'I wish I could have a face transplant for my birthday.'

'You look fine,' I soothed. 'Just stick some concealer on.'

'Yes, but it doesn't conceal, does it? It just looks like spots with gunge on. Who's ever going to fancy me in my whole entire life when I look like this?'

Rachel was at the stage of hating everything about herself: hair (yuck), face (round and pink and gross), figure (fat and disgusting and gross), legs (stumpy and gross). Like an anorexic who looks in the mirror and sees Fat, Rachel looked at Perfectly Attractive Nearly Sixteen and saw Hideous.

'Nobody's going to notice them except you,' I said. It was a strain sometimes, being a mature sixteen and a half who hadn't hated absolutely everything about herself for at least three months.

'Abby, please! You sound just like Mum!' Rachel turned her wide green eyes back to the mirror and despaired. 'And Guy's probably coming round later, and I know he's going to think I look like a pizza – I might as well kill myself now.'

I knew Guy was probably coming round later – she must have told me twice in the past five minutes. I'd never met him, but as he'd apparently lived three doors away for ever, I'd heard him mentioned now and then.

But not like this. My antennae were perking up fast. 'Do you fancy him, then?'

Rachel's face turned into a cocktail of anguish and that imploring-for-secrecy look. 'Oh, Abby! I'm madly in love with him, but *please* don't tell Lindsay. Only Cara knows, and she'll never breathe a word.'

Cara was her best friend, who also lived close by. I'd met her a few times over the years, and until then I'd neither particularly liked nor disliked her. At that moment, though, it occurred to me that Cara wasn't the type I'd trust with my secret passion. I saw her smiling as she whispered it to somebody else during maths, and the next thing you knew, you might as well have put it in the *News of the World*.

Lindsay, to whom I promised to breathe no words, was Rachel's elder sister. Then seventeen and at the heady stage of learning to drive, she was eleven months my senior. And, as it turned out, Lindsay had sussed out Rachel's little passion already. She volunteered the information right after breakfast.

The sisters were not at all alike. Where Rachel had brown hair with a hint of chestnut and big green eyes, Lindsay took after her mother. Tall and hyper-slim, she had Auntie Rosemary's corn-gold hair and blue eyes.

'Only don't dare ever tell her I told you,' she said. 'She'd be hideously embarrassed – she's known him since she was about four. If you ask me it's ever since she fell over at the tennis club a couple of weeks ago and he helped her wash the grit out.' She put on a breathy, heart-fluttery voice. '"And as his strong brown fingers gently sloshed her knee with Dettol . . ."'

Under a guilty little laugh I was empathising all too well. 'I once had a massive crush on a friend of Andrew's who called me Squirt.'

Andrew was my elder brother.

Lindsay laughed. 'Don't you ever tell him, but I once had a massive crush on *Andrew*. Still, I was only about thirteen at the time.'

'I was fourteen. I'd only just had my ears pierced.'

We laughed together. What a relief it was to be past that embarrassing stage when you still hadn't even had a snog, let alone a boyfriend.

'Anyway, it's hopeless,' Lindsay went on. 'She's just "Rachel down the road" to Guy, I'm afraid.'

'Has he got a girlfriend, then?'

'Abby, Guy doesn't really have girlfriends. He just has *girls*.'

Huh, I thought. Just like Gary Davis at home, I bet. Gary fancied himself something rotten. 'So *is* he coming round this afternoon?' I asked.

'Probably. We can play semi-mixed doubles and I'm telling you now, you'd better watch out for his lethal backhand volley.'

Better not mess up then, I thought. While I was a passable player on school courts, Mum didn't run to tennis clubs. I didn't want some Gary Davis type yelling, 'Rubbish!' and making me feel an idiot. I could bet he'd expect me to be impressed, too. He'd expect me to go all so-called subtly flirty and flick my hair, like even my best friend Emma did around Gary Davis. Well, he had another think.

As you will gather, there was a tennis court in the garden. My aunt and uncle were what my mother called 'very comfortable' and had a house to match. I didn't particularly envy Rachel and Lindsay the sports facilities, but it was hard not to covet their assorted bathrooms, one of which was Lindsay and Rachel's own. We had one and a half, and I had two brothers who delighted in filling them with noxious stinks and not opening the window on purpose.

Besides the tennis court, you could also have put in a swimming pool without losing a great percentage of lawn. Only the previous evening Lindsay and Rachel and been wailing to Uncle Matthew that if he'd only listened to them last year and put a pool in, they wouldn't be melting like lollies in the sun.

'What's wrong with that damn great pool down the road?' he'd asked. 'It's called the beach, in case you've forgotten.'

4

Yes, but that meant walking to the bus stop when it was *bak*ing, and waiting for a bus when it was *bak*ing, he was a tight old skinflint and by the way could they have ten pounds for going out? No, not between us, Dad! Each! Can you give us a lift into town, too?

Uncle Matthew was a cuddly old softie. Sometimes I envied them him, too, and not just because of the tenners. He was always there, which was more than you could say for my dad. He and Mum had finally split up when I was thirteen. Although we saw Dad regularly, it wasn't the same. Not that my folks had ever enjoyed the kind of cosy-certainty relationship I saw between Lindsay and Rachel's. Not since I was little, anyway. The six-year itch, Mum had called it: '. . . and I'm beginning to think he'll still be scratching when he's ninety-three.'

On the hottest day so far, Guy came round in the early afternoon. Psyched up to be casually unimpressed, I was perversely irritated when he was nothing like I'd expected and clearly wouldn't care how unimpressed I was, casually or otherwise.

I don't know what I *had* expected – probably some sleek, dark, thrilled-with-himself type – but he certainly wasn't it. Wearing just shades and faded old shorts, he had that chilled, beach-bum look I knew so well from *Home and Away*.

'Hi, Abby, I think I've heard about you,' he said. 'You're the London one.'

'I just wish it *was* London,' I said, which was not the kind of casually unimpressed remark I'd intended. 'It's out in the boring, suburban sticks.'

'Near enough. Lindsay, you can forget tennis, I didn't get to bed till four. Any chance of one of your old man's beers?'

While Rachel shot off to get one, he flopped on to the dry grass.

Lindsay said, 'You lazy arse. Still, I suppose it is a bit hot for bashing fuzzy balls about.'

Cara said, 'Not to mention a total waste of tanning time.' Having said that, she stripped off everything but a minute pair of bikini bottoms, and lay face up on a striped sun lounger.

I despised myself for being privately gobsmacked by this. She was so casual about it, which had to make me terribly un-cool for realising I wouldn't quite dare. Or at least, I'd feel horribly self-conscious. Nobody else turned a hair, though, least of all Guy. Still, why would he? He must have known her as long as he'd known Rachel. They'd all grown up within a few doors of each other. And as Cara's perfect, hemispherical breasts were as golden as the rest of her, she evidently did it on a regular basis.

Ironically, because it had nothing to do with taking her top off, this was when I became aware of something about Cara I hadn't consciously noticed until then. It wasn't that she was drop-dead gorgeous, although her amber eyes and honey-tawny hair would have made anybody look twice. I probably couldn't have found the precise words then, but she possessed that effortless, magnetic sensuality either you've got or you haven't. It had nothing to do with clothes or make-up, or how much you spent at the hairdresser's.

Just as well Cara's got a boyfriend, I thought. Although Rachel was the last person to be jealous of a friend who went right back to their mother's antenatal classes, going out in a pull-pair with Cara on a Saturday night wouldn't do much for her precarious confidence. Did she feel wistfully left out because Cara had Tim? I wondered. Another *Home and Away* lookalike, I'd met him the previous day on the packed beach, where he was hiring out deckchairs.

And I'd thought: Hmm, wouldn't say no myself.

Instead of tennis, we lounged on the parched lawn. While the rest of them talked things and people I hadn't a clue about, I lay on my towel with Albert Camus' *La Peste*. I'd brought it because our French teacher had said the A-level set should make a start on it during the holidays.

Actually, that wasn't the sole reason. I'd thought *La Peste* would make me look intelligent on the journey down. Maybe even French and intelligent, which would be better still. This plan was seriously flawed, I realised, after trying for ten minutes to make sense of page one on a hot, crowded train. What if anyone daft enough to be fooled suddenly addressed me in Gallic torrents and I had to say, 'Er, *pardon?*'

Still, there was no danger of that here. Pretending to be engrossed despite the hazy heat I waited for Guy to say, 'What's that you're reading?' Then I'd say casually, 'Albert Camus' *La Peste*.' I'd pronounce it 'Al*bare*' in the accent that had just helped me get an A grade at GSCE. I wouldn't even look up as I said it; I'd be too intelligently engrossed.

Ostensibly absorbed in a tale of Algerian plague, I glanced up now and then through my sunglasses. 'Abby's so *brown*,' said Rachel despairingly, slapping on Hawaiian Tropic. 'It's enough to make you sick.'

While Lindsay and Rachel were both relatively fair-skinned, I only had to look at the sun to go like a Coppertone ad. 'That's because I'm a throwback,' I said.

Guy laughed. 'To what?'

'According to our granny, probably a shipwrecked Armada sailor,' Lindsay explained. 'Her family had all lived in some Suffolk fishing village since the Stone Age.'

'Oh, right.' Guy grinned. 'And one day they fished out a soggy Manuel, and it was a toss-up between chopping him up for bait or marrying him off to the daughter who was up the duff by the swineherd?'

7

Everybody laughed, including me, though I was a mite put out at this slur on my ancestry. If she was up the duff by anybody, I hoped she'd have done better than some rancid yokel of a swineherd.

Smartass, I thought, as Guy stretched himself out on the dry grass. Under cover of my sunglasses I made mental notes for Emma and ticked things off The List. During a terminally boring biology lesson Emma and I had compiled a list of what made the perfect boyfriend. It went like this:

1. Pref. at least two years older. [Under-eighteens were so immature.]
2. At least three inches taller than you are.
3. Nice smile.
4. Nice eyes.
5. LOVELY KISSER! [V. Imp.]
6. Should pref. have car.
7. Must absolutely NOT remotely fancy Louise Hargreaves. [Louise Hargreaves thought herself God's gift to testosterone, and so, unfortunately, did most of the boys.]
8. BUT LOUISE HARGREAVES SHOULD FANCY HIM LIKE MAD.

'Can't be sure about number seven,' I'd say, 'but I could just about tick off the rest. Not that I remotely fancied him or anything, but he was nice and tanned and beach-ish. About six foot one, at least. Wearing just a pair of tatty old shorts. Longish, messy hair, sort of light brown with sun-streaks, like surfers. Blue eyes, sort of like the sea with the sun on it. Eighteen, just failed one of his A levels – his dad's really mad. Oh, and he's got a car – a lime green Beetle. Lindsay says it's a terrible old heap, but it goes.'

Yes, Emma would be impressed.

Even if I wasn't.

Well, all right, I was. Just a bit. Very reluctantly, and under cover of my shades. Through these I watched Rachel giving him another frosty Heineken.

'Anything to eat, Guy?' she asked, like an eager little slave. 'There's some cold chicken – I could make you a sandwich.'

'Thanks, Rache,' he said. 'I could force down a couple of those.'

Opening one sun-warmed eye, Cara tutted. 'Rachel, you're mad. Let him get them himself.'

You said it, I thought, knowing she really meant, 'Don't be so bloody obvious!'

Lindsay raised an eyebrow in my direction. Later she told me that feeding Guy was par for the course. Because his mother had died when he was ten and his stepmother had made it known that she had not married to be a cook, people were constantly imagining he was about to die of starvation. Wherever he went somebody was offering pizza or, 'Sit down, there's plenty for one more.'

Eventually, as it got hotter and stickier and *La Peste* was giving me a *très mal* head, I went to cool off. On the huge paved patio was an old paddling pool Rachel and Lindsay had dragged out days earlier, as Uncle Matthew was too skinflinty for a proper one. One of those huge, rigid-sided versions, it was at least eight feet in diameter, and because they hadn't changed the water since algae was starting to grow on the sides and bottom. There were also bits of leaves and grass that nobody could be bothered to fish out.

'Ugh,' said Cara, as I came back. 'You wouldn't catch me in that. It's probably a health hazard.'

Just as the water had evaporated off my skin, Guy went to cool off. There was a lot of splashing and giggles from

Rachel as he pretended to swim circuits in it. In fact, as it was about eighteen inches deep, you almost could.

Then he said, 'Shit, there's wildlife in here! Little wiggly things. I hope I haven't got any in my shorts.'

There were more giggles, though not from me. 'Probably mozzie larvae,' said Lindsay.

'And you've already got a little wiggly thing in your shorts,' said Cara.

'I shall ignore that remark,' he said. 'Anyway, how d'you know they're mozzie larvae? They could be hatchling piranhas, from eggs brought here on that scorching equatorial wind they keep telling us about on the weather forecast.'

There were more giggles, especially from Rachel. 'Don't you think he's just so *funny*?' she whispered to me.

Huh, I thought. Not *that* funny.

'I shall have to make a proper scientific investigation,' he announced. 'Rachel, haven't you got a mask and snorkel somewhere?'

There were more heat-sapped giggles as Rachel departed like an eager little puppy. 'I'm afraid they're still a bit sandy,' she said, coming back with two sets. 'But one of them might fit you.'

'Come on, then,' he said. 'I need an assistant, in case they start devouring me.'

She giggled, but shook her head, and I knew why. Close up with him in the water her concealer would wash off, and her spots would stand out like red, hatchling volcanoes. 'Abby'll "assist" you, won't you, Abby? She's got her gold medal for swimming,' she added to him.

'Brilliant,' he said. 'She'll be able to save me if I get into difficulties. Get over here, Abby.'

'Oh, all right . . .' Trying to look vaguely amused in a cool sort of way, I rose from my towel. I'd never have volunteered, as Rachel might have thought I fancied him, but as she'd suggested it herself I wasn't going to be boring.

I've done plenty of snorkelling since, but never like that. More than once he grabbed my wrist, pointed underwater at a little thing doing jerky wiggles, just as if we were scuba divers who'd found a Moray eel. As the whole thing was just so ridiculous, I stopped thinking about being casually unimpressed and laughed through my snorkel. It was certainly more of a giggle than *La Peste*.

Eventually I knelt up in the water, pushed my mask back, and said I'd had enough.

He pushed his mask back over his hair. 'You're just chicken,' he said, in jokey, teasing tones. 'In case the baby piranhas bite your bottom.'

That was when I almost went subtly flirty after all. I don't know whether it was the drops of water glistening on his skin, or just that his eyes really did look like the sort of sea you saw on postcards from Greece. I don't think it was because he'd mentioned my bottom, but I couldn't swear to that. At any rate, I suddenly thought: I bet you *are* a lovely kisser.

'Or anywhere else,' he went on. 'You've got one down your front.'

I looked down. Clinging to the wet skin just above the centre of my black bikini bottoms a big fat larva was going wiggle, wiggle, wiggle . . .

I screeched and shuddered together. 'Yeeuugh! Get it off!'

He laughed. 'Don't be so pathetic!' But he said it in teasing tones, and flicked it away with a fingertip.

The others were cracking up as I returned to my beach towel. And I laughed back, as if it were just a good giggle.

Would I tell Emma this? I wondered, putting my shades back on. *I didn't care a bit about the mozzie larvae – I just did a really girly screech because I wanted him to get rid of it. I wanted him to touch me. It was only half a second, but*

I felt bad for doing it on purpose when Rachel's so mad about him. As if I were flirting with him.

I knew what Emma would say: 'Never mind that – was it nice? Were they those really *titchy* bikini bottoms that only come just above your pubes?'

Emma and I could talk about stuff like this for hours. She always relished a vicarious little thrill.

As Guy got out of the pool a minute later, Lindsay said, 'I'm sending that up to the *Guinness Book of Records*, for the daftest thing to do on a hot afternoon.'

Rachel said, 'Well, *I* thought it was really funny.'

Cara opened an eye. 'Yes, for a prize twat.'

He came back, flicking water over Lindsay and Rachel and making them shriek. 'That's quite enough from you, Maisie.' (He called Cara that because her surname was May.)

Behind my sunglasses I was taking all this in while pretending to be absorbed in higher, French things. I wasn't prepared when Guy strolled over and picked my book up. Having scanned the cover, he grinned. 'Are you really into this, or just trying to look intellectual?'

Because I was so tanned, my wash of heat probably didn't show. 'I have to read it, don't I? I'm doing it for A level.'

At the same time, from the open french windows came the brrr-*brrrrr* of the phone. 'Oh, shit,' said Lindsay. 'I hope that's not Mum, reminding me about my driving lesson. I was planning to "forget" it and not hear the door-bell on purpose.'

She came back two minutes later. 'Thank God for driving lessons, after all. She wanted me to mind the shop for a couple of hours – she's having her highlights done. So you're the lucky one, Rache.'

Rachel groaned. 'Oh, *no* . . . Stuck in that stuffy little shop all afternoon – it's just so *bor*ing!'

Auntie Rosemary ran a little gift shop in The Lanes. She paid Lindsay and Rachel to help out now and then, but since they were never exactly desperate for cash this wasn't much of an incentive. Personally I'd have welcomed a mother who dished out casual wages. As a receptionist at the local GP's surgery, Mum could hardly ask me to take over while she had her hair done.

'Well, you have to,' said Lindsay, 'or she'll throw a fit. She said to take her cheque book – they don't take plastic at that hairdresser's. It's on the kitchen counter. And you'd better go now – it's twenty to three already. Maybe Guy could run you in.'

Rachel's face lit with sudden hope, and I knew exactly what she was thinking.

Alone with him in the car! Even if it's only for fifteen minutes, even if I'm only Rachel-down-the-road, it'll keep me going for days.

Alas, it was not to be. 'Sorry, Rache,' he said. 'I would, but the car just failed its MOT. The old man'll kill me if I drive it before it's fixed.'

Her spark of hope died. 'Oh, well, I'll get the bus.'

'I'll come with you,' I said. 'I don't mind sitting in the shop.'

We left fifteen minutes later, just after Lindsay departed for her driving lesson. 'Will you two stay?' Rachel asked the others. 'It'll save me having to lock up.'

In heat that shimmered off the tarmac and made the birds too drowsy to sing, Rachel and I ambled to the bus, a good five minutes' walk away. I said, 'Why has Guy got a nickname for Cara when he hasn't got one for you or Lindsay?'

She made a face. 'He used to have one for me, until Lindsay told him I hated it. *Polga!* As in *Olga da Polga*, you

13

know, the guinea pig books. "So how's old Polga?" he used to say – I mean, it sounds so *fat!* Like our old guinea pigs – all round and squidgy with hardly any legs.' Her face came over all wistful if-only. 'Sometimes he used to call Lindsay Spider, because she had such long skinny legs. Only she told him to put a sock in that, too, she thought it sounded hairy. God, if he'd ever called *me* Spider – oh, bum!' She clapped a hand to her forehead. 'I forgot Mum's cheque book!'

Even as she said it, a bus was approaching the stop twenty yards away. 'Look, you go back – it's on the kitchen counter. It might be twenty minutes till another bus comes and she'll go ape if I'm late.'

'She'll have left anyway by the time I get there!'

'We can drop it round – it's only round the corner. Go on, Abby – just get the next bus – I've got to run. Will you remember where to come?'

'Oh, yes – see you in a bit.'

In fact, I barely remembered where to go. I'd been to the shop very briefly the day before, after we'd been to the beach. Still, maybe Cara could remind me of exactly where to get off the bus, and which way to go once I had. I certainly wasn't going to ask Guy, in case he made some crack about whether I was intellectual enough to read a map.

As the front door was locked and I didn't have a key, I walked straight round to the back. There was a garden shed at the side of the house, and a greenhouse full of tomatoes. With the ventilators open because of the heat, that warm, fuzzy-green tomato smell hit me as I passed.

But I never asked Cara anything. Coming round the side of the house, I stopped dead.

Guy was back in the paddling pool. Semi-lying on his back, he was propped on his elbows. I couldn't see his face, just the back of his head.

Cara was on top of him. Astride him, she was leaning forward, her breasts practically dangling in his face. He was supporting her, their fingers interlaced as she smiled lazily down at him, like a cat in the sun. As I watched, too stunned to move, she gave a sensuous little wriggle that sent a flood of heat to my face. Leaning forward, she bent her head to kiss him.

With my heart thumping, I retreated as silently as I could. I went in by the side kitchen door, found the cheque book and slipped out.

At least, that was the idea.

Two

Just back round the corner of the house, I heard Cara's lazy, teasing voice. 'Not such a little wiggly thing now, is it?'

My feet sprouted roots.

Then it was Guy: a warm, rough, sexy little laugh. 'Pack it in. What if their cleaning lady turns up?'

'She won't. She never comes on Fridays.'

'Tim'd bloody kill me.'

'Stuff Tim. Who's going to tell him?'

I unfroze. Burning with indignation, I marched to the kitchen door. I opened it with no worries about creaks, grabbed the cheque book, and gave the door a good bang. That'd fix them. They'd think it was Auntie Rosemary's cleaner, after all.

Still burning, I walked very fast to the bus stop.

How *could* she? With a boyfriend like Tim slaving on the beach? And what about poor Rachel? When Cara knew how she felt about him, how could she break the First Girl Commandment? *Thou shalt not flirt with, snog or even eye up any boy thy best friend is mad about.*

Snake, I thought, as I got on the bus. Or, as I was wont to say when Louise Hargreaves was really getting up my nose, cow-bitch-slag-slut-trollop.

Under a hazy, humid sky, the sea lay like a silver lake as I got off the bus. The beach was packed. From the crowded pier with the old-fashioned helter-skelter, there echoed music and the shrieks of people on the rides. The air smelt of hot cars, of dusty pavements, of candyfloss and fish and chips. And how could *he*? I thought, eyeing hundreds of deckchairs on the crowded beach. Poor Tim!

During our two and a half hours minding the shop there were all of three customers, only one of whom bought anything. For the rest of the time, all Rachel talked about was Guy. Guy this, Guy that – and can you believe Cara says she's never really fancied him at *all*?

Somehow I kept my mouth shut. She'd be doubly devastated and I'd end up the bad guy, as tell-tales always did. I'd have given anything to call Emma, but she was undergoing the torture that is 'jolly family holiday on the Norfolk Broads'.

And I was stuck here in Brighton, bursting.

When we finally got back, Rachel tried not to look disappointed that Guy was gone. Cara was still there, lounging in the sun with Lindsay.

'He had to go,' said Cara. She even gave a lazy yawn as she said it. 'Off to spit and polish his dad's boat or something. But he said to tell you thanks for the chicken sarnies.'

'Did he?' I saw Rachel take this crumb eagerly to her heart, to take out and savour later. 'I think maybe I put a bit too much mayonnaise in them, but he didn't seem to mind.'

I was dying to tell Lindsay, but was afraid she'd tell Rachel after swearing not to. The only person I could offload it to was Fleur, who wasn't coming for another twenty-four whole hours.

My mother was the middle of three sisters. Lindsay and Rachel's mother, Rosemary, was the youngest. Fleur was my other cousin, the only child of the eldest sister, Kay.

I'd only got to know Fleur relatively recently, for two reasons. One, they lived in Yorkshire, while we lived in the middle reaches of Surrey. Two, Mum and her elder sister didn't get on. They never had, ever since two-and-a-half-year-old Kay had commanded her number-one devoted slave to take the pooey baby back to the hospital. When naughty Daddy had failed to obey she'd whacked Mum over the head with her *Just Like Mummy's* iron, causing enough damage to entail a trip to Casualty. According to legend she'd said hopefully, 'Is she dead?' but obviously I can't swear to this.

Ever since I could remember Mum and Auntie Kay had only met at whole-family dos. On these mercifully rare occasions they said things like, 'I gather you're having an extension,' with polite little smiles that might have fooled anyone who didn't know them. Fleur and I would exchange awkward smiles, feeling that making friends somehow wasn't on. It would feel like fraternising with the enemy. And although Mum always did her best to be nice to Fleur, Auntie Kay had never quite returned the favour.

From childhood I'd sensed that she didn't like me much more than she liked her sister. For a start, she always called me 'Abigail', which Mum only used when she was cross, and which I'd hated anyway, ever since finding out that it meant 'serving maid'. At Grandpa's funeral, when I was twelve, I'd heard her say to Mum,

'Abigail's looking very *sallow*, Penny. Isn't she getting enough fresh air?'

Although I hadn't a clue what 'sallow' meant, I could tell from the way Mum bristled like a mother hedgehog, that it couldn't be anything nice. 'Plenty, thank you, and *per*sonally I'd call it lovely creamy olive.'

I looked up 'sallow' that night. *Yellow or brownish, unhealthy looking.*

Thanks a lot, Auntie Horrible Kay.

That night I retreated into my fantasy of being adopted. Not only was this a great comfort whenever I was 'off' my family, it was a far more satisfactory theory than Granny's Armada sailor.

No, my birth-mother would be an Italian princess called Maria-Luisa-Teresa della Castilla-Riviera-Sorrento. She'd have run off with a penniless but dashingly romantic poet called Ladislav and given birth to me in a garret. However, her father, the brutal Prince Ferdinando, would have threatened to cut his throat and throw her into a nunnery if she didn't renounce him and give me up for ever.

This would all come to light when I was eighteen, when the beautiful Maria-Luisa-Teresa would come to inform me that I was in fact the Princess Anna-Maria-Teresa, and not an 'abigail' at all.

'I'm so very sorry,' I would say graciously to my weeping family, as I stepped into her chauffeur-driven stretch limo with all the neighbours gaping. 'I'm sure you did your best, but I always knew I didn't belong in Sycamore Road.'

Ha! That would wipe the grin off Auntie Kay's face. She'd be dying for an invitation to the sumptuous Venetian *palazzo*, wouldn't she? I might even invite her, as long as she sucked up enough first.

Back to Fleur, though. Ironically, we'd become friends just after I'd found out that there was another reason why Mum and Auntie Kay didn't get on. All those years a skeleton had been lurking in our family closet, and its name was Dad.

The skeleton leapt out when I was fourteen, two years BPP (Before Paddling Pool). One of those rare, whole-family parties was being planned at the time, for Granny's seventy-fifth birthday. In the run-up to this there were acid phone calls between Mum and her elder sister: about who was going to provide what food; and about the cake and the flowers; and paper versus proper plates; and muttered curses after phones were put down, Mum saying if Kay actually *cooked* anything it'd be a miracle, she'd get it all from Marks and decant it into Tupperware. After all of which they'd once again pretend they liked each other on the day, for their mother's sake.

It made you wonder why Mum was so keen on *Little Women*.

My elder brother Andrew was sixteen at the time, and opting out of this joyous family gathering. With his GCSEs coming up, he had to stay home and revise.

'Revising my bottom,' I scoffed to Mum later. 'He'll have that Chloe round, I bet you anything. To "test him on his physics", ha ha. Why should he get out of all those hideous old wrinklies – no, I *don't* mean Granny – saying, "Goodness, haven't you grown?" Anyone would think we might have shrunk, instead. And Auntie Kay had better not make any more "sallow" remarks, or I'll say something really rude this time. She pretends to smile, but underneath she's giving me those looks as if I've just farted and I'm trying to pretend it wasn't me.'

'Just ignore it, Abby. When someone's acting like that, the best thing you can do is be specially nice.'

'Why should I? She's never like that with Andrew or Will.'

Will was my younger brother. Only eleven at the time, he was still at the mud-magnet, soap-phobic stage.

'That's because they're *boys*, dear.'

I was incensed. 'What's that got to do with anything?'

'You'll learn.' She paused. 'Actually, there's something I ought to tell you. About why Kay and I don't get on.'

How thick could parents get? 'Mum, I *know* why you don't get on. It goes back to Auntie Kay being jealous of you being the baby instead of her. It's called *sibling rivalry*, only they didn't know about it in the olden days when you were young. And by the way, if you're off to the supermarket, could you get me some proper shampoo, not that stuff that only costs thirty-eight pence a litre?'

She hesitated. 'Why don't you come with me?'

Why not? I might get round her to buy some proper conditioner, too.

She made the revelation in Sainsbury's.

I'd always been vaguely aware that Dad had once been Auntie Kay's boyfriend, but equally vaguely I'd always assumed that Mum had picked up her cast-off. So the minor details, given alongside special-offer bath foam, gave me something of a jolt.

My mother, mistress of mashed potato, baker of cakes for school fairs, had actually stolen Dad from Auntie Kay! From the stand-out pretty one who'd never been dumped in her life!

No wonder whiffs of poison gas could still be detected now and then.

As soon as I could after that shopping trip, I confronted Andrew. He was sprawled on his bed, in a room that smelt of festering sports kit and whichever body spray his last girl guest had doused herself with.

'Did you know?' I demanded.

'Of course,' he said loftily, for he was at but one of his lofty and superior stages. 'Dad told me ages ago.'

'You could have told me! And if you're having Chloe round to help you *revise*, ha ha, while you're bunking off Granny's party, you'd better tell her not to stink the place out again. Mum's not completely stupid, you know.'

As it turned out, he didn't ask Chloe. Nor Siobhan, the other poor girl who called at least three times a week.

* * *

21

Twelve days later, on an early June afternoon that felt more like November, Andrew was standing beside me in the crematorium waiting room. While another funeral was finishing people stood about in black, murmuring things like, 'Well, at least it was quick,' and, 'Maybe it was a blessing. She was never happy after she lost Frank, and her arthritis would only have got worse.'

Although Andrew hadn't even tried to wriggle out of this one, he stood with his hands in his pockets, trying to look blasé. 'What a load of ritualistic crap,' he muttered. 'In parts of Africa they put the bodies out for the hyenas. It's what you call grass-roots recycling.'

I didn't say anything. I knew he felt terrible for wriggling out of Granny's birthday party when she'd never have another now. I felt terrible for having wished I could wriggle out of it, too.

With all this in my head, I didn't see Fleur arrive. It was Andrew's mutter that alerted me. 'Fuck me, is that Fleur? At least somebody in this family's improving.'

I hadn't seen her since Grandpa's funeral, two years previously. Then thin and painfully shy, with a mouthful of orthodontistry, she was prone to furious blushing. Her frizzy, reddish gold hair was invariably scraped back. To cap it all, she'd had a terrible stutter.

According to Mum, Fleur had not been the sort of daughter Auntie Kay had assumed would be hers by right. By this she meant gorgeous from the cradle, the type other girls would give their break-time KitKats to be friends with.

I should explain here that Auntie Kay had once been a sort of Claudia Schiffer lookalike, only with flick-ups. Family legend had it that even when she was two, old ladies at the Post Office would say, 'Dear me, she's going to be a real heart-breaker! Boys queuing all down the street, I shouldn't wonder.'

Again according to Mum, Auntie Kay had expected a daughter who'd be picked as Mary in the Nativity play, excel at ballet (while looking like an angel in her little pink outfit) and take all the rosettes at gymkhanas (while also looking prettier in her hard hat than anyone else's daughter). Over the years she had determinedly sent Fleur to lessons in these and everything else ('to give her confidence') and Fleur had obediently attended them all, while wishing she could just stay in her room and read a book.

Mum had a theory that all this pushing for reflected mother-glory was the sole origin of Fleur's stutter. ('Poor girl, it's no wonder she's a bundle of nerves.')

However, this Fleur was something else. The braces were gone. She had filled out a little, but it was her hair that struck me most. No longer scraped back, it cascaded over her shoulders in the kind of red-gold ripples I associated with old pictures of Sir What'sit and the dragon. The ones where a princess in a green medieval dress was chained to a rock for the dragon's breakfast.

Until then it had never occurred to me that Fleur was pretty, and she wasn't. She was delicately beautiful, and I don't mind admitting it gave me a little jolt.

Not that it had given her any confidence. Her manner was still terribly shy, as if she'd rather be invisible. The smile was still shy, because Fleur was the last type to start flicking her hair just because Andrew, already the source of many sighs among my friends, was there.

The service was sad and horrible. Sitting in the row in front, Fleur cried a little, and made me feel bad because I couldn't. Watching the back of her red-gold head as she fumbled with a tissue, I recalled what Granny had said more than once:

'Such a shame you hardly ever see each other, when you're both of an age.'

Afterwards, as everybody trooped out in the drizzle to look at the flowers, I found myself with Fleur. I didn't even want to look at the flowers. I hated to think of them all just dumped there to rot. The very air smelt of wet, dead flowers; of damp coats; of depressing old-ness.

'Are you OK?' I asked Fleur.

'Yes, thanks.' She wiped her eyes with a tissue. 'It's just that I c-couldn't bear to think of her in that c-c-coffin.'

I didn't like to say I couldn't bear to think of any dead body, especially in a coffin. It made me think of creepy graveyards at midnight, of rooms going cold for no apparent reason. 'Me neither.'

'And I c-couldn't bear to think of her going into that oven. What if the doctors made a mistake and she was only in a really deep c-c-coma or something?'

I didn't tell her exactly the same thoughts had haunted me. 'Of course they didn't,' I soothed, putting an arm around her. 'Mum saw her afterwards and she said you can tell. It's as if something's gone and there's just a shell.'

I was proud of this sensible, grown-up comfort, so it was typical of Andrew to stroll up with his hands in his pockets and wreck it. 'Was that your stomach I heard during "Abide With Me"?' he grinned at Fleur. 'It was like a bloody volcano.'

Fleur blushed scarlet.

I could have bashed him. Whatever Fleur's stomach might have done (and it had) did he have to point it out? 'It was a long drive!' I hissed. 'They didn't have time to stop for lunch! Just get lost, will you?'

'OK, keep your wig on!' Adding, 'Sorry, Fleur,' he got lost somewhere out of sight, where he could indulge in one of the Marlboro Lights in his jacket pocket.

Seconds later I heard the unmistakable sounds of fresh ice crunching between Mum and her elder sister.

Kay was saying, 'Really, Penny, if I'd realised you were only going to do *sand*wiches, I'd have organised the catering myself.'

Even at five yards I could feel Mum bristle. 'Well, I'm very sorry, but I had naïvely thought that *some* of us might have other things than food on our minds.'

Suddenly the tears I couldn't shed before were pricking my eyes. Granny had once said, 'It's a great grief to me, that they don't get on.'

What would she think if she could hear them? What if she *could* hear them? What if she was hovering near by, crying? Couldn't they stop it, just for a couple of hours? I wanted to scream at the pair of them, tell them to grow up. I very nearly did it, too, but two things stopped me. One, if Granny *was* hovering she'd hate a scene. Two, Fleur had heard them, too. As our eyes met, I knew she felt exactly the same as me: wretched, and ashamed of our mothers for bitching about sandwiches before their own mother was even poured into her urn.

A few yards away, Lindsay and Rachel had also overheard. They both smiled, very wryly, as if to say, 'Terrible, aren't they?' and came over.

'Horrible, wasn't it?' I said, fishing some comfort from my pocket. 'Like an Opal Fruit?'

As we stood there, sucking lime and strawberry and wishing everybody would hurry up, Rachel voiced my own thoughts. 'I hope Granny couldn't see them having a go at each other like that. She wouldn't be very happy. It's bad enough being miserable when you're alive – imagine when you're dead! You wouldn't even have chocolate to cheer you up.'

We collapsed into fits, and that was it. Without ever actually saying it, it was agreed between the four of us that Fleur and I were going to show our mothers up and be friends. Now we were old enough to get on trains, what was there to stop us?

We had a few days together at Lindsay and Rachel's that summer, and during the autumn half term they all came to me. We took the train into London, raided Miss Selfridge in Oxford Street and wandered Covent Garden, trying to look cool. The following Easter, when I was fifteen, Lindsay and Rachel's folks invited me and Fleur to join the family for a week at a ski chalet in Zell am Zee.

I knew Auntie Rosemary was complicit in this. For a couple of years after that battlefield called Two Sisters, One Man and All Hell Let Loose, she and Mum had barely spoken, because Rosemary had taken Kay's side. As the youngest, she was the favoured sister who had not put Kay's nose out of joint like poor old Middle-Mum. However, even before Dad had started to show himself as Mr Far From Perfectly Right, she'd felt bad about the rift and made friends with Mum again. Always very nice to me, she'd almost certainly thought it would be a Very Good Thing if Fleur and I had time to get to know each other properly.

While skiing was new to me, Fleur had been on two school trips, spent the whole time falling over, and hated every minute. So while Lindsay and Rachel whizzed down red and black runs we progressed together to blue, where she realised she wasn't so useless, after all. She still blushed when gorgeous Bruno said, 'Bravo, Fleur!' but we laughed ourselves sick every time we fell over. We sat outside mountain cafés with plates of chips, and talked and talked and talked.

She confessed that although Auntie Kay had never actually said as much, she knew she wasn't exactly ecstatic that we were friends. She felt so bad that her mother didn't quite like me, when Auntie Penny was always so nice to *her*. But I wouldn't ever say a word, would I?

Of course not!

She told me about being bullied at school and never telling her mother, because she'd only complain and make matters worse. She told me about hyper-confident Saffron who lived three doors away: shining star of school plays/ballet and tap. She'd known since she was about six that her mother would have liked a Saffron. She felt so bad for even saying this, as her mother would be terribly upset if she knew. I wouldn't ever say anything, would I?

It was almost the first thing I told Mum when I got home, but I knew she'd never tell.

Fleur arrived for Rachel's party at around six on the Saturday, the day after the Incident of the Paddling Pool. I was dying to offload it, but after her long hours on hot trains it was over an hour before I got her alone. We were sharing a spare room with twin beds and a built-in pink washbasin that seemed pretty flash at the time.

Then nearly seventeen, Fleur still bore the odd after-effect from her Ugly Duckling phase. A hyper-slim five foot nine should stand up straight and be proud of it, but she still hadn't quite shaken off the slightly hunched shoulders; the air of 'please don't look at me'; the eyes always on the ground.

The bedroom door had barely shut behind us when I started offloading What Abby Saw. Fleur had met Cara a few times, Guy only once. However, she recalled it all too well. 'I was only about twelve. He made some joke I didn't get and I went bright pink and felt an idiot.'

'Well, Rachel's absolutely *mad* about him. Just wait till you hear this . . .'

Five minutes later, Fleur was gratifyingly agog. 'What, actually d-*do*ing it, you mean?' (She still hadn't quite shed the stutter.)

'Any second, if you ask me. She was at him like a topless piranha.' (I was pleased with this. I thought it had a piquant little ring.)

'My God! What if you'd been Rachel?'

'I know!'

'And what about Cara's poor boyfriend?'

'Huh! *Far* too good for her, if you ask me.'

'Imagine if they'd seen you! Wouldn't you have absolutely *died*?'

I would, but I wasn't going to admit it. 'I wish they had!'

'Is he coming tonight?'

'Lindsay says *may*be. If he does, I can tell you I'm going to ignore him comp*let*ely. As for that slag Cara, if she dares start *any*thing in front of Rachel . . .'

It was a highly satisfactory conversation. I was quivering with righteous indignation and enjoying every second.

Three

With masses of Lindsay's friends as well as Rachel's and Cara's, it was a pretty good party. I remember laughing a lot, and dancing a lot, to music from the speakers Uncle Matthew had rigged up in the garden. There must have been fifty-odd revellers, and outside in the sultry air, scented with flowers and smoke from the odd spliff, I was feeling decidedly flirt-worthy. I was wearing a skimpy little dress: navy, with tiny white flowers. Like all my clothes it was dirt cheap, but looked great with a tan.

Cara's Tim was there, with a hands-off arm around her most of the time. It made me sick to see her doing the sweet-girlfriend bit.

By half eleven Guy still hadn't turned up and Rachel had given up hope. 'He's got some boys-only thing – one of his friends is off on his gap year. Lindsay says they've all probably got off their faces, gone diving off the pier and got arrested.'

By the time he finally showed up, I'd stopped thinking about him. I was flirting with someone called Sam, who had sufficiently excellent taste to evidently fancy me rotten. Just after midnight, an upstairs window opened in the house next door. With huge gardens they were set well apart, but someone had turned the music right up by then. 'Will you please keep the noise down?' roared a Major Blenkinsop type in pyjamas. 'Some of us are trying to get some sleep!'

'Shut the window, then, Grandpa!' yelled somebody, and we all cracked up.

Not long after this, Rachel had drunk enough to throw up in the bird bath. While I was fetching some kitchen roll the phone rang in the kitchen. After a few lagers I was what my granny used to call 'tiddly': light-headed, delighted with my own unbelievable sexiness, and giving not a toss about anything.

The phone was on the wall, and I was sufficiently far gone to drop the receiver while trying to answer. That set me off giggling as I retrieved it from its dangling cord. 'Hello?'

'This is the second time I've had to ask!' grated the irate voice. 'If you don't turn the noise down IMMEDIATELY I'm calling the police!'

'Velly solly, this is Chinese takeaway.' In fits of giggles at my own incredible wit, I hung up.

'Who was that?'

I spun around to find Guy standing in the doorway. His hands were thrust in the pockets of his jeans, and he wore a red bandanna thing tied round his forehead. It made him look like an Australian surfing pirate.

Still giggling, I forgot to be sniffily 'off' with him. 'Don't ask me. Some old misery.'

He grinned. 'You're pissed.'

'I am not!'

'Yes, you are. But you're quite cute with it.'

I suddenly realised that he was giving me that 'wouldn't say no' look, and no wonder, when I was so unbelievably sexy and gorgeous. What's more, he was expecting me to react accordingly. To go all so-called subtly-flirty, flick my hair and give him a giggly come-on.

In your dreams, sunshine. I put on my best, unimpressed tone. 'Why are you wearing that stupid hairband thing?

30

Do you think it makes you look cool or something?'

'No cooler than anybody else.' Leaning against the door jamb, he added a sideways, half-amused little smile. 'I really upset you yesterday, didn't I?'

'Sorry?'

'That French book. Saying you were trying to look intellectual.'

I was incensed. Did he really think I was pathetic enough to have a go at him on that account? 'Don't flatter your-self. I just think you look a prat, that's all.'

And I stalked off, triumphant.

.

If anyone had told me then, that over those two sultry days I'd helped to plant a little seed of mischief that was going to lie dormant for ages, I'd have laughed. Over the months and years that followed that seed was buried deep in the compost heap of my memory. It was fifteen years before it woke up.

During that time I left school, spent three student years discovering my alcohol limit, got a degree in English and French, and came out hungry for money. Never again would I live on Economy Baked Beans and dread letters from the bank. While London was still booming I got a job in recruit-ment that promised high rewards to good team players. I was a good team player. I exceeded my targets and was promoted. I can't say I ever found it fulfilling, but I knew after two years that I wasn't going to do this for ever.

By twenty-four I was formulating a Grand Plan; at twenty-five I started putting it into practice. First, I was going to buy a two-bedroomed flat. Next, I was going to let it, and while the rent paid the mortgage I was going to take off for a couple of years and see the world, starting with the land of the Long White Cloud. My old friend Emma, apparently content in local radio, said she was catching itchy feet. She'd come with me, at least for a few months. We decided to head first for Queenstown, for skiing and snowboarding and awesome scenery. To fund all this I'd take a TEFL course, teach English to the Far Eastern students who flocked there. Then I'd move on to Australia, the Far East and India. Part of my Grand Plan was no fixed plans beyond the first three months. I would go as the fancy took me.

With the flat bought and more or less furnished, with my TEFL course done, I was only weeks from taking off when I found out that Robbie was on the way.

Four

If you ask me, it should be against the law for your mother to spring shocks like this on you. It made you wonder what respectable divorcees were coming to.

Forty-eight at the time, Mum had naturally enough ascribed signs of his arrival to other causes. She'd started raiding the library for titles like, *Change? What Change?* and *Hot Flushes the Feng-Shui Way.* She'd started saying things like, 'This is it, then. Before you know what I'll be going to Keep Fit For The Over-Fifties. We can all have a nice cup of tea afterwards, and talk about how much fun we're going to have once we get our bus passes.'

So the reality came as a thumping shock to her. To the rest of us it was a double whammy.

'*What?*' said Emma. 'Isn't it about time your mum and dad made their minds up? They've been divorced for years!'

Although Mum urged me to carry on with my Grand Plan anyway, I put it off until after the birth. I wanted to be there when my little sibling was born and Emma wasn't as disappointed as I'd feared. 'I'll go anyway, now I'm geared up. Warm up Queenstown for you and test the bungy jumps. Do I take it your folks are getting back together?'

'Dad did make noises once he was over the shell shock, but Mum thinks it's only because he feels he has to. In any case, she says she'd never relax. She'd still be worried every time he was half an hour late back from the garden centre.'

'I hate to say it, but why is she going through with it at all? I mean, at her age?'

That's exactly what plenty of people were saying, usually behind Mum's back. 'I know they think I'm mad,' she said, more than once. 'And I dare say I am, but I just can't do it.'

Emma's parting shot was this: 'Be good, and just watch out that all this baby stuff doesn't make you go broody.'

'Broody?' I echoed. 'Me?'

I started teaching English at a school in Earls Court; the experience would make it easier to find work abroad. And if anything, I turned even less broody, which is saying something. I wasn't there for the actual birth but even afterwards, in the maternity ward, talk of after-pains and boobs like hot concrete footballs was enough to put anybody off for life.

I didn't even feel an overwhelming rush for Robbie, not at first. It was only when he was five weeks old, when he suddenly gave me a lit-up, toothless smile . . . That was when I told Emma I'd stay another couple of months, the blob was turning into a little human. And so it went on. I didn't want to miss his first steps, and how could I miss his first birthday? Once that was past, somehow I found the travel bug had passed with it. I liked my flat; I enjoyed doing it up, and letting the other room helped pay the mortgage. I enjoyed my job, teaching a United Nations of students from Kazakhstan to Mexico. I was seeing a certain Luke, who made me laugh.

Emma, meanwhile, during her first few days in Queenstown, had fallen in with a fun crowd. One of her first emails said, *We all did the scary bungy – I told the bloke who strapped me in that I'd probably wet myself out of sheer terror. And he laughed and said they all said that, but it was a mite difficult upside down.*

A few emails later it was, *Four of us are moving on to the Aussie Gold Coast next week, but I think I might come back to New Zealand afterwards. Just for a couple of weeks.*

It was over two years by the time she eventually came back, and then only for three weeks. Robbie's second birthday passed in a flash, and his third.

When that little seed began to germinate, he was four and a half.

By then Lindsay, Rachel and I had been living in south London for years. Their flat was about three miles from mine, and we saw each other at least every couple of weeks. Fleur, who'd been working in Yorkshire until May, had got a job in east London. As she was living even further out, though, we hadn't seen her much more of her than previously.

In mid July Lindsay thought it was high time we made an effort to get together. 'You know what it's like,' she said, over the phone. 'You keep saying, "We must meet up soon," but unless you actually fix something another month goes by and you still haven't. Anyway, we're having a barbie on Sunday. Fleur's coming and I've invited a few others as well. There shouldn't be any burnt-stroke-raw sausages, because we're not letting any of the blokes anywhere near the barbie. Well, maybe David, but I think we can trust him not to revert to type and think he's Og doing rare mammoth steaks outside the cave.'

David was Rachel's boyfriend, an old friend of mine from way back. She'd been seeing him a few months now and Lindsay and I were beginning to sniff a more formal arrangement. He was the kind of man I often wished I could fall for but never did: nice-looking, kind, funny and solvent. 'Lindsay, I'd love to come, but—'

'Oh, Abby! It had better be a bloody good excuse!'

As excuses went, it was cast-iron. In a rash moment five

months previously I'd agreed to ten days' camping in Brittany with Mum and Robbie. My little brother was what his nursery teacher politely called 'extremely lively', and as I didn't want Mum dying of exhaustion on a French campsite, I'd nobly pretended that camping with a small child was my idea of heaven. You never knew, there might be the odd hunky Jean-Paul to flirt with.

Two days after I got back, Fleur called. On the train home at the time, I was lost in speculation. Sitting opposite me was a fat, sweaty bloke in a white T-shirt that exposed half a hairy white gut and a cavernous belly-button. Did he get the missus to wield a Dustbuster on that? I wondered. With that handy little crevice tool?

My mobile jerked me from these gruesome thoughts, just after Fulham Broadway.

'Hi, it's me,' said Fleur. 'How was *le camping*?'

'Believe it or not, I enjoyed it. Nothing but shorts or tracky bottoms, no slap whatsoever, and I didn't go out on the pull once. How did that barbecue go?'

'That's partly why I was ringing. You'll never believe who was there.'

'Ronald McDonald? Viggo What'sit out of *Lord of the Rings*?'

'Guy.'

'Who?'

She laughed. 'Abby, don't tell me you don't remember? Bad-boy Guy? He who was rather naughty with an even naughtier girl?'

I was struck momentarily dumb.

'Abby? Are you still there?'

'Er, more or less . . . But I haven't heard Lindsay or Rachel mention him in ages! I thought they'd lost touch!'

'They had. I don't think either of them had seen him for a couple of years. Only Lindsay was at Heathrow a couple of days before, picking up a friend, but there was some industrial dispute and the terminal was heaving. She had to hang around for ages, and while she was killing time in Costa Coffee she bumped into Guy, who was hanging around waiting for his bags.'

That didn't surprise me. Only two days previously I'd collided with one of Andrew's exes right outside Earls Court underground.

'So after they'd spent half an hour catching up, Lindsay asked him to the barbie,' Fleur went on. 'She never thought he'd actually come, if only because he still lives on the south coast – he's got some boat business. I'd never have recognised him – it was only when Rachel said something about "aeons ago" that it came back. To be honest, I had a job to keep an entirely straight face when we started talking. He didn't remember me, but I wouldn't expect him to. I hadn't seen him since that party of Rachel's and even then I barely spoke to him.'

Like a video on rewind, it was all rushing back. The heat, the paddling pool, calling him a prat in the kitchen . . .

'He could see I was amused about something,' she went on. 'He said if it was a joke I thought too rude to share I was quite right – he was very easily shocked.'

'Which was supposed to make you tell him anyway.'

'Oh, of course – it was all twinkly eyed tongue-in-cheek. I was almost tempted to tell him What Abby Saw.'

'Fleur!' I had to laugh. 'You'd have made me sound like some horrible little Peeping Tomette.'

'Don't worry, I'd never have actually done it.' She laughed. 'It's funny now, to think how easily shocked *we* were. The age of relative innocence, I suppose.'

As if it were last month, that conversation with Fleur was coming back. I could see it all: her riveted face, the curtains, even the pink washbasin in the built-in vanity unit. 'I wasn't exactly innocent, just bursting with right-eous indignation on Rachel's behalf.'

'When she and Guy were always a non-starter anyway.'

'And it could have been a lot worse. After all, Cara could have made a play for him right under Rachel's nose.'

'As for him, I suppose all blokes are rampant little animals at that age, or they wouldn't be normal.'

At this point Fat Belly refolded his paper so that I was gazing at a pouty Page Three girl. Naturally enough, this brought a certain vision right back. 'Too right. Especially when Topless Totty's sitting on them in a paddling pool.'

Fat Belly lowered his paper and looked at me as if I'd just offered double pie, tits and peas.

Fleur laughed. 'No, he was hardly going to say, "Not today, thanks – I've got choir practice." Her voice turned slightly sheepish. 'I thought he'd turned out rather nice, actually. In fact . . .'

I got off the train thinking: Well, blow me. Through washout-August drizzle I walked the half-mile to home thinking: What a turn-up!

My flat was a conversion on the first floor of a Victorian terraced house. By rights the floor area should have meant only one bedroom, so my two were 'compact', but you could still swing a fair-sized hamster. The living room was light and spacious, with the original fireplace and a huge window. I'd have liked it to overlook the garden rather than the street, but one couldn't have everything.

Jeff, whose rent had been helping to pay said mortgage for the past year, was draped over the sofa. He spent half the day watching *Countdown* and chat shows, which he called 'researching his novel'. A former colleague at the Lingua Franca English School, he'd left six months ago to scrape by on a titchy private income while he wrote that novel. He still came in now and then to cover while we were short-staffed or flu was doing the rounds. It helped top up that income, left by a misguided great-aunt who'd fondly hoped a degree in Russian and Serbo-Croat would pitch him straight into the Foreign Office.

'Sod that for a game of soldiers,' Jeff had said. 'It's two years down the salt mines first, researching consequences of the failure of the vodka harvest in Turkmenistan.'

Jeff was my personal version of the gay buddy all urban girls are supposed to have. He wasn't gay, but people sometimes thought he was. Tall, pale and underweight, he had floppy dark hair and a face a colleague had once described as 'all sort of sensitive and dark night of the soul-ish'.

Jeff had cracked up when I'd told him this, which had probably exhausted him for days afterwards. After his predecessor, a girl who never stopped cleaning windows and vacuuming the curtains, I found his bone-idleness very restful.

As I slung my bag and keys on the armchair, Jeff exerted himself to raise his head. 'Any juicy snippets from the salt mines?'

I said, 'If you get off your backside and make me a cup of tea, I'll tell you an amusing little story. With a turn-up in the tail.'

'Fair enough,' he said. 'I've had a dismal day. Even the *Teletubbies* failed to raise my spirits.'

As he added a KitKat to my tea, I spiced the story right up for his benefit, especially my own outrage and banging the kitchen door so they'd think Auntie Rosemary's cleaner was about to catch them *in paddlante*.

'Spoilsport,' he grinned. 'I had no idea you were such a pious little horror.'

'I wasn't! Just upset for Rachel, never mind Cara's What's-his-name.'

But in strictly truthful hindsight, I thought, while munching a stick of KitKat, there was a smidgeon of something else. After Guy had barely spoken to me except to take the piss, I hadn't liked to admit even to myself that I wouldn't have kicked him out of the bike sheds. It had given me a green-eyed little jolt to see him with Cara when I'd thought they were just mates. There had been a touch of 'What's she got that I haven't?' The fact that it would have been a non-starter was beside the point.

Still, I was a sucker for the beach-boy look then. It was an occupational hazard of being sixteen and addicted to Aussie soaps. If it was tanned and chilled and beach-ish, I fancied it.

Then I told Jeff the turn-up. 'Sparks were evidently flying over the seafood skewers. Fleur said the tiger prawns weren't bad, either.'

I spoke to Fleur on and off over the next few weeks. Although she didn't say as much, I read between the lines that she was cautiously smitten. Lindsay and Rachel went to Corsica for a fortnight, on a holiday booked before David came on the scene. We were nearly into September before I spoke to either of them again.

During a Friday lunch break in the Lingua Franca staff room I'd just opened my Pret A Manger sandwich and the rather grimy window. The remains of August were making up for a washout summer with warm, settled weather. It was sunny outside, busy and vibrant and scruffy, but I liked the atmosphere. If you sat at that window for ten minutes, you'd see just about every nationality in the world walk past. The staff room was also scruffy: tables piled with papers and shelves over-stuffed with books. The photocopier bore a sign saying 'BUGGERED AGAIN – DO NOT FIDDLE'. Chaos and disorganisation were a daily fact of life at the Lingua Franca, but it was also small and relaxed, which was why I hadn't moved on.

Over my tuna salad wrap, I found a text message from Lindsay.

Guess what??? Clue: Rachel's gone so pink and drippy I think I'm going to have to kill her. Will call later, Love, Linds X.

I called her right back. 'Do I detect the E-word? Seven letters, ending with a trip to the jeweller's?'

'Yep, it was Corsica that did it. David missed her so much, he thought he'd better nab her before anyone else did.'

'Doesn't surprise me. Those two just "went" from the word go.'

'I hold you personally responsible, you know,' she went on, in jokey tones. 'Please think carefully next time before dragging heterosexual old friends to parties where susceptible Rachels are present.'

'I like that! It's all your fault for throwing so many parties.' Lindsay was often known as The Entertainments Committee. Whenever two or three were gathered together, she'd get on the phone to half a dozen more and call Pizza Express. 'Anyway, haven't you just done the same with Fleur and Guy?'

'I know – you could have knocked me down with a barbecue skewer. Mind you, she did look gorgeous, and playing it amazingly cool, for Fleur. I think she's turned over a new cool-leaf ever since Scott.'

'I'll believe that when I see it.' Scott was Fleur's ex. I'd only met him once but he'd belonged to that male species that makes cynics like me wonder where the catch is. And it had proved to be a very messy catch.

'Well, it evidently worked on Guy. Of course it's not

ideal,' she went on. 'What with him near Southampton and her out in the east London sticks, they only see each other at weekends and maybe once during the week, but distance often adds spice.'

'Rachel and David didn't need any spice. Give them my love, and tell them I want a shiny Cupid badge and a couple of free drinks.'

'I was coming to that. As this weather can't possibly last, I thought we could all have lunch together tomorrow, maybe by the river. I've already been on to Fleur and she's coming, with Guy, so don't you dare tell me you can't make it this time.'

I hadn't quite reckoned on being confronted with Guy, not that it bothered me. 'I can,' I said. 'Only you'd probably rather I didn't. I promised to have Robbie tomorrow, so Mum can go shopping in peace.'

'Abby! Honestly, you and your mum are like some sort of role-reversal thing. Daughter of single-parent mother, constantly charging to the rescue – it's supposed to be the other way round.'

Thank God it wasn't. 'She didn't ask,' I felt obliged to point out. 'She hardly ever does. I offered.'

'It's always you! Why can't Will or Andrew offer now and then?'

Or Dad, I thought. He did pitch in occasionally, but besides trying to run a business with too few staff he'd also had a dodgy knee for months. Since Robbie ran rings round everyone, Mum didn't trust anybody who couldn't keep up.

'It's not always me,' I said. 'Will often takes him to kick a football in the park. Andrew does try sometimes, but he's just not into small-boy things. He can't step back on to Planet Small-Boy like Will can. Actually, I'm not sure Will ever really got off it.'

She laughed. 'Point taken. But bring Robbie anyway. It'll be lovely – we haven't seen him for ages.'

'I don't know about lovely. He can still little-sod for England, you know. And he only eats about three things, and one of those is McDonald's.'

'He'll eat chips, I bet. Anywhere'll do a plate of chips. I'll call you when I've booked somewhere. Oh, and one other thing – we've got a lodger.'

'A what?'

'Well, only a temporary one. Remember Cara? Cara May, Rachel's friend?'

Five

Topless Totty? How could I forget her?

But I managed to strangle this on the way out. 'Yes, but I haven't heard Rachel mention her for ages. Wasn't she in Sydney or somewhere?'

'And Cape Town. But just before we went on holiday Rachel got an email saying she was heading back, and asking for a bed until she sorts out a job. She'll probably be coming tomorrow, too – she hasn't seen Guy for ages. We haven't told him – Rachel thought it'd be fun to give him a little surprise.'

A little surprise for Fleur, too, I thought later, on my way home. I wasn't entirely sure I'd want my new squeeze confronted with an old paddling pool, so to speak. I nearly called her, but it would smack of overreaction. Fleur didn't need thoughts put into her head. Whatever Lindsay said about her new, cool leaf, I couldn't see it ever being much more substantial than a wet tissue.

I put it down to some deep-rooted vulnerability, but something about Fleur had often attracted the kind of man they used to call cads. They tended to have perfect manners and enough non-slimy charm to fool anybody at first. Scott, her ex, had committed the ultimate cliché of sleeping with someone she'd looked on as a friend. Not that you could call it sleeping – they'd had a quickie in her car. So quick and evidently frenzied, the friend hadn't realised she'd left some evidence behind.

Fleur had found it while putting some washing on. I mean, when you find a particular shape and colour of false nail in your boyfriend's Calvins, and your so-called friend's just been complaining that just such a nail must have come off at the gym, you can't help putting two and two together.

I got off the train wishing I could share all this with Jeff. Unlike your average bloke, it was exactly the sort of thing Jeff would relish. He'd never pretend to listen while channel-hopping in the hope of finding footie, and then say, 'Sorry?' when you asked what he thought.

The trouble was, Jeff wasn't there. Ten days previously he'd announced, at forty-eight hours' notice, that he was off to Morocco. 'My creative soul needs room to expand,' he'd proclaimed, in piss-taking tones. 'Who was it who said deserts are the palaces of the soul?'

'Probably the same bloke who said you can get really cheap puff there. How long are you going for?'

'Who knows? Six weeks? As long as the spirit moves me.'

The flat seemed horribly empty as I pushed my front door open. He'd been away before, to Berlin, supposedly researching that novel. However, I hadn't known him half as well then. I hadn't grown accustomed to finding him draped over the sofa when I got home, ready to share every little detail of my day. I even missed his mess. Mine was doing its best, but it was lonely on its own.

I picked Robbie up at eleven the next morning. It was about a half-hour drive to the leafy reaches where Mum still lived in the mock-Tudor house we'd moved into when I was six. Gardens in Sycamore Road were a credit to lawnmower manufacturers and Miracle-Gro. On any given Sunday you would find the stout husbands and fathers of England spreading Weed'n'Feed, washing cars and sanding floors. There was a good deal less of the wafting smells of Sunday roasts these days, as families headed for Luigi's or River Café cookalikes, but it was still the sort of road that made my brother Andrew shudder. In fact, he'd been heard to say that if he ever thought he'd end up lawnmowing in a Sycamore Road, he'd kill himself now.

Robbie was not happy when we left. As I'd half promised to take him swimming, grown-up lunch came a very boring second. 'If you're good, I'll take you afterwards,' I promised.

'I want to go *now*!'

Robbie was an angel until he was fifteen months old, when he hit a premature case of the Terrible Twos. These had given way to the Thug Threes, and he was now halfway though the Fraught Fours. According to Mum he was a sturdier version of Andrew at the same age: big brown eyes, killer eyelashes, thick, dark wavy hair. Only Andrew had not been a brick wall disguised as a boy. Like Andrew, Robbie was also highly intelligent, which was a very mixed blessing. He knew exactly how to run rings round Mum and talking over his head was increasingly difficult. Even if you used very long words he'd often still pick up the gist.

In fact he was remarkably well-behaved at first. Because Fleur was coming from the City side, Lindsay had picked a place near Tower Bridge. If I was going to have a couple of glasses of wine this meant train and Underground, which were treats in themselves to Robbie.

As the train whizzed past fields and cricket pitches that gradually gave way to rows of south London houses, he knelt up on the seat, his nose squashed against the window.

'Look,' he said, drawing back, 'you can see where my nose was.'

'Lovely.'

'Can we go to that place where they used to chop people's heads off?'

'Maybe later. If you're very good.'

Only Lindsay was there when we arrived, at a busy riverside place with lots of glass-topped tables in the sun. 'There you go,' she said, passing Robbie a little bag. 'We've been saving them for you specially.'

It was a collection of plastic monsters gleaned from cereal packets, and his eyes lit up. 'Thanks!'

Brilliant! I mouthed, over his head.

Lindsay's corn-gold hair was gently highlighted now, cut in a sort of Meg Ryan. She worked for a big market research company, moaned about it now and then, but basically enjoyed it. At around five foot eight she was still taller than me by an inch, but we had much the same figures, hovering around a twelve.

Bearing Warehouse bags, Rachel and Cara arrived a few minutes later, minus David. 'So where is the romantic old softie?' I asked, getting up to kiss her.

'A friend had last-minute tickets for the Gunners. He was going to be all noble and turn it down, but I insisted.'

That was love for you. Long zitless, Rachel had lovely creamy skin framed by a cap of glossy chestnut hair. Although it was her natural colour, it might have been ordered specially to go with her green eyes.

'Do you remember Cara?' Rachel went on, all sunny smiles.

I hadn't seen her since Rachel's twenty-first. 'Of course! Are you glad to be home?'

Her smile was that enigmatic type that could be either

faintly bored or vaguely amused. 'Not sure yet. It depends on what turns up.'

Naturally I was comparing her to the topless piranha. Obviously she was older, fully clothed, and not about to eat anybody alive, but apart from all that she hadn't changed much. Her eyes were unusual, slightly slanted amber-brown. Then straight, her tawny hair was now tousled-chic, with the kind of highlights you only get from sun or a really good hairdresser, and she had a tan to match.

As we got stuck into the first glasses of wine, Robbie played with his monsters and watched boats on the river. In a light river-breeze the sun was shining on Tower Bridge, glinting on the water.

The conversation rapidly moved to the fun surprise in store for Guy. 'They haven't seen each other for yonks,' Rachel said blithely. 'How long is it now, Cara?'

She shrugged. 'Must be at least three years – I hadn't seen him for ages even then. He turned up at some do or other with an Italian girl in tow. She was fussing over him like a cooking-and-sewing *mamma*.'

That was interesting. There was a faint implication that she'd have liked to stuff the Italian girl into her own home-made tortellini, but maybe I was reading too much into it.

Fleur and Guy arrived about five minutes later. I saw them first, scanning the tables to find us. Over the years Fleur had acquired a veneer of confidence and a willowy grace that often turned heads. Five foot nine, she was just on the right side of too thin and still very pale in the way that can make a tan look tacky by comparison. Her hair still fell in red-gold ripples, but they were usually tamed now, held back in a clasp. She wore some simple cream dress the designer must have drawn with just her in mind.

Bingo. Fleur's face lit in her quick, sweet smile. As she waved from five tables away, there was only one thought in my head.

Guy? I'd never have recognised him, either.

Then they were upon us. 'Oh, and *Robbie*!' said Fleur, genuinely pleased to see him. 'Abby, do you remember Guy?'

She said this so perfectly straight-faced, I had a job not to laugh. 'Just about, but it was ages ago.' I took the hand he offered. 'You probably won't remember.'

All I saw was the faint relief of a man who's supposed to remember you, can't for the life of him dredge up anything, and has been wondering whether to pretend he remembers you anyway, in case you get offended. He produced an apologetic smile to match. 'I'm afraid I don't – that house was like Piccadilly Circus. Lovely to meet you again anyway.'

Perversely miffed that I'd made no impression at all, I turned to the monster. 'And this is my little brother, Robbie.'

I just caught that fleeting expression common in singles when faced with the alien species known as young children: *Right, brace yourself. Pretend you're not allergic.* Not that I blamed them. Occasionally it had occurred to me that I could hire Robbie out, as a sort of mental contraceptive: *Is your biological clock playing you up? For a mere £75 an hour you can have it taken to bits, half the pieces crunched underfoot, the rest lost for ever behind the radiator!*

Guy adopted the man-to-man approach. 'Hi, Robbie. I'm glad I'm not the only boy with all these girls.'

'*Boy?*' Robbie made his dhurr! face. Complete with cross-eyes, it went down a blast with your average three-year-old. '*Man*, you mean.'

I saw an almost imperceptible lift of Man's eyebrows.

'Well, I tried,' it said, just as a pair of hands tweaked his waist from behind. 'Hi, Fielding.'

It was Cara, who'd just nipped to the loo.

He spun around. 'Cara! Good God, I thought you'd emigrated!'

If Fleur was startled she covered it brilliantly. There was just a slight widening of her eyes. On meeting mine they said, 'Did you know?' But that was it.

Rachel was laughing. 'We thought we'd give you a little surprise,' she said to Guy.

'Ten out of ten, then. So how are you?' he went on, kissing Cara's cheek. 'Looking pretty rough, as usual.'

With the serene smile of someone who knows this is only ever a joke, she returned his kiss. 'You too, Fielding.'

We squashed ourselves at a table intended for six. Robbie sat between me and Rachel, facing the river. I was glad it was Rachel. Even after several years of teaching five- and six-year-olds, she actively liked small children. Opposite Robbie was Fleur, with Guy on her left and Cara on the other side. Lindsay sat between me and Guy.

As we chatted I gave Guy a subtle going-over. The greatest difference was his hair, though I'd think it weird if he still had those long, messy, sun-streaked locks, like whoever it was I used to fancy on *Home and Away*. With crisp, short hair, in that shade that can't make up its mind whether it's light brown or dark blond, he was a different animal. There were glints of sun in it, but nothing like before.

He was heftier, too, which wasn't altogether surprising. Unless they were nerds, eighteen-year-olds tended to turn into men. When he took off a light, linen-look jacket and draped it over the back of his chair, this impression was only confirmed. Underneath was a light blue shirt with short sleeves, and all traces of *Home and Away* stripling were gone. The arms had an altogether more businesslike air, more plentifully fuzzed with light brown. A glimpse of fuzz was also visible at the V of his open-necked shirt. I could have sworn there was damn all before.

There was no denying he made a perfect contrast to Fleur's delicate, gazelle-like femininity. Or should that be Fleur-like? As Will had once commented, 'Just as well she didn't turn out like a cauli*fleur*, then.'

Because her stutter had caused her so much anguish and bullying at school, Fleur had trained as a speech therapist. Auntie Kay had thought this a shocking waste of her looks. Apparently she'd once said to Rosemary, 'Knowing her, she'll end up marrying one of her patients, but what can you do?'

Revolting noises brought me back to the here and now. On my left, Robbie was amusing himself with his glass of Coke. Kneeling up on his chair, he blew energetic bubbles into it through his straw. When this palled, he sucked up mouthfuls and blew them back. As usual, I dithered between telling him not to be so disgusting and reasoning that at least he was happily occupied. I tried not to notice that Guy was watching him with the kind of fascination normally reserved for documentaries on, say, dung beetles.

'I think we should get on and order,' said Lindsay. 'This place is packed, in case you hadn't noticed, and they look a bit short-staffed to me.'

It was a pan-fried and wilted-spinach sort of place, but there were a few child-portion offerings, e.g., *Our home-made spaghetti, smothered in fresh, vine-ripened tomato sauce.*

Meanwhile, Robbie was fishing the slice of lemon out of his spat-out Coke. Putting it between his teeth, he then bared his yellow fangs at me. 'Lovely,' I said.

Robbie appeared to realise that Guy's eyes were on him. After eyeballing him for several seconds, his gaze moved to Fleur. 'Is he your dad?' he asked, through lemon fangs.

A ripple of mirth went round the table.

'No, he's her granddad,' said Cara, deadpan. 'Poor old thing.'

'Dhurr!' Robbie's fangs fell out as he made a face to match. 'I didn't mean *that* sort of dad, silly.' He glanced up at me. 'I meant husband, didn't I?'

'Yes, I know you did.' About to tick him off for the 'silly', I changed my mind. If Cara chose to take the mickey out of a little kid, she could hardly blame him for giving as good as he got. 'But no, he's not Fleur's husband. He's her boyfriend.'

'Oh.' Having sorted that one out, he replaced his sticky fangs, changed his mind and spat them back into his glass. 'Will told me a funny joke,' he announced. 'What flies through the air and wobbles? A jellycopter!' He hooted at this gem of wit.

Everybody was kind enough to laugh.

Guy's mouth quivered. 'Who's Will?'

Robbie made another dhurr! face. 'My *brother*,' he said, as if Guy were supposed to know. 'I've got another brother too. He's *really* old.' He eyed Guy thoughtfully. 'About as old as you.'

The real laughter that greeted this gratified Robbie no end. As his rightful place was at the centre of the universe, such attention was only fitting.

'Guy's really *really* old, Robbie,' said Lindsay, deadpan. 'Even older than me. When I was little like you, we used to go fishing for tadpoles together.'

Maybe it was this tenuous wildlife connection that hit a chord, but I saw something in her expression go 'ping!'. 'Guy, you *must* remember Abby. It was that boiling hot day when you two went snorkelling for mozzie larvae, remember? In that old paddling pool in our garden?'

Six

Rachel gave a hoot of laughter. 'Oh, my God! *I* remember that!'

Lindsay said, 'You remember, Abby, don't you?'

'Just about,' I said. 'It must have been thirty in the shade.'

Cara then spoke up. 'Weird what you remember, isn't it?' she said, with an expression of lazy amusement I soon came to associate with her. 'I wonder why certain things stick out?'

Although it sounded perfectly innocent to anybody who didn't know, I was in no doubt of what she was referring to. It was all I could do not to catch Fleur's eye.

'Because they're so daft,' said Rachel. 'I was killing myself laughing.'

'Come on, Guy,' said Lindsay. 'You surely must remember now?'

His eyes were on Robbie's bubble-blowing. 'Yes, it's beginning to ring the odd bell.'

'No wonder,' said Cara. She wasn't looking directly at him, but her lazy little smile said she was enjoying warming up any fuzzy memories. 'There was an awful lot of larking around in that pool, as I recall.'

Nobody who didn't know would read anything into it. Almost against my will I caught Fleur's glance and saw her antennae pricking right up. 'Well!' her eyes said. 'Did you hear that?'

'Just as well nobody came down with anything,' said Rachel. 'That water was manky, never mind all those horrible little wiggly things.'

'They weren't all that little,' said Cara. 'I seem to recall one or two whoppers that made me think: Ye gods, imagine a thing like that getting into your knickers!'

I had to admit, she had a genius for the innocent-sounding *double entendre,* and in other circumstances I might have found it funny. Naturally she had no idea that Fleur and I were 'reading' any of this; her sole intended recipient was Guy. His mouth only flickered as it might have anyway, but his eyes remained on the convenient sideshow of Robbie. As for Fleur, I didn't dare catch her eye.

'I'm sure you needn't have worried,' Rachel grinned. 'I'm sure no well-brought-up little wiggly would have dreamt of going anywhere near your knickers.'

'It wasn't the little ones I was thinking of,' said Cara. 'It was the ones that could almost pass as organic vibrators.'

Again, nobody who didn't know would have read anything more into it. While Rachel hooted, Lindsay looked up from her menu. 'Do you mind? I'm trying to think lunch here, not water-borne Ann Summers. Anyway, you're embarrassing Guy,' she added, with the wicked deadpan she did so well.

'I'm not, am I?' Cara shot him a glance like warm honey with a naughty little bee in it. 'And I wasn't even trying.'

'You always were trying.' Saying this in good-natured tones with barely a pinch of 'dry', he turned to me. 'Abby, you're coming right back after all. Some French book, wasn't it? You were hacked off with me for having the nerve to imply that you were trying to look intellectual.'

Blow me, he's remembered after all. And if he was trying to divert the conversation I was only too happy to help. 'Hacked *off*?' I echoed. 'I was mortified. There I was, going through my trying-to-look-intelligent phase, and you had to blow my cover.'

This brought a laugh at my expense, which was the general diversionary idea. Not that Guy laughed, exactly. It was confined to his eyes and a quiver at the corners of his mouth. If he'd dished out much of this at that barbecue, I could well understand Fleur being smitten. 'Sorry,' he said. 'But I seem to remember you getting your own back.' To Fleur he added in mock-hurt tones, 'She cut me right down to size. Accused me of *über*-cool pretensions.'

She gave him the little smile I could likewise imagine attracting him in the first place. I could see it dragging any man from the primeval male-bonding area that springs eternal around hot barbecue plus cold beers. 'And did you? Have *über*-cool pretensions, I mean?'

Lindsay laughed. 'Of course he bloody did!'

Might as well go the whole hog, I thought. 'God, it's all coming back now. That party of Rachel's. He had some bandanna thing tied round his forehead, like a pirate on a bad hair day. Now I come to think of it, I've got a feeling I said it made him look a prat.'

Lindsay and Rachel hooted in unison.

Fleur was playing along. 'Abby, how *could* you?'

'Only a prat?' Lindsay grinned. 'Pretty mild, if you ask me.'

'Well, maybe it was "D-I-C-K-head". I had to spell it, or Robbie would inevitably use it at full volume on the train home in front of some 'Disgusted, Tunbridge Wells,' type. 'I really can't remember the details – I was probably a bit P-I-double-S-E-D.'

'You're not the only one,' said Rachel. 'I seem to remember chucking up in the bird bath.'

'Sorry, anyway.' I looked directly at Guy. 'Terribly rude of me. I hope you didn't go off and cry into your beer.'

He returned my tongue-in-cheek tone with one of his own. 'I probably went off and got S-T-O-N-E-D. What else can you do when you're wounded to your *über*-cool little heart?'

Robbie then piped up. 'Why are you all saying things in A-B-Cs? Mummy's always saying things in A-B-Cs, too.'

It was going to be a bugger when he learnt to read. 'Just practising our spelling.' As he'd dropped a couple of his monsters on the floor, I bent to pick them up and give myself a mini breathing space. *Nothing wrong with Guy's memory, then. And he's still got those eyes, dammit, though I suppose it'd be a bit weird if he hadn't. Had better not look too much, in case I start the usual pointless scenario of wondering why blokes I really fancy are someone else's. Bloody Cara, though! It's just not on, talking stuff like that under Fleur's nose – I don't care whether she thinks nobody else has got a clue.*

Our waitress then arrived with her pad. I ordered the spaghetti for Robbie and something tarragon-chicken thing for myself.

As the conversation took an adult turn, Robbie became increasingly fidgety. While Rachel and I played fighting-monsters with him, I caught Fleur's eye once or twice. All she did was widen her eyes minutely, but I was fluent in eye language. *Later.*

Our food finally arrived, delivered by a harassed waitress who'd brought the wrong things for Lindsay and Fleur. And sprinkled across Robbie's pasta was at least a tablespoon of carefully torn-up, lovingly garden-grown basil.

He was immediately and indignantly vocal. 'It's got green bits!'

To Robbie, green bits were poison. 'Don't fuss,' I said. 'I'll take them off.'

Having scooped every last bit on to my own plate, I

started cutting up the spaghetti, so he could eat it with a spoon.

Robbie was again indignant. 'I don't want it cutted up! I want to suck up worms!'

'Not here, Robbie. We don't suck up worms in restaurants.'

Guy then stuck his oar in. 'I thought that was the entire purpose of spaghetti at his age. Sucking up worms.'

'Not here, thanks. He splats the sauce everywhere on purpose. Look, Robbie, I'm chopping it into lovely wiggly maggots, instead.'

'I don't *want* maggots! I want worms!'

'Tough,' I said.

'Spoilsport,' said Guy.

'Guy, do keep out of it,' said Fleur, in twitchy tones that didn't surprise me.

As far as Robbie was concerned, she might as well have kept quiet. He turned to me in triumph. 'See? And you *have* to listen to him, 'cause he's a *man* and bigger than you. She's just so *bossy*,' he added to the entire table. 'Boss, boss, boss . . .'

Shades of Will, who delighted in mischievous encouragement of the ideas Robbie was evidently born with.

Lindsay was doing her damnedest not to laugh. 'Guy, you really should M.Y.O.B. A certain *petit personne* here can *petit*-sod for *Angleterre*, you know. The elder sibling, bless her, does her best to de-*soddage* him when she gets *la chance*.'

'Thanks, Linds,' I said, with feeling. 'I'm beginning to feel out-gunned here.'

Guy turned to me. 'I should have thought a modicum of *petit-sodderie* entirely *normale* at *son age*,' he said in entirely serious tones belied only by glints in his eyes. 'Would you prefer a certified sod-free *petit* robot?'

Evidently he had no experience of the type of *petit-sodderie* Robbie was capable of. 'Now and then. Especially when we're out.' Still, I knew when I was beaten. Leaving half the worms un-chopped, I turned to Guy. 'On your own head be it. Don't blame me if this table ends up like a bloodbath.'

'Well, phew for *that*,' said Robbie, already selecting his first worm with care. 'For a minute I thought she was going to get scary. Sometimes she can get really scary, you know.'

'You're kidding!' said Guy, deadpan.

'Oh, yes she can. Even Will says, and Will's got a black belt, so there.'

He started sucking up his first worm with careful concentration. He began slowly, increasing the velocity sharply towards the end, as he'd found by experiment that this produced the best results.

Guy was observing this little ritual. 'He's bringing back the lost, innocent joys of childhood. I seem to recall splatting worms for West Sussex.'

Cara turned to Robbie. In mock-serious tones she said, 'You might not believe it now, Robbie, but Guy could be an ext*reme*ly naughty boy.'

At it again! Once more the reference was obvious, but only if you knew.

Guy said, 'You can talk,' as if referring to six-year-old stuff, but he didn't look at her. He was still eyeing Robbie, whose last effort has splatted sauce all over his nose. 'I'm sorry to say, Robbie, that Cara could be extremely naughty herself.'

All this was really beginning to get up my nose. The fact that they thought it was all going over everybody else's heads was beside the point.

'*Could?*' Cara gave a lazy little smile. 'Less of the past tense please, Fielding. I haven't been turning over shiny new leaves in the past few years, you know.'

You don't say. It almost sounded like an invitation.

He shot her a look that just missed saying, 'Enough, already!' 'Oddly enough, I believe you.'

I was beginning to feel like thumping him on Fleur's behalf. He could have ignored that one, at least.

Rachel grinned. 'She was always a devil, even in Miss Treves' kindergarten.'

That's how innocent it all sounded.

Cara gave a pretend pout. 'Do you mind? I was paint-pot monitor for at least a week.'

'Yes, until you tipped all the purple into the sand-pit. And she was queen of kiss-chase,' Rachel added to everybody else.

I bet she was, I thought.

Courtesy of Lindsay, the conversation took a different turn. 'While you're all here, could you put two weeks today in your diaries? Evening, not lunch. We're overdue for a Decorators-have-finally-finished party.'

Several years back Lindsay and Rachel had moved into a garden flat Uncle Matthew had kindly bought in their names way back, as they were bound to want a London flat eventually. (This was just one of the things that had occasionally made me wish Uncle Matthew would adopt me.) It had just been renovated, also largely at his expense.

'At least, that's the official excuse,' she went on. 'We might *just* have a drink or two to Rachel and David, too, as long as she promises not to go all pink and drippy again and make me want to puke.'

Rachel gave a pink and sheepish little smile. 'You will all come, won't you?'

'Daft question,' I said.

She raised her eyebrows at Guy and Fleur. 'How about you two?'

'Oh, we'd love to!' Fleur then checked herself, as if she

didn't want a new-ish boyfriend thinking she was organising him already. 'At least, it's fine with *me*.'

Before Guy could answer, Cara did. 'Dear me, Fleur. I should have thought you'd have him under better control by now.'

Fleur's slightly stiff tone only betrayed how Cara had got to her. 'I don't want to control him, thanks.'

Guy's response was to put a firm brown hand over Fleur's pale one and give it a reassuring squeeze. 'I'll be coming.' To Cara he gave the kind of look he might have given a sister's outrageous friend for whom he had a soft spot anyway. 'And that's quite enough from you, Maisie.'

The nickname took me right back to that steamy afternoon. He could have said it with a lot more conviction, though. Not in that semi-indulgent fashion.

Lindsay was still talking party. 'But please don't give us any rubbish about driving home – I can't bear parties where half the guests are sticking to miserable orange juice. I know it's bloody miles to Fleur's, but you'll just have to get a cab. Unless . . .' She turned to me. 'As Jeff's away, could they crash at yours? You could all come for leftover-lunch on the Sunday.'

'Yes, fine,' I said, as if I wasn't already making mental notes to blitz the bathroom, fumigate Jeff's room, etc.

With Fleur and Lindsay still unfed, Guy glanced over his shoulder. 'If that food's not here in one more minute I'm going to get seriously stroppy.'

At the same time, Robbie put his fork down. 'I've got a tummy ache,' he said pathetically. 'I don't think I can manage any more.'

Tummy ache my bottom. At the next table someone had just been served a multicoloured ice-cream in what looked like a small goldfish bowl. 'But p'raps I could manage some ice-cream,' he went on. 'Ice-cream just slips down, you know.'

Cunning little beast. This was verbatim Mum, from when he recently had tonsillitis. 'Eat some more of that first. Spaghetti's very good for tummy aches.'

He dropped the act. 'There's only maggots left! I only like it when it's worms!'

Volcano Robbie coming up. Maintain calm, firm manner, as befits rational adult in control.

This would have been easier if Guy hadn't stuck his oar in again. He wore the amused expression of a man with a *laizzez-faire* attitude to worms, who thought it now served me right if the little sod wouldn't eat his maggots. 'Your move,' he said. 'But my money's on junior. Firm principles, by the looks of him, especially when it comes to what he shoves down his gullet.'

As so often, Robbie picked up the tone. Ignoring his *See?* look, I repressed the urge to kick Guy under the table. I was damned if I was going to cave in as Mum so often did out of a combination of slavish adoration and exhaustion. 'Robbie, you haven't even eaten all your worms. Look, there are some lovely long squishy ones here.' I pointed them out with my fork.

His lower lip was mutinous. 'I don't *want* any more!'

'You've hardly eaten any of it.'

'It's *yuck*! It tastes of pooey green bits!'

I ignored him, just as those pious child experts tell you, and this was my fatal mistake. Just too late I saw what he did next. He shoved his plate away. He shoved it so hard, it shot straight across the slippery glass table.

And over the other side.

Even I'd never expected little-soddery quite like this.

Seven

If Guy hadn't been looking around for the waitress at that precise moment; if Fleur hadn't been searching her bag for something, they might have seen it coming.

It happened so fast. Tipping as it went, the dish slid straight into Fleur's lap.

She jerked and gasped.

Everybody uttered at once.

'*Shit!!!*' (Guy)

'Oh, my God . . .' (Rachel and Lindsay together)

'Oh, brilliant.' (Cara)

'Oh, *God*, Fleur, I'm terribly sorry . . .' (Me, leaping up, appalled.)

Already she was gingerly removing the upturned plate 'It's all right, please don't worry . . .'

The fact that she didn't swear made me feel even worse. Her cream lap was full of saucy maggots, with livid splashes elsewhere. Furious, I turned on Robbie. I knew he hadn't meant to shove it that far, but that wasn't the point. Never had I been so tempted to smack him, hard. 'You naughty, *naughty* boy! Sit there and don't you dare *move*!'

All this was accompanied by shocked observation from nearby tables, plus the mutterings I was used to when Robbie played up in public. Grabbing the nearest paper napkin I started picking up the solids from Fleur's lap.

Guy was doing exactly the same. 'Christ, just look at the

63

state of you. . .' His tone was fifty per cent tender anguish, fifty per cent *Just let me get my hands on the little bastard* . . . To me he added in tense tones, 'When you said "blood-bath" I hadn't realised you meant it literally.'

'It's not "literal",' I snapped, scooping livid 'maggots'. '"Literal" would be blood, not tomato.'

'For God's sake, if you're going to split hairs . . .'

Both trying to de-mess Fleur at once, our hands collided. 'I just hope this is little-soddish enough for you,' I said, dumping a soggy red napkin on the table. 'Since you seemed so keen on a demonstration.'

His response was terse. 'Thanks, this'll do just fine. If you'd like me to take him to the zoo later, I gather the tigers like a little snack around teatime.'

'Guy!' said Fleur.

'Oh, come on, Guy,' said Lindsay. 'You know you were encouraging him.'

Thank you, Lindsay. I scooped off most of the remaining solids. 'We'll have to sponge it,' I said to Fleur. 'Come to the loo and I'll help you.'

I turned back to Robbie, whose face was as aghast as it ever got. 'Stay there!' I said furiously. 'And don't even *move!*'

'Don't worry,' said Guy. 'He won't.'

Fuming and mortified, I departed with Fleur. 'I could kill him! He's just so used to getting his own way – Mum spoils him absolutely rotten.'

'Abby, calm down – it's not a massive disaster.' As we neared the loo, she lowered her voice. 'Actually, I've been dying to get you alone.'

Until then the other matter had been wiped by maggots from my mind.

'Did you *hear* her?' she muttered, as the door closed behind us.

'You mustn't let it get to you,' I said, wetting paper

towels under the tap. 'She was just enjoying a little stir.'

'"Enjoying" is the word,' she said, with feeling. 'With that sort of secret, catlike smile, as if she thought he'd be eating out of her hand in two minutes, if she only lifted a finger.'

This summed up Cara's expression pretty accurately. 'I'm sure it was just a bit of mischievous fun.' I started sponging a thigh-level splat.

Fleur dabbed distractedly at another. '*Mis*chievous?' As someone else had come in, she lowered her voice. 'You call bringing up an old sexual encounter, in front of me, mischievous? How would you like it?'

'OK, I wouldn't. But I'd try not to let it get to me.' Chucking one wet paper towel in the bin, I grabbed another. 'I'm sure this'll come out if you use a bio detergent.'

'I couldn't care less about the dress, Abby. Didn't you hear her? Whoppers getting into knickers – extremely naughty boy – why didn't he ignore her?'

It was no use pretending that it wouldn't have bothered me at all. 'Fleur, you know they go back for ever – they're basically just old mates. You've got to get this in proportion – she was only just sixteen.'

'That makes it all the worse! If she was a sneaky little tart at sixteen, what's she going to be like now?'

'Grown-*up*,' I soothed, moving on to a knee-level stain. 'You said yourself, not so long ago, that it was funny, looking back.'

'Yes, but that was before she was stirring up old paddling pools right under my nose!'

'Let her! It was a million years ago and it's you he wants, or he wouldn't be bothering to pursue a relationship with somebody an hour and a half's drive away.'

She sighed. 'I suppose you're right.' Dabbing at her lap, she made a very wry little moue. 'It's me. Not to mention the Scott effect.'

All too well I was recalling Fleur's tearful, devastated voice over the phone. Confronted, her so-called friend had resorted to cutting cruelty: *Oh, don't look at me like that – he was even more up for it than I was.*

'Will you forget Scott?' I demanded. 'He was just a reptile.'

'He wasn't at first! I just can't quite let go any more,' she went on. 'Emotionally, I mean. It's like when I was learning to swim and didn't quite dare take my feet off the bottom.'

I was still attacking the knee-level splat. 'No bad thing, if you ask me. You don't want to be in at the deep end without your armbands just yet. You've only been seeing him a few weeks.'

'Five weeks tomorrow.' She gave a 'trust *me*' little smile. 'And every night he's not with me, I wonder what he's up to.'

I tutted. 'Fleur, you're hopeless.'

She laughed, albeit a rather wry version. 'I know.'

When we finally returned to the table the mess was gone and Fleur and Lindsay's food had come at last. Guy was missing at first, but returned seconds after us. Belatedly I realised that a few splats had reached his shirt and trousers. There were damp orange patches where he'd evidently been getting the worst off. I was torn between feeling it served him right for egging Robbie on, and feeling bad for snapping at him. Then I recalled how he'd failed to ignore Cara, and thought it served him right, after all.

His humour had evidently returned, though it had a grin-and-bear-it edge. He winced as he saw Fleur's dress, with its massive sponged-out stain.

Robbie was now merely subdued. I was about to tell him to say sorry to Fleur when he pipped me. With the chocolate-eyed angel face guaranteed to get round Mum he said, 'I'm very sorry, Fleur. I didn't *mean* to.'

She smiled. 'I know you didn't, darling. It was an accident.'

Robbie then spoiled the effect by glancing hopefully at Rachel, as if to say, 'Was that right?'

She'd primed him, then. Still, at least he'd said it.

The river-breeze then picked up, making Fleur shiver in her damp dress. 'I knew I should have brought a cardigan.'

'You weren't anticipating sitting in wet clothes.' Taking his jacket from the back of his chair, Guy draped it around Fleur's shoulders. And as she snuggled gratefully into it, Robbie chose that moment to push his luck.

With a tap on my arm, he produced a whisper they could probably hear on the other side of the river. 'Can I have an ice-cream now?'

I braced myself. 'No, Robbie.'

'I said sorry!'

'I know, but you were very naughty.'

'I'm hungry!'

'Then you should have eaten your spaghetti.'

'It tasted of pooey green bits!'

'Robbie, be quiet. '

'But it was a *naxident*, even Fleur said!'

The way he could go banging on, making his point endlessly, I sometimes thought he'd end up in politics. 'That's because Fleur's very nice. It was *not* an accident – it was because you were in a horrible temper. I am *not* going to buy you any ice-cream. I'm not even going to *think* about buying you any ice-cream. OK?'

'But it *was* an—'

'Accident. Yes, we know.' This was Guy, and despite his words the eyes he fixed on Robbie could only be described as 'quelling'. In a voice to match he went on, 'But if you don't keep quiet about it, there might be another little accident. Like, my hand might just shoot across the table and accidentally give you a good wallop.'

Robbie was quelled. In fact, I'd go so far as to say he was instantly cowed. I was torn between *Hallelujah*, and thinking this was a bit rich from the man who'd thought it amusing to encourage him earlier.

As for the others, lips were bitten, except for Fleur. 'For heaven's sake, Guy, he's only little.'

Rachel said brightly, 'Anyway, does anyone else fancy something sweet and gooey?'

As normal conversation resumed, Robbie remained unusually subdued, looking suddenly so little I felt sorry for him. I whispered that it was all right, if he was still hungry I'd get him some chips. Now and then, as he dipped fries into ketchup, I saw him casting wary glances at Guy.

For his part, I guessed Guy was belatedly feeling slightly bad. Just once he spoke to Robbie again. 'Can I have one of your chips?'

Robbie eyed him with suspicion, as if it were a trick question.

Guy's mouth flickered. 'Just one?'

Robbie pushed his plate six inches towards him without a word.

'Thanks.'

I should probably have smiled at him in acknowledgement, but I was still irritated with him for egging Robbie on earlier, not to mention failing to ignore Cara. Quite apart from that, I didn't want any more eye contact that might kick off those pointless scenarios.

First cups of coffee were barely drunk when Fleur said she was sorry to be boring, but she really did want to go home and change.

After kissing everybody else goodbye, Guy brushed my cheek, too. 'Bye, then. Maybe see you in a couple of weeks.'

That's what his mouth said. The eye language was rather different: *I get the impression you're pissed off with me and pretending not to be.*

'Yep,' I said brightly. 'Sorry about the tomato-bath. Mind how you go.'

Then it was Robbie's turn. 'Bye, Robbie. Thanks for the chip.'

'Bye.' Robbie eyed him warily, but honour was at stake. 'But you weren't all *that* scary, anyway. Sometimes Abby's *much* scarier, even if she's a girl.'

I had to bite my lip.

Guy suppressed a grin. 'Well, that told me,' he said, adjusting his belt in the way of all men when they've just stood up after stuffing their faces. 'I'll say this for him,' he added to me, 'he's got B-A-double-L-S.'

'I should hope so,' said Lindsay blithely. 'Bugger off, Guy – we want to talk about you.'

Rachel and Cara left soon afterwards, and I was left with second coffees and Lindsay. With half his chips uneaten, Robbie wandered to the riverside wall, where an older child was throwing bits of bread for swooping gulls.

'I knew he'd be a disaster area,' I said. 'I'm really sorry.'

'For God's sake, Abby! You can't not take him anywhere for ever. Pity he didn't shove it all over Guy, though.' She started laughing. 'Would have served him right for egging him on. Anyway, I'm glad you didn't shoot off too – I've been dying to have a little bitch about Cara.'

This was one thing I loved about Lindsay. If she wanted to bitch, she admitted it. She'd never say things like, 'Didn't she look gorgeous?' and get around to snide comments bit by bit.

'Feel free.' I was keeping an eye on Robbie, who was absorbed in the swooping gulls. The sun was still glinting on the water, in the distance Big Ben was chiming two-thirty, and a riverboat full of tourists was sailing past to the Tower.

'She's been with us ten days now, and hasn't bought so much as a packet of teabags,' Lindsay went on. 'But I haven't said a word. Rachel would only think I'm being mean. And I'll tell you something else I wouldn't say to Rachel, as she'd really think I was being a cow. They were never an item, but I sometimes used to think Cara had a fancy for Guy. When I said he was coming today she just said, "Oh, is he?" but I swear I saw her little antennae perking up. If I said anything to Rachel she'd only say, "Oh, come on, that's just Cara," but I can tell you, if I were Fleur I don't think I'd leave her alone with him for more than two minutes.'

Never had I been so tempted to spill old beans, and I very nearly did. Only one thing stopped me. Lindsay would almost certainly tell Rachel, who'd probably pass it on to Cara. And I'd bet anything on Cara telling Guy. Given the nature of the jungle telegraph, I'd end up as some sneaky Peeping Tomette, lurking behind the kitchen curtains with my salacious little eyes popping.

No, thanks. Besides, it would smack of pointless stirring over something that shouldn't matter a damn now. 'That's hardly going to arise, is it?'

'Just as well. I've seen her in action before, not that you could exactly call it "action". She just sits there, oozing that sort of secret sexiness, you know, as if she'd turn into a rampant blue movie the instant they pressed the right button.'

Just as well Fleur couldn't hear this. 'I hope you're not thinking of David, too.'

'*David?*' she snorted. 'No, she'd never try anything with David. Whatever else, I think she really is fond of Rachel. And she's hardly going to bite the hand that's giving her a bed, so to speak.'

'How long do you think she'll be staying?'

'Until Christmas, at this rate. I don't think she's even started looking seriously for a job. Mind you . . .' She started laughing. 'I thought of something the other day that would just do for Cara. There was a magazine article about honey-traps – I thought, Yes, *per*fect! She'd have a hundred per cent success rate.'

I'd read that too, in last month's *City Girl*. The title had screamed, *I WAS A LOVE-RAT HONEYTRAP!* 'Yes, I saw that. Pays a bomb, apparently.'

'Even more perfect. She'd be able to afford her own place. She's on a Z-bed in Rachel's room at the moment, though Rachel's round at David's half the time. I can see a scenario where she stays until Rachel moves in with David – I swear she will soon – and I end up sharing with Cara by default.'

I was still watching Robbie, and the swooping, crying gulls. 'Then you'll just have to tell her you'd rather not.'

'Yes, and have Rachel think I'm a cow.' But a wicked glint returned to her eyes. 'Still, I *am* a cow. Never mind honeytraps, the other night I had a vision of her as a carnivorous plant. It oozes sweet, sticky stuff to entice its prey.'

It didn't take much guessing. Will had once had one, and killed it by over-feeding it bits of Peperami. 'Not a Venus flytrap?'

'You got it.'

'As in zips, I take it.'

'Well, I don't mean as in green and fond of ingesting bluebottles.'

We collapsed into fits.

She eventually went on, 'Cara and Guy were together a lot, you know, when she was about thirteen. Her mother was not long divorced – she and Guy's father were seeing each other for nearly a year.'

'You're kidding!'

'I'm not. Mum thought they might get married, but

71

apparently Cara's mum said she was never making that mistake again. They all went away once, *en* sort-of *famille*. They were both only children so she was with Guy a good deal. Just when her hormones were kicking in, I suppose.'

Robbie chose that moment to get bored with the bird life. 'Are we going soon?'

We went via the Tower, where I was strong enough not to buy him ice-cream from a stall. I bought him an ice-lolly, instead.

Fleur called two days later 'The stain came right out, so if you're still feeling bad, you can stop it now.'

'Thank God for that.'

'But I wasn't just ringing for that.' She paused. 'Abby, please don't tell me I'm mad – I know that already – but I did something really stupid on the way home the other day.'

Eight

I winced. 'Don't tell me you dragged up paddling pools?'

'Not quite that stupid. I said, "Were you ever involved with her?"'

Wince two. 'What did he say?'

'He laughed. He said, "What makes you say that?" so I said, "I just wondered," and he said, "Well, I wasn't. All right?"'

'True enough, isn't it? A little session of whatever it was doesn't mean "involved".'

'Yes, but I didn't mean that, did I? I meant were you attracted to her, was there ever anything between you, and he must have known I meant that. And he denied it.'

If I could have shaken her down the phone . . . 'Well, he would, wouldn't he? He could see you'd got the wind up. Honestly, Fleur, haven't you ever heard of playing it cool?'

'Abby, I could probably write a wretched *book* on playing it cool. It's just another of those things that are all very easy in theory.'

By some miracle the good weather was still with us on the day of the party. With temperatures still hovering around the twenty-five mark, I took Robbie that morning to the open-air pool. I'd been taking him on and off since he was seven months old, and with Mum and Will also doing pool duty now and then, he already swam like a little tadpole.

On my return I blitzed the flat. Just as I'd finished, Fleur called.

'I can't make it tonight, after all. Right after work last night I drove up to see an old friend in Nottingham who's just had a baby, and an hour ago she slipped and sprained her ankle really badly. Her partner's away until tomorrow morning, and she's only just moved here, so there's no one she can ask.'

'Oh, Fleur!'

'Don't tell me. The original plan was for Guy to meet me at Lindsay and Rachel's, so he's still going anyway. Sarah's Joe's flying in really early, around eight, I think, so I'll leave as soon as he's back – I'll be there by lunchtime. I've already told Lindsay. I said could he crash on their sofa – there's no need for him to come to you now.'

Naturally I thought of Cara, but if Fleur wasn't mentioning her, I certainly wasn't. 'It's a terrible shame. I hope Sarah appreciates you.'

'How could I leave her? She's a bit post-natal anyway.' She paused. 'I know it sounds really nasty, I'm probably being completely paranoid, but could you do me a massive favour tonight?'

Already I had a sinking feeling. 'What?'

'You couldn't keep an eye on Guy, could you? With you-know-who, I mean?'

'Fleur, if you really can't trust him for one night . . .'

'I knew you'd say that. I know it's horrible, Abby, but I can't help it. After all, if I'm not there, what's to stop her doing some groundwork? Saying she might pop down and see him? You can do that when you're a so-called old friend – nobody turns a hair. If you pick up any vibes – you know what I mean – you will tell me?'

It was no use pretending I wouldn't have felt much the

same. 'Why didn't you suggest he just skipped the party and came to yours tomorrow?'

'How can I? He was their friend first. Anyway, I thought if I told him to go ahead *and* stay the night there, it would kill any idea that I'm remotely jealous.'

I fought rising exasperation. 'Fleur, it's a bit late for that. If you weren't remotely jealous, you'd never have asked whether he was involved with her.'

'I know, but I swear I haven't mentioned her since. Not one *word*. Please, just keep a subtle eye open – you know what I mean. I can hardly ask Lindsay or Rachel. They'd think I was awful, when he's a friend and they introduced me.'

How could I repeat what Lindsay had said? It'd only turn her into even more of a nervous wreck than she was already. 'OK. I'm sure you don't need to worry, though.'

It was a bit late in the day, but never had I had such a salutary lesson in keeping your mouth shut.

Around five, Lindsay called. 'Abby, we have a crisis.'

'Not enough glasses?'

'I wish. Think carnivorous plant-life, beginning with V.'

Oh, please . . .

'I gather Fleur already told you she can't come,' she went on. 'Well, when I told Cara she said, "Oh, what a shame," but I swear I saw her chlorophyll light up. In fact, I almost saw her sticky little fronds unfurling already.'

'They're not fronds. They're like green shells, with fuzzy spikes round the edges.'

'Whatever. There won't be many spare blokes, so that'll give her even more of an excuse for monopolising him. I'm not having her oozing her sticky stuff at Guy tonight. Not under our roof. We need a defence strategy.'

'Lindsay, he's supposed to be your friend! I don't think it's very nice to imply that he can't be trusted for one evening.'

'Abby, I'm not sure I'd trust the Archbishop of Canterbury with Cara when she's oozing on six cylinders. Not if he'd had a few drinks and Mrs Arch was ankle-sitting. I thought you could sort of mark her, like in netball, remember? Whenever she looks like getting anywhere near goal, jump up and down and get in the way.'

This was even worse than Fleur's subtle eye. 'No way. What if anyone thinks *I'm* flirting with him?'

'I'm not talking flirting, Abby, though I'm not saying a bit of cleavage would come amiss. Just distract him. Show an intelligent interest in sailing or something. He's into all that stuff.'

'I'm not.'

'Then use your initiative. I'm not having him crash on our sofa, either. I wouldn't put it past her to wander in at four in the morning in a T-shirt and no knickers, pretending she's had a nightmare. I just called Fleur and said would she mind if he didn't stay here. There's some last-minute old friend of David's, and David's sofa's already booked.'

'You're not suggesting Guy comes here after all?'

'Yes – that is OK, isn't it?'

I tried to ignore a faint disturbance in my stomach. Of course it was OK. Why wouldn't it be? And having done it already, at least I wouldn't have to panic-blitz.

'Yes, I guess so.'

'Thank God for that – I already told David his friend can have our sofa. Look, Abby, I've got to dash – there's still masses to do. Guy was due around seven – I'll give him a buzz and redirect him. Oh, and don't forget to bring a bottle.' She gave an evil little laugh. 'A magnum of premier cru weedkiller, heh heh.'

*   *   *

My blitzing hadn't included Jeff's sty, but I'd changed the sheets, which was enough to make it habitable for me. By six I'd transferred everything I'd need, including Little Ted from under my duvet. I'd had him since I was ten days old and he couldn't sleep without me. After a shower I wrapped myself in a white towelling robe Dad had once nicked from a hotel. Mid-calf length, it would comfortably have enveloped the porkier kind of Sumo wrestler, but that was why I liked it.

While I was finishing my nails the buzzer rang.

I pressed the entryphone. 'Yes?'

'Hi, Abby, it's Guy.'

'Come up, it's up the stairs.'

En route to the door, I tightened the belt of my robe and gave myself a quick check in the mirror. Wet, combed hair. Dry, squeaky-clean face. Smile, please!

I opened the door. He wore navy shorts of the hyper-casual type, and a short-sleeved shirt in denim blue. He also wore a sea-breeze tan – and a yellow bandanna thing tied round his forehead.

'Hi,' he said, deadpan. 'Just tell me I look a prat and get the scary bit over with.'

I had to laugh. 'You shouldn't listen to Robbie, you know. I'm only really scary when there's a full moon. Come in.'

Canvas grip in one hand, ripping off headgear with the other, he followed.

'It looks a bit like a duster,' I said.

'You're not far out.' He shook out a piece of folded yellow cloth. 'More usually used for de-misting the windscreen.'

'Just as well. I'm afraid I can't say it suits you.'

He came through to my blitzed living room. The floor was the original pine, now sanded and sealed. On it lay a couple of natural cotton rugs. The two little sofas were cheap Ikea that looked non-cheap, in warm earth covers.

I'd recently re-painted it all in white, and the big bay window let in a lot of light anyway. In front of the original fireplace stood a flourishing dracaena that still hadn't gone brown at the edges. Though I say it myself, it was a quiet monument to good taste (i.e. mine) on a tight budget.

He gave a quick glance around. 'This is nice.'

I knew he wasn't just saying it. 'Thanks. What a shame about Fleur. Typical of her to come up trumps in a crisis, though.'

'Yes, I gather the baby's only about five days old. Sarah's up and down a dozen times a night, Fleur said, so it wasn't the best time to sprain her ankle.'

For a moment we stood there, in that slight, now-what awkwardness when you're thrust together with someone you barely know. I was rather conscious of being alone with someone else's bloke, who seemed to be taking up more than his fair share of space. He'd apparently grown, but then I was in my five-foot-seven bare feet. To put it bluntly, regardless of acres of white towelling, I suddenly felt it wasn't quite right to be standing three feet away from him with no knickers on.

'Like a beer?' I said brightly.

'I could murder one.'

He followed me to the kitchen. 'Brilliant weather,' I said, hunting in the fridge. 'We'll be partying in the garden. Uncle Matthew just had a sort of *Ground Force* team in to re-do that, as well.' I handed him a can of Michelob.

'Yes, I gather,' he said, ripping the top off. 'Their old man's always been – what shall I say? – very indulgent.'

'He spoiled them rotten, you mean. I don't mind admitting I was sometimes slightly green about the gills with envy.'

He laughed. 'So was I. My old man was as tight as you

78

like. Mind you, my stepmother was pretty bloody expensive. High-maintenance, as they didn't call it then.'

I'd forgotten about his own mother, who'd died. Suddenly I had a vision of a clichéd, grasping step, resenting every penny spent on her predecessor's son.

'She was good fun, though,' he said. 'Still is, come to that.'

Exit cliché, then. I was almost beginning to feel sorry for him there.

Can in hand, he leant against the counter. 'So where's your sharer gone?' he asked. 'Jeff, isn't it?'

'He's in Morocco. Contemplating his navel in the sand dunes, probably fancying himself as Lawrence of Arabia. Right, I must go and get dressed,' I added, with a briskness I wouldn't normally use. 'I'll show you to the scary west wing.'

I opened the door to my freshly blitzed bedroom. 'There you go. I've finished in the bathroom so feel free to grab a shower.'

He took one glance and turned to me. 'This is your room.'

I'd recently re-vamped it. The ceiling was Cool Blue, the walls a lighter toning shade. With a blue and white checked duvet it wasn't exactly girly, but I suppose things like make-up on the chest of drawers gave it away. 'Yes, but I'm afraid you'll have to lump it. Jeff's is a pigsty and I couldn't be bothered to fumigate it.'

'I can handle pigsties.'

'That's not the point. I dusted on purpose. I even went mad and ironed the duvet cover, so please don't be awkward.'

His mouth flickered. It was a distinctly attractive mouth: firm and soft and mobile all at once, and something in that quirky little movement had a drastic effect on me. Before you could say Time Machine I was sixteen again, right back in that paddling pool: *I bet you're a lovely kisser . . .*'

That was my first thought.

The second was infinitely worse. It was the kind of thought I liked to kid myself only other people had. In fact, if I were seven again just then and not me, I'd have said, 'I *hate* you, Abby Morland. I'm not going to be your friend any more, so there.'

Nine

But I flatter myself none of this showed.

He said, 'If Fleur finds out you've slept in a pigsty on my account, she'll probably give me a bollocking.'

'*Fleur?*' I had to laugh. 'I can't quite see her bollocking anybody.'

'Don't you believe it. She gave me a fair old bollocking the other week. On the way home, after the tomato-bath.'

His tone was light enough to tell me that it was no proper bollocking, but that she'd had a minor go at him and it had given him a jolt.

'On account of sticking my nose in to your Robbie-management,' he went on. 'And then putting the wind up him by talking accidental wallops.'

'At least it kept him quiet for a bit.'

'But I can't risk another,' he said, tongue entirely in cheek. 'So please, just point me at the pigsty.'

'Well, don't blame me if you catch something.' I went with him, to retrieve the things I'd transferred earlier. 'I've booked a minicab, by the way. I don't want to go on the tube. It's too far to walk in killer heels.'

'I'll take your word for it.' Already he was taking stuff out of his bag.

I returned to my room, nudging the door shut with my hip.

I can't believe what you just thought. Let's face, it you're actually an extremely horrible person.

What had flashed through my head was roughly this: *I hope Cara flirts rotten with you tonight. I hope I see that, 'Well, what the fuck?' look in your eyes. I hope I overhear you making a sneaky assignation with her, because then I'll know you're just another reptile, and I won't be jealous of Fleur.*

Because I was.

Naturally I felt terrible for thinking all this, which perversely cheered me up a bit. Since a really horrible person wouldn't feel terrible, there was hope.

I thought of Fleur later, cooking while Sarah put her ankle up, or changing a tiny, wriggly baby. Meanwhile she'd be thinking: What's he doing now? Is she talking to him, running the tip of her tongue over her lower lip in that oh-so-casual fashion? Looking at him with eyes that say, Come on, you know you want me . . .

My stomach contracted in empathy.

As for that 'bollocking', I could bet it was her tension over Cara coming out of a Robbie exit, so to speak. And evidently he was fooled, so she needn't worry that he was imagining jealousy in the department.

While I was still getting ready, Fleur called my mobile. 'Is he there?'

I lowered my voice. 'Not *right* here – he's in Jeff's pigsty.'

She gave a little laugh as wobbly as her voice. 'I was so relieved when Lindsay said he couldn't stay at theirs, I can't tell you.'

I lowered my voice further. 'Fleur, you sound pissed!'

'Well, maybe just a bit. I was feeling so bad, asking you to spy on him. If he ever found out, I'd die.'

If you ever found out what I just thought, I'd double die.

'Who said anything about spying? It's just that I'm a naturally observant person and I can't help noticing things. If there's anything to notice, which I'm sure there won't be.'

By the time I'd put the final touches to Party Bitch, she wasn't looking too bad. Through the odd session at the open-air pool, my Brittany tan had yet to fade to dirty olive. I don't have the dark eyes that should go with my skin. Mine are dark blue, like Dad's, and not bad when I've had a good night's sleep.

My hair isn't Armada-raven, either. It's straight, mid-brown. Although I'd once despised it as unbelievably boring (much like Sycamore Road) I quite liked it now. At least it was shiny, and in the sun or good artificial light there were gold and red lights in it. For nearly two years it had been in a sort of Jennifer Aniston, but I was overdue for a change. I just couldn't make up my mind what.

I was wearing a little sleeveless top in shocking pink silk. It was just low enough to show a hint of cleavage; just short enough to show a hint of midriff. With it I wore trousers in black, softly clinging crêpe, a chunky silver necklace, and a pair of high-heeled sandals consisting of two slivers of shocking pink snakeskin and a label on one sole that still said 'Reduced to £49.99'.

Belatedly I peeled this off, grabbed my Indian beaded bag (Accessorize sale), and an oversised black mohair cardigan. If we were partying outside, I'd freeze in just that silk top later.

Guy was in the living room. Much as I do when left alone in other people's houses, he was having a good old nose at the bookshelves. These were on either side of the fireplace, but they held more than books.

Hearing my clicky heels on the wood, he turned around. Freshly showered, his hair was still damp. He wore stone-coloured cotton trousers and a loose, short-sleeved shirt that looked like navy linen. He had a thumb hooked in a front trouser pocket in a way that has been known to turn me on. (Yes, I know I'm weird.)

Almost imperceptibly he raised his eyebrows. It was that Grade One lift that says, 'Well, she scrubs up OK.' In case you're wondering, a Grade Two says, 'Mmm, wouldn't say no,' and a Grade Three, 'Wow!'

Naturally I had been neither expecting nor hoping for either of these.

His eyes went to my toes. 'I see what you mean about the killer heels.'

'A girl has to go mad now and then.' I went over to the window and peered out, to check the taxi situation. 'I just hope we won't have to traipse the streets for a return cab later.'

'What's wrong with booking one?'

'I never do. How do I know when I'll want to come home?'

'Fair enough.'

I peered out of the window for signs of cabs, but all I saw was Lycra Shorts from over the road zooming off on his go-faster bike.

'I was checking out your photos,' Guy said. 'Are these the brothers?'

I turned around.

He was indicating a framed shot I'd taken myself and had blown up as a Mother's Day present for Mum. It was in the garden at home, on a sunny day. Both grinning, Andrew and Will were holding an ecstatically laughing, fifteen-month-old Robbie between them. 'There you go,' I'd said. 'Your three little boys all together.'

'Yes,' I said. 'That's Will on the left. He does a good line in play-fights – Robbie adores him.'

The taxi arrived two minutes later, and Guy was not impressed. 'What sort of a cab's this?' he muttered.

'It's what you call a no-frills service.'

'You don't say.'

It was a scruffy white car, but it was that sort of minicab company. I suspected that most of the drivers were illegal immigrants but fares were 'competitive', as it said on the card they'd shoved through the door.

'How's Robbie?' Guy asked, as the cab moved off.

'Still pretty horrible now and then, thanks.'

He made no polite, lying denial. 'Probably an occupational hazard of being – what – five?'

'Four and a half, but it's probably more an occupational hazard of being the centre of Mum's universe. That's why I try to de-sod him when I can.'

'Lindsay told me you're practically an honorary mother.'

'That is a gross exaggeration. Apart from the odd night's babysitting I don't usually have him for more than half a day every couple of weeks. When it's just me and him and he's not playing to an audience, he can almost be human. Believe it or not,' I added.

He laughed. 'I'll believe you. I did think he was a bit of a card. And as I said, he's got balls.'

Slowing to a crawl, the driver inched over one of the sleeping policemen that littered this residential rat-run. Lined with parked cars, it was punctuated with trees from which yellowing leaves were drifting down fast.

'I know it'll probably break your heart,' I said, 'but I'm afraid you're not on Robbie's favourite-people list. On the way home that day he said, "I don't like Fleur's boyfriend. I think he's a bit of a plonker."'

He laughed.

'He functions like a recording device,' I added. 'Replays anything he hears. That little gem was probably mopped up from Will.'

He was still half laughing. 'Did you say, "You said it"?'

'No, I was making allowances for the fact that you'd obviously had no experience of little-sod management.'

Because I was trying to tell myself I felt no such thing, I found myself acutely aware of Guy, sitting so close on a back seat upholstered in tatty grey. There was a faint, large stain in the space between us. Probably puke, I told myself, to take my mind off illicit sensations. Beer-and-kebab puke, from a bloke with fourteen earrings and a massive gut bulging from his T-shirt.

Meanwhile, the cab had almost ground to a halt. 'Cryzy people,' muttered the driver, peering out of his window to see what was causing the hold-up. 'Cryzy-bastard people making double-park – I like to string 'em up by ze short and curlies.'

'Another case of mopping up?' Guy murmured.

'Sounds like it,' I murmured back. 'You don't find that particular expression in *New Practical English*.'

As we got moving again, Guy said, 'What sort of people do you teach?'

'All sorts, as long as they're adults. Businessmen, students, people who need conversational English for their jobs, rich kids having an excuse for a glorified holiday, clubbing every night. They're the ones that can be pains. Now and then I do classes for asylum seekers.'

He raised an eyebrow. 'All human life is there?'

'A good mix, anyway.' As he'd thrown this ball to me, I threw it back. 'So what's this boat business? Rent-a-yacht or something?'

'It's a charter company. Based on the Solent.'

'Family business, I gather.'

'My grandfather started it, back in the sixties. My old man was a weekend sailor, but since he preferred law it skipped a generation. I was messing around in boats a lot as a kid – I never thought twice.'

Big business now, I thought. All those corporate jollies. 'Are you into sailing?' he asked.

'I never did any till I had a boyfriend who was mad about it. He used to insist on taking his boat out when it was freezing cold, with horrible great scary grey waves. He used to yell orders about spinnakers and ropes and things, and I never had a clue what he was on about so I did everything wrong, and he used to say, "Oh, *Christ*, Abby – what's the matter with you?" Then he used to sail the bloody thing at ninety degrees to the horizontal, and leave me hanging over the edge, praying for my life, and yell, "Great, isn't it?"'

I'd tickled him now, which was probably a bad idea. Even with no sun on them, his eyes were lit with little candles of laughter. 'Then why did you do it?'

Because I fancied him rotten, if you really want to know. 'I didn't, for long. The only boat I've been in since is a cross-channel ferry, or a speedboat. Water-skiing,' I added. 'I got hooked on holiday years ago and joined a club.'

'How often d'you get around to that?'

'Once a week in the summer, if I can. As long as it's not pouring with rain. It's not much fun in the rain. It feels like needles on your face.'

My mobile trilled. I delved in my bag, thinking: Please, not Fleur again.

The screen said, 'Mum.'

'Are you busy?' she asked, which was ominous in itself. It usually meant 'brace yourself'.

'Not for a minute – I'm on my way to Lindsay and Rachel's, remember? What's happened?'

'Well, sort of good news and bad news. Andrew called round earlier.'

This would be the good news. Andrew lived just off

Brick Lane, in a flat bought just before the area became hyper-cool, and wasn't in the habit of popping in on a casual basis. 'Well, that was nice,' I said, with an eye on the passing street. The evening sun was casting a golden wash over suburbia. On someone's gatepost sat a tabby cat like an ornamental add-on, watching the world go by.

'I don't know about "nice",' she said. 'I think I've upset him. In fact, I know I have.'

Oh, Lord . . .

'He and Imogen apparently booked a holiday a few weeks ago,' she went on. 'The Maldives, I think he said. For December.'

Imogen was his girlfriend. 'Don't tell me. You said, "Are you quite sure she's going to last that long?"'

'That's just it. It's now going to be their honeymoon.'

'*What?*' He'd been seeing Imogen for a few months, but I'd thought it was a blip. Over the years Andrew had turned playing the field into an art form.

'He said, "We thought we might as well,"' she went on.

I'd only met Imogen once. I'd had no idea it was serious, but he'd hardly have told me anyway. Details of his private life generally had to be dragged out of Andrew, kicking and screaming about their human rights. 'Is he sickening for something?' I asked. 'I mean, Imogen's lovely, I don't mean *her*, but . . .'

'Yes, that's what I thought. They've already booked venues and everything. He said, "Well, they were available, so it all tied in."'

This was the brother who'd once said loftily that he was never getting married, it was an archaic institution and totally at odds with the genetic male imperative.

Mind you, he was about nineteen at the time. 'God,' I said.

'Exactly. I said, "Look, Andrew, I hope you're not rushing into this. It's not a thing to rush into just because it "ties in".'

I was beginning to see why he'd got upset. 'Mum, you of all people should know he'd never rush into it. He's probably been thinking about it for a while – he just hadn't said.'

'I know, Abby, but it was such a shock. It's not as if they'd even got engaged!'

'He never would.' In the past Andrew had been scathingly contemptuous of such bourgeois rituals, designed only so that girls could brag about morsels of fossilised carbon on their fingers. 'You know perfectly well he'd never go all misty-eyed about it, either.'

'I *know*, Abby. Oh, dear, you're making me feel even worse now.'

Just as well I'd never gone into counselling. 'Sorry. So what did he say?'

'"Well, thank you, Mother, for that vote of confidence."' She reproduced a sardonic tone I could imagine exactly.

It made me wince. 'I can't exactly blame him. He is thirty-three, Mum, and heaven knows he's not exactly naïve.'

'I *know* that, Abby. I just worry about any of you rushing into it without being absolutely sure.'

It wasn't much use saying, 'You rushed into it, and you were sure.' 'So did he go off in a mood?'

'Well, not immediately. I said I was very happy, Imogen was a lovely girl, but I just hoped for her sake that he was really *certain*, that he really *meant* it, and only made things worse. He said, "God, no, why would I mean it? I just thought it'd be a laugh to spend thousands of pounds and have a lot of photos of people in hideous hats."'

My mind was going back years, to Andrew creeping into

my room one night when I was about nine. *I just went downstairs and found Mum crying. Her eyes were all red. She pretended she'd been watching a sad film, but it's not that. It's Dad. I think he's got another girlfriend.*

Until then I hadn't realised there had ever been any girlfriend.

'He pretended it was a joke,' Mum went on. 'He did stay for a cup of tea afterwards, only I couldn't say anything else then, because Robbie started playing Let's Bash Each Other Up, and made Andrew spill his tea all over his trousers. So he had to charge off and change before meeting Imogen.'

She paused, and when she spoke again her voice was wobbly. 'But he hardly kissed me goodbye. Just that "cross" sort of peck, you know.'

I did know. They could be like a pair of hermit crabs. Hurt that Mum could think he might end up doing a Dad on Imogen, Andrew had retreated into his sardonic shell. Wounded by sardonic shells, Mum had retreated into her hurt shell, and neither of them would stick out a little feeler.

Not so long ago, these shells had not been a problem. They'd thickened enormously around five years ago, when Andrew had wounded Mum deeply by accident. Since then, things had never been quite the same.

'He'll get over it,' I said. 'Give him a ring tomorrow.'

She hesitated. 'Yes, but could you just have a little word with him first? Explain that I only meant it for the best?'

I'd played shell-breaker before. My flak jacket still bore the holes. I wanted to say, 'No, *you* sort it out! I'm not a bloody United Nations peacekeeping force!'

I actually said, 'Tell you what, I'll have you both round for dinner and bang your heads together.'

'Oh, Abby . . .'

'All right, all right, I'll speak to him.'

I hung up with a familiar, weary feeling. 'Sorry,' I said to Guy. 'Just one of the jolly little dramas our family specialises in.'

He didn't ask what, which was just as well, or I might have told him. I wasn't in the mood for tactful shell-breaking tomorrow. I had a flytrap to think of. I'd just been showing worrying signs of being an extremely horrible person.

Meanwhile, the cab had slowed right down again. The traffic was worse than usual; at this time on a Saturday evening you could usually manage at least thirteen miles an hour. But all this stop-start-crawl was getting to Guy, I could tell. I sensed his growing tension, as if he'd like to get out and walk. The fingers on the hand that lay on his thigh flexed, relaxed and flexed again.

I tried not to notice that the hand was exactly the kind I'd choose from a Pick'n'Mix Ideal Bloke kit. Pity there was nothing to put me off. Pity he didn't splay his thighs right out, like those ape-men who manage to walk more or less upright, but have to brag to the whole world the minute they sit down that they need a hundred and fifty degrees of ball-room. That alone would almost have turned me right off. Some cheap, I'm-a-Sex-God cologne would have been good, too. All I could smell was my own, and because I'd run out of light-and-sassy, I'd misted myself with another I wasn't so keen on. In that confined space it was beginning to smell like an entire harem of heavily scented concubines.

Maybe this was adding to Guy's impatience. It wouldn't have surprised me if it were starting to nauseate him. Fleur only ever wore elusive, delicate florals. Somehow you couldn't imagine her wearing anything else.

I wound my window down, letting some good old London pollution in, and thought of floral Fleur. *I feel so bad, asking you to spy on him* . . .

I felt absolutely great about it, of course. At this rate I was going to feel like a dog told to guard the steak, to stop the cat getting it.

Still, we were nearly there. Lindsay and Rachel's street was more upmarket than mine. The interiors you spotted through windows looked like the Style sections of the Sunday supplements, which was one reason why the residents enjoyed a thoroughly professional standard of burglary.

As the cab pulled in, I had my purse ready, but Guy pipped me. From his breast pocket he plucked a twenty-pound note and passed it over the driver's shoulder.

'I'll get the return sector,' I said.

'OK.' He was already halfway out.

As I came round to the pavement side, he was standing by the driver's window while he searched for the change they never seemed to have enough of.

Guy was fingering the wing mirror. Having taken a smash, the glass was criss-crossed with tape. 'Have you heard the expression "tits on a bull"?' he asked the driver.

'I know, mite, don't need to tell me.'

'Then get it fixed. It's illegal.' He gave the front wheel a little kick. 'Your tyres don't look that great, either.'

'I tell my boss, OK? Only he never listen.' The man passed over his change. 'You want pick-up later?'

'No, thanks.' Guy pocketed the change. 'Tell your tight-arse boss I'm a police officer and I've just taken your registration.'

The cab screeched off faster than Mum's cat Pudding that time Satan wandered in and sniffed her when she was enjoying a nice little snooze. (Satan was the Alsatian from two doors down.)

Guy watched the cab go. 'Brilliant. Just what he needs, burning more rubber.'

'The poor bloke's probably an illegal. And it's not his fault if his boss is a tight-arse.'

'No, and I'm sure Tight-arse will have every sympathy when someone like you ends up in intensive care because of the state of his cabs.'

Aha! Something to put me off at last. Right or not, did he have to look at me as if I were some woolly-headed do-gooder? This type of behaviour got right up my nose at the best of times. And while I was in prime, pouncing-on-anything mood, did he have to stand in a shaft of that peculiarly golden, late-evening sun that can almost make wheelie bins look like conceptual art?

'That's an occupational hazard of cheap cabs,' I retorted, ringing the shiny brass bell on a gleaming, green-painted front door. 'This is London, you know, not down in the Sussex sticks.' (I pronounced it 'deown', like some old yokel with a straw hanging out of his mouth.) 'And least I've got sympathy for a probably illegal driver, being paid three quid an hour if he's lucky.'

'So what did you want me to do?' He shoved his hands in his pockets. 'Give him a tip?'

'God, no. He might have spent it on Polos, or some other decadent luxury.'

This came out with like PMT with lemon juice. Telling myself to get a grip, I smiled, instead. 'Sorry. I shouldn't have said that.'

'Oh, please don't apologise. I was just starting to enjoy myself.' He glanced down at me with an expression that said he almost meant it. 'But I thought you said you were only really scary when there's a full moon.'

'We must be due for one tonight, then. It might be awkward trying to get a cab later, when I've got fur all over my face.'

His mouth quivered minutely. 'You could always borrow

93

a razor and have a quick shave. And by the way, I don't live deown in the Sussex sticks any more. It's the Hampshire sticks.'

Just as he said this, my mobile trilled once more.

Mum. *For God's sake, NOW what?*

'It's me again,' she said. 'I just forgot to say, do have a lovely time tonight, won't you?'

Ten

I tried not to sound as if I'd just felt like boiling her head. 'Thanks, will do.'

'Oh, and do give my love to the girls. Two weddings coming up, now! Andrew's is planned for the sixth of December, by the way. Tell them to put it in their diaries.'

'Is it going to be a big do, then?'

'Oh, I expect so – Imogen's parents aren't exactly hard up, I gather.'

Just as I put my mobile away, Rachel opened the door, breathless and blooming. We followed her through a spacious Edwardian conversion that still smelt of paint to a garden I hadn't seen since it was done. Instead of scrubby grass and overgrown, grimy shrubs was a new area of decking bordering new green turf. There were pots of scented flowers, and draped in the new shrubs were fairy lights like twinkling dragonflies. Background music was coming from outside speakers.

My inner accountant was thinking: Shit, how much did all this cost?

'I can't believe it's the same garden,' I said to Rachel. 'It's really lovely.'

'Yes, isn't it?' she said happily. 'I'd have liked a little water feature, but Lindsay thought it'd be naff.'

We went the way of all flesh: to the bar. This was a

cloth-covered table where a dozen of the thirty-odd guests were milling.

David was doing barman duty. In a lurid, Hawaiian shirt that was almost certainly a joke, he was drawing a cork and talking to three people at the same time.

In a way, David and Rachel were like the Guy/Fleur situation. He'd been a friend of mine from way-back home, but his folks had moved away when he was seventeen and we'd lost touch. I'd bumped into him quite by chance at a charity quiz night at a pub. I was on the Lingua Franca team; he was on his squash club ditto. About ten days later I'd taken him to one of Lindsay's impromptu bashes, where Cupid had been lurking under the kitchen table.

David had wavy, toffee-coloured hair and the face of the boy next door in films where Ms Gorgeous doesn't realise she's in love with him until she thinks he's going to marry Ms Other-Gorgeous.

I gave him a kiss. 'Congratulations, you romantic old softie.'

'Abby!' He did a good line in cuddly hugs, too. 'This is my old mate Neil.'

Hmm! Exactly the sort of distraction I could do with. Tall, dark and not half bad, in a black shirt and trousers. I'd always had a little thing about men in black.

Neil was giving me a dry sort of smile. 'So you're the guilty party.'

'Sorry?'

'You introduced them. David and Rachel.'

Although he meant it to sound jokey, he didn't quite succeed. I detected a note of, *Bloody shame – I do hate to see any old mate get caught.*

I gave him a sunny smile anyway. 'Yes, it was my first attempt at matchmaking. As a matter of fact, I'm thinking of taking it up professionally.'

Guy had just helped himself to a beer when Cara appeared. 'About time too, Fielding. Come and meet some of the rabble.'

Quick work, I thought, as she led him off. He hadn't even ripped the top off his beer.

A few minutes later, I was talking to a friend of Rachel's. She was called Kirsty, and I'd met her before. Only then did Lindsay appear. 'God, what a rush – I haven't even started on the food.' She gave the small of my back a little nudge. 'Where's Guy?'

'Over there.' Cara had taken him to a little group in a corner of the garden, but because they were largely behind another lot, you couldn't see much.

She repeated the nudge, which made me wonder what on earth I was supposed to do. If Cara were planning any serious oozing, surely she'd at least wait until he'd had a few drinks?

Kirsty nodded towards the 'bar'. 'Who's that in the black shirt?'

She meant Neil, and Lindsay made a wry face. 'Forget it – he's off to work in Singapore next week, for at least six months. Excuse us, Kirsty, I need Abby to give me a hand.' She gave me another little nudge. 'Come on, Abby—'

'Will you stop poking me like that?' I muttered, as we went inside. 'I don't need it spelt out.'

'Then why aren't you doing your netball bit? Honestly, Abby, you had the perfect opportunity, coming with him and everything.'

She led me into a pristine new kitchen, all gleaming white and stainless steel. 'God,' I said, as the old one had made mine look positively trendy. 'How much did this lot cost?'

'Never mind the kitchen – we were talking flytraps.'

'It's far too early,' I said. 'She's hardly going to be oozing yet.'

'That's what you think.' She shut the door behind us. 'You didn't see her chlorophyll light up earlier. Like I said, I've seen her in action before.' She yanked open the brand-new fridge and passed me packets of oven-ready party nibbles. 'And I'm not having it. Not here.'

I piled the packets up in my arms. 'You make him sound like some helpless victim. I'm sure he's perfectly capable of fending her off if he wants to.'

'God, Abby, hasn't *any*thing I said sunk in?' She closed the fridge door with more force than necessary. 'Whether he'll *want* to is not the point. She'll wrap him in invisible threads like some rampant female spider till all he can think is, Fuck it. And then she'll eat him alive.'

'Not tonight, she can't. And make your mind up – animal or vegetable. She can't be a flytrap *and* a spider.'

'Oh, yes she bloody can.'

The doorbell rang.

'Hang on,' she said, departing.

She came back with a suspiciously sweet smile and a man on her arm. 'Abby, this is Daniel from the upstairs flat.'

I might have been forgiven for thinking my luck had changed. In his spare time, Daniel could have modelled for the pages of some Big Outdoors catalogue. When he'd moved in a few months previously, Lindsay had informed me that the Incredible Hunk was living upstairs. She had every intention of running out of coffee within twenty-four hours, popping up in a see-through top and asking him to tell her all about himself.

Unfortunately, he had. At very great length.

After introducing us, she turned to Daniel with a fake, perfect-hostess smile. 'Do me a favour, Daniel, and take

Abby off. She's getting under my feet.' To me she added sweetly, 'Daniel's got a really lovely car, Abby. She's got a bit of a thing about zoom-zoom cars, Daniel, so you'd better not mention all those go-faster thingies, or she might get over-excited.'

I made a feeble protest anyway. 'I thought you wanted a hand!'

'I'll manage. Go on, off you go.'

Four hours later I was standing on the nice new decking with Daniel and a glued-on smile. In fact it was about fifteen minutes; it just seemed like four hours. I'd made the mistake of asking about his car, as if I were really interested, and in a way I was. I used to have a fantasy of myself as a girl-racer, whizzing along in a silver Lotus, hunky blokes turning to gape after this vision with the mysterious little smile as the wind blew her hair sexily around her designer shades. *Who is she?* they would ask themselves, seized instantly with a burning desire to pursue me. In one of my steamier fantasies I had a hunk in leathers do exactly this on a Harley-Davidson. And he caught me, but I won't go into that bit now.

I listened politely as Daniel launched into a detailed eulogy about go-faster camshafts and turbo-dynamic manifolds. I said, 'Oh, yes?' and 'Really?' with my brain elsewhere.

Why didn't you stick with Guy, after all?

It's far too early. She won't be oozing yet.

Sorry, wrong answer. You just don't want to torture yourself with cosy proximity to a man who could very well inspire Harley-Davidson fantasies later. When he's going to be sleeping in Jeff's room, barely a heartbeat away through that thin partition wall.

I'd have felt the same about any off-limits bloke, but Guy wasn't just any old off-limits bloke. He was Fleur's, and that made him just about as off-limits as blokes came when you were Abby Morland.

Which brings me back to that battlefield called Two Sisters, One Man and All Hell Let Loose. And a little revelation in Sainsbury's.

Fourteen at the time, and dead chuffed with my newly pierced ears, all I had in mind was shampoo. When Mum was heavily into supermarket own-brands, this was a matter of supreme importance.

With such vital matters on my mind I wasn't really listening as Mum started the story. We were by the toothpaste; shampoo was in the next aisle and I had to have a persuasive argument ready.

'The thing is, you see,' Mum said, picking up a family-sized own-brand with fluoride, 'is that it was just like that song in *South Pacific*, about seeing someone across a crowded room. Not that it was exactly crowded – Kay had moved out by then, and it was the first time she'd brought him home. For Sunday lunch, as a matter of fact. And I'd been in the kitchen, doing the vegetables, and I think I might even have had some flour down my front, so I was hardly looking what you'd call perfectly groomed.'

You might have looked a bit more groomed if you'd lashed out on some TV-ad shampoo, I thought, though maybe they didn't even have shampoo in her day. Hadn't she once told me they used to put disgusting stuff like egg or beer on their hair, to give it 'body'?

'. . . and to tell you the truth I was always a bit nervous about meeting Kay's boyfriends anyway,' she went on.

No wonder, if she put egg on her hair. It was practically Dark Age stuff, which wasn't surprising. Mum had also told me that when she was little, the milkman used to come with a horse.

'They always made me think of advertisements for the perfect boyfriend,' she said. 'So although Kay and Daddy had arrived a few minutes previously I wasn't in any hurry. I carried on clearing up the kitchen, but then Grandpa came in and said for goodness sake take that apron off and come and have a sherry.'

Apron! I ask you. I felt quite cross with Mum sometimes, to think that although she'd been young during the so-called Swinging Sixties, she'd apparently spent her Sunday mornings peeling potatoes in aprons, instead of sleeping off pot-hazed orgies. Emma's mum had at least been sent home for smoking a Gauloise behind the science block.

'I didn't even bother tidying my hair,' she went on. 'I just went in, and there he was. Standing by the fireplace with Kay. She said, "Oh, this is Penny," as if I were the maid or something, but there wasn't anything unusual in that. But he smiled and said, "Hello, Penny. You've got some flour on your nose," and I felt as if a huge jelly had hit me in the stomach. And before we'd even finished the starters – avocado and prawn, I still remember that because he said how nice it was – I knew he felt the same.'

That was when it finally sank in. Right by the special-offer pine bath foam.

Eleven

The rest of that shopping trip was such an eye-opener, I forgot all about shampoo. As we passed the loo rolls I said, 'Why didn't you tell me before?' and she said, 'I don't know – because I thought you wouldn't understand, I suppose – it doesn't sound very nice on paper. And talking of paper, I think we'd better have a twelve-roll pack, the way it goes in our house.'

She grabbed one (own-brand, of course). 'And I thought you should know before Granny's party. Now you're older, one of the girls might just mention something.'

It took me at least until the frozen food aisle to take in all this. 'How long had she been going out with him?'

'A few months. But the thing is . . .' With her hand hovering over the frozen peas, Mum stopped. 'I didn't know it at the time, but Kay thought they were going to get engaged. She'd told all her friends.'

'Holy shit!'

'Abby!' She glanced around, as if I might have offended some old lady dithering over Aunt Bessie's Yorkshire puddings. 'But it was all in her head, Daddy told me afterwards. She'd talked it up and dropped lots of hints, and he'd sort of gone along with it – well, that's your father all over – he hadn't liked to burst her bubble.'

'She must have really loved him, then!'

'No, Abby, I really don't think she did. She just wanted

the ring and all the fuss and attention. Getting engaged was almost an end in itself in those days. He was the kind of man who made your friends jealous, so after she'd more or less told people she'd practically chosen the ring, it was a terrible humiliation. It was probably the first time she'd ever been on the receiving end, but what made it ten times worse was that it was me. She just couldn't bear it.'

Before we'd unloaded the shopping from the car, I'd learnt a good deal more.

Within two weeks of that Sunday lunch, Mum and Dad were an item and Kay was spitting nails. (*I did try, I really did, but it would have taken a saint to resist him.*)

Within five months they were married, and Kay had refused to come to the wedding. As I said, Rosemary had taken Kay's side. For a few years there had been a chasm in the family as vast as the Great African Rift Valley.

Once the shock had worn off I was rather proud of Mum, in a guilty sort of way. Of course, at thirty-seven or so she was utterly past it now, but she'd been passably pretty when she was young.

'What did she *say*?' I wondered aloud.

'Awful things,' said Mum, putting cans of tomatoes in the cupboard. 'Oh, Lord, I forgot to get kidney beans.'

'Yes, but *what* things?'

'Really nasty things, Abby, believe me. I'll never forget them as long as I live, but I'm not going to repeat them.'

Rude things, then, I thought. Maybe even the F-word, in which case it was no wonder Mum wouldn't repeat them. 'Bloody' was about her limit, and then only at times of extreme stress, like when the washing machine flooded. As for times of real emotional crisis, like when she suspected that Dad was playing away again, she'd just say cheerfully, 'Daddy's not going to be back until tomorrow, he's been held up.'

Alas for Mum, her Happy Ever After hadn't lasted long, though I think he'd held out till I was about four. After that there had been affairs on and off, and when I was just thirteen he'd left for Tina, nine years his junior. After seven months he'd come back, swearing it would never happen again, but Mum had said she was afraid it almost certainly would, and she wasn't going through all that again.

I'd been so upset with her at the time, I hadn't spoken to her for days. Ever since he'd left I'd been nurturing naïve hopes that they'd get back together, and he'd finally settle down to lawnmowing and getting the wrong washing powder on Saturdays, like Emma's dad.

Partly for this reason, I didn't feel a bit sorry for Auntie Kay. It wasn't as if Mum had stolen a Mr Perfectly Right. Auntie Kay had ended up with Uncle James: a tall, quiet, self-effacing, male version of Fleur. As Mum had often said, 'Just as well she didn't take after her mother. One Kay's enough for anybody, especially for a man like James.'

Back to that party, though. By the time I'd refocused my brain on Daniel, he'd moved on from cars to holidays.

'Yes, Manado's excellent for diving,' he was saying, 'but I suffered badly from jet-lag on that first trip. I was fit for nothing for forty-eight hours, and I must say humid climates don't altogether agree with me.'

'Very draining.' I caught Lindsay's eye, which had a wicked glint as she circulated with plates of dips and dippers. 'Well, don't look at me,' it said. 'You should have gone and done your netball bit, like I said.'

I cast a glance at the flytrap situation. She and Guy were still mingling in the far corner. Catching Guy's eye for a moment, I smiled and looked away, and then almost wished I hadn't. I wished I'd made 'Help!' eyes, but doing it without

Daniel seeing would be impossible. However tedious he was, I couldn't bring myself to be quite that rude.

Daniel was now on about the ex-girlfriend who'd accompanied him on the Indonesian trip. 'Personally, I thought it completely unreasonable behaviour,' he was saying. 'Splitting bills down the middle is all very well, I told her, but not when you've been having forty-dollar lobsters. I mean, come *on.*'

To tedious, please add 'tight git'. Just tell him you've got to go to the loo.

While I was trying to get a word in edgeways, Guy appeared at my right shoulder, bearing a bottle. 'I'm on mobile bar duty. Can I tempt you to a well-chilled Sancerre, with amusing little undertones of seaweed and rhubarb crumble?'

What perfect timing. 'Brilliant service. Slosh it out, then.'

Having sloshed, he turned to Daniel. 'I don't think we've met. Guy Fielding.'

After they'd shaken hands, Guy turned to me. 'I just checked the lunar situation and I'm sorry to say we're due for the full works tonight.' To Daniel he went on, 'Did you know Abby had a little problem with full moons? Sudden sprouting of facial hair, massive growth of canine teeth, that sort of thing?'

'Guy!' Trying not to laugh, I pretended to be put out. 'Do you have to blab it about? I told you that in confidence!'

'Sorry. I was only thinking of the cab situation, later. Do you think a paper bag over your head would work, or would you gnash it off?'

'That is ex*treme*ly insulting.' I drew myself up to my full height of about five ten and in killer heels. 'I'll have you know I make a very fetching werewolf. Anyway, I've never found it a problem. As long as I don't actually savage anybody, cab drivers usually don't turn a hair.'

To Daniel I added, 'Guy's crashing at my place tonight, you see. We'll be sharing a taxi, so I suppose he was bound to worry about whether we'd get one in the first place.'

Daniel gave the half-hearted little laugh of someone who's confronted with a puerile private joke and can't see what's remotely funny about it. 'Excuse me. I'm going to get another beer.'

Watching him depart, I gave a pretend pout. 'Now look what you've done. I thought I was in with a chance there.'

'Would that be before or after you keeled over?'

I couldn't believe he'd picked up my desperation after all. His expression betrayed the kind of conspiratorial glint that in other circumstances would have set all my quivery bits alight. It was cruel to have to tell them it was just a case of kind consideration because I was giving him a bed.

But I continued the tongue-in-cheek stuff anyway. 'Sparkling personalities aren't everything, you know. He's got a Porsche and a lot of very big muscles.'

'No pervy leanings to werewolves, though. You won't stand a chance now.' Leaning closer, he whispered, 'And I'm afraid I made it up, about the full moon. It's not due till Thursday.'

'Shame on you.' I was beginning to wish he'd left me to keel over. Gallant rescues smacked of Kind and Considerate, and you don't want good points when you're trying not to fancy someone you can't have. You want Crass and Insensitive, with a stomach-churning case of halitosis thrown in. 'I'll have to go after Daniel now. Explain that you scared him off under false pretences.'

'I've got a much better idea.' With a light hand on my waist, he turned me round. 'Come with me. I think you'll find this lot more of a laugh.'

It was no use pretending I didn't enjoy that little touch, especially as his fingers fleetingly brushed the bare skin between top and trousers. Still, I was entitled to a little morsel.

The crowd he'd just left was in a corner, near a shrub festooned with fairy lights. It was getting dusk by then, and already the first insects were fluttering around them. There were five or six people, and because I'd met most of Lindsay and Rachel's friends at least once, I knew nearly all of them.

Cara wore a slinky top and trousers in cream, and I have to say they looked stunning against a tan that looked darker still in the fast-fading light. 'Mission accomplished, I take it?' she murmured.

It had never occurred to me that he'd have informed her first. I didn't like it, and I suppose it showed.

Cara gave an infuriatingly amused little smile. 'He was under orders. Lindsay said to get his butt over there and do something before you keeled over.'

Lindsay.

I felt such an idiot. She'd paired me off with Droning Daniel on purpose, so she could send Guy to rescue me. Why had I fondly imagined he'd picked up my desperation all by himself? 'Well, he did it beautifully, but I can't help wondering why they invited Daniel in the first place.'

'Because they thought he'd kick up about the noise otherwise,' said Cara. 'He's a royal pain in the arse. And Rachel said she'd feel mean if they didn't.'

Rachel would.

During the general natter that followed, Guy stood almost within arm-brushing distance, with Cara on his other side. Shifting from foot to foot now and then, as my killer heels were digging into the turf, I wafted the odd fluttering insect from my face, and tried not to look as if I were watching for signs of flytrappery.

Almost inevitably the conversation moved on to holidays. Someone had been flotilla-sailing in Greece, which made someone say, 'You lucky cow,' and someone else say you could keep it. She'd done the same with a ruthlessly competitive boyfriend who'd nearly drowned them both trying to be first.

'There you go, Abby.' Guy nodded at me. 'Looks like you've found a kindred spirit.' To everybody else he added, 'Abby told me earlier sailing's not her favourite sport.'

Cara gave me a smile that hovered between pity and complacency. 'You don't know what you're missing. I used to crew for Guy years ago, when he was racing his little Laser.'

'*Crew?*' Guy laughed. 'That's a joke. She used to sit on the side in her bikini, topping up her tan.'

Cara gave a pretend pout. 'Come on, Fielding – you loved it. You used to say I was brilliant at distracting the opposition.'

I bet you were. 'I'd have enjoyed it rather more if I'd been able to sit on the side, topping up my tan. Only the boy-friend who was into it thought it was no fun without at least one near-death experience and hypothermia thrown in.'

'All good clean fun,' said Guy, like a send-up of some brisk-and-bracing Scoutmaster. 'Character-building, don't you know.'

'Stuff that,' I said.

'Stiffen your backbone,' he went on. 'They're all too soft these days.' He added a tiny, lethally attractive wink that that made some deep, unnamed organ lurch and shift itself in a most disturbing fashion. Lindsay and I had once discussed this lurching thing and had concluded that it must be the uterus, stirring itself for a potential delivery. 'Sort of unlocking the door, I suppose,' she'd said. 'Turning up the heating and plumping up the cushions for all those knackered little sperms.'

Well, my uterus was deluding itself. Probably out of

desperation, given the state of my love-life lately. My last relationship had drifted to an overdue close back in March. Since then I'd hardly met anyone who'd get my quivery bits going for more than a passing moment. Once or twice my inner optimist had been persuaded to go through that meat-market ritual of getting all tarted up for a night out, only to have ticked off by ten-thirty at least two of the following: boring, vain, tight, pretentious, up his own arse. Or, to have realised that his own checklist consisted of only one question: will she or won't she?

As the conversation moved on, I began to think Lindsay was at least half right. Almost imperceptibly Guy and Cara withdrew slightly, talking to each other alone. From the odd snippet I could tell a lot of catching up was going on. In non flytrap circumstances this would be entirely normal behaviour between old friends who'd hardly seen each other for ages. As it was . . .

Since Guy was half turned away from me I couldn't see his face, but I saw hers. You couldn't call it obvious flirtation, but it was that easy intimacy that borders on it. Once she caught me watching, and I had to give a quick, hypocritical smile and look away.

Just as Guy was laughing at something Cara had said, her mobile rang.

'Oh, shit,' she said, checking the screen. 'The drama queen.'

Guy tutted. 'Really, Maisie. That's no way to speak of your mother.'

Sticking the tip of her tongue out at him, she withdrew a few feet to speak to her.

Kirsty nodded towards Cara, who had her phone to one ear, one hand over the other, and a long-suffering expression. 'I take it she doesn't get on with her mum?'

'I'm not entirely up to date,' said Guy, 'but they used

to get on great. Just as long as they were a few hundred miles apart.'

Cara returned a minute later looking as if she'd just been through a particularly aggressive interview with Jeremy Paxman. 'Well, she won,' she said, ramming her phone back in her bag. 'Say hello to dutiful daughter – I said I'd go down for a few days next week.'

'Haven't you seen her since you got back?' I asked.

'Of course I have. For a day, which is about as long we can go before getting into blazing rows.' Looking almost stressed, she pushed her hair back from her face.

'But she's moving, isn't she? For the third time in two years. So now she's giving me all this emotional blackmail about "blood pressure" – that's the first I've heard of it – so I have to go down and help her sort out all the crap.'

However, she then went on, 'Guy, you'll *have* to come over and take me out for lunch, or I'll end up murdering her.' She smiled at him, and this was an entirely Cara version. 'No, scrub that. I'll come to you – she'll only invite herself along. A nice long lunch by the sea – could you take an afternoon off in a noble cause?'

He took this in an entirely relaxed fashion, as if he'd been expecting it. 'I could take a couple of hours. As long as you give me twenty-four hours' notice.'

'Fielding, you're a star.' With a smile like self-satisfied nectar, she kissed his cheek. 'You'd better give me your mobile number, then.'

I was quietly stunned. Maybe she wasn't unemployed, after all. Maybe she was secretly writing articles for *Flytrap Weekly* on 'How to Contrive A Good Old Session With Someone Else's Man Without Anyone Suspecting What You're Up To.'

How was Fleur going to take this?

Just as she'd fed his number into her phone, Lindsay

turned up, bearing plates of nibbles. 'Dig in,' she said. 'The real food won't be here for another hour.'

While hands hovered and picked, Lindsay shot me a wicked look. 'Eat something, Abby, you've got to keep your strength up. Haven't you got a netball match coming up?'

Someone said, 'Goodness, do you still play netball? Still, it must be brilliant exercise.'

'I don't any more.' I gave Lindsay the best kill-you-later look I could manage without it being obvious. 'Lindsay was having a pre-senior moment.'

Cara said, 'Lindsay, do you think Rachel would lend me her car for a few days next week?'

'Should think so – she doesn't use it much. Are you going away?' (To her credit, she didn't look as if the prospect perked her up.)

'Only down to the Drama Queen.' Cara took a bite-sized *croque monsieur*. 'She's just been on the phone, giving me an earful of emotional blackmail.'

Lindsay winced. 'Oh, Lord. You'd better stock up with Prozac.'

'It might not come to that. I'm going to escape for at least an afternoon – Guy and I are going to do lunch.'

'Oh, lovely!' Lindsay managed to say this as if no flytrap thoughts had ever crossed her brain cells. However, she was daft enough to give me a Look that spoke plenty. *See? What did I tell you?*

It was only momentary, but it was enough. And I was daft enough to glance at Cara, to see whether she'd caught it.

She had. She looked from me to Lindsay, and back again.

In an instant I knew she'd sussed it all, even down to why Lindsay had sent Guy to rescue me.

Taking another mini-*croque*, she smiled. 'These are lovely,

Lindsay. You've been very busy cooking this little lot up, haven't you?'

I had a horrible feeling that between us, Lindsay and I had just started some sort of war.

Twelve

Realising too late what she'd let out, Lindsay did her valiant best to stuff it back. 'Hardly cooking, when it's all out of packets. Right, I'm off to feed the rest of the hordes.'

She moved off without giving me any more Looks, though I knew she was dying to.

Cara said, 'I'll go and ask Rachel about the car. Be good, Fielding.' She gave me another of those infuriating little smiles. It might have said 'That wasn't very clever, was it? Still, thanks for letting me know.'

Whatever she might have had in mind, I had a feeling she now had it double.

Give a dog a bad name . . .

Pretty apt, if you just changed the gender.

I watched her head for Rachel. 'Poor Cara,' I said to Guy, like a nasty little hypocrite. 'Her mother sounds a bit of a nightmare.'

'They never did get on. Not after she was past the little-kid stage.' He glanced at the rest of the group, who were talking about something else and oblivious. Lowering his voice slightly, he moved a little away. 'Marina – that's my stepmother – used to think her mother was jealous of her.'

I was surprised he'd told me. 'That's not very nice.' Well, it wasn't.

'They're very alike,' he went on. 'Physically, I mean. Marina thought she started seeing her as competition.'

113

It was hardly unknown. 'Poor Cara,' I said, as two-faced as you like.

'Oh, she's pretty tough,' he said. 'But as you say, it's not very nice. I think she had enough jealousy from so-called friends at school.'

He said it in matter-of-fact tones, but I could tell there were layers underneath. He felt sorry for her, or he had. He was fond of her in that way you only find in friends who've known each other since before the Tooth Fairy started calling.

From Fleur's point of view, it was no use pretending this wasn't a potentially dangerous combination. 'Rachel was never "so-called",' I said.

'God, no.' His gaze shifted to the top of my head and he frowned. 'Hold still, you've got a little beastie in your hair.'

I winced. 'Not a daddy-long-legs?' I didn't mind slugs or spiders. I had no problem with the vast majority of creepy-crawlies, but ever since getting one caught in my hair when I was about ten, I had a bit of a thing about daddy-long-legs.

He brushed something away. 'Just a moth. You're in a bit of a beastie-zone here.' With a gentle hand on my arm, he moved me slightly away from the light-festooned shrubs, where masses of insects were buzzing round twinkling lights.

Then he looked down at my empty glass. 'Shall I get you a refill?'

'No, thanks.' I gave him a bright smile. 'I'll go and catch up with David.'

I had to get away. Any more brushings of hair or touchings of arms and I'd almost be tempted to nibble that steak myself. Maybe there was some undiscovered law of Nature to say that *frissons* should be in inverse proportion to the availability of the man.

114

No, that would be Sod's Law. All Nature cared about was plumping up the cushions for knackered little sperms. She didn't give a toss where they came from.

Nature was a trollop.

The man from Pizza Heaven arrived soon afterwards. The kitchen was bustling with helpers: unwrapping, cutting up, and talking at the tops of their voices.

I was on salad duty, tipping about six bags of Herb and Baby Leaf into a massive bowl.

'So how did he ask you, Rachel?' someone asked. 'Candlelit dinner and a bottle of Bolly?'

'Nothing so boring.' Shoving a pizza carton into a black bin liner, she gave a dreamy little sigh. 'It was just after Lindsay and I got back from Corsica. I was round at his, and it was absolutely pouring with rain, and we'd just run out of milk. So he nipped to the corner shop, and came back absolutely *soaked*, because we couldn't find an umbrella and it's a good three-minute walk, and when he came back, I said, "Sorry, you'll have to go back – I meant to ask you to get me a Cadbury's Caramel." I only meant it as a joke, but he said, "OK," and I said, "David!" but he shot off again, and came back like a drowned rat.'

At this point Neil appeared. 'Is this a hen party, or can anyone join in?'

'Go a*way*!' said somebody. 'We're talking girls' things.'

There was a wave of laughter as she shut the door in his face.

Rachel said, 'Where was I?'

'David had just come back like a drowned rat,' I said.

'Oh, yes. With *six* Cadbury's Caramels!' She put a broken morsel of garlic-bread crust in her mouth. 'So I said, "Dear me, I guess this must be *lurve*," like a joke, and he said, "Funny you should say that . . ." And he looked at me, all

dripping wet – him, not me, I mean, and then he said— '
She gave a sheepish little smile. 'Actually, I'm not going to
tell you that bit. But I cried buckets all over his shirt, so
it's a good job it was soaking anyway.'

'*Aaah*,' said everybody, including me.

Once the food was on the table, Lindsay poked me in
the back. 'Bedroom,' she whispered.

I joined her half a minute later, in a newly painted room
with an unmade bed and sundry items of clothing strewn
over the duvet. It smelt of fresh paint and Hugo for Women.

'Don't tell me, I know I made a pig's ear there.' Kicking
her shoes off, she plonked herself on the bed. 'Mind you,
she might have half-sussed it already. Never mind getting
Guy to crash at yours, she knows perfectly well I don't
exactly love her.' Picking up a random garment off the bed,
she tossed it towards a seagrass laundry basket. 'I suppose
she just invited herself for her "rescue" lunch?'

'Afraid so.' Sitting on the end of her bed, I loosened the
straps of my killer heels and rubbed my insteps. Just to add
to the laughs, it felt as if I had a couple of blisters coming
up. 'But it did sound as if he was just being nice to an old
friend.'

'That's exactly what she was counting on. Not that I
suppose she actually *wants* him,' she added. 'Not in an item
sense. She'll just want to prove to herself that she can get
him to want her to the extent that he just can't resist. It's
a sort of power thing. I've seen her look at people's
boyfriends, and seen them look at *her*, and seen her face.
She thinks to herself: I could get you any time I want. If
I wanted to. It wouldn't remotely surprise me if she looks
on him as a spicy little challenge.'

This struck me as all too plausible. Maybe she'd never
had an opportunity since that *in paddlante* session, and
from the way I'd banged that kitchen door I could bet it

was a case of *paddlante* hastily *interruptus*. It was entirely possible that she'd never been alone with him since, not in favourable circumstances.

Belatedly something struck me. 'Did she ever flytrap someone of yours?'

'Not quite.' She made a wry face. 'He wasn't mine – I just thought I was in with a chance. And Rachel had to bring Cara to this bloody party when I was all psyched up to knock him dead, and he never gave me another glance.'

I stared at her. 'So this isn't just about Fleur, is it? It's personal.'

'It isn't!' But this was Lindsay talking. 'OK, it *is* personal too. But I just can't bear the thought of her doing it to Fleur. I think she's really keen, you know.'

Not for the first time I wondered why she saw him as a helpless victim. 'You don't have much faith in him, do you?'

'Abby, he's a *bloke*! Don't get me wrong, I really like Guy, but I know him a hell of a lot better than you – he used to be a one-man West Sussex shag-fest.'

'Yes, but how long ago? Andrew used to be a one-man shag-fest, but some of them do grow out of it.'

'OK, but how many blokes can resist something dished up on a plate with parsley on top? When the something's *her*, oozing sticky stuff from every little frond?'

I said, 'What on earth does Rachel see in her?'

'Abby, they did everything together once. Ballet, Brownies, geography field trips – and you know Rachel. Unless it's smack in her face, she'll never believe anything nasty about anybody.'

'Just like saintly little you and me.'

She laughed. 'Abby, we're *nor*mal. Still, look on the bright side,' she went on, in black-comedy tones, 'even if he melts on contact, she'll probably lose interest. She's got a very male attitude to sex – even Rachel will tell you that. It's the chase she enjoys, and the conquest. Like I said, it's a power thing.'

For the next couple of hours, I tried to shove Lindsay's cat back in the bag. I neither avoided Guy (which would look as if I were trying to put Cara off the cat-scent) nor particularly sought him out (which would look like double-bluff). I tried to behave exactly as I would with anyone's man who was crashing at my place later.

For her part, Cara was clever enough not to monopolise him. Like me, she moved from group to group, some of which included Guy from time to time, because he was mingling, too. I even enjoyed myself, inasmuch as you can with two factors conspiring to prevent you. One, I had a couple of prize blisters coming up. I'd have taken my shoes off, but my trousers were too long for bare feet. Two, I was at any given time within twenty feet of the only man I'd felt like flirting with in ages, and I couldn't.

Despite a couple of patio heaters it turned chilly later, and by midnight most people had moved inside. One exception was Cara. As I eventually went inside, she was beside one of the heaters, warming up her chlorophyll at the Man in Black.

I passed this on to Lindsay later, while she put coffee on for the few who wanted it. 'Maybe she's given up on Guy,' I said.

'Get real,' she snorted. 'She's done the groundwork on him. Laid the flytrap.'

'You never know. She and Neil were swapping notes about Singapore. Maybe she's planning a little trip.'

'Lining him up for tonight, more like,' she retorted. 'Nice and handy, on our sofa. I shall probably have to get it treated for greenfly.'

Picking at cold garlic bread, I changed the subject and told her about Andrew.

'My God,' she said. 'What's got into him?'

'Imogen, evidently.'

She took mugs from the cupboard. 'This is getting seriously scary. I'd have thought I could at least rely on Andrew to stay on the loose. It makes me think of ponds with bugger-all fish left in them, except the ones you'd only throw back.'

'Oh, come on.' Lindsay never talked like this, which was a great point in her favour. I disapproved utterly of such Bridget-Jones-y angst. It showed a complete lack of feminist backbone, feisty independence of spirit, etc. It brought home to me the sad and shameful fact that I often had exactly the same thoughts myself.

En route to the bathroom later, I met Cara coming out.

I couldn't avoid her eye, and I didn't try to. I even gave her a smile that evidently didn't work. She paused by the door. 'Not very subtle earlier, was it?'

Shit. 'Sorry?'

She smiled. 'Nice try. Was it Lindsay's idea, or did the sainted Fleur put her up to it?'

I don't know how I didn't slap her. 'Oh, I *see,*' I said, as if it had just hit me. '*You* think that *we* think you've got a little secret agenda. Sounds like a bad case of guilt-induced paranoia, to me.'

'You can think what you like. And you can tell Lindsay, if I'd had anything naughty in mind, this would only make me think it'd be even more fun. '

'Oh, grow up.'

I locked the bathroom door, my insides churning. She'd probably look on him as even more of a challenge now, and if she succeeded, who was ever going to know? He'd never tell Fleur, and she'd certainly never tell Rachel.

But what really bothered me was not that Guy would end up helpless in her sticky fronds, but what she'd do when he didn't. I saw him making it tactfully clear even before the starters that this was just lunch; there was going to be no 'hot special' dessert. Piqued, she'd turn the situation round by telling him that Lindsay and I had been conspiring to watch him. She'd be clever enough to say it as if it only amused her, not as if she were sticking the boot in. She might even imply that Fleur had put us up to it.

But this was one thing I certainly wasn't telling Fleur tomorrow.

Guy and I left around two. Even with my mohair cardigan I was on the chilly side as we headed for the main road, and a black cab. Guy was still wearing only that linen shirt, and I wondered why men hardly ever felt cold unless there were six inches of snow. I tried not to shiver, in case he thought I wanted him to cuddle up and put an arm around me. Naturally I wasn't wishing he'd do precisely this, even though it would only be to warm me up.

Twenty yards down the road, I had to stop. 'Sorry, but I've just got to take these shoes off – I've got a couple of lovely blisters.'

He tutted, in the time-honoured fashion of all men when women are suffering in the interests of looking gorgeous. As I stood first on one leg and then the other, fumbling with fiddly little buckles, he put a steadying hand on my arm. This was entirely permissible in the interests of stopping me wobbling, which I swear I was not doing on purpose. In the newly chill air he smelt warm, with the faintest hint of tangy cologne or shaving stuff.

The pavement felt cold, but that wasn't my main problem. As my trousers were three inches too long for bare feet, I had to roll them up. The trouble was, the material was too slithery. I had to roll them up to mid calf, and even then I was doubtful that they'd stay put.

Guy held my shoes while I did this. 'Feel free to make some exasperated remark,' I said, as an occupied cab went past. 'It's probably dangerous to bottle it up.'

'I'm not saying a word.'

A little further on I had to stop again because my left trouser-leg was falling down. Once more he held my shoes. 'If you'd like a piggy-back, I only charge a tenner. I'll forget the VAT.'

A piggy-back! My arms round his neck, my legs wrapped around him . . .

What with cold feet too, I think it was very noble of me to turn him down. 'No, thanks. Far too inelegant for my image. Anyway, I never pay more than a fiver.'

It was a relief to get into a black cab a minute later. There was so little traffic, it was a much quicker journey home. I almost knew Guy would be awkward about the fare, and he was. 'Let me get it.'

Out fast, I was already proffering a note. 'Guy, will you please not *ar*gue? I'm too tired.' I was.

He pushed open the gate. There was a minute front garden, with a little paved path to the front door. Delving for my key, I didn't see the debris on the path. '*Ow!*' Hopping on one foot, I looked down. 'Bloody roses...'

Someone had been trimming the bush to the left of the path, and had neglected to pick up all the bits. A piece of stem with a choice thorn was sticking into my heel.

'Well done.' As I inspected it, Guy reached down and yanked it out. 'My God, just look at the state of your feet.'

A drop of blood was oozing into the dirt I'd picked up from the pavements.

'You'd better give them a good wash,' he said, tossing

the stem into a flower bed. 'Just in case you picked up any interesting traces of dog turd.'

I was rapidly getting to the state known as Had Enough. 'Thanks, Guy. I'd never have thought to wash them if you hadn't said.'

I stuck my key in the lock. He followed me inside, up the stairs, and through my own front door. Throwing my bag and shoes on the sofa, I said, 'Help yourself to anything,' and went straight to my room. I took my top things off, pulled the Sumo-wrestler robe over bra and pants and opened a window. It felt stuffy and airless.

After sluicing my feet over the bath, I found Guy checking out the fridge. 'How's the foot?' he asked.

'It was only a pinprick.' As I'd been slightly acid earlier, I made a conscious effort to be nicer. 'Are you peckish?'

'A bit. OK if I make myself a sandwich?'

'Help yourself. There are cheese and tomatoes in the fridge. I might even have an onion.' I found one in the rack and tossed it to him. 'There you go – I'm off to bed. Goodnight.'

'Goodnight.'

Back in my room, I found my next little problem. As I said, the only creepy-crawlies that really give me the willies are daddy-long-legs. And it was the daddy-long-legs season, and like an idiot I'd just left the light on with the window open.

Even before I'd cursed myself another fluttered in to join the half dozen already there. Maybe the brainless creatures called to each other: 'Come hither, brothers! For lo, I have found a wondrous light!'

Too tired to eject them, I took off everything but my mascara, yanked on an old T-shirt and fell into bed. After all, the chances of any of them tap-dancing on my face while I was nodding off were practically nil. Pretty low, anyway. And it really wasn't *at all* likely that while I was fast asleep my mouth would fall wide open, just as one of the leggy beasts happened to be fluttering in that precise . . .

Yeeugh!

Switching the bedside light back on, I sprang into action. On the bedside table was a mug half full of cold tea I'd forgotten to finish earlier. I tossed that out of the window. On the desk was a pile of the paperwork I kept meaning to get around to. Yes, a folded Visa statement would do nicely.

I caught the first quite easily, putting the mug over it and sliding the Visa statement underneath.

Right, out you go.

I found another clinging to the curtains. That was easy, too.

Number three was harder. It was a whopper, all its legs intact. However, it was high above the desk, too far to reach from the chair.

I climbed gingerly on to the desk, hoping it would bear my weight. It had cost around thirty-nine ninety-nine as a cut-price flat-pack when I couldn't afford anything better. I reached up and tried to 'mug' number three, but it was cunning and saw me coming. Fluttering away, it came to rest a foot to the left. Although it was just at the end of my reach, I managed.

Gotcha! I banged the mug over it, triumphant.

Only I exerted myself too violently. The sudden movement made my foot slip on the bank statement I was standing on, and under the bank statement was slippery melamine. There was nothing to hang on to, no means of saving myself. My feet went from under me; I landed on my coccyx on the top of the desk.

The desk wasn't amused. It wasn't designed for sudden,

crashing loads of nine-and-a-half-stone woman. Its cheap plastic fixings wouldn't take it. I heard the sound of cut-price chipboard giving up the fight. I felt it start to go, the end panel slanting as the whole lot did its damnedest to turn back to a flat-pack. With a rending crash the whole thing collapsed, jolting my back painfully and landing me in a shaken heap.

For a moment I thought I'd broken something. My back hurt. My coccyx hurt. The mug was smashed to bits on the floor, and Visa statements lay all round.

I was gingerly starting to move when the door burst open.

Guy stood stock still on the threshold. 'Christ! I thought—'

It was the stuff of nightmares. He was gaping at a sprawling heap in a short, glorified T-shirt, and nothing else at all.

Thirteen

Whatever eyeful he got, it was only for a millisecond. 'Go *away!*' Yanking my T-shirt down, I struggled to sit up. 'Haven't you ever heard of knocking?'

Ignoring me, he came right in. 'What the hell happened?'

'Nothing! Bugger off, will you?' Hot with embarrassment, I tried to get up without revealing anything else, which isn't so easy when you're starting from a sprawling heap. 'Did you have to barge in like that?'

'I'm sorry, all right?' he said, in terse tones. 'I just had this crazy idea some psycho was trashing the place – are you all right?' He took my arm, helping me up.

'Do I *look* bloody all right? Would you be bloody all right when your bloody desk's just collapsed underneath you?' I winced again, rubbing my elbow.

'What the hell happened?'

'I was practising table dancing, what d'you think?'

As this rang in my ears I added, 'If you really want to know, I was catching daddy-long-legs.'

He bit back a grin.

Suddenly I was close to tears of pain and mortification. 'Go on, have a good laugh! Now push off, will you?'

'Look, I'm sorry.' He gazed from me to the wreckage and back again. 'You must have copped a few bruises.'

'You'll cop a few if you don't get out of—' I was interrupted by the *beep beep beep* of the smoke alarm.

'Oh, Christ,' said Guy. 'My cheese on toast . . .'

As he shot off, I yanked my Sumo robe back on and stared at the wreckage. I heard Guy say, '*Shit*!' The smoke alarm was still going *beep beep beep beep beep beep beep beep* . . .

'Can't you shut that thing up?' I yelled.

'What with?'

Charging to the living room, I grabbed a magazine from the coffee table, charged into the smoky kitchen and waved it under the alarm.

The beeping stopped. I turned to the draining board, where Guy had dumped the grill pan. Amid the remains of burnt-on melted cheese were two black pieces of toast.

'Just a tad overdone,' he said.

'Feel free to make some more. I'm going to bed.'

As I turned to go, he caught my arm. 'Look, I'm sorry. I didn't mean to laugh.'

He wasn't laughing now. He was looking down at me with the kind of concern that almost made me dissolve. I knew if I did he'd take me in his arms, say, 'There, there,' and stroke my hair. And I couldn't handle it.

I went acid, instead. 'Oh, feel free,' I said, shaking him off. 'It *was* pretty bloody hilarious, especially as I've bruised myself to bits.' I stalked to my room and shut the door.

As Sod's Law really had it in for me that night, I then managed to step on a splinter of smashed mug. It was the tiny, final straw that made my eyes well up at last. I picked out a minute shard that hadn't even drawn blood.

Guy tapped on the door. 'Abby, I'm sorry.'

That only made me leak more. 'Bugger *off*!'

'Do you want me to come and get rid of any more beasties?'

I wiped my eyes on my sleeve. 'I just want to get to bed, OK?'

There was a pause. 'Goodnight, then.' I heard his retreating footsteps.

Only then did I realise that the leggy brute that had caused all the trouble was still there, on the wall above my desk. That was where humane ejection got you. If it was still there tomorrow I'd go and buy some fly-spray. Serve it right for resisting arrest in the first place.

I got into bed, making mental notes never again to go to any social occasion where I was asked to watch, perform netball duty on, or in any other respect have any dealings whatsoever with any man I was attracted to, who was also seeing someone else. I made a particular note never to do any of the above during the daddy-long-legs season. It was a recipe for wishing to God you'd stayed at home, watching the fifty-ninth re-run of *Only Fools and Horses*.

After a couple of minutes a tap at the door jerked me out of this lot. 'Abby?'

For God's sake, now what? 'If you want Worcester Sauce it's in the cupboard!'

'Nothing like that.' He paused. 'It's just that you left something in the other room.'

I couldn't think what, but at least it wasn't a vibrator.

'Your little friend,' he went on. 'I found him under the duvet. I told him he was welcome to stay, but he wasn't having it.'

My eyes closed. Little Ted. How could I have forgotten to retrieve him?

What could I do? Only summon the shreds of my dignity, try to pretend I didn't feel like a total prat. 'Hang on . . .' Yanking my Sumo robe on again, I padded to the door, taking care to avoid the smashed mug area.

I opened the door to find Little Ted looking right at me. Holding him at chin level, Guy wore an almost entirely serious expression. 'He said he wasn't sharing a bed with a hairy great sod like me, thanks very much.'

My eyes started pricking all over again. 'Well, that was

extremely rude of him.' I reclaimed Little Ted from his hand. 'He's a little bit set in his ways, I'm afraid. It's his age.'

'No problem. I used to have an elephant called Jumbo. He could be very difficult.' He smiled. It was the last kind of smile I could cope with just then: a warm, gentle, quivery little killer. 'Sure you don't want me to get rid of any more long-leggetty beasties?'

'I think the last one died of a heart attack with all the commotion.'

'Goodnight, then.' He leant forward and brushed my cheek with his lips.

'Night.'

When I finally hit my pillow again I did leak a few tears into it. But I swear they were only down to the bruises.

I awoke feeling stiff, sore and morning-after-ish. With a mortifying rush the night before came back so fast I groaned and pulled the duvet over my head. This was no help; it was so stuffy I had to come straight up again for oxygen.

The bedside clock said twenty-five to eleven. If she'd left Nottingham early, Fleur could be here any minute. The thought of Fleur was almost enough to send me back under the duvet. She'd be dying to get me alone for a flytrap report, hoping there'd be nothing to tell. And I couldn't *not* tell her – if the lunch date came out anyway it'd look infinitely worse.

If Fleur took it philosophically, though, I'd make myself a daddy-long-legs sandwich.

And eat it.

I thought of going back to sleep, but sounds of life were wafting through my open window. Screeching magpies and somebody's lawnmower, just for starters. Then I heard sounds of Guy: the hushed kind you get when somebody's trying not to make any noise.

I peered round the door before dashing for the bathroom, making sure the coast was clear. It's a whole lot easier to gather the shreds of your tattered aplomb if you've had a shower first. From the faint sounds of the radio I knew he was in the kitchen, but the door was ajar. I nipped to the bathroom, where steam still misting the mirror told me he'd not long left it. A faint scent of male shaving stuff hung in the warm, humid air. It was odd how I noticed it, when I never noticed Jeff's. It had the unfortunate effect of conjuring up visions of him stepping from the shower in all his dripping glory, and standing like that in front of the mirror to shave.

About to turn the shower on, I changed my mind. A bath would soothe my bruises, and a hefty dose of Pink Grapefruit bath foam would drown out any remaining whiffs of Guy.

I've always found that a bath is one of the best places to sort out your thoughts. Maybe water performs some psychological version of washing the dust off them, so you can see things more clearly. Obviously there were two reasons for last night's rush of attraction. One, a man-shaped void in my life. It was a long time since March.

Two, forbidden fruit. If he were available, calling three times a day and sending flowers, I'd almost certainly go right off him inside a week.

Hmm. Quite sure about that, are you?

Well, no. But attractions were like tans, I thought, eyeing my own brown bits. If you didn't top them up, they faded right away. After this weekend I'd probably hardly see him anyway. Out of sight, out of mind.

With Guy thus reasoned away, I thought of other things.

Hermit crabs. Shells.

As I said, things between Mum and Andrew had never been quite the same since a certain Sunday lunch, just after she'd found out that Robbie was on the way.

129

As I'd arrived first, she'd given me the news in the kitchen.

I'd nearly dropped the gravy boat. '*Preg*nant?' I'd echoed. 'You can't be!'

'I am. I've done a test.'

I'm afraid to say that horrible visions had instantly shot through my head. Until a couple of months previously she'd been friendly with a widower called Donald, since gone to live in Spain. He was very charming in an old-fashioned, blue-blazer sort of way, but quite a bit older than her, and looked it. Until then I'd imagined that their relationship was purely platonic: trips to the theatre in Guildford, and so on. The thought of her up to anything else with Donald, who had age spots on his hands and called me 'My dear', made me feel vaguely ill.

'Er, I suppose it was Donald?'

'*Donald?*' Bewilderment was written all over her voice. 'For heaven's sake, Abby, we were just friends!'

'Who, then?' *Please, not that plumber you said was a 'very nice boy'. Please, not that friend of Will's who said, 'Your mum's still pretty fit, isn't she?'*

'Oh, Abby, who do you think?'

It had happened on Will's birthday. Then living fifty miles away, Dad had come over bearing cheques, and had stayed for an early supper. It had to be early, as Will was going out to get off his face with his friends. After a couple of drinks Dad had stayed the night. There was nothing so unusual in this; they were friends again by then. More than once he'd slept in Andrew's old room.

After Will left, they'd sat on the sofa with a bottle of wine and an old film. And not just any old film: one they'd happened to see during their first, heady weeks.

I couldn't take it in. Not long before she'd told me that she'd come to look on Dad as a sort of wayward child she despaired of, but would never cease to love.

'You always said you'd never have him back!' I said.

'I was lonely.'

'You've got masses of friends!' (Such was my level of sensitivity at the time.)

'Oh, Abby. Not that kind of lonely.'

As Will and Andrew had arrived soon afterwards there was no time to give them early warning. Quickly sensing that something was coming, they'd managed to keep their jaws from dropping. They'd even managed to say something appropriately nice.

We were eating in the dining room. It was only when Mum went to the kitchen to get the pudding out of the oven that they let their full-scale shock out. As we all stared at each other, I spoke first. 'Well, at least it wasn't Donald.'

Will said *sotto voce*, 'And they talk about irresponsible kids! A bit bloody embarrassing, isn't it?'

It was just Andrew's bad luck that he didn't utter first. As his words are engraved on my memory, I'll quote them verbatim: 'Christ,' he said, 'if Dad has to go fathering sprogs at his age, couldn't he do it with a twenty-seven-year-old, like normal blokes?'

He never meant Mum to overhear, but she did. I can still see her, white-faced on the threshold. As her words are also engraved on my memory, I'll quote them, too: 'I'm sorry, I forgot the oven glove.'

After my bath I twisted my wet hair into a scrunchie, pulled on some light blue linen trousers and a white T-shirt.

Guy was still in the kitchen. Sitting at the little pine table with a mug and yesterday's *Evening Standard*, he looked up as I came in. 'How are the bruises?'

'Better after a soak in the bath, thanks.' He was wearing the shorts he'd arrived in yesterday, and a loose, short-sleeved khaki shirt with an open neck. With bare feet as well, he looked very Easy Like Sunday Morning. 'How did you sleep?'

'Fine. I made some coffee.' He nodded towards the cafetière. 'It should still be hot.'

I could already smell it. From other scents in the air I gathered that he'd made himself some toast, too, though there was no debris lying around.

While I was pouring, I heard him turn a page of the *Standard*. 'I might be able to fix that desk, if you'd like me to take a look.'

'God, no! It's very kind of you,' I added hurriedly, 'but it's really cheap old chipboard – the fixings have been torn right out.'

'I could probably still do it. A few brackets and a screwdriver . . .'

Which would mean a trip to the DIY, at least for the brackets. 'Thanks, but it was pretty cheap and nasty – I'll be glad of an excuse to cart it off to the tip.'

Having milked my coffee, I was faced with one of those tiny dilemmas that seem enormous at the time. The kitchen table was titchy, with just two stools. Sitting opposite him would mean eye contact at roughly two feet and you could hardly avoid knee contact, either. I didn't want either of us to have to say, 'Sorry,' at any accidental touch, as if the other might have thought we'd done it on purpose.

So I leant against the counter with my mug. 'Have you spoken to Fleur?'

'Yes, just before she left.'

As he said it, his mobile rang in his breast pocket.

I knew at once that it was Fleur. I could tell from the way his slight frown disappeared and his expression softened. 'Hi,' he said. 'Where are you?'

His voice had softened to match. I hated myself for the little green twinge that contracted my stomach. I started putting the milk away and so on, so it wouldn't look as if I were listening.

After half a minute he said, 'It should have a little symbol on. Check your manual if you're not sure. Or ask someone.'

Then it was, 'OK. See you soon.'

I heard him make the faintest kissy sound into his phone. 'Take care. Bye.'

I was still pretending to tidy up, which wasn't so easy after my blitz yesterday.

'That was Fleur,' he said, as if I didn't know. 'At the last services on the M1. Her screen-wash has run out and she's not sure where to fill it up.'

From his tone I knew he wished he were there to do it for her, and I couldn't help wondering why no man ever seemed to feel like that about me. Probably for the same reason I hadn't asked him to get rid of my daddy-long-legs last night. I'd never ask a man where to put my screen-wash. I'd be expecting him to say, 'Jesus, Abby, are you really that clueless?'

'She'll find it,' I said. 'So don't start worrying that she'll pour it into the coolant thing instead.'

He frowned. 'I hadn't thought of that. Do you think I should ring her back?'

'Guy, I was joking!'

He grinned. 'So was I.'

'I should hope so!' But I laughed, and he was verging on it, and for a moment I felt perfectly at ease with him. 'Sorry I told you to bugger off last night.'

'My fault. And you were under duress.'

'And I really have to apologise for Little Ted. As hairy great sods go, I've seen an awful lot worse.'

'I'll take that as a compliment.' He smiled, and for perhaps two seconds there was nothing else. Just his smile and mine and the soft background of Capital FM.

Suddenly brisk, he stood up. 'Right, I'm off to stretch my legs and buy a paper.' He pushed his chair smartly under the table. 'Anything I can get you?'

'A *Sunday Times* would be good. Shall I give you directions to the paper shop?'

'I'll find it. See you later.'

Even before the front door had closed behind him, I had the uncomfortable feeling that I'd somehow driven him out.

As if you suddenly had 'I fancy you' written all over your face, you mean.

Oh, don't be ridiculous.

I started doing useful Sunday-morning things, like shoving washing in the machine and checking what I was supposed to be teaching my first two classes tomorrow. But through it all I still had the uncomfortable feeling that I'd betrayed a hint of something. Enough to make him think it diplomatic to take himself off.

And the more I thought about it, the more irritable I became. What did he think I was going to do? Strip off and ask him to kiss my bruises better? How dare he feel uncomfortable with me? Me! What about the bloody flytrap?

Oh, come on. More than likely he simply wanted to buy a paper and stretch his legs. Exactly as he said.

I started scribbling a lesson plan, though other things were constantly intruding into the complicated matter of question tags:

He's been gone rather a long time, *hasn't he?*

You must have really frightened him off, *mustn't you?*

That is complete BOLLOCKS! *Isn't it?*

He'd been stretching his legs for a good forty minutes when the doorbell finally rang.

Only it wasn't him.

'Fleur! Guy's not here – he nipped out for a paper.'

'I know – I met him at the end of the road. I'd been driving round and round, trying to find somewhere to park. He said he'd see to it – he's just dropped me off.' With a guilty glance over her shoulder, she stepped inside.

'Oh, Abby, I feel so terrible about last night, you can't imagine. He was so sweet just now. What would he think if he knew?'

Then I realised that the faint rose flush under her skin was at least partly due to a lovers' reunion. I imagined him getting into her car, followed by the kind of kiss that said he'd missed her like hell last night.

Again I hated myself for the little green twinge in my stomach. 'Calm down, he's never going to know. In your place I'd probably have done exactly the same.'

'No, you wouldn't.' Under her translucent skin, the flush of rose deepened. 'Sarah's ankle wasn't that bad. I didn't really need to stay at all.'

Fourteen

I stared at her. 'Fleur, what are you saying?'

'It was like a test. I knew you'd tell me if you picked up any vibes. I thought: If he passes this, I'll be able to trust him.'

I didn't know what to say. I couldn't possibly say what I was thinking, i.e., 'Have you ever thought of seeing a shrink?' 'Fleur, I really do wonder about you sometimes.'

'I know you think I'm off my head.' With a tiny 'trust *me*' smile she followed me to the kitchen and sat down. 'But it just seemed meant, somehow. Sarah *was* a bit low and post-natal. I knew she was dying for me to stay, so that sort of justified it.' She looked up. 'And now you're going to tell me I got myself all worked up over nothing.'

'Almost nothing.' Giving the gist, I saw from her face that she now felt marginally less guilty. At least she hadn't been worrying for nothing.

'I knew it,' she said. 'Asking in front of everybody like that, so it looks all innocent – why couldn't he just say he was busy?'

'How could he? Whatever else, they go back a hell of a long way and the way she asked, he could hardly refuse. I honestly didn't pick up any vibes on his part. I'm sure he's well aware that she wouldn't need much encouragement, but I really can't see him giving her any.'

I might have given her a certificate saying: *Flytrap Test, Passed with Merit*.

'You won't ever tell Rachel or Lindsay, will you?' she asked anxiously. 'I'd feel so bad when he's their friend.'

What was the point of telling her Lindsay didn't quite trust his zip control, either? 'Are you kidding? Anyway, forget it. Do you want a really good laugh?'

I told her about the daddy-long-legs débâcle, playing up the farcical aspects, so that by the time Guy came back, saying he'd had to park two streets away, she was laughing helplessly.

She greeted him with soft smiles, sweetly grateful to him for taking the trouble. It set up more green pangs in my stomach that made me love myself not at all.

Within an hour we were due to meet the others at some gastro-pub, but I chickened out. I didn't want any more encounters with Cara. I certainly didn't want to risk any more Looks from Lindsay. Besides all that, I didn't want to see Guy and Fleur all sweetly couply over lunch. So I made some excuse about feeling a bit rough/having masses to do, would they please make my apologies?

When I called Lindsay that evening she was very out of sorts. 'Why didn't you come? There I was, all hungover, having to field the odd knowing look from Cara as if I hadn't a clue there was anything to give me knowing looks about.'

I fought a compelling urge to spill out full histories, from paddling pools to Fleur's call the day before. But old sayings were flitting into my head: hornets' nests, least said soonest mended, too many cooks stirring molehills into mountains. 'That was another reason I didn't come. In case you started giving me any more Looks for her to pick up. What if she goes stirring it up with Guy? She might even imply that Fleur put us up to it.' (I said this innocently enough, I think.)

She snorted. 'Get real. And even if she did he wouldn't believe her. He must have sussed Fleur by now. He'll know she'd never be that sneaky.'

That's what you think. Thankfully it was almost certainly what Guy would think. 'So were there any flytrap vibes from Cara over lunch?'

'Nothing you could put your finger on – she's too canny. I nearly didn't go myself – I was feeling pretty rough.'

She did sound pretty evening-after-ish. 'What time did you get to bed?'

'Gone four. Once everybody had gone Neil said he was hungry, and I ended up doing him beans on toast.'

What was it with men and late-night snacks? 'You should have let Cara do them.'

'She'd gone to bed. I should have told him to do them himself, especially after he made some so-called joke about David "getting caught". It got right up my nose.'

I was recalling Neil's remarks. 'He made some crack to me, too. About me being the "guilty party" for getting them together. If you ask me he just fancies himself slightly more than the average. No signs of greenfly on the sofa, then?'

'Not so's you'd notice, but I might spray it anyway.'

That evening I phoned Andrew.

Despite his 'fathering sprogs' remark, Andrew was not a callous jerk. He'd have given anything to take it back, but the damage had been done. Mum had been bitterly wounded. *I suppose he'd rather I just got rid of it. I suppose he thinks it's not decent. Oh, don't look at me like that, Abby, I wasn't born yesterday.*

Only after Robbie was born did I feel they were getting back to normal, but I still sensed the rift hadn't quite healed over.

He was actually in when I phoned.

'Andrew Morland.' He always answered as if he were at work. (Corporate lawyer, in case you're wondering.)

To start sweet, I launched into song. *'You're getting married in December . . . Ding, dong, what a turn-up for the books . . .* Sorry, that last bit doesn't quite scan, but congratulations anyway.'

'I gather you've spoken to Mum.'

'Yes, last night. She didn't *mean* it, you dope. She's terribly upset now, that she's upset *you*.'

His tone was both weary and sardonic. 'How the hell would you feel? Implying that I was going to screw Imogen about like Dad screwed her – hasn't it occurred to her that that's precisely why I've never contemplated this before? Because I never felt certain I wouldn't want to do just that?'

Aaah. Sweet, really. 'OK, I get the message. Look, why don't you invite her for lunch with Imogen? Maybe with me and Will too – she'll be so anxious to be nice it'll smooth any feathers. Just call her as if nothing's happened and try to sound as if it was your own idea.'

'I won't have to try – I already thought of that. Only it'll have to be here: I'm not up for taking Robbie out anywhere civilised.'

'Then buy a throw for that white sofa. Robbie and white sofas just don't go. Oh, and one more thing – if Imogen hasn't picked her bridesmaids yet, would you ask her to think of me? At this rate I'm never going to have my turn at wearing a lovely long pink dress.'

There was a taken-aback silence. 'God, Abby – I don't know. She's got two sisters . . . We haven't got around to anything like that.'

I laughed. 'Gotcha! Can you really see me in a long pink dress? I'd look like Nightmare Barbie.'

During that week a different lunch was on my mind: Guy and the flytrap, and what Fleur might be thinking. She called me late on the following Sunday night. 'I didn't say a word. In fact, when he told me he was going to be seeing her I made a point of saying how nice, do have a lovely time, and all that.'

I hope you didn't overdo it.

'But I think he must have realised I wasn't a hundred per cent ecstatic,' she went on, 'because over this weekend he made a subtle point of telling me he'd been unexpect-edly busy that day, he was back at work just after three and didn't even have a glass of wine.'

She probably had overdone it, then. But at least he was intuitive enough to pick up undercurrents, considerate enough to put her mind at rest, and grown-up enough not to sulk over her unspoken angst. One way and another, all this was giving me another worry, i.e., that he was too good to be true. But if Cara had done any stirring, he was evidently keeping it to himself.

Andrew's 'healing' lunch also went fine, and the next few weeks flew by. I was busier than usual at work. On the last day of her Turkish holiday, a colleague was involved in a bad accident and flown home on a stretcher. Since she was going to be off work for weeks, I was detailed to muck in with the TEFL course she was down to lead. I was thrown in at the deep end with wannabee teachers, many of whom were planning to use their new skill to fund overseas travel, just like I had. I empathised with their nerves on being thrown in front of a class on day two (and mostly making a hash of it) but since the students were there for the purpose, getting virtually free lessons, nobody complained.

On top of that I was roped in by another colleague to help with a very amateur charity Christmas pantomime involving Cinderella, half the 'cast' of *EastEnders* in a pub called Ye Vic, and a pair of ex rugby pros as the Ugly Sisters. Since he was back from his musings in the sand dunes by then, I took Jeff along to a read through where he was promptly written in as Idle Jack, the wicked stepmother's droopy toy boy. Jeff came up with so many ad-libs, he ended up co-editing the script.

Robbie had started 'proper' school and came home proudly with his reading books. Before I knew it we were well into autumn and Hallowe'en pumpkins were in the shops. Dad's dodgy knee was sufficiently better for him to offer to take Robbie to Center Parcs for half term, and Mum was only too glad of a few days' peace and quiet.

Friends and colleagues bemoaned the end of summer, but I didn't mind chilly autumn fingers snaking round my neck. It went back to early years, but I'd always loved this season: the smell of woodsmoke, the golds and russets of falling leaves, the prospect of dressing up as a ghost and trick-or-treating. I'd loved Hallowe'en and Bonfire Night: the sparklers, the smell and whoosh of fireworks, the faces round the bonfire, your breath coming out all frosty, baked potatoes held in woolly-gloved hands.

And after all that, the magical run-up to Christmas.

Only when I spoke to Fleur did I give more than a fleeting, secret thought to Guy. During those few days with her mother Cara had looked up other old friends, one of whom had offered her a job. 'Apparently it's with some corporate entertainment outfit,' Fleur told me. 'Guy said he deals with them now and then – day sails for managers on conferences, that sort of thing.'

I'd already heard something of this from Lindsay. What

Fleur was actually trying to say, of course, was that she wasn't entirely happy that Cara was just down the coast and might be dealing with Guy professionally.

'Don't get the wind up,' I said. 'She's hardly round the corner, is she? It must be a good hour from Brighton to Southampton.'

'I'd feel a whole lot better if he wasn't so far away from me. Still, at least she doesn't wear lurid false nails.' She gave a sheepish little laugh. 'Do you know I actually dreamt of that the other night? I still wish I'd put that nail in Scott's dinner. I wish he'd said, "What's this?" Then I'd have said, "You tell me," and thrown a glass of wine over him.'

'It's called the Law of Delayed Brilliance, Fleur. We only ever think of these things afterwards.'

'But it's not just her. He's only got to tell me he's off to the gym and I imagine all sorts. I swear the main reason Nails went to the gym was to pick up men.'

'You always get a few of those. A friend of mine calls them the Sweaty Slags. He said he wouldn't touch them with a bargepole – he'd catch athlete's dick.'

This was a complete lie. I said it to lighten her up, and I might as well not have bothered.

'Sometimes I call his mobile just to see whether he answers,' she went on. 'And if it's off or he's not answering, I wonder why.'

This was turning into a master class in the destructive power of jealousy. 'Fleur, we all feel like that sometimes. Just do your best to hide it, that's all.'

From mid-October almost the only topic of Mum's phone calls was Andrew's wedding.

E.g., 'Did you realise it's a five o'clock ceremony? At the beginning of December it'll be pitch dark, and it'll make the dinner terribly late for Robbie. Still, I suppose it was all they could get at short notice.'

A few days later it was: 'Did you hear Imogen's having her two little nieces as flower girls? I can't help thinking it'd be nice if they asked Robbie to be a pageboy.'

'Mum, he'd hate it! Sissy little velvet breeches – you know he'd never wear them. He'd play up like mad.'

'That's not the point, Abby. I still think they could have *asked*.'

My invitation arrived on the second of November: *Mrs and Mrs Clive Burridge request the pleasure,'* etc. A 5 p.m. ceremony at St Michael and All Angels was to be followed by reception, dinner and dancing at the Welford Castle Hotel. As all this was in Derbyshire, it meant an overnight job.

Lindsay phoned that same evening. 'My invitation says "and guest".'

'So does mine.'

'That's different – you're his sister. I hope you haven't magicked up a man since I last spoke to you, I don't want to be the only Blokeless Wonder.'

She'd recently been seeing someone called Baz, but he'd only lasted three weeks. 'There was another great new love in his life,' she'd said. 'And I do draw the line at competing with a bloody i-Pod.'

'I did think about Jeff,' I said. 'I thought any arctic undercurrents between Mum and Kay would be great material for his novel, but it clashes with his dress rehearsal.'

'Just as well you're not playing Cinders, then. I take it Fleur's bringing Guy?'

I felt a disturbing little stirring in my stomach. 'I don't know.'

* * *

Fleur called the following evening. 'I'm not sure how to play it. Taking someone to a family wedding smacks of "serious", and I don't want him thinking I'm making assumptions. Mum's dying to meet him, and knowing her she'll come across all over-eager and frighten him to death.' She paused. 'You know what she said when she heard Rachel was engaged? "You'd better get a move on, Fleur. You don't want to end up on the shelf."'

Not for the first time I gave thanks that Mum never said things like this. She rather tended to the reverse. 'Look at me,' she'd say. 'And don't ever rush into it.'

'On the other hand, I'd feel bad if I *didn't* ask him,' she went on. 'I'm sure he'd like to see Lindsay and Rachel's folks. He once told me that Auntie Rosemary was very kind to him after his mother died, and I know he always got on well with Uncle Matthew. What would you do?'

This was such an unsettling question, it was very difficult to give an honest answer. 'Tell him it's entirely up to him.'

I came home two days later to find Jeff back in his usual position on the sofa. 'Your ma called,' he said. 'And from the sounds of it I should fortify yourself before calling back. A shot of vodka at the very least.'

My heart sank. 'Did she say what?'

'Nope. But she sounded as if she wanted to grill someone's wedding tackle. With the owner attached.' He grinned. 'Funnily enough, I rather think it's the dashing bridegroom.'

Fifteen

Andrew had put his size ten right in it again.

Mum's voice was quivering with hurt. 'I phoned him earlier to ask about the reception dinner, could they possibly order something child-friendly for Robbie, and do you know what he said?'

My heart plummeted to approximately basement level. 'What?'

'He said maybe it'd be better if Robbie didn't come at all! He said, "From a purely practical point of view." I mean, how *could* he? His own brother! At a church wedding, when I know for a fact that Andrew doesn't believe in *any*thing, just because anyone who *is* anyone round Imogen's way gets married in that particular church. What does it say in the C of E service, I should like to know? *Marriage was ordained for the procreation of children!* And he's implying that his own little brother won't be welcome - I wouldn't mind betting it's Imogen's parents behind it, too. I've got a good mind to tell those Burridges to stick their invitation right up their bottoms.'

I called Andrew ten minutes later. 'If you don't want little sods, you should have said so in the first place! Why put ". . . and Master Robbie Morland" on Mum's invitation if you don't want him?'

His tone was wearily resigned. 'Abby, she misconstrued

it completely. If I thought Robbie would even enjoy it I wouldn't have said it, but he won't. If he's not tear-arsing around he'll probably be bored out of his mind.'

'So are you suggesting we leave him Home Alone? With the TV remote and a few packets of crisps?'

'Oh, don't be ridiculous. I thought he'd have a lot more fun staying over with a friend. And you know perfectly well Mum'll be in a permanent state, trying to keep an eye on him.'

'Then *I'll* keep an eye on him. So get on the phone to Mum now and grovel. If you were trying to rip open old wounds, ten out of ten for effort.'

After hanging up, I slumped on the sofa in front of the TV. 'I can feel the wedding from hell coming up,' I said gloomily to Jeff. 'At this rate I shall be digging out my flak jacket. Why can't we be like that lot?' I was referring to a family of about fourteen on the screen: wrinkly old grannies, young macho types, gorgeous women and cherubic babies and children, all happily smiling as they sat in a sun-dappled garden under a grape vine. This was naturally all down to the enormous dish of *penne al forno* in delicious sauce, which some radiantly happy woman was taking out of the oven.

'They're Italian,' said Jeff helpfully. 'And I do hate to shatter your dear little illusions, but telly is not always a mirror image of life, especially when it's an advertisement.'

'Maybe it's the pasta,' I said. 'Maybe if we all ate more pasta we'd turn into *Little House on the Prairie*.'

Andrew did some serious grovelling and Mum did not shove her invitation up any Burridge bottoms. She was still hurt, though. She'd got it into her head that 'those Burridges' didn't want any young children they weren't absolutely forced to put up with, like the little flower girls, who were their own grandchildren and therefore entirely different.

She thought Andrew was only too happy to go along with this, especially where Robbie was concerned.

So there were still slight tensions when W-Day dawned.

By then the networks must have clocked up at least fourteen million phone calls on Andrew's wedding, and that was just Mum to me. What to wear (too dressy, too undressy), who was buying what off the present list, whether Dad was going to bring his current partner, Wendy ('At least she's a vast improvement on that Liz'), and the vexed question of Best Man Will's hair ('Shaved! If he doesn't grow it before the day, I shall be absolutely *mort*ified').

As I was chauffeuring Mum and Robbie, my mental countdown went like this.

Ceremony at 5. Therefore, because going to hotel first to change and hotel ten miles from church, need to be ready by 4.

Therefore, need to arrive hotel by 3 latest.

Therefore, as journey should take 2 1/2 hrs, need to leave by 11, to allow for traffic, lunch stop, etc.

Therefore, tell Mum we have to leave by 10.30. That way, stand outside chance of getting away on time.

Therefore, leave flat by 9.30 to allow for traffic.

On the way out I collided with the girl from the downstairs flat. 'Off somewhere nice?' she asked, eyeing my things.

'My brother's wedding.'

'Oh, lovely!'

'Lovely. Oops, I forgot the stain remover.'

'*Stain* remover?' She frowned.

'For when we play Happy Families,' I explained. 'Blood on the carpet, you know.'

She laughed, and I didn't like to tell her I wasn't joking. The previous evening my dear mother had phoned with this: 'I just spoke to Rosemary, and she said Kay's just had one of those laser face-lifts! Typical, isn't it? And her outfit cost about six hundred pounds, apparently. Well, if it makes her happy to make me look like a haggard old frump by comparison, good luck to her.'

You will deduce that the Great Rift Valley had not shrunk to a two-inch crevice.

Still, it was a lovely day for December: sparkly sunshine and crispy blue sky. I arrived at Sycamore Road with my best 'We're all going to have a lovely time!' smile, which just goes to demonstrate my sunny optimism in the face of experience.

'Thank heaven you're here,' Mum said, before I could even say her hair looked lovely. 'The hairdresser just left and if I hadn't just paid her thirty pounds I'd be tearing it all out. I wasn't going to put him into his new things till we got there but Robbie's dug his heels in already. You talk to him – I've got a splitting headache coming on.'

Robbie was lying on his stomach on the sitting-room floor. Absorbed in a video, he was dressed in his Superman outfit. As Mum had picked this up at his school Christmas Fayre a week previously, she had only herself to blame.

I perched on the arm of the sofa. 'Are you wearing that for the wedding?'

His hair was still un-brushed. That would be another battle before we were very much older. 'What's wrong with it?'

'Nothing exactly, it's lovely, only Mummy thought it'd be nice if you wore the grown-up shirt and trousers she bought specially.'

'Well, I'm not. I'm wearing my Superman outfit. I can't see what on earth's wrong with wearing a Superman outfit. I bet Superman would wear his, if he was going to his brother's wedding.'

Bribery? No, I couldn't resort to that. The only guaranteed bribe was Chessington World of Adventures, which was closed until Easter.

I beat a retreat to the kitchen, where Mum was raiding

her pharmaceutical supplies. 'Just let him wear it,' I said. 'What does it matter?'

She knocked back two Hed-Eze with a glass of water. (At least, I hoped they were Hed-Eze.) 'I dare say Andrew'll have something to say. I'm quite sure Imogen's parents will have something to say.'

'Let them. Anyway, if Robbie won't even wear a shirt and trousers, you'd have had to sedate him to get him into a pageboy's outfit.'

'That's not the point, Abby. They still could have *asked*.'

We eventually departed at ten past eleven, but I still had to turn back half a mile down the road. 'Oh, Lord, I left Robbie's swimming things on the bed,' Mum said. 'You did promise to take him in the morning.'

I had. The Welford Castle Hotel had 'every possible facility in beautifully landscaped grounds' and charged accordingly.

Mum sat in the back with Robbie, in case he tried to dismantle the door handle. 'It'll be lovely to see the girls,' she said, as we passed Carpet Heaven. 'And David, after all these years.'

David had once lived in Chestnut Road, which ran parallel to Sycamore. During our junior school years Mum had been on PTA cake-stall terms with his mother.

'I gather Fleur's bringing her boyfriend,' she went on. 'What's his name again?'

'Guy. Guy Fielding.' Merely saying his name aroused something that had been sleeping. As if to prove it, I felt a nervous little *frisson* in my stomach.

'Oh, yes. Isn't he an old friend of Lindsay and Rachel's?'

'Yes, he used to live down their road.' *I don't know why you've been kidding yourself. Let's face it, you've been thinking about him on and off ever since Fleur told you he was coming.*

'Oh, yes, I think Rosemary said.'

Mostly off, though.

'Kay's very keen to meet him, according to Rosemary.'
Yes, but what about the 'on' bits? 'Hardly surprising.'

'Oh, no. Between you and me, I expect she's very slightly peeved that Rachel's got engaged first.'

They weren't anything you couldn't tell your granny. Except perhaps for how you felt when he rescued you from Daniel, and that conspiratorial glint in his eyes. 'Probably. She told Fleur to get a move on, she didn't want to end up on the shelf.'

'She didn't!'

It was no use pretending this was just shock. She couldn't quite hide a slightly guilty gratification that Kay could be so unfeeling to her own daughter.

Still, Mum needed something to put her in a good mood. *'She did, but don't you dare repeat it.'*

'Abby, what do you think I am?' After a pause she added, 'So do you think it's serious, then? Fleur and this Guy, I mean?'

'How should I know?' *At least I haven't had any fantasies about him. I haven't even had that one where I've just been water-skiing and he's unzipping my wetsuit.*

'But you have met him?'

'Once or twice.' *Or the Harley-Davidson one. Mind you, I'm not sure I could see Guy in leathers. Could see him in a wetsuit, though.*

'So what's he like?'

Do you have to keep on about Guy? 'Nice enough.' *He'll be in a suit today, won't he? I wonder what he'll look like in a suit?*

'That doesn't sound terribly enthusiastic.'

'Mum, what d'you want me to say? He's nice, he's nice-looking, he's got the usual number of arms and legs.' *With any luck he'll look really boring in a suit, so stop thinking about him. It's your perverse subconscious working him up*

150

because he's off limits. Like craving baked potatoes when you're on the Atkins.

As I overtook a huge van saying Police Horses, Robbie took his headphones off. 'I want a drink.'

'I'd *like* a drink *please,*' said Mum automatically. 'Anyway, not now. Wait till we stop.'

'I'm thirsty *now!*'

'No, Robbie. You'll spill it all down your front and have to wear your other things after all.'

That shut him up. In the mirror I saw him put his earphones back on. I'd got him a Horrid Henry CD, but at least it wasn't *Horrid Henry Goes To The Wedding*.

Mum said, 'I just hope Will's hair's grown a bit. Last time I saw him it can't have been more than a quarter of an inch all over.'

Best Man Will had gone up the previous evening, with his girlfriend.

'I don't want anyone sniffing that he looks like a skinhead,' she went on.

Think about something else, like how you're going to keep Robbie quiet in the church. Not sure the little devil's ever actually been in a church. He'll probably say 'bollocks' in front of Those Burridges on purpose. Just as the vicar's said, 'Let us pray . . .'

'Especially not Kay,' she went on. 'Though I'm sure she'll find something to be sniffy about.'

Charging her anti-Kay batteries nicely, isn't she? Working herself right up till Kay will only have to twitch an eyebrow and she'll pounce.

'She's had botox as well, you know. Rosemary told me.'

'Probably needs to. That's the downside of all those expensive holidays in the sun.'

'You know what she'll say, don't you? "Dear me, Penny, you do look *tired.*" Just like last time.'

Last time was Uncle Matthew's sixtieth, several months previously. 'She won't! You'll look gorgeous once you've got your face on.'

I might as well have saved my breath.

'With that sort of pitying little smile,' she went on. 'I don't know why she can't just say "worn out" and have done with it.'

'You don't look worn out!' *All I need on top of this lot is illicit yearnings. I hope to God this is all in my head. What if Guy and Fleur are looking into each other's eyes, going all touchy-feely, and I get that nasty green feeling in my stomach?*

'I will compared to her. I suppose I could say, "Oh, you do look *well*, isn't it amazing what laser-lifts can do?" but I'm certainly not going to descend to that sort of level.'

You're getting green feelings already, just thinking about it. You're working yourself up, just like Mum's working herself up about Kay.

'And did I tell you what she said the other week? When she phoned to make sure our outfits weren't going to clash – as if *that* mattered?'

'Mum, please! Can't we at least *start* this wedding in the right frame of mind? You know, like normal people?'

That did it. Put her right in the wrong frame of mind, I mean. 'I really don't know what you're talking about,' she said, with offended dignity. '*I'm* certainly not the one who ever wants to dredge up old wounds.'

'That's exactly what you *are* doing! Psyching yourself up to find anything to pounce on – if you ask me you'd actually *like* Kay to give you pitying looks, just so you'll have something to bitch about.'

'Abby!'

Please now take the above offended dignity and multiply by twelve.

Why didn't you keep your big mouth shut? Wasn't diplomacy supposed to be the order of the day? And by the way, you're in the wrong lane, you're about to miss the M1 slip road. 'Oh, hell – get out of the way, will you?' This was to a black SUV in my path as I tried to move over. The driver hooted sharply as I cut across, and I muttered something very rude back.

I turned on to the motorway.
M1 AND THE NORTH.
LUTON 24
WEDDING FROM HELL 12O
HAVE A NICE DAY!!

Sixteen

'And another thing,' she said to the back of my head, 'since you seem to think I'm the bad guy here—'

'I don't!' *Heaven help me, count to ten, calm down.* 'Look, I'm sorry I said anything, all right? Let's just forget it and have a lovely day.'

'As if I ever wanted anything else!' She paused. 'I was only going to tell you the other thing she said, just before hanging up.'

Eight, nine ten . . . 'What?'

'She said, "I must say, I think it's rather peculiar, getting married after dark in the depths of December." *Rather peculiar*! How do you like that?'

'Mum, take no notice! Auntie Kay is an evil old hag.'

'Abby! I wouldn't go quite *that* far.'

But she was mollified, I could tell. I sensed mollification emanating from the back seat in bucket loads.

'I hope Andrew's remembered to book a babysitter,' she said. 'Though if he hasn't, I really won't mind filling in. I wouldn't want you to miss out later.'

'Mum, we've had this out already. If anyone ends up having to babysit, it's not going to be you.'

Since Andrew had not been far off about Mum being in a permanent Robbie-state, I'd told her I'd take charge of him from start to finish. Will would be willing, but I couldn't expect the Best Man to do much Robbie-duty, still

154

less the bridegroom, and Dad would have his elderly mother to look after. I knew Lindsay and Rachel would help, and probably some of the others. This way Mum could enjoy her status as mother of the bridegroom. She could wallow in her top-table glory without worrying about sticky fingers, or what he was up to now. In order that she could also get ready in peace and sleep in tomorrow morning, I'd got Andrew to scrap the triple room he'd booked and make it two. Yes, all this was very noble of me. I didn't expect any reward in heaven, but a small lottery win would have been nice.

'Well, it's very good of you,' said Mum. 'And don't think I don't appreciate it. But to go back to Kay, do you remember what Andrew used to call her? It used to worry me sick in case it ever got out.'

The Witch of West Wittering . . . It was where they'd lived when they were kids.

'Mum, I haven't heard him say that in *years*.' I paused for effect. 'He's got another name for her now. "Double-u double-u double-u dot."'

'Abby!' But she laughed.

'But I think my own little nickname's better,' I added.

'I didn't know you had one.'

That was because I'd only just thought of it. 'Well, I have. AK 47, though I suppose I should add a half a dozen years to that.'

'Abby!' She laughed again.

At least I'd put her in a good mood.

Built of grey-gold stone, the Welford Castle Hotel stood on gently rising ground and wowed Robbie on sight. 'It's got castle bits!' (As it was more like a rambling stately home, he meant the odd bit of battlement.) 'Is it a *real* castle? With dungeons?'

Should I say, Only for really bad boys? 'You never know.'
'Wow!'

As Mum had called to say we were nearly there, Will
was watching for us.

I drew up outside. Robbie shot straight at Will, who
swept him up in a hug. Dressed in tracksuit bottoms and
T-shirt, I guessed he'd been checking out the fitness suite.
Will had never possessed Andrew's dark, drop-dead looks.
His eyes were light blue, his hair mid-brown with reddish
glints. In the nicest possible way his face had a slightly
bashed-about look, but his smile could warm a corpse at
ten paces.

It certainly warmed Mum. 'Well,' she said, kissing him,
'your hair still looks a bit like a lavatory brush, but never
mind. Where's Andrew?'

'Upstairs, yacking his nervous guts up. Relax!' He laughed,
seeing Mum's face. 'I was joking.' After doing porter duty
he parked the car while Mum and I checked in.

It wasn't the sort of place where you want to arrive dishevelled and journeyed-out, brushing bits of Robbie's crisps
from your trousers. However, any grandeur was more than
compensated for by five-star comfort that settled around
you like a goosedown duvet. I had an impression of flowers,
warm reds, old golds and polished wood. A huge log fire
was burning near reception, and a wide, turning staircase
led to the first floor.

While we waited for the lift Mum gave an 'over-his-head'
nod at Robbie. 'He's going to wear his Superman outfit,'
she said, with pointed brightness. 'We thought it'd be nice
to be a little bit *diff*erent. Nobody else'll be wearing a
Superman outfit, will they?'

If she thought this might work, she was deluding herself.
'No,' said Robbie, like a blithe brick wall. 'That's why *I'm*
going to.'

156

Just as he said it, the lift arrived. Two people were waiting to step out.

'Fleur!' said Mum. 'How lovely!' – (kiss) – 'and dressed already – we shall have to get a move on. And you,' she turned to him, 'must be Guy.'

He produced a perfect, family-meeting smile. 'Hello, Mrs Morland.'

'Oh, Penny, *please*! I can't say I've heard all about you, because I haven't, not really . . .'

While this sort of thing went on for another thirty seconds, I slapped a smile on, as if my stomach was behaving entirely normally. When those lift doors had opened he'd been standing right in front of me. For a direct hit from those Greek-island eyes, I could hardly have placed myself worse.

After the niceties with Mum and Will, he got around to me. 'Hi, Abby, how's it going?'

'Great!' *Please, don't kiss me, I don't think I can handle it.* 'How about you?'

No kiss. 'Pretty good. Reasonable drive up?'

'Yes, we made very good time.'

He wore a very non-boring suit of mid-grey. The jacket was undone. Underneath was a crisp, mid-blue shirt. The tie had blues and reds in it, and wasn't horrible at all.

His eyes went to Robbie, who was half hiding behind Will. 'Hi, Robbie.'

Robbie wore a wary, suspicious look. 'Hi.'

I tapped Mum on the shoulder. 'Come on, we really should be going.'

While Will took Mum's things into room 215, I took Robbie into 214. There were twin beds, covered in quilted jade and pink that matched the curtains.

Tempted to raid the mini-bar for a large anything, the first thing I did was find a cartoon channel on the television. 'I have to hurry and get ready now,' I told Robbie.

'Will you watch the cartoons quietly while I have a shower?'

Strangely enough, he wasn't already jumping on the beds or tearing open the packets of biscuits on the tea and coffee tray. 'You didn't tell me *he* was coming.'

Just hearing him say it made my stomach misbehave all over again. 'Who?'

'Him! Fleur's boyfriend.' He paused. 'Did you tell Mummy what I did that time? You *said* you wouldn't.'

No wonder he'd been hiding behind Will. 'Of course I didn't!' As he'd known she'd certainly be furious with him for once I'd been very tempted, but on the other hand she'd also have been utterly mortified.

'Yes, but what if *he* does?'

I make no apologies for what I said next. My stomach was still in post-lurch. My brain was saying, *All in your head? Ha! All you need on top of this lot is Robbie playing up.* 'If he sees you being naughty he probably will. So you'd better be very *very* good.'

'I will!'

'Then how about putting on the things Mummy bought specially?'

With a heavy sigh, he looked down at his beloved scarlet and blue. 'All right, then. If she really wants me to.' Pathetically he added, 'But it's my *very best thing*! How come everybody else can wear their very best things and not me?'

It was like a tug at my heart. When he could little-sod at such advanced levels it was easy to forget just how young he still was. 'All right, then. As long as you're very good as well.'

Just as I was locating my sponge bag, there was a tap at the door.

I opened it to find Mum, in tears. 'Oh, Abby. Just come and see . . .'

Robbie followed me next door. On the dressing table of

her room was a huge basket of flowers. Amongst cream and pink roses were forced spring blooms. Scents of early hyacinths and narcissi filled the room.

She handed me a little florist's card. On it was written:

> *Thank you for everything.*
> *All my love always,*
> *Andrew.*

She was dabbing her eyes with a tissue. 'They were here already. Will said, "Blimey, have you got a fancy man?" but I suppose he knew . . . Oh, dear, just look at me, going all weepy already . . .'

I went back to my room thinking: Andrew, you're not such a dickhead after all.

Much of the clan was assembled in the foyer when we went down. While I was catching up with Rachel, Lindsay and David, Guy and Fleur joined us, with AK 47 in tow.

I hadn't seen her since Uncle Matthew's sixtieth. There was no denying she looked chic and elegant, in antique gold. (Mum was in jade, so no problem there.) Her beautifully cut hair was still blonde, and she could easily have passed for forty-three until you got close up. I saw at once that Guy had surpassed her expectations. She looked like the cat whose kitten has not only got the cream, but the smoked salmon, too.

She bestowed on me a relatively gracious smile. If I were Mum in her best anti-Kay mode I'd say this was entirely due to the fact that Fleur was 'Guyed' while I was merely 'Robbied', but that wouldn't be very nice.

'Well, Abigail!' she said. 'You're looking very nice.'

Blimey.

'She looks gorgeous,' said cuddly old Uncle Matthew. 'How are you, Lady in Red?'

It was a slim red dress, with just a hint of cleavage, and though I say it myself, it suited me. 'Thanks, Uncle Matthew.' I gave him a kiss. 'I'm fine.'

'But no significant other to appreciate you?' said Kay sweetly. 'What a shame. Still, I expect you're just hyper-choosy.'

Not very nice, but probably correct. Even at two paces I felt Mum gently bristling.

Auntie Rosemary pitched in. A more 'ordinary' version of Kay, she was also more cuddly, in an elegant way. 'There's not exactly much for the girls to choose *from*. At least half of them seem to be gay nowadays.'

'And there's absolutely nothing wrong with being choosy, Kay,' put in Mum. 'Excuse me, I must go and speak to Will.'

Good start.

As she gently bristled off, Guy glanced down at mini-Superman, who was half hiding behind me. 'Is Robbie trying to show us all up?' he asked. 'I feel sartorially boring by comparison.'

With a suspicious look, Robbie took himself off.

Guy raised his eyebrows at me. 'Was it something I said?'

'Oh, no,' I said. 'It's just that he's got the wind up in case you tell Mummy about that very bad thing he did before.'

He laughed, but stopped abruptly. 'You did tell him no way?'

'Afraid not. I told him you very well might, unless he was very, *very* good.'

Everybody but Guy laughed, but he was verging on it. It was betrayed by a flickering mouth and eyes that followed Robbie, now fled to the sanctuary of Mum.

160

He turned back to me. 'I see,' he said, looking me straight in the eye with a particularly lethal glint. 'So I'm a nasty bastard now, as well as a bit of a plonker?'

'A *what*?' With a 'dear-me' little laugh, AK's eyes went to the cream and smoked salmon, and back to me. 'Abigail, you surely didn't call Guy any such thing?'

'It was Robbie,' I explained. 'He and Guy didn't quite hit it off before.'

Guy gave AK a smile of perfect, self-deprecating charm. 'Entirely my fault, I'm afraid.'

Her return smile had an almost roguish quality. 'I'm not sure I quite believe *that*, but never mind.'

Guy turned back to me. 'Do I gather you're using me, then? As a nasty-bastard bargaining tool?'

'Sorry.' I gave him the best apologetic smile I could manage, while wishing there were anything to put me off. You'd think he could at least have taken on that pasty winter pallor that makes you think how unappetising a man would look with his clothes off. 'But it was too good an opportunity to miss. If you could practise a few cold-and-quelling looks, like the scarier sort of teacher, I'd be grateful.'

'At this rate I'll be practising them on you.' He fixed me with a scary-teacher look that didn't quite work. 'This is the third time you've told me the dog ate your homework, Miss Morland. What have you got to say for yourself?'

Er, I wish you could keep me in after class. 'We never had a dog. I used to say I'd left it on the bus.' At that moment I saw Dad and his mother emerging from the lift. 'Sorry, must just go and say hi . . .'

At least Andrew and Imogen didn't have the headache of divorced parents who weren't speaking, I thought. Partly greying, but still possessing most of his hair and not much more waistline than when he was thirty, Dad was looking pretty good in a dinner jacket. During the past twelve years he'd re-married, re-divorced, and lived with a certain Liz for fifteen months. His current partner, Wendy, hadn't come in the end. As they were short-staffed at Fillup and Smyle, a pair of off-licences they co-owned in Hertfordshire, it would have meant shutting one of the shops for an entire weekend. Fillup and Smyle was just the latest in a long line of businesses Dad had embarked on. His entrepreneurial ventures were much like his love life. He'd put his all into something for a few years until the itch for new challenges would get the better of him.

In the past I'd gone through very ambivalent stages with Dad, part of me almost hating him for what he'd put us all through, while the rest of me couldn't help loving the father who'd taught me to swim, who'd checked the wardrobe for witches and read ad-libbed bedtime stories of Paddington Bear, with Little Ted as the co-star who didn't care for marmalade sandwiches but loved Nutella (like me). And over the years other people's experiences had made me realise he could have been an awful lot worse. At least he'd always made an effort to see us, he'd never been mean with maintenance, and as for violent tendencies, he'd barely even squash a caterpillar.

Midge, his mother, was on his arm. We'd never been allowed to call her Granny or Grandma – she said it made her feel old. Having buried two husbands in ten years, she'd often said it was just as well Dad's father had left her early on, or it would have been three. ('It's a wonder I never murdered him. I did love him, but oh, dear . . .')

'Never heard of dinner jackets at a wedding,' she said, once we'd caught up. 'Still, I suppose I'm out of date.'

'I suppose they thought morning suits would look weird,' I said. 'As it's the evening.'

But her eyes were already elsewhere. 'Well, here's Andrew! Dear me, doesn't he look handsome?'

He did, though often I just didn't 'see' it. A touch over six foot, he was just the right side of too thin, but there was nothing limp about him. His dark eyes could go from sensitive to cynical in a heartbeat. Although his hair was darker than mine, with a slight wave, his skin was paler. Just now it looked as if this was due to last-minute panics and lack of sleep.

Just before he left, I took him aside for a moment. 'Well done with the flowers. She nearly cried her mascara off.'

His smile was rueful, fifty-fifty with relief. 'Thank God for that. I thought she might assume they were Imogen's idea.'

'No, your cred's sky high.' I kissed his cheek. 'Off you go, then, you handsome beast. Good luck.'

Moments later we were ushered into a fleet of sleek black cars. I sat in the back of one of these with Robbie, with Mum in the front. The air was clear and crisp, with a bright moon.

'You must be very good in the church,' Mum told Robbie. 'It's God's house, you know, so you must be very quiet and not fidget, and think nice thoughts even if you get bored.'

I wasn't so sure I'd be thinking nice thoughts, especially if Guy was sitting anywhere near me. It was all very well telling my inner horrible person that 'coveting thy cousin's boyfriend' wasn't on, but she wasn't listening. In fact, I had a feeling she had him lined up for that wet-suit fantasy during the boring bits.

It was easy to see why anybody who was anybody wanted to get hitched at St Michael and All Angels. Complete with lofty spire and lych-gate, it was set beside a village green, amid ancient stone cottages and the inevitable olde-worlde pub.

'Such a shame it's not summer,' Mum said, as we got out of the car. 'Still, it all looks very pretty by moonlight.'

Inside, organ music was already playing softly, and lack of summer had been more than compensated for. All along the length of the aisle, huge arrangements of white flowers and winter greenery were dotted along the ends of the pews. At the sharp end, a mass of candles threw their soft light up to medieval stained glass. In the left-hand corner a tall Christmas tree twinkled with a thousand tiny white lights. And just in front of the front left pew was a crib with beautifully crafted figures. There was real hay in the manger, and straw round the ox and ass's feet.

We sat in the front pew: Robbie on my right, with Mum on his right, Dad beside her, and Midge on the end, as she wasn't very mobile. 'Can't be very High Church, then,' Mum whispered. 'Not if they've got a Christmas tree. Where on earth are the boys? I hope to goodness Andrew's not having last-minute nerves.'

Robbie was struck with uncharacteristic awe. He gazed up at the stone vaulting, and down at the embroidered hassock at his feet. 'Why are there cushions on the floor?'

'They're for kneeling on,' Dad explained. 'Some people like to kneel for the praying bits.'

He wrinkled his nose. 'It smells funny.'

Like all medieval churches, it smelt of ancient stone and battered copies of *Hymns Ancient and Modern*.

Within a minute the second pew was filling up. Rachel and David, Lindsay, Fleur and Guy were settling themselves right behind us. I turned around, as you do, and we started that semi-hushed nattering people only do in churches. Further back people were saying things like, 'Don't tell me you've forgotten the camera?' and, 'For heaven's sake, turn your mobile off.'

As I caught Guy's eye, he nodded towards Robbie. Having taken one wary look, Robbie snuggled very close to Mum, who'd put an arm around him.

Guy's mouth flickered. Leaning forward he murmured, 'So how long do I have to be the bad guy? Can I come clean after the service?'

'No way!' I whispered. 'There's the dinner to get through, and the speeches, if he hasn't fallen asleep before then.'

Fleur whispered, 'Guy's very upset, you know. He was planning to be very nice and de-plonkerise himself at least.'

'No chance,' said Lindsay wickedly. 'Once a plonker, always a plonker.'

Guy gave her a gentle whack on the thigh with *Hymns Ancient and Modern*.

Lindsay laughed. Anyone could see she'd come determined to enjoy herself with reckless abandon, whoever he was.

'It's only for tonight,' I told Guy. 'Tomorrow you can be Mr Nice Guy all you like. I could send him to jump on you around seven, if you like. With his swimming things.'

Amusement glinted in his eyes. 'Why do I get the impression you've got it in for me?'

'Oh, she's often like this,' said Lindsay gaily. 'Evil. You could always dance with her later. Trample all over her toes.' To me she added in a very audible whisper, 'He always was a pretty crap dancer.'

'He isn't!' This was Fleur, half laughing.

'You wait,' Guy said to Lindsay. 'Once I've pulped Abby's toes, it'll be yours.'

Rachel nudged me. 'Look, there are Andrew and Will. I bet Auntie Penny'll be having a little weep any second.'

Now it was too late to worry what he might have left undone, Andrew really did look heartbreakingly handsome.

Black-tied Will just looked like Chilled Will, only rather better.

'Where have you two been?' said Mum. 'You left before us!'

'I took him into the Hand in Hand for a quick one,' grinned Will. 'To steady his nerves.'

'Hi, Tiger.' Lifting Robbie out of the pew, Andrew put him on his shoulders.

'For heaven's sake!' said Mum. 'His feet!' But I knew she was touched. Andrew was really pulling the stops out today, mending fences for England. Robbie was grinning from a great height.

'Quick, Abby' said Mum. 'A photo of the three of them, before it starts . . .'

Robbie was only just set down when Mrs Burridge and her eldest daughter turned up. You'd think Mum had never had a 'Those Burridges' thought in her life. As Andrew introduced her and Dad, she was overcome with happy-weepy warmth. The mother of the flower girls was called Fiona, and nice as pie. Imogen's mother, was a slightly anxious faded blonde, full of apologies for not having met before. 'It's all been so very hectic, you see . . .'

'Oh, I can imagine, *please* don't apologise . . .'

Within a minute, a bustle at the back of the church told us the bride was arriving. As Andrew and Will watched, expectant, sister Fiona nipped up and whispered something to Andrew. He then whispered to Will, who grinned and came over.

'Come on, Superman,' he said, lifting Robbie out of the pew. 'They've got a job for you.' With a wink at Mum, he whisked him off.

'What on earth . . . ?' said Mum.

We soon found out. As the organist struck up, all eyes turned to the back of the church. Imogen was on the arm of her father, a tall, spare man. Imogen's light-gold hair was swept back; her pale face luminous and serene. Over a simple white velvet dress she wore a cloak of the same, with a face-framing hood. Her bouquet was white, just touched with green. She looked like the Snow Princess.

Just Andrew's face as he watched Imogen coming up the aisle would probably have tested Mum's mascara to the limit, but that wasn't the end of it.

Behind Imogen were the flower girls. Angelic-blonde, they were only about four and six. In dresses of Christmas red with green sashes, they carried little baskets of snowdrops. Circlets of snowdrops lay on their hair.

Bringing up the rear was Imogen's other sister. Wearing a simple dress of forest green velvet, she carried a white posy tied with red ribbon.

And in between, looking sheepish but decidedly pleased with himself, was Superman.

Seventeen

I'm glad to say I had no wetsuit thoughts during the ceremony. It kicked off with 'Away in a Manger', which can make me go a bit throat-prickly even without a choir, never mind Robbie looking like an angel in the wrong kit. Even Dad was pretending he'd got something in his eye.

Having learnt the words for his school Nativity play, Robbie sang out with gusto. Once or twice he glanced across at us, grinning as he sang. Once the ceremony started, he and the flower girls were restored to their parents. It was too much to ask them to stand still any longer.

Robbie was tickled pink. 'I think I did it *quite* well, didn't I?' he whispered. 'Imogen needed a Best Boy, you see.'

By then I think Mum was in love with Those Burridges for ever.

He didn't even fidget much through the service. It was the beautiful old King James version, though naturally without the 'obey' bit.

'*I, Andrew Thomas, take thee, Imogen . . . forsaking all others . . .*'

I did try not to look at Dad here.

There were a few photos in the church, as they could hardly take them outside. Afterwards guests formed an orderly rabble for the ushers to ush back into cabs.

In the crowd, I was momentarily crushed up with Fleur and Guy.

'You've smudged your mascara,' he said, glancing down at me.

'Only a bit,' said Fleur. 'And I'm sure she'd rather you didn't point it out.'

'I'm getting my own back,' he said, gently mock-miffed. 'For the nasty-bastard bit.'

'Scary-by-proxy,' I said. 'It's a lot less exhausting than being scary myself. Still, even scary people can get a bit weepy during "Away in a Manger", you know.'

'So I saw.' He raised his eyebrows. 'I was all ready to pass over my flash, wedding-suit handkerchief – it'd make a change to use the bloody thing for once – but you seemed to be well supplied with Kleenex.'

It gave me a weird feeling to know he'd been watching me. Weird and fuzzy, and not altogether comfortable.

Back at the Welford Castle Hotel, more photos were taken on the sweeping staircase and in the chandeliered room laid out for drinks. For the first twenty minutes of the reception, I managed to avoid Guy. On my second flute of champagne, I was in a group with Lindsay when he and Fleur joined us. Moments later, up came an old friend of Andrew's I'd met a few times, but not for years.

'Snap,' I smiled, as she wore a red dress very similar to mine.

We kissed, in the daft way you do at such functions even when you can barely remember the other person's name. 'I nearly wore' – mwah – 'black,' she said. 'In mourning at Andrew being so prematurely off the market.'

They'd had a very brief relationship. Her name was Nicola, and one reason I remembered was because Andrew had sometimes referred to her as Nickerless. Tall and statuesque, with a deep, creamy cleavage and a tumble of dark hair, she wore exactly the same sexily mischievous smile I remembered from before.

I introduced her to the others, and five minutes later was beginning to wish I hadn't. She was one of those women who, perhaps unconsciously, gravitate towards the men in any given gathering, address any conversation *at* the men, and give them two-thirds of the eye contact. She didn't confine it to Guy, but as she gave the third husky peal of laughter at something he'd said, I saw Fleur's smile freeze around the edges.

Chill out! I thought.

Seconds later, Fleur took matters into her own hands. With an expression of sweet apology she said, 'Guy, I think I left my mobile in the car. Would you mind? I'd go myself, only all that gravel round the car park will wreck these heels.'

The barest flicker crossed his face. 'Are you sure it's not upstairs?'

'No, I haven't used it since. I think it's in the glove compartment.'

'OK. Won't be long.'

As soon as she could do it discreetly, Lindsay drew me aside. 'What's the matter with her?' she muttered. 'I know that Nicola was on the flirty side, but she wasn't that bad. Is Fleur actually *try*ing to come across twitchy and neurotic?'

My thoughts exactly. 'Maybe she did just want her mobile.'

'Like hell. I bet you ten quid it *is* upstairs. It's miles to the car park – I bet you Guy's gone all that way for nothing.'

I could bet he had, too. I wondered whether that tiny flicker was the tip of an iceberg of exasperation, of which nine-tenths was submerged. However, Robbie jerked my mind off this. Although there were few child guests, he'd found a couple of slightly older boys. Flush-faced and hyped-up, these three were playing some sort of 'catch' game. Charging around guests' legs, Robbie bashed into some old boy of eighty-odd and nearly made him spill his drink.

I grabbed Robbie's arm. 'I'm so sorry.'

Old Boy gave a genial smile. 'Don't worry, my dear. Nice to see the youngsters having fun.'

'All the same,' said a much younger man, with some asperity, 'if you could perhaps exert *some* sort of control . . .'

Can't you see I'm trying to? 'Sorry. Will do.' I took Robbie off. 'Calm down! You nearly made that poor old man spill his drink!'

'I didn't mean to!'

'I don't care! Do you want Guy to see you bashing into people? Remember what he said before? He told Fleur the only thing for horrible little boys was a really good wallop!'

I hadn't meant to say anything like this, but there it was. Evil.

And undeniably effective.

'I *won't* do it any more!'

'Promise?'

'Cross my heart and *hope to die*!'

As he shot back to his new friends I dumped my empty glass on a passing waiter's tray, grabbed another and headed back to adult company.

About ten minutes later it occurred to me that I hadn't seen Robbie for a bit. As I needed a little pit-stop anyway I had a quick look on the way, but there was no sign of him or his partners in mayhem. The loos were just around the corner, in a square, russet-carpeted area. I was on my way out again when Guy emerged from the lift right opposite. With him were Robbie and his new friends.

Robbie's eyes lit on me first. 'Aha! *There* she is!' He marched up with an expression I didn't quite like the look of. 'You told me a big fat fib,' he said accusingly. 'Guy was only joking about wallops, weren't you?'

He looked up at Guy, who'd strolled up with a barely suppressed grin.

'In *fack*,' Robbie went on, fixing accusing eyes back on me, 'he said he had a good mind to give *you* a good wallop, for telling porkies.'

Guy was still trying not to let that grin see daylight. 'Robbie, that was only a joke, too.'

Robbie's friends were smothering giggles.

'*Well?*' demanded Robbie.

When under attack, attack back. 'Don't you "well" me! Where have you been? I was looking for you!'

'*Play*ing,' he said, cheeky as you like. 'Any injections?'

'*Obj*ections,' I said. 'And yes, I have, when you go off without asking.'

Guy said, 'I met them on the way up. I've pointed out that larking about in lifts is not a great idea, so they're packing it in now.' He looked down at the trio. 'Aren't you? Go on, off you go.'

As the three of them scampered back to the reception, Guy turned to me like a man trying to pretend he was pissed off, and not remotely succeeding.

'You had a little talk, then,' I said. 'Might have known the little devil would spill my evil beans.'

'I don't think he would if I hadn't asked. All I did was have a minor go at them for mucking about in the lift, and he was looking at me as if I were Saddam Hussein on a bad day.'

'Ah,' I said. 'That would be the wallop effect.'

He was still suppressing a grin that was possibly more lethal for being kept in. 'Abby, if you keep spreading these scurrilous lies about me, I won't be responsible for my actions.'

If you keep giving me this kind of eye contact at two feet, neither will I. 'Oh, come on. If you weren't itching to give him a good wallop at that spaghetti lunch, I'm Mother Teresa.'

'Don't you come all reasonable-argument with me. My thoughts are between me and my own inner brute.'

Much like mine, and my own inner bitch. 'I seem to recall something about feeding him to the tigers, too.'

'Ah.' He raised his eyebrows in acknowledgement. 'That was my outer brute.'

I stifled a laugh. 'You do realise you've now undermined my devious authority completely?'

'Serves you right.'

He looked so hideously attractive, trying to pretend he was mad, I couldn't resist a bit more. 'Well, you did say you were going to trample my toes later. I was just trying to make sure you got your money's worth.'

He looked down at my feet, and back again. 'You bet I will. My outer brute's warming up nicely.'

Something told me this conversation was beginning to overstep that delicate, invisible line, but that didn't stop me pursuing it. 'Huh! It won't stand a chance against my outer Fairy-Elephant, especially not if we get a Lambada.'

He laughed.

It was like a sweet, green sword in my guts. 'You'll be laughing on the other side of your face later. I'll have you know I nearly got slung out of my ballet class at the age of five, for galumphing and doing "naughty toes" on purpose.'

'You'll have to fill me in on "naughty toes", I'm afraid.'

'Then your education's woefully lacking. Pay attention, please . . .'

Looking down, I pointed my left foot in its new black suede, tilted it upwards and back, and repeated. '*Good* toes, *naughty* toes, *good* toes, *naughty* toes – see?'

I looked up into full-frontal, glinting blue eyes, and my heart gave a drunken little lurch, followed swiftly by a near case of cardiac arrest.

Bearing down on us at two paces was AK 47, wearing a smile like a hawk that's just spotted its dinner. 'Oh, there you are, Abigail! I do believe your mother was looking for you just now, wondering what you were up to.'

Her voice was as light as faintly metallic goose down. She put a very slight emphasis on 'up', smiling at Guy as she said it.

There was no mistaking the insinuation.

'I was on a Robbie hunt,' I said. 'But Guy had already found him. The little devil was playing in the lift.'

'With a couple of other little devils,' Guy added. 'Right, back to the party . . .' He shot an entirely charming smile at AK 47. 'See you later.'

I went with him. AK departed for the ladies, which was where she'd evidently been heading when she'd seen us.

'Why does she call you Abigail?' Guy murmured, as we threaded a path through the throng.

Probably because the old hag knows I hate it.

I only just managed not to say this. 'Because it's my name, I suppose.'

He glanced down at me. 'You don't look like an Abigail.'

'Thank you.'

We happened to 'thread' past Mum on the way back. 'Were you looking for me?' I asked.

In happy mid-chat, she was nearly as flush-faced as Robbie. 'No, not specially – is everything all right?'

'Yes, all under control.'

I made no comment as we carried on, and neither did

Guy, though I was certain Kay's agenda hadn't escaped him.

Back at the group we'd left, Guy passed Fleur a minute silver phone. 'There you go. It was upstairs, after all.'

'Oh, Lord, was it?' She gave a guilty little wince. 'Poor Guy – I'm so sorry I sent you all that way in the cold.'

'I should think so.' Slipping an arm around her waist, he gave her a little squeeze. 'Could be dangerous, a delicate plant like me. All that gravel wrecking my heels, too.'

Lindsay gave me a subtle Look. *Told you, didn't I?*

I looked away before anybody else caught it. Quite at random I turned my eyes to the throng and caught AK looking directly at me from perhaps five yards away.

My response was automatic. A quick, plastic smile before turning away.

'Abby, are you OK?' asked Lindsay. 'You've gone a bit pink.'

'It's the fizz. Always goes straight to my face.'

It was nothing of the sort. It was the sudden realisation that my aunt had been watching me. Watching for signs of anything resembling what she thought she'd seen a few minutes before. *Like mother, like daughter . . .*

And I didn't even have the satisfaction of righteous indignation.

Eighteen

Maybe it was the Lanson, after all. Two glasses on an empty stomach never encouraged circumspect behaviour. Knowing I was bordering on flirtation, I'd gaily carried on anyway. And if AK's antennae had picked it up at six paces . . .

I couldn't risk anything else like this.

The trouble was, I wasn't sure it was just me any more. I'd never kidded myself that Guy found me about as alluring as a dung beetle, but neither had I flattered myself it was much more. Back there, though, I thought I'd caught a whiff of something else.

Chemistry.

Sod's Law, wasn't it?

The chatter suddenly hushed. A gong was banging. 'Ladies and gentlemen, boys, girls and Superman!' boomed an MC voice. 'Dinner is served.'

I already knew from the seating plan that Guy and Fleur were at the same table. Like the others, this was a round ten-seater, not far from the long, raised, top table. An arrangement of white flowers and greenery sat in the centre of a glass bowl, surrounded by floating white candles. Also with us were Lindsay, Midge, the genial old boy (who turned out to be a great-uncle of Imogen's) and two late-twenties males who turned out to be her cousins. Placed

176

between these two, Lindsay seemed entirely happy with the arrangement.

My own placement could have been worse. Guy was three seats to my right. On my immediate right was Robbie, next to Fleur.

A goody bag at Robbie's place kept him amused while we introduced ourselves. Among other things it contained a plastic 'champagne' bottle of bubbles. Opening this at once, he managed to spill half the contents over the cloth.

Along with adult starters, mousseline of salmon and prawns, came the child-friendly food Andrew had ordered. 'There you go, Superman,' grinned a waiter, putting a plate before him.

'Hey, that's mine!' said Guy. 'I ordered chicken and chips with no green bits.'

He did it so well, Robbie believed him. Fallen-faced, he looked up at me.

'Silence, Earthling.' I shot Guy a quelling glance to match. 'This was flown in specially from Planet Krypton. You have to eat mere human food.'

'Not green bits?' He made an aghast face that made Robbie hoot. It was increasingly obvious that far from being wary of him, Robbie now had Guy down as a Thoroughly Good Bloke.

'*Lots* of green bits,' I said. 'Maybe even broccle-trees.'

As broccle-trees were his worst green-poison, Robbie hooted with glee.

'I'm not so sure Guy is a mere earthling.' Lindsay shot him a wicked little grin. 'I've heard rumours that he's actually a Zogite in humanoid form.'

'Watch it, Lindsay.' Guy shot her a look much like her own. 'If you blow my cover I'll be in dead trouble.'

'He's liable to trans-mute at any time,' Lindsay explained

to Robbie. 'Which means he bursts out of his humanoid-suit and turns into a hideous Zogite blob.'

'But I try not to do it very often,' Guy said. 'Fleur's not mad keen on the green, warty bits.'

'No,' said Fleur. 'Pity you didn't do it earlier, though. In front of a certain Nicola.'

She said it like a joke that isn't, quite, and I couldn't help glancing at Guy. There was a flicker of exasperation, but even as he did it Fleur knew she'd gone too far. 'Just kidding,' she said lightly, patting his hand.

All this went right over Robbie's head. 'Do it, then,' he said to Guy.

'Do what?'

'Turn into a blob!'

'Ah.' Guy raised his eyebrows. 'That could be a problem. I have to plug myself into my control centre first, eat half a dozen green jellies, and so on.'

Robbie hooted. 'You know what I think?' He pointed his fork at Guy as if it were a gun and he was taking aim. '*I* think you're talking a load of old bollocks.'

Although the ripple that went round the table was only mirth, I couldn't let it pass. 'Robbie, you know perfectly well that Mummy's told you not to say that word.'

'Oops!' Acting to the crowd, he clapped a hand to his mouth. 'So she did. Cos it means willyballs and it's rather *rude*.' He chortled blithely at his own risqué wit.

'Now, now,' said Midge. 'Enough of that. Eat up like a good boy.'

For half a minute he ate up like a good boy. Then he said to Guy, 'Me and Abby are going swimming in the morning. D'you want to come?'

Heaven help me. 'Of course he doesn't!' I said, before Guy could utter. 'We'll be going very early, when every-body else'll still be asleep.'

'Yes, but it'll be really *bor*ing with just you!'

'Then we won't go at all!' I almost snapped it. 'Now just eat up and be quiet.'

Against all my expectations, he behaved reasonably well for the rest of the meal.

There was a lot of good-humoured talk that got steadily merrier, the food was lovely, and good wine flowed, though I was watching my intake of this. As if trying to compensate for before, Fleur smiled and talked in a quick, bright way that struck me as slightly forced and tense underneath.

I wondered whether she was expecting Guy to have a go at her later, about Nickerless. Was she imagining the bedroom door closing behind them, him tossing the key on the bed, turning exasperated eyes on her? *Look, Fleur, I've just about had enough . . .*

If so, he was suppressing the signs. His manner was just the same: warm and relaxed, with an ever-present hint of protectiveness. If anything, I thought the scenario would be reversed. I imagined her saying, *Look, I'm sorry – about that Nicola – I don't want you to think—*'

Relax! I saw him taking him in her arms, soothing her. *Forget it, OK? Let's just go to bed.*

This was not the best thought to eat by. It added little green bits to my *filet en croûte*, and I don't mean broccletrees. Still, Mum was clearly having a ball on the top table, and by the time the coffee arrived Robbie was flagging. Andrew had booked a babysitter from eight-thirty; at this rate I'd be able to hand him over before the rest of the evening got going. As one of the flower girls was carried off, fast asleep in her father's arms, I crossed my fingers.

* * *

As the speeches started, I arranged Robbie's nodding head in my lap. Without my having to ask, Fleur gently took his legs across her own. She smiled at me: a soft, between-us smile that constricted my stomach. Why did he have to be involved with her? Why couldn't it be some utter bitch I couldn't stand? Then I could have told myself that all was fair in love and war, and played dirty with a clear conscience.

Will's speech was short and full of laughs, but nothing too risqué, as Mum had said she'd murder him. Andrew's was also short, and a model of diplomacy. Somehow he managed to give full credit to Mum for her single-parent hard work, without casting any reprobate light on Dad. At any rate, I saw Mum get her tissues out again, while Dad just basked in slightly sheepish pride.

I looked down at Robbie. Asleep, he still looked as if babyhood was only yesterday. His long eyelashes curled on the infant delicacy of his skin.

I caught Fleur's eye. 'Sweet,' she mouthed, and smiled.

'When he's asleep,' I mouthed back. Stroking his hair gently, I hoped I could get him upstairs without waking him.

Hollow laugh. The moment I tried to move him he woke and his second wind kicked in. 'There's going to be a disco! My friends are staying up!'

The disco was the kind you always get at mixed-age dos like weddings. It kicked off with good old Elvis. To the *aaah*-making strains of 'Can't Help Falling in Love', Andrew and Imogen drifted over the floor.

More energetic stuff followed, anything with an irresistible beat that wouldn't frighten the grannies. For over an hour I was barely off the floor. I danced with everyone from one of those cousins to Robbie, though in his case I use the term loosely. His idea of dancing was bouncing up and down like a Pogo stick, or whizzing round on the spot. The only person I hadn't danced with was Guy, who was barely off the floor, either. He even danced with AK, who took on an almost flirty air as he did a rock and roll with her. I don't know why Lindsay had said he was a crap dancer. His rhythm beat at least eighty per cent of the other men on the floor.

Andrew and Imogen left shortly after ten, but only for the bridal suite. A car was coming at six, to take them in chauffeured style to Heathrow.

The music then resumed. While I got my breath back after a daft 'Viva España' with Will, Lindsay flopped beside me. 'Just look at your folks.' She nodded towards the floor, where they were dancing together to a slow one. You couldn't call it smooching, just slow movement in time to the music. They were talking as they danced, like old friends.

'Do you ever wish they'd get back together?' she asked.

'I used to, but they never will. I'm just glad they get on.'

While I was still sitting with Lindsay, the moment I'd stopped expecting came to pass. After the next number, off the floor came Guy and Fleur. 'My feet!' said Fleur, easing off her shoes. 'I knew I shouldn't have worn such pointy toes.'

The DJ said, 'And if that one didn't warm you up enough, here we go with "Hot Hot Hot" . . .'

'Dead right it is.' So saying, Guy took his tie off and undid his top button. Having done that, he turned to me. 'Come on, Abby – your turn. Enough of this bone-idle wallflower bit.'

'Will you listen to him?' Lindsay grinned. 'Like some hairy-legged games teacher telling you to stop slacking.'

He tossed his tie at her. 'You'll be next. There's far too much slacking going on around here.'

181

I pretended to protest. 'It's all right for you lot! You'll be slacking in the morning, while I'm being jumped on at unearthly hours.'

'Pathetic excuse. You'll have to do better than that.' Taking my hand, he pulled me to my feet. 'I'll get you lot fit if it kills me.'

The contact was already quickening my pulse. I can't even pretend I was racking my brains for any more excuses. When I'd danced with everybody else, it would have looked odd to refuse.

And I didn't want to. There was no possible harm in 'Hot Hot Hot', after all. Apart from a fleeting hand on my waist as we moved on to the floor, he barely touched me. Half the time we were cracking up at someone doing a David Brent impression right beside us. It was only our eyes that touched, in mutual laughter.

In any case, we never made it to the end.

'So sorry to interrupt . . .' It was AK, appearing at Guy's shoulder with a bright smile.

But it was me she spoke to. 'Abigail, dear . . .'

Dear?

'I don't want to bother Penny, but I really do think someone should see to Robbie.'

I suddenly realised I'd barely seen him for ages. She nodded towards a table a good way from where I'd been sitting with Lindsay. At my last check he'd been happily playing Beggar My Neighbour with his new friends, slurping Coke and telling me to go a-*way*. And I'd gone, blessing whichever genius had thought to include mini playing cards in their goodie bags.

But Robbie's second wind had run out. He was in a kneeling-up position, his top half horizontal on the white cloth. His head wasn't even pillowed on his arms. They were flexed either side of his head.

'He just sort of *zonked*,' explained one of the other boys. I scooped him gently up in my arms.

Guy had come with me. 'Let me take him.'

'It's fine!' With Kay still hovering, I couldn't have this. 'I'll just take him to say goodnight to Mum . . . Yes, I *know* he's out for the count,' I added, seeing his face, 'but if she doesn't kiss him goodnight, something terrible might happen.'

Leaving him to digest this law of Mother Nature, I found Mum nattering to Helen Burridge. Robbie was duly kissed, with a, 'Bless him, he's been *so* good. But don't you carry him all that way, Abby – let Will or your father take him.'

However, as Will was dancing and Dad was nowhere to be seen, I returned to our table for my room key.

Lindsay passed me my bag. 'Abby, let Guy take him! He must weigh a ton and it's miles down those corridors.'

'I already offered,' Guy said. 'But I was spurned.'

'Abby, for heaven's sake!' said Fleur. 'You'll get back trouble. Just take him, Guy.'

So Robbie was transferred. As we left the ballroom, the DJ was back with Elvis. Nobody else was waiting for the lift. There was just me and Guy, and the sleeping Robbie in his arms.

And the liquid gold voice of The King, drifting from the ballroom.

Are You Lonesome Tonight?

Nineteen

Would I have ended up dancing that one with him? Up close and personal, or at least at a distance of three respectable inches? Hand in hand, my other on his shoulder?

Get real. Even without Hawk Eye watching you'd have made some excuse. If he hadn't first.

'Elvis again,' I said, pinging the 'up' button.

'Yes, pretty rubbish for keep-fit purposes. You could do that in a Zimmer frame.'

His tone was light and jokey, but suddenly I knew it was masking something else. I hadn't imagined that whiff of chemistry. I wasn't even looking at him; my eyes were fixed on the descending lift light, but I felt it like a sudden electric field. 'I really can manage Robbie, you know. You don't have to be noble.'

'Oh, come on. If you spurn me again, I'll sulk.'

I didn't trust myself to look at him. If I did, I knew it would be an acknowledgement, a conscious betrayal of Fleur. 'Well, I can't have that—'

The lift doors opened. We stepped in and I pressed '2'. 'To be honest, I'm surprised Robbie lasted this long.'

'Probably didn't want to miss anything.'

'Probably.' I was watching the little red light go from 'G' to '1'.

Here it stopped. The doors opened, but nobody was there.

184

The doors slid shut behind us. I still didn't look at Guy. It was as if something else was hovering in the silence. I knew he knew it was there, and he knew that I knew. Much like commuters on a train, with a weirdo muttering to himself, we were pretending it wasn't there.

'You never know, he might sleep late in the morning,' he said.

'Are you kidding?' I glanced at Robbie's face, sideways over his shoulder. His lips were just slightly parted. He looked like a painting of a sleeping baby angel. 'Whatever time he goes to bed, he still wakes at the normal time. He'll just be whiny and horrible later.'

The doors opened.

It was hushed on the landing, and down the long, softly carpeted corridor. Outside one or two rooms were room service trays, put out for collection. Neither Guy nor I uttered as we walked to 214.

I'd already met the babysitter. I'd had to let her in, explain that I wasn't sure what time I'd be needing her. 'Aaah, bless,' she whispered, seeing Robbie's face. 'He's had a busy day.'

I turned down the covers on Robbie's bed; Guy laid him gently on the crisp white sheet.

I had to look at him then. 'Thank you, Mr Porter,' I whispered.

'No problem,' he whispered. 'See you in a bit.' With a light pat on my waist, he departed, shutting the door quietly behind him.

'He's nice,' whispered the babysitter, taking Robbie's left shoe off while I did the right. 'He your boyfriend?'

'God, no.'

'Of course not. Silly me.' She glanced at the other single bed. 'You'd be a bit cramped, wouldn't you?'

'Not to mention in dead trouble.' I started easing the Superman kit off. 'He's my cousin's.'

She laughed quietly. 'Oh, well. Can't win 'em all.'

Leaving Robbie in his underwear, I pulled the covers over him.

'Off you go, then,' whispered the babysitter. 'And don't worry about your little boy – he'll be fine.'

I didn't bother correcting her. 'Actually, I've changed my mind.' I nodded apologetically towards the other bed. 'I've had a rather busy day, too.'

After she'd gone I shut myself in the bathroom. There was about an acre of mirror over the washbasin. All the better for gazing at yourself and seeing – what?

A chicken.

A scaredy-cat.

After all, what could possibly happen? At the most, a couple of dances with him, probably to something like 'Blue Suede Shoes', given the DJ's Elvis kick.

But rock and roll meant hand-holding. It meant twizzling into someone's arms, however briefly.

No, far better to stay here, away from masochistic little pleasures. Away from Kay almost certainly watching like a spy-satellite. Excuses for my shameful boringness would be easy enough to find tomorrow.

I turned the bath taps on, emptying a freebie bottle of gel under the flow. With a bit of luck there might even be a film worth watching afterwards. Once he was out for the count, Robbie would sleep through earthquakes.

While I wallowed motionless in the bubbles, that Elvis song replayed endlessly in my head. *Are you lone-some to-niiight?*

Maybe Kay gave Robbie some instant zonk-drug. So she'd have a good excuse for prising my talons off Guy.

Not that I had any talons on him.

'Are You Lonesome Tonight?'

I am, now you come to mention it.

'*Dee-dee dah-dee, dee-daaah . . . ?*'

'*Dee-dee dah-dee, dee-dah-dee, dee-daaaah . . . ?*'

With closed eyes, I thought myself into Guy's arms, with no respectable three inches between us. From chest to knee, you could not have slid a sheet of paper between us. I felt his arm around my waist, the warm chest under his shirt. I felt the side of his face brush my hair, the shivering caress of his fingers over the material of my dress. I'm not sure how this then turned into my wetsuit fantasy, but I guess the bath had something to do with it. I didn't feel bad about it, not when I was so nobly forgoing the rest of the evening.

At any rate, he was in a wetsuit, too. His hair was wet, the sun glistening in the drops of water on his skin. He was looking at me with eyes that said I looked pretty damn good in black neoprene, but he'd like me a lot better out of it.

Like some help out of that thing?

A soft knock at the door dragged me out of this. I sat up with a jerk from the bubbles, my heart racing. 'Who is it?'

'Me!'

My heart-rate subsided. For a moment I'd actually thought it might be Guy. 'Hang on . . .'

I pulled on a hotel robe over my wetness and opened the door.

Lindsay winced. 'Sorry, I hope I didn't wake Robbie.'

'No chance, he's out for the count.'

She looked down at my wet legs. 'Why didn't you come back down?'

And here's a lie I made earlier . . . 'He started to wake up and I didn't like to leave him with a stranger. And to tell you the truth, my bed suddenly looked very enticing.'

'Abby! How boring can you get?'

'Oh, come on. It must be half eleven already, and I won't have the luxury of sleeping in.'

'OK, I'll let you off this time. See you tomorrow.'

I returned to the bathroom, thinking 'boring' was at least one up on 'chicken'. The bubbles were nearly all gone, not that I fancied getting back in the bath now. I let the water out, washing my wetsuit fantasy with it. It just wasn't the same if you had to go, 'Now, where was I?'

In any case, it was a pretty hopeless fantasy to start with. You'd need to have been skiing on a private lake. In a heat-wave. With a handy waterproof rug in the boat, because you could bet any lakeside grass would be covered with Canada goose shit. And even then you could bet some old bugger of an angler would turn up and get his maggots out.

'Are you awake?'

I roused to Robbie's max-volume whisper. (He thought it didn't count if you whispered.) 'No!' With a glance at the clock, I turned over. It was twenty to eight.

'Yes, you are!' He came round to the other side of the bed. 'I've got my swimming things on already, look!' He was wide-eyed, perky and expectant.

It was a twenty-five-metre pool, almost completely surrounded by glass. Outside, in the grey dawn light, lay landscaped lawns and trees. By the entrance was an attendant's desk with a pile of fluffy towels, but nobody at it. Nobody was in the pool, either. The turquoise water lay calm and pristine. The air was warm and humid, smelling of chlorine and rubber.

Signs around the pool said, 'NO DIVING' and 'THIS POOL IS NOT SUPERVISED. CHILDREN UNDER 12 MUST BE ACCOMPANIED BY AN ADULT'.

Having learnt to swim without armbands at eighteen months, Robbie jumped in before you could say 'get your things off'. Until recently he'd still resembled a freestyle tadpole, but he was beginning to get the hang of front crawl.

I dived into the deep end anyway, and after a couple of lengths I felt awake and more or less human.

Robbie scrambled out of the deep end. 'Do a leg and a wing!'

This was a favourite game, but we usually only managed it once before an attendant blew his or her whistle. It involved taking him by one wrist and the same-side ankle, swinging him back and forth over the side and letting go on the last count. He was getting heavy for this sort of thing, but I wasn't going to be boring.

'A leg and a *wing*,
To see the *king*,
A one,
A two,
And a jolly good – THREE!'
Splosh!

He'd just sploshed for the third time when I heard a voice behind me. 'Can I be next?'

My heart jumped almost to my tonsils. 'Guy!'

'Morning.' He wore a pair of loose combats, a T-shirt, and a rather morning-after smile. 'Glad to see I haven't missed all the fun.'

'Why aren't you in bed, like normal people?'

'I've got Robbie's problem. Heavy night or not, I still wake at sparrow-fart.' Deadpan he added, 'And how could I turn down a gracious invitation like that?'

So bor*ing with just you* . . . 'Quite easily,' I said. 'I hope Fleur's not feeling abandoned.'

'No, she was half asleep. Mumbled something about,

"No, you go, I'd come if I could wake up," and curled up again like a puppy.'

'Hi, Guy!' Robbie waved from the water. 'Look what I can do!' Glancing over his shoulder, he made a face of abject terror. He then swam five yards as if Jaws were after him (well, he was), yelled and thrashed for three seconds with his extreme-agony face, then 'died' and floated, spread-eagled, on his front.

He then popped up. 'That was "Death by Jaws", only most of me would be in his tummy, of course.'

'Will again,' I explained.

'Bravo!' Guy clapped enthusiastically. 'Can you swim a length?'

'Course I can! Just watch!'

While he struck out with a lot more energy than style, Guy watched.

But not in silence. Without taking his eyes off Robbie he said, 'Tell me the truth, then. Did you chicken out last night?'

Twenty

Every tiny hair on my skin prickled. 'Sorry?'

He turned to me with a grin. 'Of the Lambada. Or anything else that might have involved toe-trampling.'

'Oh, yes.' I tried to laugh as if nothing else had crossed my mind. 'No, it was just a case of disgraceful slacking. *Was* there a Lambada?'

'Even worse. The Gay Gordons and a tango.' He nodded towards the side. 'I'll get my kit off . . .'

I dived back in. *I swear he meant something else there, too. I swear he knows why I didn't come back down. But at least Fleur knows he's here. It's not as if he's sneaked off.* On reaching the far end, I turned around and got my breath back.

Or rather, watched Guy de-kitting. The trainers and combats were already discarded; he was just pulling off his T-shirt. He wore a pair of loose black swim shorts, and it was no use pretending the body was a disappointment. It was firm and lithe, with the kind of musculature that fits perfectly under the skin without screaming, 'Get a load of me!' There was just enough fuzz on his chest, tapering down over a firm stomach into those shorts. He didn't take his watch off. I don't know why I noticed that.

Having adjusted the waist of his shorts, he did a running dive in, a fast front crawl to the end, an underwater turn, and back again.

Well, it was too much to hope that he'd be a rubbish

swimmer. Be he ever so gorgeous, I can't do with a man who does that flappy, side-to-side, amateur crawl.

Robbie was scrambling out again. 'Abby! A leg and a wing!'

I swam back, passing Guy halfway.

He watched from the other end, as I did two more legs and wings. However, this was enough. 'No more, Robbie. You're getting too heavy.'

I didn't intend this as a cue for Guy, but I suppose it was inevitable. While I got a few lengths in, he did half a dozen legs and wings. Robbie shrieked with joy. Guy swung him harder than me, and threw him further.

Meanwhile, three kids came in. Two girls and a boy I didn't recognise from the wedding, they were fifteen or sixteen. Instantly the place was ten times noisier. The boy pushed one of the girls in; there were lots of shrieky giggles and yelling at each other.

Thinking Guy had more than done his bit, I got out. From the bag I'd dumped at the side of the pool, I took half a dozen coins from my purse. 'That's enough now!' I called to Robbie. 'Guy wants to swim. Dive for these, instead.'

I threw them at random. As this was his next best game, he was wriggling to the bottom almost at once.

I went to a point halfway down the pool and sat on the edge with my feet in the water, watching Robbie. I think I knew Guy would join me, but I wasn't looking at him. I was wringing water from my hair, smoothing the odd strand from my face.

He surfaced beside me, flicking his head like a wet dog, and wiping the water from his face with the back of his forearm. 'He's a handy little swimmer,' he said, nodding towards Robbie.

'So he should be. I've taken him often enough.'

With one lithe movement, he was out. He sat beside me, about eighteen inches to my right.

Like me, he was watching Robbie diving for coins. 'Good game.'

'Yes, it keeps him quiet for five minutes.'

Although we weren't even looking at each other, I knew he was as aware of me as I was of him. I could almost feel the heat of his wet body. 'I'm surprised nobody else from the wedding is here,' I said.

'Maybe all the energetic types have gone for a run, instead.'

'And the non-energetic types are sleeping it off.'

'Can't blame them. It is Sunday morning.'

I don't know when I'd ever had such a conversation. The words were mere small talk, yet every nerve ending in my body was quivering with awareness.

My eyes were on the far end of the pool. Having collected his coins, Robbie was hanging on to the side, watching the teens. They were chasing each other round the side, pushing each other in with shrieks and giggles. There was a lot of noisy splashing and the poolside was awash. I said, 'Someone's going to slip any minute. Do you think we should tell them to cool it?'

'Are you kidding?' He turned to me. 'They'll think we're a couple of killjoy old farts.'

But he was half-laughing. His mouth hovered on a full-scale smile, his eyes lit from within. 'Speak for yourself,' I said, deadpan, while my heart did a massive back-flip. 'I'll have you know I take poolside safety very seriously. I once spent an entire summer as a lifeguard for the council.'

'What, with one of those whistles?'

'Yep.'

'In a pair of shorts, sitting on top of one of those lookout posts?'

'Yep.'

'Saying, "Oi, you over there! Cut it out!"'

'All the time.' His eyes were doing possibly illegal things to my insides, but I couldn't look away. 'We used to get a very rowdy element, you know. Boys of a certain age, showing off . . .'

Very fleetingly, his eyes swept over my sleek black Speedo. 'I bet some of them played you up on purpose.'

'I doubt it. The council T-shirt was specially designed to make you look like a sack of dead cats.'

His mouth flickered. 'Very wise. Or some of the rowdy element might have been very tempted to throw you in.'

'They'd never have dared. I could be extremely scary, you know.'

'Oh, yes?'

I knew exactly what was coming. I suppose I'd almost said it on purpose. I could have taken evasive action, slipped into the water, but I didn't. Instead, just as I knew he was about to make a grab for me, I stood up.

He was on his feet before you could say, 'Open invitation.' Two firm hands were suddenly on my waist. 'Not nearly scary enough . . .'

If he'd used anything like full force, I'd have been over the side in a second, but he didn't. That would have defeated the object. As it was I was fighting him, bracing my feet and laughing. 'Get *off*!'

'This is what you get for slacking . . .'

In the brief struggle as he forced me towards the edge, his arms went right around me. My back was against his warm, wet chest. 'Let *go*!'

Stop it, I love it . . .

'In she goes . . .' But we went together. He let me go in mid-air, there was a massive splosh, and we surfaced about three feet apart.

My heart still racing from the brief, illicit thrill, I trod water and pushed my hair back from my face. 'That was extremely irresponsible,' I said, trying not to laugh. 'I've got a good mind to report you to the management.'

'It was a temptation too far.'

Don't tell me . . . 'This kind of thing can be highly dangerous, you know.'

I knew it was double-speak, but it came out before I could stop it.

His eyes flickered in acknowledgement. 'Not that dangerous. Not before breakfast.' He pushed a clinging strand of hair from my cheek.

On the surface it was such a casual little touch, but the effect on me was out of all proportion. It felt as if about five million volts were in his fingertips.

So it was just as well Robbie was jumping up and down at the side. 'Throw *me* in, Guy! Throw me!'

With a glance at me, Guy hauled himself out and chased an excited Robbie to the deep end. 'Be careful!' I called, partly to cover my internal churnings, partly because I was still conscious of the slippery, awash poolside.

I swam to the shallow end, telling myself there was no reason to feel guilty. It was only the most minor flirtation. Nothing had actually happened.

On the other hand, we'd never have done 'nothing' if Fleur were here.

He wouldn't have sat next to me.

I'd never have issued that open invitation.

He'd never have touched my face like that.

Oh, shit . . .

With my arms spread across the bar, I watched him chuck Robbie in. The teens were still at it; anyone could see there was some flirty stuff going on there, too. They were chasing each other, the girls shrieking and pretending to fight as the boy chucked them in. 'Be careful!' I called, as Robbie scrambled out and one of them nearly fell over him.

Guy then hoisted Robbie on to his shoulders, ready to jump in together. 'Do a *big* jump!' Robbie yelled, wriggling with excitement.

Guy waited a moment, as one of the girls surfaced in front of him.

Meanwhile the younger was shrieking, 'I'll get you!' as she chased the boy around the side. They dodged and darted right behind Guy.

It was the girl who pushed him. Giggly and over-excited, she gave him a shove as she passed. Right on the edge, holding Robbie's ankles, he went over the side.

It seemed to happen in slow motion. Aghast, I saw him hit the water not nearly far enough out. I saw Robbie's head fall back with the force, hitting the side as he fell.

I raced to the other end.

Robbie surfaced gasping, his eyes wide with shock.

Already around him, the water was awash with blood.

Twenty-one

The next minute was a chaotic blur: Robbie's terrified crying, my own panicky leap into the water while Guy was already carrying him to the steps. The wet, the blood my own fear, all wrapped up in the smell of chlorine.

Dripping with water and blood, I knelt on the wet floor with sobbing Robbie on my lap, trying to see the damage. Fragments of first-aid horrors were flashing through my brain: *head injuries, fractured skull, bleeding into the brain* . . .

Guy brought a towel, putting it to Robbie's head. 'Let me!' I grabbed it from him. 'For God's sake call an ambulance!'

As I held the towel to his head, Robbie sobbed and sobbed. The teens stood white-faced, silent. Sick with fury, I turned on the girl who'd pushed Guy, thinking it'd be a laugh. 'How could you be so *stu*pid? You stupid, stupid brat!'

Tense-faced, Guy said, 'Abby, for God's sake. This isn't going to help.'

'Shut *up!*' I turned on him like a whirlwind. 'It's your stupid fault too – I *told* you to be careful!'

At that precise moment, Fleur turned up. Pristine in jeans and a pink sweater, her horrified face took in this bloody carnage. 'My God, what happened?'

I was still trembling with shock and anger. 'Stupid bloody messing about – Guy, will you please, for God's *sake*, call an ambulance?'

Already he was pulling on his combats. 'That could take bloody hours. I'll drive you to the hospital.'

'We don't even know where it is!'

'Then I'll find out. Fleur, stay with Abby – help her get dressed – I'll be right back . . .'

Minutes later I was in reception with Robbie in my arms. While Guy was bringing the car around, Fleur was trying to call Mum from the phone at reception. 'She's just not answering!'

'She's probably in the shower.' I looked out, to see Guy's car already screeching on to the gravel. 'Look, I can't hang around. Just keep trying – no, on second thoughts will you tell Dad first? Let him break it. Thanks, Fleur, I've got to go . . .'

I stepped out into freezing air, thick with a misty chill. Guy was already opening the passenger door. He had some green four-wheel drive with a tow-hook on the back.

'Where are we going?' cried Robbie, in between shuddering gasps.

'Just to see a doctor. It's all right.'

'I don't want . . . to see a doctor!' As he associated them with stitches after a cut foot, this set him off again. 'I want Mummy!'

'She'll be coming soon, sshh, it's all right . . .' Dad could drive her to the hospital. They'd be twenty minutes behind us at the most.

Only after a couple of miles, when Robbie was back to shuddering gasps, did Guy open his mouth. 'It probably looks worse than it is. Scalp wounds can bleed a hell of a lot.'

'Since when are you a doctor? It's not his scalp I'm worried about!'

He shut up until we were there. Dropping me off at Accident and Emergency, he went to park.

Inside I was met with the calm manner of professionals, but the 'head injury' alert signs were obvious. 'Dear me, Robbie, have you been in the wars? Can I just take a little look?'

Robbie took one look at that white coat, and howled.

The next few minutes were a nightmare. Robbie clung to me, howling as if they were about to mince him alive. Eventually a second nurse was called and I was gently asked to leave him to the pros, who were used to it.

Robbie's screams followed me out. I felt sick, anguished for his pain and terror.

Guy was there as I emerged, in the usual waiting area with hard plastic chairs and old magazines. As he came over, hands shoved in his combat pockets, I knew he was about to come out with some soothing platitude, like, 'Don't worry, he'll be fine.'

My voice came out tense and taut. 'Don't say *any*thing, OK?'

He spoke anyway. 'I just called Fleur. Your folks are on their way.'

My stomach churned afresh, my mouth dry. 'Mum's going to be beside herself . . .'

After a long pause he said, 'Shall I get you a coffee?'

'Out of those machines? It's like dishwater!'

He walked away.

I could still hear Robbie crying. In my head, endlessly, I saw him fall. I saw that sickening crack; the back of his skull hitting that hard, tiled edge. Gazing unseeing at posters about HIV and skin cancer, I tormented myself. When I could see there was an accident just waiting to happen, why hadn't I told those kids to stop charging around the pool?

Because you were obsessed with illicit, passing thrills. A few minutes earlier Robbie could have hit his head and drowned and you wouldn't even have noticed.

And then there was Fleur. Even with Robbie's wails echoing in my ears, I thought of her. What if she'd turned up two minutes earlier? What if she'd seen us in the water, witnessed him brushing that wet strand from my cheek?

The arrival of Mum and Dad jerked me out of this. Tense and anxious, Mum hurried up. 'Where is he? Why aren't you with him?'

'They sent me out.' I nodded towards the cubicle.

'Well, they won't send *me* out.' Grabbing Dad's arm, she charged through.

Where Guy had been when my folks came in I don't know, but she hadn't noticed him. Now he came up. 'Look, I'll clear off – I'm only in the way. I'll see your folks later, issue apologies, and so on.'

Part of me knew I should say 'It wasn't your fault', but the other part wouldn't let me. I was too full of guilt to let him off the hook when he was the cause of so much of it. All I said was, 'OK. Thanks for the lift.'

When we arrived back at the hotel, Mum and Dad took Robbie. I was just out of the shower when a continental breakfast was sent up, courtesy of Dad.

I didn't want it, but a crowd of scavengers solved this little problem. Lindsay, Rachel and David came to hear the drama from the chief witness.

'Trust Guy,' said Lindsay, digging a spoon into a mini-pot of strawberry jam. 'Just what you can do with on a morning-after, not that you exactly qualify for morning-after.'

'But it wasn't exactly Guy's *fault*, was it?' said Rachel. 'Not from what I gather.'

David sat beside me on the bed. 'He looked like shit at breakfast.'

200

'What do you expect?' said Rachel. 'He was probably worried sick about Robbie.'

'Not to mention the sight of all that blood.' Lindsay sucked another scoop of jam off the spoon. 'He didn't even have anything cooked. It was a lovely buffet, too. I made a pig of myself on the pancakes.'

'Poor Guy,' I said lightly. 'I'll have to catch him before he goes and apologise for ruining his appetite.'

I shooed them all out soon afterwards, saying I had to pack and tart myself up. This was true, as immediate family was invited to the Burridges' for lunch. However, after pulling on smart casual I grabbed my key and went to look for Fleur and Guy.

Particularly Guy. I knew I'd been vile to him earlier, and if I didn't catch him soon it'd be too late. With still-wet hair, I hurried to the lift. Checkout time was coming up, so there was a fair chance they'd be gathering up their things.

Their door was ajar. Thinking they'd already gone, I tapped on it. 'Anyone at home?'

'Come in.' It was Guy's voice. I pushed the door open and saw him zipping up a suit carrier.

'Where's Fleur?' I asked.

'Saying goodbyes. Probably looking for you.' He chucked a washbag into a leather bag, zipped it and straightened up. 'I gather the hospital gave a tentative OK?'

'More or less, although obviously he's got to be watched for a bit. Paleness, vomiting, unusual sleepiness . . . Mum was pretty philosophical about it, in the end.'

'Yes, I gathered. She told me Will practically used to have a season ticket for Casualty.'

I hadn't been there when they'd spoken. 'I guess he did. He was always breaking something or cutting himself.' In a rush I added, 'Look, I'm sorry I was such a snappy cow earlier. It's just that I was worried sick.'

'I think I worked that one out.' But his brisk manner faded, his eyes softening. 'It wasn't exactly my idea of Sunday-morning laughs, either.'

I was within a heartbeat of saying, 'I'm so sorry,' and kissing his cheek. If he were anybody else, I would have. 'That'll larn yer,' I said lightly. 'Serves you right for not staying in bed, like normal people.'

He responded in kind, with a lopsided little smile: 'Too right. Blood all over the car seats, too.'

'Send me the bill. Look, I've got to dash. Have a safe journey home.'

I kissed him after all. It would have seemed odd not to. Not that you could call it a kiss – just the briefest grazing of his cheek against mine. 'Bye.'

'Bye.'

I went to find Fleur and pretend I was only looking for her in the first place. I found her in reception, in a pre-departure gathering of the clan. It was the usual mixed-dither group of those still paying bills, those about to go, those saying, 'Oh, Lord, I think I've left a top hanging behind the bathroom door.'

Doing my own farewells, I spoke to Rosemary first. 'Poor little Robbie!' she said. 'Thank heaven he's all right – after he looked so sweet yesterday, too! I can't wait to see the photos.'

'Yes, and poor Guy!' said Kay, in the bright metallic tones she so often polished up for me. 'What a thing to happen when all he wanted was some healthy, early-morning exercise.'

Like a dart at a bull's-eye, this was aimed directly at me. *I haven't forgotten yesterday*, she might have said. *Bit of a coincidence, you two being there together, wasn't it?*

But her tone was so ostensibly casual, nobody else would have picked up a thing. Lindsay said, 'I don't think he'd have got much serious swimming in anyway. Robbie asked him to come.'

Thank you, Lindsay. 'Yes, he was only being noble, and I was in such a tizz I ended up biting his head off.' To Fleur I added, 'But I just saw him upstairs and put it back.'

As she laughed, I thanked heaven telepathy was a gift bestowed on so few.

Uncle Matthew said, 'Come on, Rosie, or we'll be here all day.'

'Yes, and I must dash.' I glanced at my watch. 'We're due at the Burridges' in half an hour, and I still haven't packed a thing.'

It was gone four when we finally got away. 'Well, apart from poor little Robbie,' said Mum, watching his sleeping head in the back, 'I really think it all went beautifully. And those lovely flowers Andrew sent!'

The basket was in the boot. 'No more than you deserved.'

'Yes, but when he had so much else to think about! I told Kay, of course. I don't think even she found anything to sniff about, though I'm sure it wasn't for want of trying. And between you and me, I didn't think her suit was all *that* special. I'm sure I've seen something much the same in Marks.'

Although I was dying to tell Jeff about my Guy-thing, I didn't. He could be a bit of an old woman with gossip and because he naturally saw them now and then I was afraid he might let something slip in front of Rachel or Lindsay. But because I had to tell someone, I told Heidi, the colleague I was closest to at the Lingua Franca. I knew Heidi would empathise. Not long back she'd told me she'd once suffered months of agony on account of a secret passion for a sister's boyfriend.

'If Fleur's really that paranoid, I can't see it lasting long,' she said. 'After a decent interval you could give him a call. Of course, if he dumps her and then starts seeing you, she's going to think he dumped her *for* you, which could be just a tad awkward.'

This conjecture set up nervous butterflies in my stomach. 'I'm not flattering myself he had a massive thing about me. It was just a little whiff of chemistry.'

'It couldn't be much else at a family wedding, could it? He was hardly going to pounce on you and rip your knickers off.'

I did wish she wouldn't say things like this, not when I had a class in two minutes. How was I supposed to concentrate on countable and uncountable nouns with this kind of image in my mind?

'But he still might,' she whispered wickedly, on her way to her own class. 'There's something to keep you warm when you're tucked up in bed tonight.'

In bed was one thing. I just didn't want to think of it in front of a whiteboard.

'Now, how about "friends"?' I said brightly to my lower-intermediates.

'Like on TV?' said Mexican Anna.

'No, Anna, like in *your* friends. You can count friends.'

'I can't count zem. I have too much friends for count.'

'Yes, but if they were all here, you could. So we say, "I have too *many* friends to count."'

'Big problem for me,' grinned Juan-Carlos, 'is I have too many *girl*friends for count.'

Juan-Carlos was from Argentina. About twenty, he was the class clown and Romeo combined. 'Lucky old you. Now—'

'*Lucky*? You call lucky, so many girls have so much hots for me? Is make me knackered.'

Whatever the topic, he always brought it back to sex. 'That's quite enough hots, thank you. And we don't say "much" or "many" hots. Just "the" hots.'

'Why?'

'We just do.'

'Ze girls are mad,' said Anna scornfully. 'Any smart girl, she have colds for him. *Many* colds.'

I moved swiftly on to hair, money and milk.

On Saturday night, exactly a week after the wedding, Mum and Robbie came to the last night of the pantomime. In a hall more used to playgroups and Weight-Watchers, it was a sell-out. During the interval I was manning the coffee stall when Mum said, 'Oh, I forgot to tell you! I had a call this morning, from Fleur's Guy! Said he was so glad to hear there weren't any lasting ill-effects, and could he pop in tomorrow, on his way back from Fleur's! It can't *really* be on the way, of course, but I don't suppose it's a massive detour. He said he's got a Christmas present for Robbie – isn't that nice?'

'I hope it's something really really *cool*,' Robbie piped up.

Over his head, Mum made an 'Oh, Lord' face. 'Whatever it is, Robbie, be sure to say thank you very nicely. Even if it's something you've already got.' To me she added, 'But I must say, it's very kind of him. I think he felt rather bad, you know – I can't think why when it was hardly his fault. Anyway, he's coming late afternoon. Six-ish, he said, so I did think it'd be nice to ask him to stay for supper. Would you come over, too? It'll be just me and Robbie otherwise – maybe a little bit boring for him – and with four of us it might be worth doing a roast.'

A roast. Heaven help me.

'I've got a nice leg of Welsh lamb in the freezer – I thought you might bring Jeff, too.'

Jeff! With Jeff and Mum and Robbie, where was the possible harm in a roast in Sycamore Road?

Jeff was only too willing. As he said later, when the entire cast and crew piled into the nearest pub, 'I love your ma. She does a mean roast spud, too.'

As the hour of Welsh lamb drew near, I was doubly glad I'd kept Jeff in the dark about my Guy-thing. Had he known, he'd have been winding me up non-stop, making remarks about the aphrodisiac properties of Mum's gravy. As it was, he was as innocent a chaperon as Jeff could ever be.

As I pulled into the Sycamore Road drive, Guy's green SUV was already parked on the road. The mere sight of it got my flutters going for England.

We entered to the smell of roast lamb and potatoes. I found them all in the kitchen. Done fifteen years back in now-battered farmhouse pine, it was far from *Homes and Gardens* and hardly ever tidy, but always warm and homely. As always when she could smell a roast, Mum's cat Pudding was sitting on the table, pretending she wasn't interested. Robbie was excitedly crashing a remote-controlled truck into the fridge. 'Look what Guy brought me! It was s'posed to be for Christmas, but Mummy said I could open it now.'

'Lovely! Hi, Guy!' He was perched on the edge of the table, his arms folded.

'This is Jeff.'

Guy de-perched.

'The lodger.' Jeff grinned, shaking his hand. 'The useless, lazy git, but I expect Abby's mum's told you that already.'

'Oh, *Jeff*. . .' Pink-faced from the cooker, Mum gave him a kiss. 'I'm quite sure I never said *git*. I'm so glad you've come, though. Guy can't stay to eat – he's got to dash.'

My stomach contracted. 'Oh, what a shame!'

'Yes, it's a crying shame when it smells so good.' With

a smile at Mum, he glanced at his watch. 'But it's high time I was off.'

That's when I knew something was up. There was nothing in his voice or manner, but the eyes that met mine were different. As if a cool veil had come over them.

While he said his goodbyes, I wondered what on earth had happened. 'I'll see him out,' I said brightly, and shut the kitchen door behind us. I badly wanted to say, 'What's wrong?' but couldn't get it out. 'How was Fleur?' I asked, as we crossed the hall.

He stopped. 'You'll hear sooner or later. We've split up.'

'My God.' I swallowed, hard. 'Since when?'

'Since this morning.'

For a wild moment I thought that explained it. There'd been a fraught parting; he was emotionally drained. 'I'm really sorry.'

'I think we both knew it was coming to the end of the line.' He hesitated, as if about to say something, and then apparently decided against it. 'Look, I've got to go.' His voice matched his eyes. Cool and detached, like a stranger who'd taken one look and decided he didn't like me very much.

I couldn't bear it. Neither could I understand it. For a wild moment the thought shot into my head that Kay had been stirring, telling Fleur we'd been up to something, and they'd rowed on that account. Had he furiously denied it, accused her of being a paranoid wreck?

I couldn't ask him outright, but I had to say something. Finding the right words in three seconds was impossible, and as it turned out I didn't have to.

About to open the door, he paused. 'By the way, I should congratulate you on a job well done.'

His cool, sardonic tone desiccated my throat. 'Sorry?'

'Your little undercover role at Rachel's engagement party.

207

I had no idea I was under surveillance.' He pulled the door open, and cold, damp air rushed in. 'If you ever decide to apply to MI5, I'll write you a reference. Goodnight.'

Twenty-two

Like a slap in the face, the door closed behind him.

For a moment I was too shocked to move. I felt sick, as if I'd been caught in something shameful. Assorted thoughts were crashing round my head like dodgem cars. *What the hell happened? What on earth possessed her to tell him? I just can't believe she'd do it. Has the flytrap been stirring, after all? Run after him, quick* . . .

But almost as fast as guilt had hit me, came something else. Already the defence was forming in my brain. 'You think it was my idea? You think I *want*ed to do it? Was it my fault Fleur was a mass of insecurity?'

But how could I say anything like this? It would be like bad-mouthing Fleur. It would only add to whatever he probably already felt.

With something else forming in my head, I yanked the door open. *Look, I'm sorry, I know it wasn't very nice, but it wasn't her fault she was in a bit of a tizz* . . .

I thought of all this just too late. Running down the path, I was just in time to see his tail lights disappearing down the road. Only when they'd finally vanished did I realise I was shivering.

I walked back up the drive. By some mercy the front door hadn't banged itself shut. Inside, I stood with my back to the door, churning with that sick, shaky feeling.

The kitchen door opened. Out wafted the smell of roast lamb and Robbie.

'Mummy wants you,' he pronounced. 'She says will you come and lay the table?'

I was profoundly glad of Jeff during that meal. His ability to amuse, his re-hashes of Idle Jack, took the pressure right off me. While Mum and Robbie laughed and I pretended to, I turned it over and over in my hurt, increasingly angry, mind.

'Now, who's for blackberry and apple crumble?' said Mum brightly.

Keeping it to myself on the way home was no longer an option; I'd have blown a gasket. For the first few miles of lashing midwinter rain, I offloaded it to Jeff. Everything. Vibes at the Welford Castle pool and all.

As high-speed wipers battled cats and dogs, my anger steamed up the windows. 'Anyone would think it was my idea!' I fumed. 'You should have heard the way he spoke to me! I can't believe I ever let myself fancy him. God help me, I actually *liked* him!'

Jeff gave a deep yawn. 'I wouldn't waste any sleep over it. As they say down in Much Shagging by the Marsh, nadgers to him.'

I fumed on regardless. 'Why did he have a go at me? God, why didn't I tell him to have a go at the bloody flytrap? If it hadn't been for her sneaky little innuendoes over that lunch, Fleur would never have been in a state in the first place! But of course, she's his *friend*, so it's perfectly all right for *her* to make remarks right under Fleur's nose about the time she was sitting on his dick in a paddling pool . . .'

Jeff sighed. 'I wish I could meet this flytrap. Sounds like all my adolescent fantasies come true.'

'It's not funny!' I fumed on for a few more miles, until I realised Jeff was lost in one of his periodic switched-off modes. 'You're not even listening, are you? You could at least listen, when Mum's just stuffed you full of Sunday roast!'

'Sorry.' He came to. 'I was just trying to see it from his side, that's all.'

'Well, don't!'

'Oh, come on. What if you were at some do your bloke couldn't come to, and you found out later that a mate of his, who you thought an OK sort of guy, was taking notes in case you were sniffing round someone else?'

'You make it sound as if I was wired up with a recording device! God, *I* was the one who told Lindsay she should credit him with a bit more zip-control!'

'OK, OK. But I still don't think you'd be over-chuffed if it were you.'

I knew I wouldn't. I'd hate it. But then, if I were ever in a position where some fleeting, ancient flame was trying to warm up steamy memories right under my boyfriend's nose, I'd ignore him completely. Or else I'd give him one of those looks that wither parts other looks can't reach, and then ignore him. 'I bet you anything it was Cara,' I said, finally shoe-horning my little Corsa into a space I counted myself lucky to find at all. 'Fleur would never have told him in a million years.'

But I didn't call her the minute I was in the door. I needed a stiff glass of something first, and a few minutes for conscious calming down.

As I started keying her number Jeff said, 'Look, go easy. She's probably in a bit of a state.'

She's not the only one. But I did go very easy at first. When I knew exactly how she'd be feeling I could hardly do anything else. 'I just saw Guy, over at Mum's.'

'Abby! I knew he was going, but I didn't know you'd be there!'

'Mum was doing a roast. She invited me and Jeff over.' I paused. 'He told me you'd split up. I'm really sorry, Fleur. What on earth happened?'

'Oh, Abby, it was awful . . .' There was a snuffly noise, as if she were wiping her nose on the fourth soggy tissue. 'He was supposed to come last Wednesday, but he made an excuse. I didn't believe it – I thought there was some-body else. While we were eating last night I heard his phone beep for a text message. He didn't bother checking – it made me wonder who it was. So later, while he was in the bathroom, I checked.'

I winced. 'Don't tell me he caught you?'

'What do you think? Just as I was reading a message from someone who works with him . . .'

'Oh, Fleur . . .'

'It was awful,' she went on. 'He said, "Forgive me for asking, but have you been making a habit of this?" He took the phone from me and checked. He said, "It's Peter. Satisfied now?" I still couldn't utter. Then he said he knew I'd never quite been Miss Tender Trust, but this . . . And something snapped in me, and all this stuff came out . . . I said how could I trust him when he'd lied to me? And he said, "What lie?" And I said, "Cara! You told me you were never involved with her!" And he said, "I wasn't!" and I said, "Oh, no? What about that bloody paddling pool?"'

My eyes closed. 'Fleur, what were you thinking of?'

'I don't know, Abby. I'm really sorry . . . He was so stunned, it was all over his face. He said, "Who the hell told you that?" So I had to tell him. And then I started crying and all this other stuff came out about Scott – I'd never gone into detail before – and how I'd never thought he'd do it, either, until he did . . .'

I could hear her sniffing, wiping her nose. I fought the urge to say, *Get on with it!* 'So what did he say?'

'Not much. He just went quiet. Gave me tissues and things, and said all there ever was with Cara was some adolescent messing. He was sweet, really, but even before we went to bed I knew it was over.' I heard her sniff again. 'I knew there wasn't going to be any repair job with sex. He just sort of cuddled me to sleep.'

Even that, when I was still hurt and angry, was enough to trigger green pangs in my stomach.

'He was tossing and turning in the night,' she went on. 'So in the morning, I saved him agonising. I said we'd both been kidding ourselves, it was never going to work when we lived so far apart. He tried to hide it, but it was still horrible to see that sort of relief on his face.'

Why hadn't it occurred to me that she'd have delivered the *coup de grâce*?

'*You* finished it?'

'Only because I didn't want to put him through it.' I heard another snuffly nose-wiping. 'He'd probably been awake half the night, dreading an emotional scene. I didn't want him shuddering every time he thought of me in future.'

It's a weird fact of life that you can feel desperately sorry for someone and want to shake them at the same time. 'Fleur, I'm not mad or anything, but why did you tell him about getting me to watch him at that party?' I paused, choosing words with care and extreme difficulty. 'He had a bit of a go at me about it.'

'Oh, Abby, I'm so sorry!' Her voice was aghast. 'I'd never have told him, only he asked, and by then I just couldn't bear to lie to him. You're not upset, are you?'

Twenty-three

What could I say? *Yes! Don't you think there are times when a nice little lie is best?*

'A bit. In fact he was decidedly off with me, but I suppose I can't altogether blame him.' It cost me a lot to say this, but I didn't want her any more upset than she already was. 'But don't worry about it. How the hell did it come up?'

'It was just before he left this morning. He said, "Look, don't get upset, I'm not going to throw a fit, but did you ask Abby and Lindsay to watch me at that party you couldn't come to? In case I started sniffing around Cara?"'

Cara. This is beginning to smell of her after all.

'I couldn't believe he'd found out. I said, "No!" But then I couldn't bear to lie to him, and I said yes, maybe I had, but not *Lind*say! Lindsay had nothing to do with it. And it wasn't because I was afraid of him sniffing around Cara, it was Cara sniffing around *him*. And he said, "What's the difference? You still had me down as up for it."'

Vaguely I was aware of Jeff making, *What?* faces, but already Fleur was going on, 'Abby, I felt so bad . . . But then I said if he'd suspected all this time, why hadn't he said? And he said he hadn't suspected anything till a couple of weeks ago, when he saw Cara at some semi-work do. He said she'd been rather obviously available before, but he'd ignored it. Only this time it was more full-on, and he'd had to get blunt and tell her it wasn't on. Particularly

214

as they were both friends of Lindsay and Rachel, when I was their cousin.'

'Get *blunt*?' At last I could give vent to a few raw feelings. 'Why didn't he tell her he'd never be up for it anyway, he'd be afraid of catching something? Why didn't he tell her he wouldn't be up for it even if he'd been stuck on a desert island for fifteen years, catching the sort of crabs you can at least *eat*?'

She gave a wan ghost of a laugh. 'I have a feeling he thought something like that. At any rate, she got nasty. She said he might like to know just what sort of friend of his Lindsay was, for a start. She hadn't exactly trusted him to keep his dick to himself – you and she had been conspiring to keep him away from her at that party.'

So now she's dropped Lindsay right in it, too.

'But the thing is, he didn't buy it,' Fleur went on. 'He thought she was just making trouble out of pique. He told her he didn't believe a word of it, and he didn't.'

'Until this morning?'

'Until last night. But I feel awful about Lindsay now, because I'm sure he thinks she was in on it. I swear he thinks you involved her.'

Me? Why do I have to be the bad guy?

'But how on earth did Cara suss it out?' she went on. 'And what made her point the finger at Lindsay?'

'Because she *was* in on it, Fleur. And I didn't have to involve her – she'd got the wind up all by herself.'

When I finally related all this to Jeff, he offered the helpful opinion that it was the juiciest little pile of shite he'd ever seen hit the fan. Was I now going to fan it on to Lindsay?

I couldn't face it that night. While sleep eluded me, again and again I saw Guy in the hall at Sycamore Road. I saw his cool, detached eyes; heard his super-chilled voice. God, why hadn't I shot after him, given him a few biting truths? In my head I tore his car door open, had a screaming row with him right there in the road. '*Me?* Why are you having a go at me? What about bloody Cara? If you'd had enough manners to ignore her sneaky little remarks, Fleur would never have been in such a state in the first place! Were you flattered? Was that it? Did it pander to your pathetic little ego?'

In my head I banged the door and stalked off, triumphant.

It helped not at all.

After a bad night, I fanned the shite on to Lindsay the following evening. I told her the whole lot at last: paddling pool, Fleur's angst, everything but how I felt about Guy. I didn't quite trust her to keep it to herself.

As I'd feared, Lindsay was appalled. True or not, she couldn't bear him to think she hadn't trusted him not to screw around behind Fleur's back. Much of this came out as venom towards Cara, not that I blamed her in the slightest for that. 'Even Rachel's gone off her now, you know,' she said. 'She's given up calling – she says Cara never calls *her* any more. I think she's finally beginning to realise she was just using her back in the summer for a free bed. Anyway, I'm going to tell her the whole lot now, and if that doesn't cure her of the flytrap for good, I'll have her certified.'

The following evening I had an email from Fleur.

Just to make clear . . .

Abby, I felt so bad about Guy having a go at you, I just sent him this:

216

< *Dear Guy,*
< *Don't get the wind up, I'm not asking for a*
< *reconciliation, but I just want to say one thing. I*
< *know you must have been up to here the other day,*
< *but I wish you hadn't had a go at Abby about that*
< *party business. I think she was a bit upset, and I*
< *don't blame her when it was hardly her fault. She*
< *never wanted to do it – I should never have asked.*
< *If you were going to have a go at anybody, it should*
< *have been me.*
< *But thanks anyway for not hitting the roof – I know*
< *I must have tried the patience of a saint sometimes.*
< *Love, Fleur*

I wouldn't have thought anything could unsettle me more than I already was, but that did. Would he feel bad when he read that? Was I now going to get some sort of apology, and if so, by what means? I couldn't see him asking Fleur for my phone number, but he might just ask for my email. And if he did, what sort of tone would he use? Cool and polite? Warm and wry, with a hint of 'sorry I was such a dickhead . . .'?

I called Fleur briefly to say I hoped she was feeling a bit better, thanks for putting him straight but I really wasn't that bothered. I felt I had to say this last, to cover up how I really felt.

I found his reply the following afternoon, though it wasn't sent directly to me.

Fwd: Just to make clear . . .

Abby, this came this morning from Guy. I've been dithering about whether to pass it on, but thought you'd rather know. It's my stupid fault again, I was in

217

such a state it *must* have come out all garbled, but I
think it explains why he was 'off' with you. He's got
the wrong end of the stick over timing.
I'll put him straight, I promise.
Love, Fleur X

< Hi, Fleur, thanks for that. I'm sorry if you were
< upset that I said anything to Abby, but if you want
< the truth, it wasn't just the 'surveillance' bit that got
< to me. I know you're close to her, and I'm willing
< to believe that she had your best interests at heart,
< but I still can't accept that she was remotely justified
< in raking up minor juvenile shenanigans that
< happened half a lifetime ago. All it achieved was to
< worry you unnecessarily about shenanigans that were
< never going to happen. I hope I made that clear the
< other day, at least.
< Whether you pass this on to Abby is entirely up to you.
< I won't say you didn't try my patience now and then,
< but any paid-up saint would have found you a
< breeze. I wouldn't have missed it.
< Take care,
< Guy

I felt so sick, I don't know how I got through my next
class. Only later did other emotions start to kick in.

Hurt and angry, I had a good old fume to Jeff that night.
'How *could* he? If I hadn't told Fleur before, I'd never have
told her afterwards! She's about the last person who needs
fuel for her insecurities! Do I really come across as the kind
of bitch who'd rake up muck over something that happened
a million years ago? And will you please turn that *bloody*
television off?'

Draped in front of *Macho Action Man With Lots Of Girls*

Doing Kick-Boxing in Leather, Jeff zapped it.

'I mean, just what sort of person does he think I am?' I fumed on.

'I don't think you really want an answer to that one. But I suppose you can't blame him for getting the wrong end of the time-stick. Fleur was probably in a right old tizz.'

'Then why didn't he say something the other night? Why did he just look at me as if I were something he'd picked up on his shoe?'

'Abby, forget him! If he's enough of a dickhead to think you'd do something like that, he's not worth getting wound up over.'

'How can I help being wound up?' It would have hurt that anyone would think that of me. From him, it was like a lash of barbed wire on my heart. 'I really liked him! I thought he at least liked me!'

'*Liked?*' he echoed. 'From what you told me the other night, you were picking up the odd vibe. And maybe that's another thing that got to him. Pots and kettles.'

'What?'

'Water-based variety,' he said. 'Pots fooling around in paddling pools, kettles fooling around in swimming pools at weddings. You did mention a little bit of fooling around in a swimming pool. I don't want to use the long H-word, but it might just have occurred to him.'

Hypocrite . . .

'I mean, as *he* sees it,' he went on, 'after putting the wind up Fleur over naughty little wet flytraps, you weren't above a bit of the same yourself.'

It was just another lash on my heart. 'Jeff, nobody could call it "fooling around" at that pool! Virtually nothing happened!'

But whichever way you looked at 'virtually nothing', it still added up to 'something'.

Until then I hadn't replied to Fleur. Thinking I'd only give myself away if I spoke to her, I sent a text saying: *You're right, it would certainly explain it. He evidently thinks I'm dead handy with a wooden spoon. Hope you're feeling better, xxx.*

Barely an hour later came a call from Lindsay.

'I called Guy, like a sort of "feeler",' she said. 'Asked if he fancied coming for supper on Saturday.'

'And?'

'I wish I hadn't bothered. He was very slightly "off" with me – said he was tied up. I feel absolutely terrible, when we were friends so long. I know we lost touch for a few years until the summer, but while we were all living at home he was almost the brother I never had. When I was about six we had chicken pox together, for God's sake. We drew around our best scabs with felt pens. And he was round at ours so much after his mother died – it's not much fun going home after school to an empty house when you're only ten.'

Despite everything, a poignant little ache contracted my stomach. I thought of the after-school chaos that had always reigned at Sycamore Road: noise and spag bol and *Neighbours*, Will squashing strawberry yoghurt into the carpet, Mum making 'Lovely!' noises as I told her I'd been picked for the netball team . . .

'And it's not as if I wasn't partly justified, was it?' Lindsay went on. 'The bloody flytrap *was* sniffing around him.'

'But he wasn't playing, was he? That's the point, Lindsay. He never was going to play.'

'Do you have to rub it in? It's all right for you – you'll probably never see him again!'

Evidently.

After another bad night, I had a call from Fleur. 'I thought you'd like to know I just put Guy's messy sticks straight.'

'You spoke to him?'

'I didn't trust myself over the phone. I thought I might come over all emotional and make him think: *Oh, shit . . .* I emailed him. I've just sent you a copy – I thought you might like to see what I said.'

Might like? I found it a couple of hours later.

Subject: Wrong end of stick

<Dear Guy,
<So sorry, I'm not going to go on about all this till
<next Christmas, but I think you're under a little
<misapprehension over Abby. I evidently didn't make
<it clear, but anything she told me about juvenile
<shenanigans was at the time, not recently. I
<wouldn't want you to think she's the sort of person to
<deliberately stir up trouble. In fact, the way I carried
<on, I'm sure she heartily wished she'd never told me
<at all.
<In case I didn't make this clear either, anything she
<happened to see on that hot day I'm never going to
<mention again, was quite by accident.
<That's all. (You can heave a sigh of relief now.)
<Love, Fleur

What would he think when he read that? At the very least he had to feel slightly bad. Feeling as if a storm cloud had at least partially lifted, I went that night to do some long-overdue Christmas shopping. While I was battling crowds of people, all equally desperate to cross the last presents off their lists, Fleur called again.

'I just had a call from Guy. Said yes, he had got his sticks all arse about face, sorry about that, had I told you? And when I said "sort of", he said in that case

221

perhaps he'd better have your email and drop you a line.'

O hallelujah. 'I'm not sure I want one now.' I said it jokily, to cover up my relief. 'I was rather enjoying my Evil Stir-Queen role. Still, it's nice of him to bother. How are you feeling now?'

As I put my mobile back in my bag a few minutes later, it started to rain. Cold, miserable rain that could have turned into snow with only marginally more effort. On the wet, dark streets, people cursed as they put up umbrellas, cursed that they didn't have any, cursed other people poking spokes in their eyes.

Me, I felt as if the sun was just poking through the clouds again. I gave five pounds to the carol singers belting out 'Ding Dong Merrily' in the rain.

That was the nineteenth of December. I checked my inbox the following day with all the anticipation of a kid lifting the last little windows on the Advent calendar. But there was nothing from Guy. There was nothing on the twenty-first, nor the twenty-second.

By the evening of the twenty-third my expectation had turned to bitter let-down. 'What's he waiting for?' I demanded of Jeff, having checked my inbox for the tenth time that day. 'Next Christmas?'

'Abby, it's the party season. He's probably out getting hammered.'

'More than likely. Why would I be a priority?'

'Oh, sod him.' He actually zapped the TV and un-draped himself from the sofa. 'Come on, let's at least go for a couple of drinks. You're going to drive me crazy, checking that laptop all night.'

'I've got presents to wrap!' That was my excuse. In between Sellotaping, and cursing fiddling curly ribbon, I checked my inbox every twenty minutes, while making inroads into a bottle of good red Bordeaux earmarked for Mum's on Christmas Day.

By ten-thirty there was still nothing from Guy.

'I've got a good mind to send him one myself,' I fumed, while opening the second bottle meant for turkey. 'To tell him not to bloody bother anyway.'

'You do that. And tell him nadgers from Jeff.'

The way I was feeling then, nadgers would be the least of it. I had visions of him in a bar somewhere, pissed out of his head in a Santa hat, asking flytrap lookalikes if they'd like to pull his cracker.

Subject: Arsehole.

No, perhaps not.

Subject: Just to make a few more things clear

Dear Guy,

No, scrub that, whoever puts 'dear' in emails anyway?

Just a quickie to say Happy Christmas, and not to bother dropping me any line. To be frank, I wouldn't want one from anyone who evidently had me down as the Evil Stir-Queen.

Yes. Good start.

In between slurps I added a few more paragraphs of incisively worded English. I then read it all through, well pleased with my literary genius. I was wasted in EFL. Why wasn't I writing leaders for *The Times*? 'Come and check this out!' I called to Jeff.

He came and read it over my shoulder.

'What d'you reckon?' I asked.

'A masterpiece. I like the "piranha in lip-gloss".'

'Me, too. Am I brilliant, or what?'

'Genius. What's that about Little Ted?'

'Can't explain now. Too complicated.'

'And the spinnakers?'

'Didn't I tell you? He's a sailing nut.'

'Oh, right. How about a PS, then? "I'm three sheets to the wind as I write this, but, hey, it's making me feel a whole lot better?"'

It certainly was. '*In vino veritas . . .*' I hit 'send'.

Jeff said, 'Er . . .'

I looked over my shoulder. 'What?'

'Oh, nothing. Only I never thought you were actually going to send it.'

'Why the hell not?'

'Because, my little petal, you're just a bit rat-arsed. I thought you were just letting off a bit of steam.'

'It was the truth!' I turned back to the screen.

Message sent.

'Well, OK,' said Jeff. 'What's wrong with a good old dose of unvarnished now and then? Like I said, nadgers to him.'

Twenty-four

I slept like a log that night. Rousing with a heavy, muzzy head, I recalled a horrible dream. I'd dreamt I'd sent Guy an incredibly rude email that would put him off me for life, not just for Christmas. Jeff said never mind, he'd take me for a couple of drinks, there was a computer nerd in the pub who could zap incredibly rude emails if you just bought him a couple of pints.

Then I woke up properly.

Bits of that email floated back to me all day. As my head cleared, I veered between two lines of thought.

One: even if it was pretty over the top, it *was* only a good old dose of unvarnished, and if he couldn't take it like a man I wouldn't want to know. It was no more than he deserved after not even a line of mild apology for thinking I was a mischief-making bitch.

Two: oh, God, what have I done?

After loading the car with presents that afternoon, Jeff and I decanted ourselves to Sycamore Road. As he had no family to go to, Mum wouldn't hear of him not coming. What with Will and his girlfriend also there, plus Robbie's excitement, my mind was partly taken off other things. Andrew and Imogen had gone to her parents. This led to a revelation from Mum, while I was preparing some gourmet cat cuisine, aka chopping up disgusting turkey innards for Pudding's supper.

'Andrew only told me the other day, but Imogen's father was diagnosed with cancer back in July. That's why they rushed the wedding. They'd originally planned it for next summer, but Imogen was afraid her father wouldn't be well enough, or even that he might not still be here.'

'God.' As Pudding was already trying to save me the trouble of preparation, I gave up and let her steal it off the chopping board. 'Poor Imogen. But why on earth didn't Andrew say before?'

'Her father didn't want anyone but immediate family to know. Andrew said he's a very private person – he didn't want everybody feeling sorry for him.'

I thought of the tall, spare man, looking so proud on Imogen's arm. 'How is he now?'

'Doing quite well, apparently, so fingers crossed. But of course she'd want to be with him for Christmas. Just shows, doesn't it? You have to make the most of every day, and not worry about little things.'

One 'little thing' was still very much on my mind, however. In between putting out carrots for the reindeer and drinks with the neighbours, I checked my inbox on Mum's computer, a cast-off of Andrew's.

Inbox 3.

Two were spam. Viagra. Hot teens up to no good with ast*r*sks.

The third was from Emma, my old friend who'd gone a-travelling without me. After ten days in Queenstown she'd fallen for the Sean who'd strapped her into her bungy jump harness. They'd finally married two years previously. She'd come back for three weeks for the wedding, gone back with him, and I hadn't seen her since.

She'd sent a round robin, to an address book of multitudes.

Sorry! Didn't get around to cards, usual disorganisa-
tion, plus Sean was in hospital with appendix. Had to
drag him to emergency room, the idiot was being all
macho. Will be in proper touch soon, hope you all
have a great Christmas, Love Emma.

While sending a quick reply – *Poor Sean!, etc.* – I agonised
over sending Guy another *Sorry, I was a bit pissed when I*
sent that, I didn't really mean any of it.

But I did. And why should I apologise when he's sent
me not a word?

By the time Jeff and I returned home late on Boxing Day,
there was still nothing. Crunch time came on the 27th.

Subject: just to make a few more things clear.

With my heart in my big e-mouth I clicked it open.

Hi, Abby. Glad to see you're not the type to mince
words. Prime meaty chunks in gravy hit the spot so
much better. Sorry anyway for wrong assumptions and
failure to check facts. Can only offer the excuse that
things were a tad fraught when it all came out. In
fact I did send you a line, but I guess it got lost in
the system.
Guy
  By the way, just one spinnaker is the norm.

Underneath was my own, entire message.
This is what I read:

Just a quickie to say Happy Christmas, and not to
bother dropping me any line. To be frank, I wouldn't

want one from anyone who had me down as the Evil Stir-Queen.

Just a few points to go with your Christmas pudding:

One: Neither Fleur nor I would have given your juvenile shenanigans another thought if not for Cara bringing them up right under Fleur's nose at that infamous spaghetti lunch. The fact that you thought her references were going right over everybody else's heads was no excuse for failing to ignore them. It was no wonder Fleur got the wind up – anybody would have.

Two: I make no apologies now for 'spying' on you at that party. I always fancied myself in MI5 anyway. After the way you practically rolled over and purred when Cara invited herself for lunch, I was almost beginning to think Fleur was right to get the wind up. If you're short of ideas next time, I suggest asking Father Christmas for The Idiot Bloke's Guide to Looking a Complete Pushover.

Three: in my non-humble opinion you show a woeful lack of judgement in being friends with Cara at all when anyone can see she's a piranha in lip-gloss. Though I know men are invariably too thick to see these things when someone like that's fluttering her eyelashes in their faces.

Four: to go back to the shenanigans you thought I raked up recently, just for the record, I thought you were a complete arsehole to be fooling around with Cara at all when she had a boyfriend. (Yes, I do realise this sounds quaint, but I was only sixteen and ever so slightly more idealistic than I am now.) I also thought Cara a complete bitch to be fooling when she not only had a boyfriend, but also knew that Rachel

*had a crush on you. I don't suppose Rachel will mind
my saying this – I expect you were aware anyway.*

*Five: funnily enough, my opinion of Cara has not
changed.*

*Six: Lindsay had absolutely nothing to do with any
'spying' – I claim that dubious honour for myself.
Though I might add that Lindsay had her own ideas
about Cara, and from what I've gathered since they
were entirely justified. (See point five, above.)*

So put that lot in your spinnakers and hoist them.

Abby

*PS And by the way, Little Ted told me afterwards that
he couldn't give a stuff how hairy you were – he was
just scared shitless in case you were bi.*

Naturally I refreshed Jeff's memory of all this.

'What the fuck's all that about Little Ted?' he asked.

'Never mind that!' Feeling sicker than ever, I scrolled
back to Guy's own message. 'What does he mean, he sent
me a line? What if there's an email floating round in cyber-
space?'

He put a soothing arm around my shoulders. 'Abby, it'll
be an excuse. It's easy enough to blame it on the system,
like the post. Even when it wasn't crap I used to blame the
post.'

'And just look at this bit – prime meaty chunks in gravy
– is that supposed to refer to dog-food? Implying that I
was spewing out bitch-food, I mean?'

'Probably exactly what he said – that you weren't dishing
up mince.'

I had a horrible feeling it was the other.

He was scrolling back to my own message. 'I thought
you told me Lindsay was in on it. So why did you tell him
she wasn't?'

229

'God knows. Because she was so upset, I suppose. And I didn't want Cara to have the satisfaction of making trouble between them.'

Over the next few days I waited for a little lost email to find its way to my inbox. And with each day I felt increasingly convinced that Jeff was right; it was an excuse. In which case, any apology I was drafting in my head was not only entirely undeserved, he was a lying excuse for a man and I shouldn't be wasting any precious sleep over him.

On the 30th I had a call from Lindsay that made me think at least I'd achieved something. 'Seems I was worrying for nothing,' she said. 'While I was home I saw Guy for a couple of drinks, and he was perfectly normal. Thank God for that – I'd have hated it if we'd fallen out.'

There you go, then. Even the darkest e-abuse can have silver linings.

But I said not a word about it. First, although she'd very likely laugh, she'd want every detail, and if I didn't spill beans she'd only ask Guy. Two, she was quite astute enough to know I'd never have got so steamed up over anyone who left me cold. I could almost see her saying wickedly, 'Abby, is there something you're not telling me?'

Having talked myself so well into the 'lying excuse for a man' viewpoint, I managed a pretty good New Year's Eve. The following afternoon I called Fleur, to say Happy New Year. 'How was Christmas?' I asked.

'Not bad, except that I had a massive row with Mum.'

I had an ominous feeling. 'Why?'

'She was on about Guy, asking why we'd split up, was there someone else? She meant him, of course, she assumed he'd done any dumping.'

'I hope you told her it was you?'

'I told her the truth – well, most of it – I just couldn't

be bothered to pretend. I said I had a feeling he was working up to ending it, so I saved him the trouble.' She paused. 'Please don't get upset, Abby, but she started saying things about you. Said she'd seen you flirting with him at Andrew's wedding – was I sure there was nothing between you two?'

God help me. I was right about the stirring, then.

'I was so mad with her, I can't tell you,' she went on. 'I told her I was sick of the way she's always having little digs at you, she was a nasty-minded old woman, and banged out of the kitchen.'

As far as I was concerned, of course Kay would be Stir-Queen. But I'd have felt a million times better if I could have told myself it was just her malicious imagination. 'I'm not upset – I had a feeling she thought something of the kind. She happened to see us right after he'd found Robbie mucking about in the lifts. We were only laughing about what a little devil he was.'

'I just knew it'd be something like that. I *told* her.'

But a minute nuance in her voice told me she hadn't 'just known'. After AK had sown a tiny seed of doubt, Fleur had needed to ask me herself. And as I'd known she would, she'd believed my half-truth reply.

It's all been for the best, I told myself. If, and it was a colossal *if,* Guy and I had embarked on any kind of relationship soon after Fleur, I'd never have heard the last of it. Cold war between Mum and Kay would have reverted to hot war, with WMDs thrown in.

Then came the fifth of January.

I was just coming in from the street when I met the girl from the downstairs flat coming out of her front door. 'Abby, I've been meaning to catch you! Hang on . . .' Popping back in, she came out with a couple of envelopes. 'I'm terribly sorry, it was my idiot boyfriend. We went away just before Christmas – he picked them up with mine by mistake and I forgot to put them back out. We only got back yesterday. They're probably Christmas cards – I hope you haven't been put out that anyone had forgotten you.'

'Oh, no, please, don't worry about it . . .'

I went upstairs checking envelopes. One was little and I recognised the handwriting. As it was from one of those very old friends I hadn't seen for ages and probably never would again, I hadn't missed it.

The other was large, with distinctive, unfamiliar handwriting. I checked the postmark. Southampton, 20th December.

With my heart in my throat, I drew out a glossy card. It was a reproduction of an old painting: a boat tossing in a dark and stormy sea, under angry pewter skies.

I hardly dared open it. Inside, on the left, was something about the RNLI Lifeboats. Entirely supported by voluntary contributions. The purchase of this card, etc.

On the other side, under the printed *Merry Christmas*, was written,

> *Hi, Abby. Sorry it's not very seasonal, but lifeboats are dear to my heart.*
>
> *Hope this reaches you before Christmas. I gather from Fleur that I should never be trusted with sticks again. I'll have them labelled in future: pick up this end, dummy.*
>
> *I'm sorry if you've been upset by all this. In a few weeks' time, when the dust's worn off the holiday season, maybe I'll see you to say all this properly. Please give my best to your mother and say hi to Robbie for me.*
>
> *Happy Christmas, if I'm not too late, and Happy New Year anyway.*
>
> *Guy*

Twenty-five

If I'd felt sick before . . .

Over and over I read that card with only one thought in my head. Having sent that, what must he have thought when he got my email?

Jeff said, 'Well, that'll teach you to fire off e-mouthfuls when you're hammered. Maybe you could get some software that gives you a little pop-up: "There was an error in the 'pissed' field. Your message has *not* been sent. It will be put into rehab until you've sobered up."'

'Oh, bugger off!'

As I stomped out, he followed. 'Look, it's not as if he actually said he'd give you a call, is it?'

'Of course he wouldn't, so soon after Fleur!'

Again and again I re-read that one line: *In a few weeks' time . . .*

A diplomatic little window, banged shut in his face.

Yes, but only very little. He'll be thanking God he didn't open it any further. By now he's probably locked it, too. Not to mention draped wild garlic all around it, to keep the evil she-demon out.

But I had to reply. After agonising for over an hour, I wrote this:

<u>Subject: Seriously Scary</u>

Hi, Guy,
I only just got your card – it was mis-delivered. But
thank you anyway, and many [many? yes, leave that]
apologies for my email. I was completely pissed [no,
scrub that] *slightly off my face when I wrote it. I*
didn't really mean any of it [hang on, do I really
want to go all abject-cringe here?] *I won't pretend I*
didn't mean a word of it, because I'm afraid I did
mean some of it, but I do realise a lot of it was
uncalled for, not to mention scarily over the top. So if
it put you off your turkey I'm very sorry.
Love [no, perhaps not]
Very best wishes [no, too formal]
Happy New Year
SS Abby

Before I could change my mind, I hit 'send'.
There. The ball's in your court now.
He lobbed it back the following evening:

Subject: Off your seriously scary face

And there was I thinking it was all down to a full
moon. But no problem – a few meaty chunks never
hurt anyone, though I have to send apologies for
scaring the shit out of Little Ted. And no, I wasn't put
off any turkey – in any case, it was goose.
Happy New Year to you, too.
Cheers,
Guy

I went to bed that night with the smell of goose all around
me. Beautifully stuffed, perfectly cooked goose.

* * *

As it seemed the sensible option, I looked for silver linings. I wouldn't have to imagine Kay's triumphant, 'I knew it!' I wouldn't have to feel terrible, confessing to Fleur. I wouldn't have to stock up on antidotes to poison gas, for resumption of hot war between Mum and Kay.

Over the next few weeks I pushed Guy to a private little room at the back of my mind. Although the smell of cooked goose still hung in the air, there were a few nice pictures on the walls. That one of him with Little Ted; certainly one of him just before he threw me in the pool. There was also a shot of his face in the hall at Sycamore Road, but I needed that. It was good to take a good long look at it when I was reminding myself of how little I was missing. Especially when I'd never had it in the first place.

Against all my expectations, the first rain-sodden weeks of the New Year flew by. The usual flu bugs were decimating our staff room, which meant I was covering several hours a week of other people's classes, sometimes without even ten minutes to prepare. Jeff was summoned from his so-called 'research retirement' to help out. He never prepared anything anyway; he relied on a quick squint at the teacher's book and his own innate genius. Now and then I also saw the bloke who'd played Baron Hardup in the pantomime. He was fun and good company, but I think we both knew it was never going to get heavy. We were just a couple of singles enjoying a double act now and then.

Before I knew it the first daffodils were splitting their buds, telling everyone to cheer up, spring was on its way. And in spring, a young woman's fancy turns to weddings.

Or against them, as the case may be.

'I know it sounds horrible, but I'm sick to death of it already,' said Lindsay, over a Saturday lunch at the end of February. 'When I went home the other weekend there was nothing but wedding. Between them Mum and Rachel must have had about fourteen *Bridal Heaven* mags, and each of *them* had about ten supplements on hair, dressing up Rover as a page-dog – you name it.'

Rachel had booked it months back, for the one August Saturday her chosen venue could offer. She'd set her heart on a lovely, olde-worlde hotel about ten miles from home, where they'd do the whole thing from ceremony to guest chuck-out the next morning.

'You wouldn't believe what it's all going to cost,' Lindsay went on. 'I think even Dad nearly had a heart attack when he saw a provisional figure. And you know who David's having as his best man?'

'Who?'

'Neil! Singa*pore* Neil,' she added, as I looked blank.

'Oh.'

'What d'you mean, "oh"? Having ordered only a meagre salad and demolished it, she was now picking at my *pommes lyonnaises*. 'After he made those cracks about David "getting caught"?'

'Yes, he was a bit full of himself.'

'You can say that again.' She speared another morsel of crispy spud. 'He'd better not make any more cracks like that in his speech, that's all.'

'You'll have to dance with him,' I said, winding her up on purpose. If she carried on scoffing my lunch at this rate, I'd have to force myself to fill up on Death by Chocolate. 'It's down in holy writ that bridesmaids have to dance with the best man. There's also that quaint, olde English custom of the bridesmaid snogging the best man 'ere ye sun hath set on ye confetti.'

Making a face, she sprinkled some salt over my remaining *pommes*. 'I'll wear baby-pink frills first. God, Abby, I know it sounds really horrible – don't ever tell Rachel – but there's something a bit sad about being your younger sister's bridesmaid. I swear some of Mum's friends are starting to think I'm a closet lezzie.'

'Don't be daft!'

'OK, but they'll be thinking something. Like, Dear me, poor old Lindsay . . .' Spearing another morsel, she went on, 'And I bet you I'll still be man-less, just when I could do with one.'

Lindsay hadn't had much luck since disappointing Baz. 'It's months away! Anything might happen by then.'

Her eyes went gloomily to the window. It was a lovely, spring-like day, with daffodils nodding in tubs outside. 'I bet you it won't.'

'Oh, come on.' Following her gaze to the sunny street, I changed the subject. 'Thought about summer holidays yet?'

'I've *thought*, all right. I can't help thinking, when just about everybody at work's planning a holiday *à* couply *deux*. Even Dopey Di, who must be forty-three and hasn't had a boyfriend in years, has met some bloke who wants to go walkies in the Dales.'

So much for that change of subject, then.

'Have you thought?' she went on.

'I've had to.' I gave a guilty little wince. 'Mum's been mentioning Brittany again, in that tentative, "If you're not doing anything else . . . " way. And I've been saying, "Erm, I'm not sure just yet . . . "'

Lindsay made an 'ouch' face. 'It'd be very noble of you, but you were noble last year. Aren't you overdue for something a bit more exciting?'

I was. After all, Mum would be the first to say, 'You're only young once . . .'

'So where d'you fancy?' I asked. 'Personally I've got a little yen for Mykonos.'

We booked it three days later, for September. I did feel

slightly bad when I told Mum, but if she'd been counting on my company, nobody would ever have known. 'Oh, lovely!' she said. 'You're sure to have a brilliant time with Lindsay.'

The weeks continued to whizz by. May arrived with its darling buds, fresh, newborn greens and fluffy white candles on the horse chestnuts. Something about this time of year always made me restless, itchy for change. Maybe it was some primeval migratory instinct, but the prospect of Mykonos wasn't enough to shift it. Then I had an email that sharpened my urge and focused it.

<u>Subject: This year, next year, sometime, never</u> . . .

Twenty-six

It was from Emma. She hadn't been in touch since that Christmas Eve email, but then neither had I.

> *Hi, Hag-face, hope you're still there! Isn't it about time you made it out to the land of Lord of The Rings? There's always a bed here, as I've told you about ten million times. And I've got an extra reason for wanting you to come now. Don't faint, but I'm expecting the patter of tiny rugby boots, at least that's its fate according to Sean, if it's a boy. (I wouldn't let them tell me when I had the scan.) It wasn't exactly planned, but we're both pretty chuffed now we're over the shock. It's due in September. So if you fancied coming out for a month or so around Christmas, you could do some babysitting. (Only joking.) Better still, go back to plan A, let the flat and come out for six months. Do Oz as well, though if you like it better don't dare tell Sean.*
>
> *So how about it?*
> *Love, Emma XXXX*
> *PS My tits are getting absolutely HUMUNGOUS!'*

This fired me right up. It put a zing in my blood, a tingle of Plan and Purpose. If I gave the Lingua Franca enough notice, I could probably talk them into a few months' unpaid leave. I wouldn't go for Christmas, I'd stay with Mum and Robbie for that, but I'd go right afterwards. As long as Jeff stayed on the flat wouldn't be a problem, and letting my room would help pay the mortgage. That wouldn't be a problem either – there was always the odd student in some horrible dump who couldn't wait to get out of it.

I told Fleur over the phone. I'd only seen her once since Christmas, but we called each other regularly. 'I wish I could come with you,' she said. 'Only it's not so easy for me to take unpaid leave, especially when we've got waiting lists a mile long.' She paused. 'Did I tell you Scott had been in touch?'

'*What?* What did he say?'

'It was a text. Saying he'd felt really bad ever since, he couldn't stop thinking about me.'

'I hope you told him to bugger off?'

'Even better. I deleted it. And if he sends any more I'll delete those, too.'

I was impressed. 'Fleur, I do believe you're getting hard-headed at last.'

She laughed. 'Yes, there's hope for me yet.'

I was still seeing Rachel and Lindsay every couple of weeks, but towards the end of May Lindsay called with this: 'Guess what? Mega-wedding of the year is off.'

'*What?*'

'Oh, I don't mean Rachel and David are off, just that wedding. There was a bad fire at the hotel they'd booked – part of it was virtually gutted. No way is it going to be fixed by August and everywhere else she might even consider is booked solid.'

'Oh, God.' My heart constricted for her. 'Poor Rachel.'

'Don't tell me. For forty-eight hours you'd have thought

the end of the world was nigh. Still, by last night she'd perked right up. She and David rolled in with half a dozen *Weddings in Paradise* brochures and Plan B. Rachel said it was getting ridiculous anyway. Mum was wanting to invite all sorts of people she hardly even knows and David thought it was turning into a bit of a circus.'

'Weddings usually do. How's your mother taking plan B?'

'Rachel hasn't told her yet. If you ask me Mum and Dad'll end up going anyway. When it comes to the point, she'll feel awful if they're not there.'

Over the next couple of weeks plan B evolved into plan C. Parents would be invited, especially as David was the only son of a widowed mother. Rachel and David were also banking on a few friends coming along, as it wouldn't be a proper 'do' otherwise. Uncle Matthew had done a deal with the hotel on half a dozen rooms, as it was still all going to cost a hell of a lot less than plan A.

They fixed on Barbados, for the third week in July.

Rachel called herself, to tell me. 'I do hope you can come, Abby, especially after you introduced us. David and I'll be heading for one of the other islands afterwards, but the general idea is for everybody else to stay for the whole week. It's hardly worth going all that way just for a couple of days.'

You could say that again. Whether Uncle Matthew was picking up room tabs or not, I was thinking arm-and-leg flights. I was thinking extras in an expensive hotel. I was thinking Mykonos in September, and New Zealand right after Christmas.

And then I thought of soft white sand fringed with palm trees. I thought turquoise Caribbean, and long rum cocktails with hibiscus flowers in them. To be frank, I was thinking of those posters they plaster on hoardings in the street to make you sick in the depths of winter. Or even, it must be said, in the depths of the type of summer that's a washout from the second week of Wimbledon onwards.

'It sounds pretty horrific,' I said. 'But I'll be very noble and force myself. Just let me check work for the leave situation first.'

In the end, this consisted of telling Jeff he was covering for me whether he liked it or not, and hoping he wouldn't have the energy to object.

A week later I heard that Rachel's friend Kirsty was coming, with her boyfriend, plus another couple I knew slightly, and two friends of David's ditto, with their partners. 'Rachel did ask Fleur, but the leave situation's too tight, and she's going away in August anyway,' Lindsay told me. 'And you'll never believe who with.'

I hadn't spoken to Fleur for a bit. I'd left a couple of messages, but she hadn't got back to me. 'Who?'

'Bloody Scott. She's got back together with him.'

'*What?*' No wonder she hadn't called back. She'd have been afraid of bluntly worded opinions.

'You said it. No use saying anything, though. Neil's still coming – wouldn't you know it? – all the way from Singapore. I shall rely on you to stop me saying anything too rude when he gets right up my nose. Oh, and one other thing – I'll tell Dad he's paying your air fare.'

Occasionally it irked me that she could still make me feel like a poor relation. The fact that Uncle Matthew would probably offer anyway was beside the point. 'Don't be daft – I'll get a cheapie off the internet.'

'I don't see what's daft about it. He's paying mine.'

'Lindsay, that's different.'

I did find a cheapie on the internet. It was with one of those holiday airlines that usually provide three whole inches of leg room, but at least it was the right dates.

I eventually spoke to Fleur, and she told me about Scott. He was genuinely full of remorse and she'd forgiven him.

'Please don't have a go at me,' she said. 'I can't help it – I'm never going to be much more hard-headed than a boiled egg. Except for those first lovely, buzzy weeks with Guy, I never quite got him out of my head. I suppose I was always wishing and hoping me and Guy into a bigger thing than it was. I wanted another *it* so badly.'

Now you tell me. 'I just hope you're doing the right thing.'

'I'm sure he's learnt his lesson, Abby. Everybody deserves a second chance, don't they?'

Can I have that in writing? So I can throw it back at you when he breaks your heart again?

But I didn't say it. For all the use it would be, I might as well read Robbie *Horrid Henry* in Latin.

Inevitably, all this dragged Guy out of that private room in my head. I'd sneaked in now and then, usually after glimpsing on a crowded street the back of a head that looked just like his, until I got a proper look and the sudden leap of my heart turned into a little ache. I'd think it was only a matter of time before Lindsay called one day, saying, 'Fancy coming round on Friday night? I've got a few coming for nosh in the kitchen. Guy said he might make it, by the way.'

Only she never had.

After Fleur's call, I talked myself into a more proactive attitude. Now she was so evidently over him, what was to stop me taking a first step? But not via email, it was too detached. What was to stop me saying to Lindsay, 'Oh, by the way, I suppose you couldn't give me Guy's number?'

'*Guy's?* Er, OK, but why?'

'Because actually, I've fancied him for ages, only it was a tad awkward, what with Fleur. I thought I might give him a call.'

'Oh. I see.' (Pause for awkward little titter.) 'Well, OK,

only, erm, I don't want to be off-putting or anything, but the last time I saw him I happened to say I'd seen you the other day, and he said, "Oh, yes?" and changed the subject.'

Maybe not.

Next, Mum phoned to tell me she'd had a call from her younger sister. 'I know Fleur can't make it to Rachel's wedding, but apparently Kay and James are now going and Rosemary thought it'd be nice if I came, too! She even said it'd be lovely to have Robbie!'

I felt bad for my first, gut reaction. It'd be lovely for Mum, and there was no denying that Robbie was marginally more human since starting proper school, but he was still only five. However Mum would intend it otherwise (and she would), bang would go my idle lying in the sun. Bang would go whole days of lazy-coconut chilling, or any reliable peace. In the unlikely event that I found myself in mid chat-up with any promising hunk on the beach, there would be a tap on my arm. 'Ab*bee!* You said you'd come swimming with me!'

'So what do you think?' she said.

Er . . .

'Because the thing is, I'm not so sure it'll be a good idea,' she went on, before I could reply. 'A whole week, at an entirely adult do like that? He can be enough of a handful on a campsite, never mind a smart hotel. It's not as if it's going to be just family, is it? All those friends of Rachel and David's . . .'

She said it. I could just see those politely glazed 'Oh, shit,' expressions. I saw carefully oiled bodies, cursing under their breath as he inadvertently flicked sand over them. Given a carefully oiled body within ten yards, Robbie would manage to flick sand/sea/pool water over it. And knock its drink over, and tread wet, sandy feet over its beach towel.

'And such strong sun!' she went on. 'I'd go mad trying

to keep him out of it. I'm not sure I'd be very good in that sort of heat anyway.'

Having thought she wanted me to talk her into it, I was beginning to wonder. 'There's bound to be a certain amount of shade. As for Robbie, I don't suppose he'll cause a diplomatic incident. If you'd really like to go, don't let him put you off.'

'Of course I'd love to go to Rachel's wedding! Well, if you really think I'm making a fuss about nothing, I'll tell Rosemary yes. Could you possibly check for another two seats on that flight? Oh, and one more thing, in case you're thinking you'll end up looking after him half the time, you won't. I'm not having it, not this time. You'll have more than enough with your own one of these days.'

A week later she went down with some vicious spring flu bug she described as 'just a cold' at first. It was three weeks before she got even half her stuffing back, during which time neighbours rallied round and Will and I did what weekend duty we could. Andrew and Imogen descended one Saturday, taking Robbie ice-skating, and Dad turned up on a non-Robbie Sunday to pitch in.

But five weeks after the flu first hit, much of her former stuffing was still missing. A neighbour said bluntly, 'She needs a holiday. A proper, child-free one, with nothing to do but please herself.'

And you should have Robbie, was the implication. Still feeling slightly guilty about Brittany anyway, I felt bad, and resentful for being made to feel bad. Nobody ever expected Will or Andrew to Robbie-sit because Mum was under the weather.

'I know it's none of my business,' she went on, 'but if you could have him while she went to this Caribbean wedding it'd do her the world of good.'

As I said, blunt.

'But I suppose that's not on,' she went on. 'Since you're supposed to be going too. Maybe you should ask your father. It's high time he did a bit more of the hard work, if you ask me.'

After a fair amount of thought, I called Dad that night. Yes, he could have Robbie, though taking time off would be tricky. As long as Mum didn't mind Robbie spending most of the time in Fillup and Smyle, no problem.

But Mum did mind. 'You know your father – he'll let him stuff himself with Coke and crisps for an entire week. Anyway, I told Robbie the other day that I'm taking him and I couldn't possibly disappoint him now. He's already hopping with excitement about going on a plane – and he's promised to be gooder than gold.'

So that was it until a few days later, when a call from Will changed everything.

I called Lindsay to fill her in. 'So it's just going to be me and Robbie, after all.'

'Yes, I heard. Poor old Auntie Penny's already been on to Mum, all apologetic in case anybody's offended. Not hacked off at getting lumbered again, are you?'

'What do you think?'

'Yes,' she said unhesitatingly. 'And feeling bad about it, and pretending you're not hacked off to everybody but me.'

We were leaving on a Saturday morning. On the previous Tuesday evening, Lindsay called. I was curled up in front of *EastEnders* at the time. Jeff was out, at some alternative poetry reading in the scruffier type of pub. He went to these now and then for two reasons. One, he was into this kind of thing. Two, they were frequented by women who went for sensitive, dark-night-of-the-soul types.

Or, as Jeff put it, were after the more literary type of shag.

'Don't faint,' she said, 'but I've found a man to bring to this wedding after all.'

'Lindsay!' Instantly agog, I zapped the TV volume. 'Is he nice?'

'Of course he's nice! Would I be bringing him otherwise?'

'Where did you find him?'

She laughed. 'Don't get worked up, it's only Guy.'

Only Guy? I felt as if a massive, fuzzy jelly had hit me in the stomach. 'Not "man" as in "item", then?'

'Alas and alack. I popped down to see the folks on Saturday, but Mum was doing my head in. Wedding this, wedding that – I ended up calling Guy on the off-chance that he'd like me to treat him to supper.'

Why hadn't I anticipated this? I knew she'd seen him now and then. She'd said they'd lost touch once – she was damned if they were going to do it again.

'Of course we got talking about the wedding,' she went on, 'and he joked that he was going to sulk about not getting an invitation. So I said why didn't he come, Rachel would be chuffed to bits. He's just booked a seat on the same plane.'

Help! Have I got time to buy new bikinis? Book proper leg wax? Bikini wax? Surgical removal of Scary Personality Traits?

'Oh, lovely!'

'I told him you and Robbie were coming, by the way,' she went on. 'And he said to tell you not to worry, there wouldn't be any dangerous swimming pool activities this time.'

Well, how am I to take that?

Until Jeff rolled in around midnight, this question gave my stomach plenty of churn-fodder. 'It never occurred to me that he'd be coming!'

'So what if he is?' He tossed his scruffy, 'literary' jacket over the armchair. 'The beach'll probably be crawling with Scandinavian blondes – I don't suppose you'll have to say more than, "Hi, had any good e-mouthfuls lately?"'

'It's not funny!' I threw a cushion at him. 'Go and make me a cup of tea.'

'Yes, dear.' He then put his grinning face around the kitchen door. 'You still fancy him, then?'

Our flight left from Gatwick. Most of the others, including Lindsay, Guy and Neil, left on a slightly earlier flight from Heathrow.

At least, that was the theory. In practice theirs was eight hours earlier. Having sat on the ground for an hour and a half, we were told to get off again while they fixed an engine. By the time we eventually took off, over six hours late, Robbie was already whingey and horrible – and we still had eight and a half hours to go.

We landed at nine local time, two in the morning in real money. I was worn out, almost sick with exhaustion. After waiting at the baggage carousel with the zonked Robbie in my arms, I emerged into air like a warm, humid blanket.

Out of the throng of meeters, greeters and tour reps, someone called, 'Abby!'

'Lindsay!'

She hurried over. 'You didn't have to come!' I protested. (Kiss.) 'I wasn't expecting anybody!'

'Don't be daft – you must be shattered. Guy, take Robbie – he must weigh a ton.'

And there he was. After nearly eight months. In light, cotton trousers, an open-necked shirt. Tanned. Fresh from a few hours on the beach, probably with a kip in the sun thrown in, followed by a good, long shower and dinner.

And there was I. Weary and dishevelled. My white top

smeared with chocolate and traces of yucky aircraft food from Robbie's fingers. My trousers stained with his spilt Coke. Fragrant with the same aircraft food, smelly aircraft loo, and those nasty little wipes they give you with the salt and pepper sachets.

'Hello, Guy,' I said.

'Abby.' With a smile that melted my heart, he came up and kissed my cheek. 'Lovely to see you again. It's been too long.'

Except that he didn't. That was the version I'd been imagining on and off all week, complete with slightly husky voice. (All that suppressed passion, you see.)

Silly me.

'Hi, Abby,' he said. 'Pass that lump over – you look like a zombie on a bad day.'

Twenty-seven

'Thanks, Guy,' I said. 'You're looking pretty good your-self.' My arms tightened around the dead-weight lump. At least he was hiding much of my gruesome state. 'I'll hang on to him. He'll only wake up and whinge otherwise.'

'Then let me take this.' He relieved me of an over-weight flight bag, the strap of which was cutting into my shoulder. 'Why was it delayed?'

'Some "minor" engine fault. Still, I'm glad they found it before take-off and not halfway across the Atlantic.'

'That's a very philosophical attitude when you're so obviously knackered.'

'Guy!' said Lindsay, half laughing. 'That is *not* very complimentary.'

He raised his eyebrows. 'Sorry. Wait here while I find a cab.'

He departed into the mêlée, leaving me with Lindsay. In a pristine little white slip dress and kitten-heeled sandals, she looked as if she'd just come from smart-casual dinner. 'You do look just a teensy bit rough,' she explained.

'I can't think why.' But I gave her a worn-out smile. 'What's the hotel like?'

'Small and chilled, right on the beach. My room's next to yours.'

'Have the others gone to bed?'

'You're joking – they've gone to some *Harbour Lights*

club in Bridgetown. Except for the assorted folks, of course. Rachel and David were going to come and meet you but I said no, Guy and I honestly weren't bothered – oh, look . . .'

Guy was waving from a line of cabs.

'For heaven's sake go and party with the others,' I said, as we made our way over, Lindsay trailing my wheelie-case. 'I'll only feel bad otherwise.'

'Don't be daft – you'll need a hand with Robbie and everything.'

'Lindsay, I can *man*age. I'm sure they'll have a porter.' As we reached the cab, Guy was loading my flight bag into the boot. 'Guy, I need that, it's got my purse in it. And will you please take Lindsay off to that club – she's making me feel bad and I'll only fall asleep on the way anyway.'

'She's being awkward,' said Lindsay. 'She's got her being-awkward voice on.'

'In that case . . .' Guy fished out my flight bag '. . . maybe we'd better not argue the toss about it.' He slung my wheelie-case in, banged the boot shut, and slung my flight bag on the back seat. 'We'll see you in the morning, then.'

Preoccupied with transferring Robbie and getting in beside him, I didn't realise he was up to no good until I saw him actually passing notes to the driver through the window.

It was a sort of exasperated last straw. 'Guy, what are you doing? I've got local money!'

'Abby, shut *up*,' said Lindsay. 'It'll save you fumbling in your purse the other end. You can buy him a drink tomorrow.'

'Take her away,' Guy said to the driver. 'She needs her bed.'

* * *

251

During the forty-minute drive to the West Coast hotel I was too dozy to take much in. I was conscious only of Hot Abroad: unfamiliar sounds wafting through the car windows on warm, tropical air. By the time we arrived I was nodding off. I had a hazy impression of a white, colonial-style house with no door. The whole place was open to the air; reception led straight out to gardens, where I could just see a glimpse of pool.

Carrying the still-sleeping Robbie, I was led down garden paths lit by lamps in the grass. The air was warm and soft, with a background chorus of loud chirping. I was shown into a large, ground-floor room with twin double beds. After tucking Robbie in, I opened sliding glass doors to a little terrace with a table and two chairs. Beyond a low wall was the sand, and barely twenty paces distant was the sea, quick-silvered with moonlight. From somewhere came the soft lilt of a steel band. The beach curved around to the right. Fringing the sand were trees hung with lamps. A lone couple strolled along the edge of the sea, hand in hand.

I slid the door shut and collapsed into bed.

Still on his home clock, Robbie woke before dawn, bursting for breakfast and action. After keeping him going with a packet of foresight-biscuits, I took him out into warm almost-hush. As the odd tiny bat flitted past on its way to bed, last night's chirping was beginning to be replaced by birds. Telling Robbie he must be absolutely quiet, I took him to explore. The rooms were laid out in low, staggered blocks around gardens dotted with trees and luxuriant with flowering shrubs. A pool lay within staggering distance of the beach.

Robbie shrieked, 'Look!'

Clapping a hand over his mouth, I was just in time to

see a couple of monkeys, one with a baby clinging to its belly, shoot off in alarm. 'Sssh! You've frightened them away. Be very quiet and they might come back.'

They did, which kept him amused for ten minutes. But as the light intensified, telling me the sun was rising behind the trees, we headed for the beach.

Apart from a man sweeping the sand and a fellow guest laying towels over a couple of sun beds, it was deserted. The sea lay like a smooth, blue jelly, washing the beach with minute, rippling waves. In both directions the beach stretched in little curving bays, each fringed with green, one after the other, as far as the eye could see. Except that the sun had yet to light it all up, it was exactly like something out of a brochure.

I was sitting in the soft sand, watching Robbie paddling in the wavelets, when a voice behind me said, 'Hi. How long have you been up?'

My stomach gave a perfect little back-flip. 'Ages.' I stood up, dusting sand off my swimsuit, and wondering why on earth I hadn't put on something marginally more fetching than my black Speedo with an old T shirt on top. 'But I hadn't expected to see any of you lot just yet.'

On the soft sand, I hadn't heard him approach. A pace away, barefoot, in just a pair of blue swim shorts, he gave me an up-and-down appraisal. 'You look a bit brighter than you did last night.'

'That wouldn't be difficult. It's probably been scientifically proven that a nine-hour flight with a small child turns into nineteen even when you haven't been delayed six hours first.'

'Hi, Guy!' Suddenly seeing him, Robbie bounced up. 'Guess what we saw!'

They might have seen each other only last week. After Robbie had told him about the monkeys, and Guy told him about a mongoose he'd seen yesterday, he nodded up the beach. 'Fancy a wander?'

I don't know why I hesitated. I suppose I was worried about Robbie pestering him to death.

'It's perfectly safe,' he added. 'Aside from the giant, flesh-eating sea urchins and the eight-foot crabs, of course.' His mouth gave the barest flicker. 'That's why I need you along. Someone seriously scary to frighten them off.'

I could see I was never going to live this down. 'Well, if you put it like that . . .'

If I'd suggested a walk with just me, Robbie would have been whinging all the way. With Guy along, it was another matter. As we walked in wet sand to the curve of the bay, he chattered non-stop, pausing now and then to pick up a piece of bleached coral or sea glass. In between Guy said things, like, 'So how have you been?' and I replied in kind.

So far, so rather better than last night. On the other hand, it was no use pretending there wasn't a certain constraint between us. Shadows of e-abuse and his own misapprehensions hung between us like an invisible cloud, and with Robbie running up every ten seconds to show us some bit of flotsam, it was difficult to broach the subject.

As we rounded the corner of the bay Guy said, 'I gather your mother's not been well.'

'She's basically just exhausted – it was some post-bug thing.'

'And you're doing Robbie duty again.'

'Yes, but don't think it's out of any saintly nobility. Fate sort of chucked it at me and there wasn't anywhere to duck.'

He raised his eyebrows.

'OK, I could have ducked,' I said. 'But I'd only have felt bad afterwards. I'd arranged for Dad to have him, so Mum could have a peaceful week here, but she didn't want Robbie running round Dad's off-licences for a week, stuffing Coke and crisps. Plus he was so excited about going on a plane – he'd never been on one before. So that was it, until she started talking to an old school friend she met up with recently via Friends Reunited. She told her the mere thought of the heat here was making her even more ragged than she was already, and Jean said—'

'Hey, come and look!' Having run on ahead, Robbie had found a mini black porcupine, aka a washed-up sea urchin. It was still alive, its sharp black spines waving weakly. Guy chucked it back in the sea, but Robbie was already calling him to look at something else.

After that it turned into a sort of us-boys walk, with Robbie claiming Guy's attention much of the time and me lagging behind. I was quite happy with this, for two reasons. One, I'd just been rabbiting on about Mum like one of those people who respond to a simple, 'How are you?' by telling you every gruesome detail. It was probably nerves, which leads me to reason two: the inner Abby was in a bit of a tizz.

Any faint ideas that he might have 'worn off' were deader than Danny Diplodocus. I'd known that as soon as I'd laid eyes on him last night, but I'd been too exhausted for the full G-force to hit me. Now was another matter. There was no mistaking that misbehaviour of organs that are normally as quiet as hibernating dormice. There was no mistaking that sudden acute awareness of somebody else, of everything from the tiny gold flecks in his eyes to the fuzz of brown on his forearms.

As if none of this were unsettling me I idled along past villas half hidden in their gardens, and another little hotel you'd hardly know was there. Where gardens met sand, flowers had fallen from the shrubs. Pausing to pick up a frangipani blossom, I inhaled its delicate, lemony scent.

A few yards ahead, Guy waited for me to catch up. 'Are you always this slow in the morning?'

'I is chillin',' I said. 'Anyway, what's the rush?'

He tutted. 'What sort of attitude is that?' he said, in the same old-school scoutmaster send-up he'd done before. 'Frightfully un-British. I hope you haven't come here with any subversive ideas about relaxing and enjoying yourself?'

Up close in only those blue shorts, he was a bit too much for the inner Abby to cope with. 'That *would* be a tall order, in a horrible place like this.' I nodded at the placid aquamarine sea. 'I mean, just look at it. I call it very inconsiderate of Rachel and David to drag us all this way.'

'Too right. What was wrong with Bognor?'

'Or Worthing.'

'*Skeggie*,' he said.

I laughed, and so did he.

This was more like it. Maybe not a breaking of ice, as nothing was frozen solid, but at least a warming-up of the water.

'So how's the boat business?' I asked, as we carried on.

'Good. We're pretty busy.'

'But you still found time to get away?'

'I was overdue for a break. OK, a week in the Caribbean's a pretty grim prospect, but I always had a soft spot for Rachel.'

As the conversation carried on like this, I became aware of something else hovering between us. It was like an invisible balloon, labelled, 'Chemistry – December 2003'. It was only a little one, very wrinkly and depleted, but I was relieved to sense it at all.

As for either of us sticking a pin in it, let alone re-inflating it, I knew that wasn't going to happen now. Months-old chemistry needed time to warm up, particularly when there were only tiny whiffs of it in the first place. It was an unstable substance, all too easily dispersed into the atmosphere, especially when it hadn't been stored in the right conditions.

As we were rounding the corner into the next bay Guy suddenly broke off what he was saying. 'Robbie! Don't touch those!' He ran to where Robbie was picking something off the sand.

Alarmed, I ran after him. The ground was littered with small green fruits. 'What are they?'

He nodded towards a large tree with small, dark green leaves growing at the edge of the sand. Taking Robbie's hand, he led him to it and pointed to a wooden sign on the trunk. 'What does that say?'

'Man – manch . . .'

'Manchineel. What else?'

'F – fruit, leaves, sap – what's sap?'

'Like tree blood,' I said.

'Fruit, leaves, sap, poi – poi –'

'*Poi*sonous,' I said. 'Which means they'll make you very ill, all right?'

'OK.' He scampered off.

Guy raised his eyebrows. 'I'd completely forgotten about them.'

'Have you been here before, then?'

'The old man brought me, years ago. I was only about ten or eleven. We stayed at the Coral Reef, further up the coast.'

To the right you could see two more curving bays, each fringed with green and gold. A few boats were moored in the placid water. I looked back the way we'd come, and saw it was further than I'd realised. 'I don't know how far you were planning to go, but it's time Robbie and I turned back. He'll be getting hungry.'

'Not surprising.' Guy glanced at his watch. 'It's nearly lunchtime back home. But I'd better head back, too – I promised to wake Lindsay.'

I called to Robbie, and we began retracing our footprints.

'Are there any more hazards I should know about?' I asked, as we carried on. 'Apart from those eight-foot crabs and flesh-eating urchins, I mean?'

'Only from the bar. After one too many rum punches on the beach last night, Rachel nearly didn't make it to dinner, never mind out clubbing.'

I imagined them all enjoying sundowners while I was stuck on that wretched plane with Robbie saying, 'How much *long*er?' for the forty-second time. 'Did I miss a gorgeous sunset?'

'No, it fizzled out.'

My eyes were on my bare toes, squishing into the wet sand. 'I heard about a million somethings chirping last night,' I said. 'Any idea what they are?'

'Oh, nothing to worry about. Just the giant tropical version of *daddy-long-legs highly scaryus.*'

'Don't!' But I laughed.

He smiled. 'They're tree frogs. Little tiddlers. You're not likely to find one sharing your shower.'

'I wouldn't mind. I'm rather fond of frogs.'

He glanced across at the T-shirt I'd pulled on over my black Speedo. 'So who's Crazy Daisy?'

'An après-ski bar in Austria. I won this in some silly game, but there was so much schnapps flowing I can't remember what it was.'

'Lindsay tells me you're off to New Zealand.'

'Yes, but not till after Christmas.'

Robbie chose that moment to come running up. 'Look what I've found!'

In his hand was a small, dead crab. 'It's all stinky and fishy! Smell!' He shoved it under my nose.

I turned my face away. 'Robbie, for heaven's sake . . .'

Guy tutted. 'Come on, Robbie. You don't show girls things like that.'

'Why not?'

'Because they don't appreciate them. What you do is wait until they're not looking and shove them down their T-shirts.'

Robbie hooted. He positively exploded with glee.

I put on the appalled big-sister face he was hoping for. 'Don't you dare even *think* about it!

'Hee hee . . .'

Guy was suppressing a grin. 'Sorry. You'll have me down as a bad influence.'

'Believe me, you couldn't possibly be worse than Will.'

Robbie was still hooting. Evidently it was the most deliciously puerile idea he'd had all year.

'You couldn't do it, anyway,' I said, as we carried on.

'Oh yes I could!'

'Oh – no – you – couldn't!' I said, like a pantomime villain. 'I've got eyes in the back of my head and I run too fast. Anyway, you couldn't reach.'

This evidently gave him the idea. Still giggling, pulling at Guy's arm, he produced a whisper that could probably have carried across the water to Antigua. '*You do it!*'

Fleeting visions shot through my head: Guy making a grab for me; me darting off with feigned shock-horror. Guy laughing, chasing me for a few yards; me letting out a few fake girly shrieks as I finally let him catch me. Guy holding me captive long enough to do

the foul deed; me pretending to shudder for Robbie's
sake . . .

It was coming to something when I was hoping for
crumbs like this.

Twenty-eight

Robbie produced another devil-glee whisper. 'Go on, *quick*!'

'Robbie, stop it!' (I felt obliged to say this, for the sake of form.)

Guy glanced down at Robbie. 'I wouldn't dare.'

Robbie hooted. 'Yes, you would!'

'That's what you think. She might come over all scary on me.'

Bugger. He said this almost as if he meant it.

'That's why it'd be *fun*!' Robbie emphasised this with a mini long jump in the sand.

'Not for me, it wouldn't. I never do anything seriously dangerous before breakfast.'

And just what's that supposed to mean?

'Do it after, then!' said Robbie.

'Robbie, e*nough*!' I felt obliged to say this, too. 'It was just a silly joke and it's not funny any more. Go and throw it in the sea.'

I watched him run to the water and toss it in. 'I just hope he doesn't find any more. If he starts shoving them down anyone else's T-shirt I'm going to be in dead trouble.'

Guy wore the expression of a man who thinks he'd better not laugh in case it pisses you right off. It made me want to punch him. You know, the kind of punch that results in the man laughing as he fends you off, and ends with

261

you melting in his arms. 'Point the victims at me,' he said. 'I'll take full responsibility.'

'Dead right you will. Oh, look . . .'

About fifty yards off, Rachel and David were strolling arm in arm along the waterline. They waved, I waved back, and half ran towards them. I needed a diversion from Guy – he was doing my stomach in.

As I hadn't seen either of them for three weeks there were huggy-kissy reunions, with lots of 'Poor Abby!' over the flight.

Guy strolled up seconds later. There followed the kind of chat you'd expect on an early-morning beach, but Robbie was quickly getting restless. Saying I'd see them all later, I took him off.

In mid-chat, Guy stayed on.

Robbie and I ran most of the way back, chasing each other along the line where the wavelets met the sand. Our own beach was still virtually deserted. Except for a man putting out pairs of sun beds with umbrellas and two or three people swimming, the hotel seemed to be still sleeping. Although the actual beach was still shadowed by trees, the sun had risen enough that the water further out was lit up, sparkly turquoise.

There was a huge, semi-circular swimming area roped off with buoys, presumably to keep motorised boats out. About fifty yards out was a little raft, where a man was just climbing the steps.

I was so hot and sticky after running, it was unbearably inviting. 'Come on,' I said to Robbie, stripping off my T-shirt. 'I'll race you to that raft.'

As I ran up to dump our T-shirts and key under a palm-thatched hut, I saw Guy out of the corner of my eye, coming back along the far end of the beach.

I didn't look in his direction. I didn't want him thinking I was hoping he'd come and join us.

O blissful vitamin sea. It wasn't quite warm-bath temperatures, but the shock was minimal. I let Robbie reach the
raft first, and even before I'd climbed the steps he was lying
on his front, peering over the side. 'Look at the fish!'

The middle-aged man already there said, 'If you bring
some bread later, you'll see swarms of them. My wife's been
bringing her leftover toast every morning.'

I lay on my front with Robbie, my head pillowed on my
arms, gazing into about twenty feet of water so clear, you
could see sandy ripples on the bottom. Little fishes, striped
in black and yellow, pecked and darted at the algae-covered
sides of the raft, and at the ropes that held the raft in place.

'Look, there's a blue one!' said Robbie.

'So there is.' Intense, purply blue, it was like a piscine
jewel.

A speedboat hummed past, rocking the raft gently in its
wake. The sun was warm on my back as I gazed down at
the fish. I was in a little piece of paradise, but all I could
think of was Guy.

And that crab. You'd think he might have done it anyway,
just to make an innocent little child's day.

It was a far cry from the Welford Castle pool. He hadn't
needed much encouragement to indulge in mildly flirty
horseplay then. When Fleur was still in the equation, too.
But maybe that was the whole point. He'd known nothing
would come of it, not then. Maybe it was just a safe,
amusing diversion in a relationship that was going nowhere.

Robbie said, 'Look, there's a funny long one!'

There was. It looked like a short, brown pencil with a
long snout.

I should get him a mask and snorkel, I thought. He was
so fascinated, he didn't utter again for at least a minute.
All around us was sun-warmed, sun-sparkled, turquoise
peace until I heard the sound of someone swimming

towards the raft. My practised ear detected Hard Front Crawl; it had Guy written all over it.

'Do they do long string-poohs, like goldfish?'

Why did all small boys suffer from crapomania? 'I expect so.'

The sound of Hard Crawl was louder. Robbie and I were facing away from the beach, but I didn't look round. I waited for it to stop, for the raft to rock as he climbed the steps, but it carried on past us, about twenty-five yards beyond the boundary rope.

'Look, there's Guy!' said Robbie.

'So it is.' Pretending to be engrossed with the fish, I glanced up just long enough to see him pause, tread water, and flick it from his face.

'Come and see the fish!' called Robbie.

He swam up more slowly, stopping in the water a bare foot from us. On purpose I didn't watch him come, but I was aware of every stroke.

'Pretty grim sea,' he said, putting a hand up to the raft. 'I'm not sure I can take much more of this.'

I wasn't sure I could, either. Just below me, his wet skin glinted in the sun. His eyes had taken on the colour of the sea around him, and they were looking directly at me.

'Yes, I know what you mean,' I said, as if I hadn't just been wishing he'd stuff a dead crustacean down my T-shirt. 'What's the point of sea that doesn't give you a good, bracing shock when you get into it?'

'Too right. Full of these verminous little fish, too. It's a bloody disgrace.'

'I thought you were going to wake Lindsay.'

'I did, but she was pretty dozy. Said to give her twenty minutes.'

He swam round the other side and climbed the steps,

saying, 'Morning,' to the the middle-aged man *en route*.

'Time I was off,' said the man. 'My wife'll be waiting to go for breakfast.' There was a colossal splash as he jumped in. The fish all darted back under the raft in alarm.

Guy sat a couple of feet to my left. I stayed put, gazing into the water with my head on my arms, pretending I was only interested in the fish. As if he were giving off an electric field, I was acutely aware of him. My peripheral vision told me exactly how he was sitting: left knee up, the right bent sideways. His right hand lay on his knee, a bare few inches from my ribcage. I was conscious of his wet skin, the light brown fuzz on his legs. It was so quiet I could even hear his breathing.

Suddenly bored, Robbie jumped up. 'Throw me in, Guy!'

'Robbie, don't start pestering,' I said.

'He's all right.' Standing up, Guy swung him over the side. One, two, three, *splosh*!

As the fish had all shot under the raft again, I sat up. 'You'll be at this all day if you're not careful.'

Still standing, he glanced down at me. 'I'll tell him when I've had enough.'

Robbie surfaced about three feet from the raft, grinning. 'Now Abby! Throw Abby in!'

Guy tutted. 'Come on, Robbie. Now you're really trying to get me into trouble.'

His tone was light and dry, as if he really meant it. 'Robbie, stop *pes*tering!' I said it sharply, so there'd be no doubt that I meant it, too. If Guy didn't want to play, then neither did I.

Robbie blew me a watery raspberry before doing a duck-dive.

'Right, that's it,' I said to Guy. 'See you later.'

I dived in and grabbed Robbie as he came up. 'Come on, we're going for breakfast.'

'I'm not hungry!'

'Well, I am, so tough.'

He started swimming slowly, in a grump. We were barely halfway back when Lindsay appeared on the ground-floor terrace, next to mine. She waved, I waved back, and from behind me I heard Guy yell, 'Coming in?'

Dressed in a white bikini, she walked down to the edge of the sea, put a toe in, and stepped back. 'Too cold!' she called back, using her cupped hands as a microphone.

'Too *cold*? Right, that's it . . .'

There was a splash as he dived in. He overtook us at a flat-out crawl, emerged on the sand, and chased Lindsay, who ran off, shrieking. He caught her, swept her up in his arms, and ran with her back into the sea.

There was a lot of shrieky mirth. 'You bugger! I'll get you for that . . .'

A chase to the raft ensued, with a lot of splashy laughter. I knew it was different with Lindsay, but that didn't stop me feeling a bit like a kid at a birthday party. The one who thought she was going to get the pass-the-parcel prize when the music stopped, only she didn't.

Yes, it was pathetic.

Robbie was still in a grump when we hit the beach. 'Why couldn't we stay with Guy? It's so *bor*ing with just *you*.'

I grabbed his arm. 'Listen to me, you little stinker. If you're going to be horrible I'll change the tickets and take you straight home. You are *not* to pester Guy or anyone else, and if you're rude or cheeky to anybody, especially me, we'll stay in the room *all - day*! Do you understand?'

Apart from the usual zoo-like table manners he behaved reasonably well at breakfast. This was a communal affair, at a long table where the entire party had eaten the night before. Lindsay and Rachel's folks were already there, with

David's mother, Helen. Except for a roof against the rain, the dining room was alfresco. Our table was at the outside edge, bordering on the gardens and pool area. Flutters of birds flocked near by, constantly chased away by the waiters, but now and then a bolder one would flit to the table. Twice a tiny black and yellow bird ventured to the sugar bowl, staying just long enough to dip a delicate, curved beak into the contents. 'What are those little yellow birds called?' I asked the waiter topping up my coffee.

He grinned. 'We call them yellow birds.'

Guy and Lindsay turned up twenty minutes after me and Robbie, but I spent most of breakfast catching up with Helen, who wanted every last detail of the family. Rachel's friend Kirsty was also there, with her boyfriend Mike. Apart from Neil, everybody else had yet to surface.

I hardly recognised Neil. His hair was a lot shorter, and he'd grown one of those little beards Lindsay often referred to as a Mr Wonderful. I half expected her to mutter something when we collided at the fruit end of the buffet, but evidently she'd made up her mind not to be rude. She'd even said a crisp, sunny, 'Morning!'

And there was no denying it rather suited him.

After breakfast I took Robbie to the little hotel shop, where we found a child-sized snorkelling kit. After my Evil Big Sister bit, I felt bad enough to add a pack of Jolly Roger playing cards, a set of beach bats, two bars of Cadbury's Fruit and Nut and a packet of crisps. I knew I'd been taking out other feelings on him, feelings that had nothing to do with his behaviour.

While I was paying, Rosemary came in, looking for postcards. 'What a shame about Penny,' she said, selecting sunsets and hummingbirds, 'but I'm sure child-free lakes will perk her up no end. To tell the truth,' she added, 'I was rather hoping a week together might mend the odd fence between her and Kay. This veiled antipathy is so silly after all this time.'

'I think it's gone on too long,' I said. 'It's a habit they can't get out of.'

'Probably.' She gave a wry smile. 'Matthew did tell me I was flogging a dead horse.'

I took Robbie to the pool to try out his gear, so it was gone ten before we hit the beach. By then I was wearing a new, hot-pink bikini bought the day before we'd left. It was the most expensive one I'd ever lashed out on, and worth it. How cut can make such a difference to a few scraps of fabric I don't know, but it fitted and flattered.

The trouble was, the man I'd intended it to impress was otherwise engaged. As I sat in the edge of the wavelets, keeping cool while Robbie snorkelled in the shallows, he was busy with boaty things. Along with a boy from the watersports hut, he was dragging a catamaran into the sea.

Armed with hat and T-shirt, Lindsay ran down from her sun bed. 'I'm going sailing with Guy,' she called, on her way past. 'See you later.'

I watched him hold the boat at the edge of the water. I watched him give Lindsay a hand on to the canvas deck. I watched him push it out, haul himself on board and mess with ropes and sails.

As a bigger wavelet washed over my feet, two pairs of legs appeared about a yard to my right. 'So annoying,' Auntie Rosemary was saying, 'but that's what comes of charging into Boots just before they close. I could have sworn I bought *water*proof cream, but it turned out I picked up the insect-repellent stuff, instead.'

'I think mine's both. Oh, hello, Abigail. I didn't see you there.'

'Hello, Auntie Kay.' She hadn't been at breakfast, and I hadn't seen her since Andrew's wedding. She wore a black and gold one piece that had never come cheap, with sunglasses that hadn't, either. She had the kind of tan that had probably come from a tanning shop. Her blonde hair was carefully coiffed. She looked expensive, in a way that made me think Monte Carlo rather than a chilled place like this. 'Sorry to hear that Uncle James couldn't make it,' I added. Rachel had filled me in on this earlier, and I was sorry. Quite apart from the fact that Kay was more palatable when diluted, I liked Uncle James.

'He was unexpectedly busy at the last minute,' she said. 'A panic on, someone over from the Santiago office – you know how it is.'

I didn't know much about the kind of engineering Uncle James was involved in at director level, but I knew he was exactly like Fleur in that he'd never be the one to say, 'Sod it, I'm going anyway.'

'I hope you've recovered from your dreadful flight?' she went on.

'Oh, yes, thanks.'

'An occupational hazard of charters, I expect.'

She'd have come British Airways, of course. Probably Club.

Shading her eyes, Auntie Rosemary was gazing out to sea. 'Is that Lindsay and Guy on that boat?'

Further out in the bay, the catamaran was catching the breeze, the sail filling as it began to skim the aquamarine water. 'Yes,' I said. 'It looks lovely and breezy out there.'

Kay was shading her eyes likewise. 'I must say, those two seem to be getting very friendly.'

The implication was obvious. It almost made me laugh.

Rosemary did laugh, but it was a slightly embarrassed version. 'I really don't think there's any of that sort of "getting", Kay. They've been friends since they were little.

Matthew used to say Guy was the brother the girls never had.'

'I do realise that, Rosemary. But you never know, do you? And I must say I was beginning to wonder last night. During dinner, the steel band, you know . . .'

'Oh, *that*. Well, yes, but I'm sure there wasn't anything in it. At least, nothing occurred to *me*.'

'I don't suppose it would. But I flatter myself I'm rather good at picking up these things.' She looked down at me. 'What do you think, Abigail?'

I think you're trying to wind me up, you old hag. You're trying to make me think that any ideas I might have had are being stuffed by Lindsay. Maybe you even believe it, but if so, you're way out.

Not that I quite said this. 'Don't ask me. But Lindsay once said thank God she never did fancy him – it'd feel too much like incest.'

Rosemary laughed. 'There you are, Kay. Not that I'm saying it wouldn't be rather nice – I've always had a soft spot for Guy – but I'm perfectly sure there's absolutely *noth*ing between those two. Come on, we were supposed to be going for a swim.'

As they waded in, her words were echoing in my head. 'Perfectly sure . . .'

'Absolutely *noth*ing . . .'

Twenty-nine

If Kay had intended to wind me up, she'd succeeded. Once she'd put the idea in my head, it refused to be shifted. I thought of that horseplay in the water, earlier. I thought of how upset Lindsay had been that he was 'off' with her, all those months ago. I thought of her determination not to lose touch again.

Had she been nursing a little spark, too? What if it had suddenly hit her when she'd met up with him again, invited him to that barbecue? The barbecue when he'd then gone for Fleur?

If that was it, she'd never have told me. Lindsay could be decidedly cagey about sparks unless she knew they were reciprocated. She'd once said it made you look such a fool when nothing came of them.

I watched for the boat to come back, but by eleven it still hadn't. By then Robbie had made friends with a couple of other kids, and was clamouring to go with them to the pool.

While I sat on the edge with my feet in the water, watching a noisy Death By Jaws competition, Rachel came to join me. At the nearby pool bar, David was ordering drinks to take back to the beach.

'All ready for tomorrow?' I asked.

'Except for shifting my things into Lindsay's room. Mum says I can't possibly share a room with David the

271

night before.' She made a wry face. 'Terribly "bad luck",
apparently.'

'It'll add to the sense of occasion,' I said. 'It wouldn't be
very weddingy if you were both getting ready together,
would it?'

Splashing water over my thighs and shoulders, I began
to think it was high time I got Robbie out of the sun.
There was the odd cloud to take the heat off, but despite
a breeze the intensity was obvious.

'Look!' Rachel pointed at a nearby shrub with red, bell-
like flowers. 'A humming-bird!' I could almost have
mistaken it for a large moth. Iridescent greeny-blue, it
hovered round a blossom before darting to another.

My mind was still consumed with other things, however.
'Don't laugh, but I heard Kay telling your mother earlier
that she thought Lindsay and Guy seemed to be "getting
very friendly".'

'She didn't!' Rachel laughed. After a pause she went
on, 'Mind you, you never know. I always think it's so
sweet when old friends get it together. When something
finally goes *ping!* at least you already know you like each
other.'

My breakfast mango was beginning to churn most
horribly with a fillet of flying fish. I wouldn't normally eat
fish first thing, but it was in the interests of being adven-
turous while on holiday. Flicking my feet casually in the
water, I said, 'I think Kay mentioned something about a
steel band last night.'

'Oh, that. Well, maybe I can see where she got the idea,
then. It was playing during dinner – there's a little dance
floor under the stars. They started playing 'Island In The
Sun', and Lindsay said it was so gorgeously corny she just
had to dance to it, and dragged Guy up.'

My stomach contracted.

'Of course, I was having a gorgeous little smooch with David,' she went on, 'but now you come to mention it I did think Lindsay and Guy looked rather sweet together.' She turned to me with a smile of dawning, happy possibilities. 'Imagine if my wedding helped do a *When Harry Met Sally* on those two! Wouldn't it just be lovely?'

Guy and Lindsay didn't come back till around lunchtime, just at the point when I finally had to take Robbie back to the room. Keeping him in the shade would have defeated anybody.

We returned to the beach around three. Those of the wedding party who hadn't gone for siestas were draped over blue plastic sun beds near the water. The sea lay like burnished silver in the afternoon sun.

Lindsay called to me. 'Here, Abby, I've saved you a bed.'

It was on her left. On her right was Guy, apparently asleep under his shades.

After slapping sunscreen all over a wriggling, protesting Robbie, I handed him the bottle. 'Now, will you be a good boy and put some on my back?'

Unhooking my bikini top, I lay down and rested my head on my arms. 'Just a little, OK? Squeeze the bottle gently.'

About half a pint of gloop landed instantly between my shoulder blades.

'Oops!' He clapped a hand over his mouth.

'Oh, *Robbie*! You little devil – that stuff costs about twelve pounds a bottle!'

Lindsay started laughing. So did Rachel's friend Kirsty and her boyfriend, Mike.

'Suck it back into the bottle!' I told him.

'*How*?'

The next thing I knew, Guy was on his feet. 'Pass it over, Robbie. Before she really blows a gasket.'

His lazily sun-warmed voice was quite enough to send an instant *frisson* through me, let alone the prospect of him de-glooping my back.

But I protested anyway, for the sake of form. 'Now look, Robbie! You've woken Guy up from his nice little nap.'

'I was only dozing.' Squatting in the sand beside me, he started scooping the cream off my back. I heard a sucky noise as he squished it back into the bottle.

'*Now* can I go in the sea?' demanded Robbie.

'Go on, then.'

With my head pillowed on my arms, I pretended to be intent on him, while Guy started part two of the exercise. 'How d'you want it? Marmalade or Marmite?'

'Er, sorry?'

He tutted. 'Wake up, Abby. Thick or thin?'

'Oh,' I said. 'Make it Nutella, then. Sort of in between.'

He began Nutella-ing.

There was no hint of 'lingering' or 'sensual' in the way he did it, but I wasn't complaining. His hands were light, firm and gentle all at once. It was hard to restrain a shiver when they moved to the nape of my neck, pausing to brush away strands of hair that had escaped my scrunchie. They moved in quick, light circles to the sides, and I had a job to restrain a shiver here, too. With my strap undone and my head resting on my arms, the sides of my breasts were exposed and his fingers came within a whisper of them.

I was beginning to understand what they meant by 'exquisite torture'.

It was over all too soon. 'There, you'll do.' (I thought he might have added a little pat on my expensively hot-

274

pink bottom, but 'twas not to be.) 'Happy cooking. Now, where's the top of this bottle?'

'Oh, Lord knows, he probably dropped it in the sand . . .'

He had. I was treated to a close-up of Guy's fuzzy-brown legs as he did a top-hunt.

'There you go.' He tucked the blue-topped bottle into my beach bag. 'Right, I'm going to cool off. Are you coming, Lindsay?'

'Not now,' she said lazily. 'I'm far too comfortable.'

'Bone idle,' he tutted. 'I shall have to take drastic measures later.'

She gave a lazy little giggle, as if more chucking-in might be on the cards before she was much older.

This only re-kindled my doubts. Could Kay really be right? After all, she'd picked up my own vibes before, like a heat-seeking missile.

Behind the cover of my shades I watched him stroll the few paces to the water. Given that lithe, loose-limbed walk, plus a firmly muscled back view, this was just another masochistic exercise

'Did you book a babysitter?' Lindsay asked, in a dozing-off voice.

'Yes, just before breakfast.' Although David had already had a stag night, Neil had missed it. He'd said he couldn't possibly do Best Man unless David was off the leash for his last night of freedom, and the hens were retaliating.

My 'cooking' session didn't last long. During the rest of that afternoon I discovered a blunt truth about single 'parenting' in an otherwise adult party. You're constantly on edge about the child's pestering: 'D'you want to come swimming/snorkelling/play beach bats with me?' After both Guy and Neil had played beach bats with him, Uncle Matthew had taken him snorkelling and Lindsay and

Rosemary had played several games of Beggar My Neighbour, I thought they'd all done their bit. I carted Robbie and his Jolly Roger cards off to the pool, pretending I wanted to go anyway. I then felt fed up and isolated. I thought about ordering a Big Bamboo from the pool bar, especially after the barman told me it'd blow my head off.

But I was saving myself.

Later, as the setting sun cast liquid gold on the sea, I was hitting the rum punch. Still in swimsuits, with sand between their toes, the entire wedding party was on the beach.

The Guy/Lindsay situation was still tormenting me, but I couldn't make my mind up. To anyone who knew them, they looked like intimate friends on holiday together, having a laugh. But then anyone who knew them had preconceived ideas.

Aware that I was watching non-stop for evidence, I stood ankle-deep in the sea, watching Robbie playing in the shallows. Sucking my second sundowner through a straw, I began to see what Guy meant about bar hazards. The rum punch was so moreish, it was easy to ignore the kick under that deceptive, sugar-and-lime innocence. One too many and I could well have thrown discretion to the soft trade winds. The way the sun was gilding Guy's entire body from hair to bare feet, I might have been tempted to do the kind of thing that seems such a great idea when you're half pissed, like tipping the ice from my glass down the back of his shorts. On holiday with Emma, I'd once done precisely this to some hunk I fancied rotten. I'd been hoping he'd run after me and exact delicious revenge. Instead he'd crossly shaken it out and said to Emma, 'Is your friend always such a pain when she's pissed?'

So it was just as well I had to stay sober for watching Robbie.

When the sunset was getting into its stride, Guy appeared at my left shoulder.

'I told you it was a washout last night,' he said. 'It must have been waiting for you.'

'Well, that was very kind of it.' The rays of the setting sun were exploding on the horizon, like the giant burning spokes of a bicycle wheel. The fluffy clouds were washed with fire.

I was washed with tingle. He was standing so close, the hairs on his arms were within shivering distance of my own. 'I wish I'd got my camera,' I said. 'But I left it in the room and I'm afraid that if I go back I'll miss the finale.'

'It's better in your head. At least you won't lose it when your hard disk goes into meltdown and you've forgotten to back up.'

'I wouldn't have that problem. I've still got a good old Push Here Dummy.'

He laughed and nodded at my nearly empty plastic glass, as real ones were banned on the beach. 'Like another one of those?'

'Not on an empty stomach.' *Just keep standing right there.*

He picked up a little piece of bleached coral and tossed it at the water. 'So what was that you started telling me this morning? About Friends Reunited and nowhere to duck?'

'Oh, that.' Having eaten my rum-punch cherry, I stirred the melting ice with my straw. 'Well, Mum told Jean the thought of the heat was making her feel like a wet rag, and Jean said how about Austria, then, a friend of hers had a chalet on a lake. And Mum told Will lakes and mountains were her idea of heaven, but he was absolutely *not* to say a word to me, as I'd feel obliged to bring Robbie here on my own.'

'But he did?'

'Of course he did. And although half of me wanted to thump him, he knew I'd only have thumped him anyway if he hadn't.'

'Your famous scary factor again. Here, d'you want mine? I'm not much into these.' He passed me the cocktail stick from his own glass, with its cherry.

'Yummy,' I said, thinking it would have been a far better sign if he'd popped it into my mouth, instead.

'Couldn't Will have done the honours?' he asked.

'He's on a course half this week. And he's got hardly any leave left anyway.'

Robbie came running out of the water. 'When are we having our dinner? I'm *starv*ing!'

I glanced at my watch. 'In five minutes. I've ordered you a burger and chips in the room.'

It was just as well I had, as he'd never have lasted till dinner. Exhausted from hours of swimming, he zonked out five minutes after the babysitter arrived.

The hens ended up at a glorified pub a few miles down the coast. There was a buffet of barbecued steaks and king-fish, plantains and candied sweet potatoes; local spicy chicken and black-eye beans. With live, open-air music and perfect-rhythm locals to dance with, it was a fun enough evening until the heavens suddenly opened. Within seconds a few fat drops turned into dense tropical sheets that sent everybody scurrying inside.

A few minutes later I found Rachel wiping her eyes in the loo. 'What is it?' I asked. 'Don't tell me you're nervous?'

That set her right off. 'Oh, Abby – what if it rains tomorrow?'

We left just after midnight. In another drenching shower we ran to taxis. 'It's not going to rain tomorrow, is it?'

Rachel asked the driver plaintively. 'I'm getting married in the morning.'

He gave a velvet-brown chuckle. 'We call it liquid sunshine. But don't worry, dear. In Barbados the sun always shines tomorrow.'

Although I was tired, sleep eluded me. There was too much in my head, and it wasn't the thought of next month's Visa bill. After tossing and turning for twenty minutes I tiptoed past the sleeping Robbie, slid open the glass door and stepped out on to the little terrace.

It had stopped raining. The air was warm and moist and still. It smelt of wet sand and green, growing things. I could just hear the lapping of wavelets. The chirping of the tree frogs was louder than ever, as if a good downpour was their very best treat. I had wildlife company, too. Just under the outside light, clinging to the rough, coral-stone wall, a little lizard was waiting for unwary insects. Pity I couldn't take him home, I thought. He'd come in very handy during the daddy-long-legs season.

With my feet up on the little table, I was getting absorbed in the book I'd grabbed from the airport shop, when muted laughter made me look up. A young couple were strolling at the edge of the sea, arm in arm. They were barefoot. His trousers were partly rolled up; her shoes dangled by their straps from his hand.

A pang of envy seized me. Of all the places to rub in your singledom, this had to be the worst. Why was I sitting here with only a lizard for company, when a thousand tree frogs were chirping love songs?

Gradually a fantasy took shape in my head. I was sitting here, but not in the oversized T-shirt adorned with dolphins. I'd be wearing slinky silk pyjamas, like you should when you're about to be waylaid by the man you've been fantasising about. I'd be gazing at the sea, thinking how heart-stoppingly gorgeous it would be if suddenly, out of the warm tropical night, a familiar voice said softly—

'Hi. Can't you sleep, either?'

Thirty

Shame it was only Lindsay, peering round the dividing wall from her own terrace.

'No,' I whispered. 'Is Rachel asleep?'

'Zonked.' She climbed over her own wall, back over mine, and sat in the other chair. She wore a long cotton kimono in black and cream.

For a moment we sat in silence, gazing at the beach. There was just the shish of wavelets on the sand, and the tree frogs. My little lizard was still lurking on the wall, watching for potential snacks. 'Why couldn't you sleep?' I asked.

'I don't know. Too many things going round in my head.'

You're not the only one. 'Like what?'

'Oh, nothing. Stuff.' For a minute or two we talked about the rain, and what on earth would happen tomorrow if it chucked it down when the entire do was supposed to take place in the gardens. During a pause she turned her head.

'Hear that?'

I had. Running behind our rooms, on the 'front door' side, was a covered path. Another path at right angles to this led through the gardens to the main building. Out of the hush emerged soft footsteps and muted male voices.

'The stags, I bet,' I said. 'Trying to be quiet and not wake anybody up.'

Moments later, beyond the last beachfront room to our

left, two male figures stepped on to the sand. They strolled a few paces before pausing, facing the sea and talking softly. Unmistakably they were Guy and Neil in that easy, male-chat stance, half turned towards each other. I will admit to a major flutter-moment just on seeing him. There was something about the back of his head, in the way he stood with his right hand shoved in his trouser pocket, that just did it for me. Though the way I felt just then; the way he took the top off a boiled egg would probably have done it, too.

'Trust Guy to get matey with Mr Wonderful,' muttered Lindsay.

'Oh, come on. He's been relatively human so far. He even played beach bats with Robbie this afternoon.'

'Yes, I saw.' She picked at a loose thread on her kimono. 'Remember how I thought the flytrap was going to give him itchy greenfly?'

I stifled a laugh. 'Oh, yes. You had visions of her sticky little fronds ravening round his stamens. Or is it pistils?'

'Don't ask me. Biology was never my strong point, especially when it came to how buttercups make out.'

'I think it's pistils. Sounds vaguely male, doesn't it? Though I expect that's the *pis* bit. Connotations of the loo seat up, and all that.'

'She didn't, though.'

My eyes were on Guy. 'Sorry?'

'The flytrap. She never got anywhere near his pistils.'

'Just as well. She might have given him a dose of ball weevils, too.'

'I did, though.'

For a moment I thought she was joking, but that was before I saw her face. '*When?*'

'When d'you think? Look, I'll tell you tomorrow, OK?' Half rising from her chair, she uttered a soft whistle.

Turning as one, they saw us and came up. I was almost too stunned to appreciate Guy's thumb hooked in his belt.

'So what time do you call this, you dirty stop-outs?' Lindsay asked. 'Guy, I need you,' she added sweetly. 'There's a bloody great cockroach in our bathroom – I'll never sleep with that running around. Could you come and eject it without waking Rachel up?'

'Probably not,' he said, 'but I'll give it a go.'

'What cockroach?' I said. 'You didn't tell me about a cockroach.'

'Didn't I? It's a whopper with three-inch feelers.' Already she was stepping on to the wall. Guy took her hand as she jumped down. 'Night, you two,' she said.

Guy said, 'Sleep tight.'

After watching them disappear, Neil turned to me. 'Good night?'

Never mind that – *what's the hell's all this about your pistils and Lindsay?*

But I just said, 'Great, thanks. How about yours?'

'Pretty good. Still, better call it a night . . .'

He melted away, leaving me in that state known as 'whacked in the face with a jelly'. Except for a security guard wandering past with a torch, the beach was deserted again. All I could hear was the *shish* of the sea and the overhead chorus.

And my own thoughts.

Neil! What on earth had happened? Apart from the obvious, I mean. How could she drop a bombshell like that and leave me waiting till tomorrow for the juicy details? Even more importantly, why did she have to whisk Guy off like that? A few minutes out here would have been lovely. I might even have got a little goodnight kiss to send me to bed happy. A brushing of lips on cheek; that lovely, grazing of his cheek against mine—

283

Ow! A sudden sting on my ankle told me some blood-hungry insect had just bitten it. I stood up, about to go in, when my breath caught in my throat.

On the far horizon, where indigo sky melted into the sea, stretched a fuzzy, ghostly, pearly-silver arc. I'd heard of such things, but I'd vaguely connected them with Narnia or Middle Earth. With enchanted woods, or the kind of Greek goddess who spent half her life as a sea nymph.

'You still here?' The soft whisper made me jump. Guy was stepping over Lindsay's wall. He'd come out so quietly, I hadn't heard a thing.

I pointed at the horizon. 'Look!' I whispered.

'A moonbow.' Coming to stand just on the other side of my little wall, he followed my gaze. 'Haven't you ever seen one before?'

'Never! Have you?'

'Once or twice, when I've been out at sea, at night.' His voice was as low as mine. With people sleeping both sides and upstairs too, it had to be.

It was already fading. As the last of the fuzzy arc melted like mist in May, I turned to him. 'I hope that wasn't a bad sign.'

'A bad sign of what?'

'Rain. You know, like a ring around the moon.'

'It's a sign that it's raining out there, anyway.'

'I just hope it stays there. Rachel was worried in case it rains tomorrow.'

'David was worried in case Rachel was worried.'

'Rachel was worried about that, too. In case David was worried about her being worried.'

His soft laugh sent a warm, woozy rush through me. Of course, Sod's Law dictated that Robbie would wake any second, announcing that he'd wet the bed, but until then

I was making the most of it. He was still on the other side of the wall, but no more than eighteen inches away. 'Did you manage to catch the horrible beastie?'

'Oh, that,' he said. 'Yes, I sent it off with a flea in its feelers.'

Hushed laughter turned our eyes to the right. The young couple I'd seen earlier were strolling back in the soft sand, arms round each other's waist. As they came closer I could see that the girl's hair was wet and his shirt was slung over his shoulder. I absolutely knew they'd been into the next bay, which was more secluded.

'No prizes for guessing,' Guy murmured. 'Skinny-dipping, I bet. They've used his shirt as a towel.'

Lucky buggers. 'They'll catch cold,' I said, as tongue in cheek as I could in the circumstances. 'And someone really should have warned them about those giant, flesh-eating urchins.'

His mouth flickered. 'I'd forgotten about those. I believe they're largely nocturnal, too.'

'It was a dangerous exercise, then.'

'Highly dangerous.'

Suddenly I thought I detected a leak from that chemistry-balloon. I could tell from the way his eyes lingered fractionally longer than necessary before a muffled giggly shriek from Miss Skinny-Dip tore them away, damn her.

'What about those eight-foot crabs?' I asked, in case he crisped up and said, *Well, time for bed* . . . 'I hope they're not nocturnal, too.'

'Ah,' he said, deadpan, shoving a hand in his pocket. 'I'm not sure I should tell you about those. They have a particularly nasty way of lulling their prey into a sense of false security. I wouldn't want to give you – oh, shit—'

With a frown, he looked up. 'Here we go again – I'm getting splatted.'

285

Already a few fat drops were landing on his shirt, and within another heartbeat scores more were joining them.

He raised his eyebrows. 'They really know how to do rain here – I'll make a run for it.'

'You'll get soaked!'

'It won't kill me. I'll see you in the morning.'

He shot off through teeming, increasingly deafening sheets.

If this was liquid sunshine, you could keep it.

I woke from a coma-like sleep, wondering where on earth I was until I saw the curtains: turquoise blue, with hibiscus-coloured splashes.

Oh, yes. Barbados. Morning.

Oh, yes. Last night. Guy. What a waste of a moonbow.

And Lindsay and Neil! Bloody hell . . .

I thought about this for about ten seconds.

Robbie's very quiet. How come he's still—

I sat up with a jerky start. His bed was empty, the covers flung aside.

I was out of bed in a flash, pulling that T-shirt back on. Somehow he'd unlocked the sliding doors, which were open a crack. In a complete panic, I shot outside, scanning beach and sea.

Oh, GodohGod . . .

Only then did I see the note. On a sheet of hotel writing paper it was on the outside table, held down by pieces of bleached coral.

I found Robbie on the beach, just outside. We've gone for an exciting explore. Didn't like to wake you.
Guy.

Ah. How sweet of him.

Underneath was a line of writing that looked like the crawlings of a spider that's half drowned in a pot of ink: *Pleaz dont be croS.'*

Beneath was added, *Especially not with me.*

I wasn't quite sure how to take that.

Dressed in shorts and T-shirt, I stepped back on to the veranda twenty minutes later, combing my wet hair. There was some fluffy cloud around, but most of the sky was tranquil blue. At nearly nine o'clock the sun was sparkling on the sea and the first sun-worshippers were stretching themselves out to cook.

There was still no sign of Guy and Robbie, but a few of the wedding party were up. A couple of David's friends were on the raft and Neil was halfway to joining them.

Sitting down to wait, I scraped a chair on the tiles, and the sound brought Lindsay's head round the dividing wall. 'I was beginning to think you were in a coma. Don't tell me Robbie's still asleep?'

'A noble babysitter let me have a lie-in.' I showed her Guy's note.

'Oh,' she said. 'Good old Guy. Glad he's making himself useful.'

'Yes, he's a glutton for punishment. Is Rachel up?'

'She's doing her nails.' In a short denim skirt, she came around and sat on the other chair.

I lowered my voice. '*Well?*'

Thirty-one

She made a face. 'Sorry. I hope you weren't awake half the night, in suspenders.'

'Why didn't you tell me before?'

'Because he made me feel like shit and I've been trying to forget it.'

My eyes went to Neil, just climbing on to the raft, and back to Lindsay.

'Don't you dare tell anybody,' she added. 'I never even told Rachel. She'd have told David, after swearing blind not to. I've only told one person, and that wasn't till the other week.' She paused. 'That's why I was so glad he could come. To give me a bit of moral support.'

It took a moment for this to sink in. 'You told *Guy*?'

Misunderstanding my reaction, she made a face that said, Don't you get it? 'Abby, after you've checked each other's bottoms for your best chicken-pox scabs, there's not much that's off limits. Anyway, he's hardly judgemental in these matters.' She paused. 'It was when I saw him the other week. After a few drinks I ended up staying over. We were talking about all sorts, and it all came out.'

I had to ask. 'Have you been trying to make Neil think there's a budding little thing between you and Guy?'

'No! Don't tell me Neil asked you?'

'God, no. Only Kay said something. She thought you two were "getting very friendly".'

She made a face. 'She should keep her nose out. I just didn't want to be floating around "spare" anywhere near Neil. When Guy made noises about coming I thought:Yes! If I was "with" an old friend, I wouldn't be spare, would I?' She paused. 'OK, it wouldn't have bothered me if Neil got the wrong idea, but that certainly wasn't the intention.'

I was thinking of last night. 'Was there really a cockroach in your bathroom?'

'Of course not. I was just having a fit when I saw them together on the beach. I thought Guy might have been saying something, so I had to get him away and check that he hadn't.'

'And had he?'

'No, and just as well, because I'd kill him.'

My eyes returned to Neil, who'd just dived off the raft. 'What the hell happened?'

Her tone took on a warning note. 'Look, don't start giving him dirty looks, will you? The last thing I want is for him to think I'm still upset enough to be slagging him off.'

We were interrupted by the sound of Rachel calling, 'Lindsay?'

'Here,' Lindsay called. 'With Abby.'

Rachel put her head round the dividing wall. 'Morning, Abby! Is it my imagination or has that face pack made me more like a killer tomato than I was already?'

'It's your imagination,' I said. 'You've just got a little bridal glow already.'

'D'you reckon? I wish I'd brought some of that green make-up that tones you down. Where's Robbie?' she added, as it hit her that the noisy one was missing.

'Guy took him off.'

'Oh, did he? That was nice of him.' She turned to survey the beach. 'Don't you just love that view?' She indicated the gentle curve of the bay, with its fringe of feathery green. 'I thought I might get the photographer to take some shots with that in the background. Everybody barefoot in the sand with a hibiscus in their hair. Of course that might be a bit difficult for Dad when he's hardly got any, but I suppose he could tuck it behind his . . .' Her voice tailed off. 'Oh, no . . .'

The sparkle had just gone off the water. At the same time a little wind whipped up, flapping the beach umbrellas.

Rachel's face creased with anxiety. 'Oh, *please*, not today . . .'

The sky ahead was blue, but here you soon worked out that the weather came from the Atlantic side of the island, from the east. As one, the three of us climbed over the wall, stepped back and stared up at the sky. Moving swiftly from inland, over the tops of the trees, was a swathe of grim and businesslike cloud. Even as we watched, the first fat drops began to fall.

'Oh, no . . .' As the sun worshippers ducked under their umbrellas or ran for cover, Rachel's face crumpled. 'Please, God, don't let it rain on my wedding day.'

'It probably won't last long,' I said, with a lot more conviction than I felt.

'Are you kidding?' She was nearly in tears already. 'Just look at it!'

Shooting me an 'oh, Lord' look, Lindsay put an arm around her. 'Come on, let's go for breakfast.'

Left to myself, I sat under cover, watching through dense wet curtains as squillions of tiny splats blanketed the sea. Neil and the others were swimming back PDQ.

As they approached, my mind was full of Lindsay's revelation. What on earth had he done to make her feel so bad? Lindsay was hardly the type to indulge in self-loathing over the odd mindless shag: at least, no more than anybody else who's woken up to find Mr Seemed Quite Nice Last Night snoring beside her in the morning.

As for Guy, it was all as clear as a nice clean windscreen now. She was merely 'with' him. She looked on him as a supportive male rock, 'hers' for the duration.

This minor complication didn't spoil the little leap of my heart when I saw Guy and Robbie coming. In pelting rain they were running around the corner of the next bay. During the last few yards Guy swept Robbie up and dropped him over the wall.

'It's *warm* rain!' Robbie chortled. 'I'm not cold a *bit*!'

'No, but you're all wet. Run and get a towel.'

Guy was on the other side of the wall. From his soaked hair, water was dripping all down his face. The hair on his chest and arms were soaking; his eyelashes were soaking; his soaking shorts clung to his thighs. He looked like Mr Wet Dream, with a heart-fluttering little smile thrown in. 'We really must stop meeting like this,' he said.

OK, he didn't. He said, 'Bloody weather – looks like you were right about bad signs.'

As I said, a complete waste of a moonbow. 'Yes, poor Rachel's in a right old tizz. Come in quick, before you drown.'

'No, I've got to run. Urgent business.' And with a quick smile, he shot off once more into teeming sheets.

What could be so urgent? With a horrible feeling it was an excuse, I went inside. There were wet, sandy footprints all over the floor and more sand on the bed, where Robbie was lying on his stomach. Already channel-hopping for cartoons, he was stuffing his face with Cadbury's chocolate.

'Who said you could have that before breakfast?' I took it away and started drying him properly. 'I'm not cross, but you must never go off like that without me, all right?'

'I didn't go off!' Impatiently he tried to wriggle away

from this annoying female attention. 'I was only just playing right outside!'

I bit back replies about other nice 'friendly' men who might have passed by instead of Guy. 'I was worried, that's all. I need to know where you are.'

'You *did*! Guy wrote you a note, didn't he?' He suddenly got the giggles, much in the bottled-up way he had over the dead crab.

'I hope you haven't found any more smelly dead things,' I said.

'No, but it's a bit *rude*.' He was giggling worse than ever.

'What?'

He put a hand over his mouth, as if that would keep his bubbling mirth from boiling over.

What on earth had they been up to? 'Robbie, if you don't tell me, there won't be any Cokes today. Or chocolate, either.'

'It's just – hee hee – when Guy creeped in to find a piece of paper – hee hee hee – to tell you where I was – heeheehee—' He almost doubled up.

Suddenly I was catching on. I hadn't slept in that T-shirt, and I could be a messy sort of sleeper. 'What?'

'Hee hee hee – one of your *bosoms* was poking out of the covers!'

That was school playgrounds for you. Six months ago he wouldn't even have noticed, let alone found it funny. 'There's nothing funny about that, Robbie. Bosoms aren't rude.' (Funny how I was fighting a little flush, though.)

'They are when *boys* can see them, hee hee . . . But don't tell Guy, cos I was laughing, and he said it wasn't funny.'

'Quite right, too.' Thank God I wasn't snoring with my mouth open. Poking-out bosoms gave me another feeling altogether.

* * *

Breakfast was back at that long, wedding-party table. Because it was at the edge of the semi-open dining room, it was impossible to ignore the rain still falling in sheets only feet from Robbie's Rice Krispies. Although Rachel was putting on a brave face, I knew she felt like crying rivers to match.

David, AK and Guy had yet to appear, but everybody else, especially Uncle Matthew, was saying, 'I'm sure it'll clear up later,' in those hearty tones that said they were privately sure of precisely the reverse. The local paper said, 'partly cloudy with scattered showers', but according to our waiter it said that nine days out of ten anyway.

Just as Robbie and I had nearly finished, Guy turned up. He wore khaki shorts with combat-style pockets and a white T-shirt.

'About time too,' said Lindsay. 'We'd just about given you up.' Her eyes went to the plastic bag he was carrying. 'Don't tell me you've been shopping?'

'I had some urgent business.' He shot a tiny wink at me. 'Taking out insurance policies.'

From the bag he took a pink, mini-umbrella. 'Here you go – this one's for the bride.' He tossed it to Rachel, who started laughing. 'And the bride's mother . . . catch . . .' He tossed a tartan one to Auntie Rosemary, who started laughing likewise. He continued with more to other major players, finishing with a green one, adorned with frogs. 'And this – no fairytale connotations intended – is for David.'

By then everybody was laughing, including our waiter.

And me. My relief that his 'urgent business' wasn't an excuse was profound.

'And the rest of you . . .' he pinched a morsel of bacon from Lindsay's plate, '. . . can bloody well buy your own.'

She was still laughing. 'You idiot. Go and get some breakfast.'

Auntie Rosemary was regarding him fondly. 'It was a very kind thought, Guy. Though I'm sure we could have borrowed some from the hotel, if necessary.'

Lindsay raised her eyes to heaven. 'Mum, you've missed the *point*. That wouldn't have been insurance, would it?'

Robbie tapped my arm. 'I've finished. Can we go swimming now?'

'Robbie, dear, it's pouring!' said Rosemary.

'I *know*!' he said blithely. 'That's why it'll be *fun*!'

It restored my faith in human childhood to think that rainy swimming beat the cartoon channel. 'Come on, then. I'll take you to the pool for a bit.'

After twenty virtuous lengths, I sat under a palm-thatched hut, with an eye on Robbie. The rain had just about stopped, but it was still heavily overcast. Feeling slightly chilly in my wet black Speedo, I pulled a towel around my shoulders. Everywhere was dripping. Water dripped off the roof of the hut, splashing on to the end of the green plastic mat I was sitting on. There was hardly anybody else there: one forty-something couple reading papers and glumly checking the sky now and then, and the parents of the boy Robbie was playing with.

Of similar age and inclinations, he'd arrived the previous evening. They were enjoying a noisy competition to see who could do the splashiest bomb.

The voice came from behind. 'Hi. Don't tell me you've been in, too?'

'Oh, hi, Guy,' I said, as if he were anybody I was pleased to see. 'Yes, I thought I'd get my hard exercise out of the way.'

In the same white T-shirt and shorts, he slung a newspaper on the sun bed next to mine and sat on the side. 'I could do with some hard exercise myself,' he said. 'I just had enough breakfast for a pig farm.'

'You earned it,' I pointed out. 'First Robbie, then charging off to the shops – your insurance went down a blast.'

'Let's just hope it works.' He peered out at the wet, sunless gardens. 'Doesn't look great so far. I might ask for a refund.'

'At least the rain's nearly stopped. Our taxi driver last night told us they call it liquid sunshine.'

He raised very dry eyebrows. 'That'll be straight out of "Quaint Local Sayings to Keep the Tourists Happy". They're probably paying someone to dream them up.'

'That's a very cynical attitude, but I wouldn't be surprised. Still, at least you made Rachel laugh. I wouldn't have thought anything could make her laugh this morning.'

He gave a wry little smile. 'That was the general idea.'

How many people would think of it, though? Let alone charge to the shops and actually do it before breakfast? It was one of those heart-twisting moments when you realise that you like someone so much, remaining 'just good friends' will nearly kill you. 'Thanks for taking Robbie this morning. I had a gorgeous long sleep.'

'Yes, I thought you could probably do with it.' His gaze went to the noisy bombing in the pool. 'Wot, no Jaws?'

'You missed that bit. They had a competition to see who could "die" most gruesomely.' By logical brain connection, Jaws made me think of swimming at night, which led to those skinny-dippers and thence to other perils. 'You were going to tell me about those eight-foot crabs. Forewarned is forearmed, you know.'

His mouth flickered. 'Are you sure you're up for this? It's pretty horrific stuff.'

'I'll try not to scream.' As I was draped lengthways on

my sun bed, and he was sitting sideways, I thought this was a good time to swivel round. Tucking my bare legs up, I half-turned into a more friendly position.

He leant slightly forwards, his arms resting on his thighs. Nice, hunky brown-fuzzed ones. His forearms were exactly the same, in a forearm fashion. 'Their favourite prey, of course,' he said, deadpan, 'is a tasty, well-fed tourist. They prefer the young ones, often found wandering in pairs at night.'

Oh, if only we could stay here and talk lovely daft rubbish all morning. 'Well, they would.'

'Don't interrupt. So what these crabs do is lie in wait in their lairs. And while they're waiting, they sharpen their pincers on their built-in pincer-sharpeners.'

He said it so straight-faced, I had a job not to laugh. 'Sounds nasty.'

'I did warn you. The trouble is, pincer-sharpening's on the noisy side, which rather gives the game away. So – and here's the really sneaky bit – over millions of years the noise has evolved to sound exactly like tree frogs.'

'You're kidding!'

'That's old Mother Nature for you. She plays dirty. So just as your hapless tourists are strolling in the moonlight, saying, "Ooh, look at the sea!" and "Just listen to those dear little tree frogs!" – suddenly, out of its lair—'

His darting tweak at my knee made me shriek.

'I thought you weren't going to scream,' he grinned.

I was still laughing. 'You idiot . . .'

'Don't you "idiot" me. A serious lecture on the local wildlife and that's the thanks I get.' His eyes suddenly shot to somewhere over my left shoulder. 'Morning!'

My own eyes followed.

'Morning, you two!'

If I'd stopped to make a metallurgical analysis of the voice at the time I'd have said thin gold leaf over steel. The owner was Kay, and she wore a smile to match. 'Well, Abigail! I was just passing when I heard a giggly shriek that sounded highly suspicious, so I've made a little detour to see what's going on.'

Of course she said no such thing. Coming right up in a pair of navy tailored shorts she said, 'Well, Guy! I've just been hearing all about your insurance. It looks as if it might even be working, too – the rain's just stopped.' If anything, the gold-leaf smile increased by a fake carat or two. 'Have you seen Lindsay? I just wanted a little word.'

And if you believe that . . .

Guy said pleasantly, 'I guess she's on Best Woman duty, with Rachel.'

Meanwhile, as if I had something to hide, I'd swivelled back from my 'more friendly' position. I despised myself for letting her make me feel caught in the act, but I couldn't help it. 'Have you just had your hair done?' I asked, like Niece-Hypocrite Star, but I couldn't think of anything else to say. 'It looks very nice.'

'Heavens, no.' She patted her smooth blonde bob. 'I'm sure the beauty salon's fine, but I'd never trust a hairdresser I don't know.'

Behind her shades (she was still wearing them despite the lack of sun) I absolutely saw her in a quandary. What she'd really have liked, I swear, was to retreat to a first-floor poolside room with a pair of binoculars. As she had a beach-front room, though, this was not an option. She knew she should carry on in that direction, where she'd evidently been heading when she saw us, but couldn't quite bring herself to go.

For a fleeting instant my eyes met Guy's. Naturally he

had no idea of Kay's conjectures about him and Lindsay, but I'd have bet a hundred quid he was recalling that incident at Andrew's wedding. I'd have bet another hundred he was feeling a retrospective, guilty pang for our whispered chemistry when he was still seeing this woman's daughter.

At any rate, our reaction was identical. It came from the almost certainly shared feeling that not to do it would be ill-mannered. At the exact moment I said, 'Take a pew,' he said, 'Why don't you sit down?' Taking Robbie's damp towel, he shifted up and wiped raindrops from the end of the green plastic mattress.

She hesitated only minutely. 'Well, maybe for just a minute.'

She'd barely arranged her navy raffia bag beside her legs when Robbie scrambled out of the pool. 'Joe's got to go to the shops with his mum and dad,' he announced, running up in a shower of drips. 'Hello, Auntie Kay!'

To her credit, her wince at the drips on her bare legs was minimal. 'Hello, Robbie. Have you been swimming in the rain?'

'Course I have! You get wet anyway, don't you? I'm *starv*ing,' he added to me. 'Can I have some chocolate?'

'No way. You had some just before breakfast.'

He turned hopeful eyes on Guy. 'Will you come in the pool with me?'

'Not just now.' Suddenly brisk, Guy picked up his paper. 'I was on my way to check my emails. See what's been happening down the salt mines. And by the time I'm through with that . . .' he glanced at his watch, '. . . it'll be time to make myself beautiful.'

Robbie hooted.

'It's not funny.' Guy gave him a gentle whack on the head with his *Independent*. 'When you're as old as me, it

takes a long time to get your socks on. I'll see you lot later.'
There was just a moment's eye contact as he said this, but
nothing Kay could have 'read' if she'd seen it.

Left with Kay and Robbie, I felt years of swallowed
resentment turn to a flood tide. As if a five-year-old wasn't
enough, why did she have to descend like the chaperone
from hell? What had I ever done to make her hate the
thought that he might be attracted to me? To wishful-think
it was Lindsay, just so that I couldn't have what had once
been Fleur's?

'I don't see *why* I can't have any chocolate,' Robbie
complained. 'It's hours and *hours* till lunch!'

'Oh, go on, then.' Delving irritably in my bag, I shoved
twenty Barbados dollars at him. '*One* bar, no crisps, and
come straight back.'

'Well,' said AK brightly, as his bare feet scampered off
up the path, 'maybe it's time I went to get ready, too.'

'Yes,' I said. 'No point in staying now Guy's gone, is
there? Absolutely no need to watch that I'm not sticking
my tongue down his throat behind Lindsay's back.'

Thirty-two

This wasn't one of my nearly-said-its. I did say it. Accompanied by a hot beating of my heart, the words tumbled out on that pent-up tide.

She actually flushed. It was barely discernible under her tan, but I saw a tinge of dull red even in the V of her white linen shirt. Because of the shades I couldn't see her eyes, but I didn't have to. It was a moment before she spoke, in tones that weren't a hundred per cent controlled. 'Really, Abigail, I think you must have got a touch of the sun yesterday.'

My own voice wasn't altogether crispy-cool, either. 'You know exactly what I mean. But just for the record, there's absolutely nothing between Guy and Lindsay. *Nothing*. So if I were you I'd stop dropping hints that there is. You'll only feel a fool when you're proved wrong.'

I saw her swallow, as if she felt a fool already, but she covered with a light little laugh. 'Are you trying to tell me there's something between you and him?'

'I'm not trying to tell you anything. But I might point out that whatever might or might not be going on between anyone, it's absolutely none of anybody else's business.'

She picked up her bag. I thought she was leaving without a word, but maybe it took her a few seconds to find any. 'As I said, it's time I was off.' Standing up, she added smoothly, 'I do hope you'll be in a sweeter frame of mind for the wedding.'

300

And on mules of soft bronze leather, she went.

Left in that hot, heart-thumping state, I wished I'd said a hell of a lot more. I wished I'd given her a prime mouthful, with a few 'evil old hags' thrown in.

Robbie came running back with two small bars of Fruit and Nut and a handful of change. 'I know you said only *one* bar, but the lady said they'd run out of the big ones, so I'd better have two. You can have one, if you like,' he added graciously.

Yes, I could do with a fix. 'Thank you.' Ripping the wrapping off, I stuffed two chunky squares in my mouth.

'Will you play catch with me in the pool?'

'Yes, great idea.' *You be Auntie Kay and I'll be Jaws.*

Pool catch was dubious therapy. On the one hand, it let me work off that hot, heart-thumping state. On the other, it let rational Abby back from the sidelines.

That was very clever, wasn't it? All you've achieved is to make her think you were trying to tell her something.

Oh, shut up.

Please yourself. But who's going to look the fool now if those whiffs of chemistry disperse into the atmosphere after all?

With all this in my head I wasn't feeling exactly sunny by the time I finally dragged Robbie from the pool, but at least the weather was. As I picked up wet towels, the only remaining cloud was the fluffy white variety in a sky of Wish-You-Were-Here blue.

As Lindsay said afterwards, it was almost worth the rain for Rachel's ecstasy when it cleared up. The ceremony took place in the gardens, under a little, white-painted gazebo. It was draped with a riot of flowers, frantically culled from the grounds by a posse of staff as soon as the rain had stopped. Hibiscus of red, pink and white, yellow bell-like flowers, red-hot cat's tails and delicate, pale blue plumbago combined with lush greenery in an orgy of colour. Everything sparkled with newly washed freshness, raindrops glistening on a million petals.

Arriving at the last minute with Robbie, I was just in time. Along with a white-robed vicar from a nearby church and the photographer, the assembled guests were waiting with cameras poised for Rachel to appear on Uncle Matthew's arm.

'What a rush,' I said. 'I don't think my hair's even properly dry.'

'Stuff it, you look gorgeous,' said Lindsay. 'I love the dress.'

'Thanks.' I'd bought it specially. It was a strapless thing in clingy cream crêpe, splashed with stylised red and pink flowers that looked vaguely tropical. The slightly ruffled hem fell from just above the knee on the right, to mid-calf on the left.

Guy gave me an appreciative once-over, and I can tell you, I appreciated it. 'She matches the gardens,' he said. 'Hot and tropical.'

'Not as hot and tropical as Lindsay,' I said, eyeing her slip dress in hot pink.

Guy wore smart-casual navy cotton trousers, with a short-sleeved shirt in blue and white stripes. Like all the other male guests, he'd pinned a buttonhole of white and feathery green to his shirt.

Wearing a simple, strapless dress of cream silk, Rachel arrived moments later. She carried a little posy of pink and white, and a few matching flowers were pinned to her hair. Beside her, Uncle Matthew wore a smile of fond pride. As for David, his smile as he watched her arrival made my little Cupid badge glow like a halo. After all, I was glad I'd been relatively restrained with my dear aunt earlier. Just before Rachel's wedding was hardly the time for pouring out everything I'd been storing up since I was about eight.

I spoke not a word to Kay, though nobody would have noticed. After the ceremony champagne flowed and the party tripled in size. Swim-suited guests pausing on their way to the beach or pool were pressed by genial Matthew to join the party. Rosemary was heard to say to David's mother, 'I must say, I was very dubious when she first suggested a wedding away, but it's all turned out beautifully. And I've really never tasted wedding cake like it. The chef told me they soak the fruit in rum for *three weeks*!'

'Dear me,' said David's mother. 'I'll have another piece of that, then.'

Kay handled herself as if nothing had happened, not that I was watching her on purpose. I caught her eyes on me more than once, but if she was looking for signs of anything, she was disappointed.

And she wasn't the only one. Guy behaved to me almost exactly as he behaved to Lindsay: chilled and friendly and fun. But we were never alone for a second, though I made no effort to contrive this, and neither did he. I knew Kay had made him feel that any move he might make now would be taken as proof that her way-back suspicions were justified; that he'd been unfaithful to her daughter in thought if not in deed. Given that he must have known how paranoid Fleur was, he probably still felt some residual guilt. He'd be telling himself that this was not the time, he was only waiting for a more appropriate moment. Besides all that, there was Lindsay. Right beside him much of the time, she evidently looked on him as 'hers' for the duration, and I had a fair idea he was well aware of this.

I told myself all this, and half of me believed it. The other half was saying, *Believe it, then, if it makes you happy.*

Just don't discount the possibility that it's fantasy-wish projec-
tion, which is psycho-babble for wishful thinking. And we
know someone else who's been indulging in that lately, don't
we?

The little matter of Lindsay and Neil was a minor distraction. I was far more aware now of her manner towards him,
and vice versa. Nobody would have guessed a thing. She
certainly didn't deliberately avoid him; she was casually
bright, with just a tinge of the lemon juice Lindsay was
known for anyway. To her he was pleasant with very slightly
wry nuances I'd never have picked up if I hadn't known.
He didn't seek her out; in fact I spoke to him far more.
During a second snatch of conversation I found myself
thinking that if I'd only just met him, I'd be wondering
where the catch was. Any full-of-himself stuff was toned
down, and his short speech made no allusions to anyone
'getting caught'.

But a good part of the do, for me, was spent chasing
Robbie. When he wasn't spilling Coke he was disappearing
altogether with his new friend Joe. After one frantic, ten-
minute hunt I found them playing Knock Down Ginger
on the first-floor garden rooms: knocking on doors and
running away.

After Rachel and David left, for a late-afternoon flight to
St Lucia, there was a general drift back into swimsuits and
on to the beach. With a few others, Uncle Matthew took
Robbie off for a ride on the banana, a yellow inflatable
towed behind a speedboat.

I swam to the raft, where Lindsay was flaked out in the
gold of the sinking sun. It was the first time we'd been
alone since the morning.

We watched the banana zoom past about fifty yards out.
There were a lot of shrieks and yells as the banana-goers

bounced up and down, trying to tip themselves off. 'Just look at them,' said Lindsay. 'Talk about a load of big kids. I bet they were all dying for an excuse to go on that thing.'

I wished I were on it myself, right behind Guy, but Uncle Matthew had gathered enough volunteers before I even found out. I think he was trying to give me a little break, bless him.

But Lindsay's mind was elsewhere. 'I expect you're panting for Part Two?'

'Part Three, actually.' I stretched my legs out in the sun. 'But I do seem to recall you telling me before that you gave him a little late-night nibble.'

'I did!' With a hollow little laugh she clasped her arms around her knees. 'Suddenly it was just us – everybody else gone, Cara in bed . . . It was nearly four o'clock by then, and well . . .'

'You don't have to spell it out.' Both a bit the worse for wear, chemistry suddenly fizzing all over the place . . .

'It was as if somebody had suddenly taken a lid off a pan. One minute we were talking and I was making him beans on toast – the next we were at it like a pair of ferrets.'

She paused. The boat was zooming past again, and the banana-goers had just bounced themselves off. A lot of hilarity was echoing across the water.

While I watched Guy haul life-jacketed Robbie back on board, Lindsay went on. 'When I woke up there he was, still asleep, looking all rumpled and unshaven but rather sweet all the same. I thought: Bugger it, why do you have to be going away?'

There was a long pause. 'And then he woke up. He looked at me all fuzzy for a moment, but then he smiled and said, "Hi." And I said, "So when can I come and see you in Singapore, then?" I was just being a little bit wicked, I swear. It was a wind-up, until I saw his face.'

I was cringing in advance.

'That "Oh, Christ" expression, you know,' she went on, her voice faltering slightly just at the memory. 'And I wasn't quick enough to hide my reaction. He actually said it then. He said, "Look, I'm sorry, I thought it was just a bit of fun."'

'Oh, Lindsay . . .'

'The thing is, it *was* just a bit of fun until then. I felt so stupid, I went the other way. I laughed. I said, "It *was*! Marginally better fun than my Jolly Pink Giant, especially when his batteries are flat."'

I made a wincey face.

'I know,' she sighed. 'He really knew he'd upset me then – there was "Oh, Christ" all over his face. So I said, "I'm going for a shower," and left him. And while I was still in the bathroom Rachel and David came to clear up – thank God he was out of my room by then – and that was it. I managed to get him alone long enough to say that I'd appreciate it if he didn't share it with David, and he got all stroppy and said what the hell did I take him for? So I said, "A passable shag, if you really want to know," and gave myself away all over again.'

She gave a hollow little laugh. '*Hell hath no fury . . .*'

'I don't think even the old Bard would call that "fury". But if it's any consolation, I'd never have guessed. I thought you just weren't mad keen.'

'Part of me hates him. He sent a postcard about two weeks later. To me and Rachel. It said, "Thanks for the bed, I had a great time, Neil."'

'He'd probably have sent that anyway.'

'I know, but it felt like double-speak.'

I watched the banana zoom into the next bay. Another speedboat buzzed past, towing the kind of skier that makes it look dead easy to do one-hand turns with a shoulder brushing the water. The raft rocked gently in the boat's wake.

'I'd almost put him out of my head until this wedding was on the agenda,' Lindsay went on. 'I always knew he was probably going to be Best Man, but a normal wedding, just a day, wouldn't have bothered me. And you know the worst thing?'

'What?'

'He phoned, about three weeks ago. Ostensibly it was to ask about presents, but then he said, "I gather you're not bringing anyone to this wedding." So I said, no, I wasn't. And he said, "Neither am I. Maybe we could do dinner or something."' She paused. '*Or something!* "You'll be up for another shag," in other words.'

'Maybe it was just a figure of speech.'

'Abby, you didn't hear him. I swear it would have sounded more romantic coming from Robbie.'

'So what did you say?'

'What d'you think? "I don't think so, thanks." As if the mere thought made me yawn.'

To stave off a post-wedding anticlimax, Uncle Mathew had booked an en masse meal that night, in a cliff-top restaurant. For the following day he'd also booked the entire party on the Jolly Roger pirate cruise. We danced on deck to island rhythms that were still pounding in your blood twelve hours later; we walked the plank that said *Dead Men Tell No Tales;* we swung off ropes into clear, aquamarine water. It was a corny riot. Robbie was in Pirate Heaven.

We didn't get back till late afternoon, and from that evening the party formed into loose groups. The two couples who were friends of David's were one such, with Neil, as he knew them from before. The two couples who were friends of Rachel's formed another. The assorted parents made a third.

And then there was us: Guy and Lindsay, me and Robbie.

We went sailing together, skimming in the trade-wind breeze up and down the coast. Like the others, we hired a mini-moke for trips out, but since Robbie grumped at the mere suggestion of leaving the beach and pool, it had still barely left the car park by Wednesday evening. Through all this Guy was nice and friendly and chilled. He was everything I could wish, except for one thing. Whatever was there, and I knew something was, it was lurking under a surface of relaxed, sun-warmed foursome.

But we were never alone. As his body-clock adjusted Robbie started sleeping later, and when he did wake he was bursting for breakfast, so there were no more early-morning strolls along the beach. During the day there was always Robbie or Lindsay, and very often both; or one or two or three of the others; or a beach vendor or jet-ski operator, or the pool bar waiter coming to say Robbie had signed for a Coke, what was my room number, please?

Whenever I got my sun cream out, hoping for a repeat of before, Lindsay said, 'Here, let me . . .' During pre-dinner drinks there were always others in the bar, and during dinner there were always the assorted parents, and a few of the others as well. I thought of sitting on my terrace late at night, but after being on the go all day I knew I'd probably fall asleep anyway. Which might be all very well, but I had a horror of him finding me zonked in a chair with my mouth open. Dribbling.

Still, there was the odd, delicious crumb to savour. Towards sunset on the Wednesday, with the sea so flat and golden-calm, I couldn't resist some very expensive water-skiing, he came on the boat to 'spot' and make sure Robbie didn't fall overboard.

Somewhat out of practice, I was a mite nervous as I slid my front foot into the binding of a beautiful pro ski and fastened the Velcro on the gloves. With Guy watching from the back of the boat I was wondering whether I'd even get up first time.

'Ready?' called the driver.

I gave the thumbs-up. The line went taut.

Oh joy. Up first time like a cork, and although I did some of my best-ever turns in a lovely, swinging rhythm, I didn't feel once as if I'd leant just a bit too far.

At the end of fifteen minutes, though, I felt the lack of practice in my arms and shoulders. As the boat wheeled around to pick me up the strain had left them fit for nothing, certainly not for clambering back in.

Not that I'd have tried anyway. Leaning over the side, Guy popped me out of the water as if I weighed no more than Robbie, and believe me, hauling any adult into a boat takes serious muscle.

The brief, wet contact was delicious, even with that pesky lifejacket in the way. 'I'm impressed,' he said, as I unbuckled it. 'I'm not sure I dare follow that.'

But he did, and I was glad he wasn't intimidated. If there's one thing that gets right up my nose, it's a man who sulks because you can do something better.

I thought of enlisting Lindsay, but she had blinkers on where Guy and I were concerned. Because she wasn't looking, she just hadn't 'seen' anything. She'd hide it, of course, but in the Neil-circumstances I had a feeling her first, gut reaction would hold echoes of the playground: *You can't play kiss-chase with him! He's MY friend!* She'd then feel bad and over-compensate. She'd be just a bit too obvious in taking Robbie off, so we could be alone. He'd know exactly why she'd done it and think we'd been conspiring. She might even have a word with him, having sworn she wouldn't, and I didn't want that either.

I yearned for just half an hour. No Robbie. No Lindsay.

No anybody else. Just Guy, me and the right moment. The oxygen of opportunity, with a box of matches thrown in and no liquid sunshine whatsoever.

By the Thursday afternoon, I was beginning to think I had more chance of finding a Caribbean iceberg.

Thirty-three

The day did not begin well. Robbie was so noisy and cheeky during breakfast that even Guy told him tersely to pack it in, and Lindsay was doing her best to suppress her irritation. She'd been vaguely irritable the previous evening, but as she suffered from it anyway I'd put it down to PMT.

Tense and irritated with Robbie myself, I urged them to take a trip out. 'At this rate we'll have hired that moke for nothing. No, I'm not coming,' I added firmly, as they started to argue. 'Sightseeing and Robbie just don't go – he'll only be bored and whiny. If you two don't get to see anything of the island I'll only feel bad.'

They left with no further argument, and I was glad to see the back of them. I was even glad to see the back of Guy. It was part of the devious plan I'd hatched over breakfast. If Robbie was going to be horrible, I didn't want to see irritation building up all day, especially not from Guy. By the time he and Lindsay returned, around Happy Hour with a bit of luck, I'd have worn the little horror out completely. I'd leave him with the babysitter I'd already booked, as we were eating out that night, at a seafood place on the south coast. And after that dinner I'd contrive something with Guy, somehow. I was almost desperate enough to do a Lindsay: call him after we'd all gone to bed and pretend there was a massive cockroach in the bathroom. Only when he came to get rid of it, I'd tell him there was no such thing, I just had to see him alone. This strategy naturally involved a certain risk of humiliating rejection. He might run a hand awkwardly over his neck and say, 'Look, I know there was the odd vibe between us, but if it's all the same to you I'd rather stick with the status quo.'

If he did, at least I'd know. I might get on that plane miserable, but at least I wouldn't be wishing I'd had the guts to try.

Having expected Guy and Lindsay back for sunset, I was startled to see them return just as Robbie and I were finishing lunch by the pool. On the hottest day so far, we were sitting well in the shade.

'It was just too hot,' Lindsay said irritably, as they joined me at the lime sorbet stage. 'And we kept getting lost – just you try reading a map like that – it's a maze of little lanes. And Guy was doing my head in because he just *would* not stop and ask.'

'It might have helped,' said Guy tersely, 'if you'd bothered to give the map a glance now and then, instead of constantly complaining about every bloody thing.'

At that precise moment Robbie accidentally knocked his glass over, spilling half a fresh lime squash all over the table. As few drips splashed on to Lindsay's top, I saw her bite back a muttered expletive.

'Sorry,' I said, swallowing one of my own. 'I'll take him back to the room for a bit.'

Possibly twenty minutes later, while he was absorbed in the cartoon channel, I went to drape a couple of rinsed-out swimsuits over the terrace wall. I'd have been back inside in thirty seconds if I hadn't heard Lindsay's voice wafting from inside her room. Just audible, it was still decidedly tetchy.

'So what is your point, exactly?'

Guy's tense voice replied, 'My point *is*, Lindsay, that if you go out of your way to give a guy the impression that you wouldn't touch him again with a ten-foot bog-brush, you can't blame him for taking the hint.'

I'm afraid to say that going back inside didn't even occur to me.

Lindsay said, 'And just what's that supposed to mean?'

'If you really want me to spell it out, that you're pissed off with him. You want him to try it on again, just so you can tell him to sod off.'

'I don't! And I don't know why you're in a mood with *me*.'

'I am not – in a mood.' (Said with enunciated grit.)

'Yes, you are. You're in one of those trying-to-pretend-you're-not moods. You don't have to stick with me just because we came together, you know. If you want to go and chat up those lissom, oiled French girls you were eyeing up yesterday, I'm not stopping you.'

'They're Belgian.'

'Belgian, outer-bloody-Mongolian – who cares? If you're suffering from moody pressure in the gonads, then go and get your end away. At least it might lighten you up a bit.'

'Oh, for Christ's sake—'

I heard her 'front' door closing with something just under a bang.

Well.

The mention of Belgian girls didn't bother me. He hadn't been eyeing them up anymore than anybody else, and besides, I had a shrewd idea that they were the more discreet type of lesbian.

As for Neil, had I been blind?

Answer: yes. I didn't blame Lindsay for wanting a chance to tell Neil to sod off, but Guy was dead right about him taking the hint. During the past couple of days we'd hardly seen him. He and the other friends of David's had taken themselves off much of the time in a pair of rented mini-jeeps.

Guy went sailing shortly afterwards, alone. Unlike when Lindsay, Robbie and I were sitting on the flat deck, he really put his foot on the HobieCat gas this time. I watched him pick up the wind and streak up the coast with one hull at about eighty degrees to the horizontal.

He's working off something, I thought. *The nautical equivalent of kicking the cat.*

Around four, I took Robbie to snorkel around the raft. On its way to the horizon the sun was washing the beach with gold. Nobody else was there. I'd only been there two minutes when Guy skimmed back into the bay, waving as he passed about thirty feet away. As I'd been hoping for precisely this, my stomach gave a nervous little flutter. Watching him drag the boat up the beach and stop to chat with one of the watersports boys, I uttered a silent prayer to anyone who might be listening. *Please, let him stop passing the time of boaty day. Please, let him come here, while there's nobody else . . .*

And someone heard me. Guy gave Watersports that friendly 'see you, then' clap on the shoulder. My pulse started that pitty-patty stuff as he strolled to the sea and did a running dive in. Surfacing ten yards out, he flicked his head and carried on.

I had a good tan by then. It made my hot-pink bikini look even better. Propped on my elbows, I stretched my legs out and watched his lithe, easy crawl.

The raft rocked slightly as he climbed the steps. 'Hi.'

'Hi.' He flopped down about eighteen inches to my left, scattering a few droplets over me in the process.

For a moment neither of us spoke. Bathed in sun, we gazed together at the sun-washed beach. The sea was tranquil aquamarine, shot with rippling gold like Thai silk. On either side the further bays curved gently into the distance, fringed with lazy coconuts and feathery green. Quietly absorbed near-by, Robbie was singing softly and tunelessly to himself through his snorkel.

With my legs stretched out in front of me, I cast a glance at my Whisper Pink toenails. Flexing my toes back and forth, I thanked heaven I'd given myself a proper pedicure. At times like this you need to know that any parts your object of desire might have his eye on are groomed to within an inch of their cuticles.

Guy said, 'Abby, are you doing "naughty toes" again?'

His tone sent a wobbly *frisson* through me. It was that warm, jokey intimacy that only heralds one thing. 'Unconscious habit,' I said, in much the same tone. 'I was admiring the view.'

'Yes, still pretty horrible, isn't it?' He wrapped his arms around his knees. 'This time next week you'll be looking back with a shudder, thanking God you're back home.'

'Don't.' I couldn't even pretend to play along. 'I can't believe we've only got two more nights. Holiday Sod's Law, isn't it? The more you don't want to leave, the faster it goes.'

'Come on,' he chided. 'That's the half-empty attitude. Think of forty-eight more hours. Clause two of Holiday Sod's Law says the last forty-eight hours are invariably the best.'

Some warm, roughened nuance told me he was building up to something. I savoured the anticipation, the sensation of tiny hairs shivering on my skin. 'That makes it all the worse when you get on that plane.'

'All the more reason for making the most of it while you're here.'

He wasn't looking at me as he said it, but I knew he was

about to. Any second he was going to turn to me, and I was going to turn to him, and—

'Abby! I need a poo!'

Je-SUS! I turned to the popped-up face in the mask. 'For heaven's sake, Robbie, we've only just come! Why didn't you go before?'

'Because I'm just trying to annoy you, OK?'

All right, he didn't say this.

'Because I didn't need to go *then*, did I? Only now I do. Very *bad*ly.'

I couldn't keep back my exasperation. 'Trust him,' I said to Guy. 'I'll have to go.'

'No, you don't.' As I was about to get up, he caught my wrist in a firm grip. 'You can go by yourself, Robbie. You're not a baby.'

'I can't work the room key!'

'Then go to the one in reception. You know, near the entrance.'

'That's miles! I need to go *soon!*'

'I'm sorry, I'll have to take him,' I said. 'Even if he could work the room key he'd never find it in my black hole of a bag. And even if he did, he'd only drop it in the sand or lock us out.'

His own exasperation was obvious, but repressed. He let go my wrist. 'All right. You know best.'

As I was waylaid by David's mother just outside our room, it was a while before I was back on the beach. There were three people on the raft, but no sign of Guy. Swallowing my crushing sense of let-down, I went to sit by Lindsay, who was by herself on a sun bed halfway to the sea. 'What happened to Guy?' I asked, as casually as I could.

'Don't ask me. He said did I want the moke, because if not he was going out.'

My stomach contracted like a pain. 'Where?'

'How should I know? If you ask me, he was going off in a huff. He was in a mood with me earlier.'

I could hardly say I'd been listening, or that any mood was probably now down to me. A mood that came of bitten-back remarks about over-protective mollycoddling.

'And just look at her,' Lindsay went on.

She meant Kay, who was sitting by herself in a little chair designed for sitting at the edge of the water with your toes in it.

Or rather, not just by herself.

'It's positively embarrassing,' Lindsay went on in a mutter. 'I heard Dad joking to Mum yesterday, something like, "Is she hoping to get lucky, then?" and Mum got cross, but only because she was embarrassed for her.'

Obsessed with where Guy had gone, and when he'd be back, I couldn't have given a stuff whether Kay was chatting up the entire West Indies cricket team. But my eyes took her in anyway. Squatting next to her chair was one of the roving jet-ski operators who passed by now and then. These guys thought nothing of investing fifteen minutes' good-humoured chat in trying to persuade you to spend twenty dollars. Lindsay and I had christened this particular operator Lennox, as he looked rather like Lennox Lewis. And over the past couple of days he'd been investing a good deal of time in Kay, who was evidently enjoying the attention.

'I swear she actually thinks he fancies her,' Lindsay went on. 'She doesn't realise it's just a sales pitch. As for him, he probably thinks she's after a gigolo. I'm sure I saw the watersports boys having a giggle about it yesterday. I mean, just look at her!'

I had to admit, there was a slightly flirty element in her body language. You could hear it in her voice, too: that arch note of, 'You're a very naughty boy, but I like it.' More than likely he was saying things like, 'Your husband must be crazy, letting you loose all alone on Barbados.' He'd said much the same to me and Lindsay.

'Your mum would never carry on like that,' Lindsay went on. 'And neither would mine. Or David's.'

Guy, where are you? 'For God's sake, Lindsay, does it matter?'

'Abby, it's embarrassing! If Mum were here, I'd have a word. I'd get her to go and tell her to stop acting like some desperate old slapper.'

'Just as well she's not here, then.' That morning she and Uncle Matthew had taken themselves off for a two-day trip to Grenada. 'I wouldn't quite say slapper, either. Bored, well-off fifty-something who wouldn't say no, might be more like it.'

She gave a soft snort. 'Terrified-of-getting-old fifty-something might be even more like it. That's what Mum thinks. She's got a theory that Robbie didn't exactly help there, either.'

'*Robbie?*' I almost laughed. 'What on earth's he got to do with it?'

'What d'you think? Just as Kay was getting stuck into her HRT, there was Penny suddenly bursting with fertility. Blooming.'

She was. It was well after the birth that exhaustion had kicked in. 'Kay would never have wanted a baby at that age!'

'Of course she wouldn't, but all that late blooming only rubbed it in that her own hormones were coming on prescription. What's more, it was proof that your old man still fancied Penny even though they'd split up long before. Mum thinks maybe that rankled, just a bit.' She looked around. 'Where is Robbie, anyway?'

Not for the first time, or even the seventh, in the past few days, I had a panic moment. For the umpteenth time he'd done a disappearing act. One minute he was splashing in the shallows, the next he was gone.

But back within seconds. As I panic-scanned the beach, he came running from the garden side. 'Joe's in the pool! Can we go to the pool?'

I dragged him back to the beach for Happy Hour and sunset, which I absolutely refused to miss. Only there was still no sign of Guy, or Lindsay, either.

As Kirsty's Mike passed me a rum punch, I asked if they'd seen either of them.

Mike said, 'I don't know about Guy, but I think Lindsay's gone for a run. I saw her head that-a-way.' He nodded up the beach. 'She was in shorts and trainers, looking pretty businesslike.'

By the time the sun was spilling molten gold on the sea, there was still no sign of either of them. As my second rum punch went down, I could still feel that sudden, firm grip on my wrist. Only now it felt like an aching band round my heart. Why couldn't he have waited? All right, Robbie's timing was exasperating, but was that my fault? Had he really gone off in a huff on that account?

While Robbie devoured his burger and chips in the room that evening, I tried calling Lindsay's room for the second time.

Nothing. Where *was* she? I tried every room, even Kay's, but there was no answer there, either.

Minutes later, while I was drying my hair, there was a tap at the door.

It was a girl from reception, with hair in beautiful, intricate braids. She wore a pristine white blouse and an anxious expression. 'Sorry to disturb you – are you one of the wedding party?'

'Yes?'

'Are you a relative of Mrs Hammond?'

Kay. 'Yes, I'm her niece. Is anything wrong?'

I don't know why I asked. I'd already seen it on her face.

Fifteen minutes later, having charged all over the hotel looking everywhere I could think of for Lindsay, I ran up the wooden steps that led to the first-floor rooms. Sick with apprehension, I knocked on Guy's door.

After several seconds there was no reply, but I was sure he was there. Hearing faint sounds of talk radio or TV news, I knocked again. 'Please, come *on* . . .'

'What's up?'

It was Neil. Dressed for smart-casual dinner, his hair still damp, he was strolling along the wooden walkway.

'Kay's had an accident in the moke,' I said rapidly. 'The police have just been. They want a relative to go to the hospital and I can't find Lindsay anywhere – you haven't seen her, have you?'

'Not since this morning – we were over at Crane Beach.' His eyes had widened, his expression suddenly sober. 'Anything I can do? What about Robbie?'

Just as he said it, Guy opened his door at last. Dripping wet, he was still fastening a towel around his waist. 'Sorry, I was in the shower.' Even as he said it, he saw from our faces that this wasn't a social call. 'What's happened?'

I repeated what I'd just told Neil.

'Christ,' said Guy.

'She went off in the moke – I don't know what happened, but it sounds pretty bad. I thought Lindsay might just be with you.'

He shook his head. 'I haven't seen her since around four.'

'Where the hell *is* she?' I fretted. 'Mike saw her go off for a run hours ago and it's pitch dark now. Where on earth can she have got to?'

'For God's sake don't start worrying about Lindsay,' said Guy. 'She'll be chilling in a beach bar somewhere.'

'I hope so – I've been having visions of her slipping on rocks or something. Will you tell her I've had to shoot off? Thank God the babysitter's just come, so there's no problem about Robbie.'

Guy's wet face looked down at me. 'Do you want me to come with you to the hospital?'

'Would you?'

'Just give me two minutes.'

Thirty-four

Since I'd had two rum punches, he'd downed a beer from the mini-bar, and neither of us had a clue where the hospital was, we left the moke in the car park.

My stomach was in knots as we headed for Bridgetown in a heavily air-conditioned cab. As this felt freezing on my wet hair, we asked the driver to switch it off. We opened a window instead, and the warm night air rushed in.

'I'm beginning to think I'm a jinx on weddings,' I said. 'First Robbie, now this . . .'

'I don't see why you should get all the credit. It's probably me.'

I managed a sick little laugh. 'And I couldn't very well say it to the police or the hotel, but even if she's conscious, Kay's hardly going to want to see *me*.'

Feeling I shouldn't have said it, I glanced across at him in the dark back of the cab. 'Sorry, but in case you hadn't gathered, I don't enjoy Most Favoured Niece status.'

'You don't have to apologise. Even if I hadn't picked something up, Fleur told me.'

It was a relief that he knew. 'It really doesn't bother me. It's all so pathetic and ridiculous – dates back to Mum "stealing" Dad.'

'Yes, I heard about that.'

'It was Cold War for years. I suppose some of the antipathy just rubbed off on me.'

'Fleur thought there was another reason.' He paused. 'She said that when you were both kids, when she was all shy and skinny and awkward, and couldn't say a stuttered boo to a goose, you were the opposite – bouncy and outgoing. She thought her mother resented you because you were everything she thought Fleur should have been.'

My heart and stomach constricted. 'Now you're making me feel terrible.'

'Sorry.' He took my hand. 'That wasn't the idea.'

My eyes met his in the dark, his hand squeezed mine, and my heart gave a drunken little lurch. 'But I don't know about "bouncy",' I said. '"Lippy" would be more like it.'

He smiled. 'Nothing's changed there, then.'

I don't know a few little words like that can have 'this is it' written all over them, but they did. I just knew, and a wave of 'at last' washed over me.

'I'm glad you wanted me to come,' he said.

His warm, slightly husky tones only made my own voice wobble around the edges. 'Of course I did, you dope.'

There was a moment of that warm, lovely silence where you both absorb relief-making truths. 'I wasn't taking anything for granted,' he said at last. 'And it's been a hell of an arse the past few days. People, people everywhere . . .'

'You said it. I was beginning to think I'd have to call you in the dead of night, pretending there was a giant *daddy-long-legs scaryus* in the bathroom.'

He laughed softly. 'If I hadn't thought you'd only trash the place getting rid of it yourself, I'd have planted one.'

'I wish you had.'

For a moment there was nothing but that moment where you both drown in each other's eyes. He ran a fingertip down my cheek. Then, at last, came that heart-stopping moment where eyes drop to mouths . . .

My head turned to swimming wooze. It was a gorgeous,

323

tantalising little starter of a kiss; warm, firm and tender, and full of promise. However, with the cab driver right in front, it didn't progress any further.

I didn't care. It would keep. As I sat back with his arm newly curled around me, everything felt warm and 'right' and lovely – until I remembered why we were in that cab. Who'd have thought Kay would provide the oxygen? And what would she think if she knew?

Then I felt terrible to be having such horrible-person thoughts when she was lying in hospital in God alone knew what sort of a state. All they'd told me was 'cuts and fractures, and possible internal injuries'.

'I feel awful,' I confessed, as warm air wafted through the window. 'I feel I should be experiencing a rush of something for Kay, but I don't. I do feel bad for her, and terrible for Fleur and Uncle James when they'll be so worried, but I feel like a complete hypocrite, zooming off to the hospital as if I love her. As if she were some lovely auntie who was always sweet to me at birthday parties.'

'You're not a hypocrite.' Taking my left hand in his own, he gave it a little squeeze before resting both on his thigh. 'What else could you do?'

We talked of other things for the rest of the journey, much of it relating to Lindsay and Neil. Sounds and smells of the tropical night wafted in through the windows: tree frogs, hooting horns and music from bars we passed, all on soft, humid air that smelt of damp earth, growing things, and whiffs of food from roadside stalls.

We were met at the hospital by reassuring calm in lilting Bajan accents. It could have been a lot worse. She had a broken arm, a couple of broken ribs, concussion and cuts and bruises, but nothing more serious. No, nobody else had been badly hurt. She was woozy but conscious – would I like to see her?

Leaving Guy in the waiting room, I went in. And whatever I hadn't felt for her before, at least part of it hit me now. She looked pathetic and diminished. Quite apart from the arm and ribs, there were cuts to her face and head. Part of her hair had been shaved away.

I think she was half asleep, but her eyes opened when I approached.

I knew she'd hate me seeing her like this. 'How are you feeling?' I whispered.

Her eyes closed. Tears trickled from their corners.

'Is there anything you want?' I asked. 'I can bring anything tomorrow.'

'I want James,' she said. 'Tell James I want him.'

'Of course! I'll call him as soon as I get back. '

As there seemed no point in staying any longer, I returned to the waiting room.

Guy, meanwhile, had been calling the hotel. 'I spoke to Kirsty,' he said. 'Lindsay's turned up – she's on her way.'

We waited until she arrived, looking distraught. I'd hardly given an update when she said, 'It's all my fault.' Taking a seat, she looked at me. 'She came and sat next to me after you'd gone. I wasn't in the mood for talking anyway, let alone when she started on about Fleur, she was off to Tuscany with Scott, he was so *charm*ing, wasn't it nice that she was back with him? I swear she hasn't a clue why Fleur dumped him before – I really had to bite my tongue. She even managed to imply that you' – she looked up at Guy – 'were just a very second-best blip.'

'No skin off my nose,' said Guy.

'That's just Kay,' I said. 'Anything connected to her always has to be best.'

'Well, it was skin off *my* nose – it made me so mad, I really had to swallow my tongue. So when she finally started on about jet-ski Lennox – didn't I think he was attractive, and so re*mark*ably persistent? – she might just give it a twirl after all – I really opened my big mouth.'

'Oh, Lindsay.' I winced. 'You didn't.'

'I did.' To Guy she added, 'She was doing the flirty bit with him earlier. So I said something like, "Yes, well just watch out that he doesn't think you're willing to pay for more than his jet-ski."'

I winced again.

'She said, "Just what's that supposed to mean?" and I said, "Well, if you carry on flirting with him like that, that's what he's going to think." '

Guy said, 'Christ, Lindsay . . .'

She turned on him. 'Don't you think I feel bad enough? She just went off without a word – how was I to know she was going to go off in the moke when she was upset?'

He put an arm around her and gave her a squeeze. 'I'm sorry.'

'No, you're right.' She wiped a guilty tear from her eye. 'I should never have said it, especially given what I wasn't supposed to know.'

'What?' I said.

'Uncle James has left her.'

'*What?*'

'He has. Only a couple of weeks ago. She'd been very naughty with her tasty young landscape gardener, and not as discreet about it as she'd thought. Apparently one of the neighbours sussed something out – there were whispers around the golf club and Uncle James found out. He said he wasn't going to be made a fool of any more, and moved out.'

I could scarcely take it in.

Lindsay took a sip of my own tepid coffee. 'She was devastated, according to Mum. She'd never thought he'd find out, let alone leave her. She said it was just a bit of fun and excitement. She thought Uncle James would come back in a couple of days, he was just trying to make a point, but he hasn't. She can't bear the thought of all their friends finding out he's left her on account of a bit on the side with Landscape Joss.'

'Christ,' said Guy, tossing his plastic cup into the bin. 'Lady Chatterley has a hell of a lot to answer for.'

'But nobody's supposed to know,' Lindsay went on. 'So you two don't, either, OK? She's been hoping to sort it out before anyone else finds out.'

'But she's surely told Fleur?' I asked.

'I expect so, but I can't very well ask when I'm not supposed to know.'

She gave one of those guilty, appalled little laughs you can't help, however much you try. 'Dad's been making the most awful jokes about "earthy garden tools". And Mum's been saying, "Matthew!" and trying not to laugh.'

I'm afraid there was general mirth then, though of the guiltily stifled variety.

Only then did I remember what Kay had said. 'I asked her if there was anything she wanted. And all she said was, "James."'

Lindsay put her face in her hands. 'Oh, God . . .'

We took a cab together. As it was big enough to take three in the back, I sat in the middle, with Guy on my left. Lacing his fingers through my own, he tucked my hand between his right thigh and my left. In the circumstances maybe I shouldn't have felt such a lovely tingly glow, but it was a G-force I couldn't resist. I was thinking of how easily it could have been me feeling bad now instead of Lindsay. I was thinking of the other day; of all the things I might have said. What if I'd told her that for years Andrew had referred to her as the Witch of West Wittering? What if I'd said Dad had at least had the great good taste to prefer Mum, God knew what Uncle James saw in her, it would just serve her right if he went off with a twenty-two-year-old bimbo?

What if she'd gone off in the moke after that lot?

'We'll need to sort out her insurance,' I said. 'Quite apart from medical bills she'll never be able to leave on Saturday now.'

'And somebody needs to call Fleur,' said Guy. 'It's probably best if she tells her old man.'

'I'll do the phoning,' said Lindsay. 'As it was partly my fault.'

'No, it wasn't,' said Guy. 'So stop beating yourself up about it.'

'Where were you, anyway?' I asked her. 'You were gone hours.'

'I just had to get away.' She sighed. 'I ran up the beach till I was shattered. Then I sat down in the sand and a Rasta beach vendor came by, offering jewellery and ganja.' She gave a little laugh so hollow, it was almost vacuum-packed. 'I could have done with some of that, only I hadn't got any money on me. There was quite a nice haematite necklace, too. I told him if he came by the hotel tomorrow, I'd buy it. We ended up talking, and he was so chilled and funny we were still there when the sun went down. He said he'd walk back with me in case anybody else waylaid me, and get the bus by the hotel.'

She paused. 'But when we were still about half a mile away, guess who we bumped into?'

I had a flash-insight moment. 'Not Neil?'

'How did you know? Apparently he'd come to check that I wasn't crawling back with a broken ankle. And to tell me about Kay, of course.'

'So you told him to sod off?' said Guy.

She put on a sheepish, slightly defensive tone. 'I wouldn't exactly say that. It *was* rather sweet of him to worry.'

'We'll take that as a no, then,' I said.

Guy gave my hand a conspiratorial little squeeze. 'Hallelujah. Because quite frankly, Lindsay, you were starting to do my head in.'

She returned his good-natured tone with much the same. 'And you can bugger off, too.'

Biting back a laugh, I turned to Guy. 'Where were you, anyway? You were gone for hours, too.'

'I nipped down to the airport. I'm only wait-listed for Saturday so I thought I'd put some personal pressure on. And on another purely practical note,' he added, 'by the time we get back, we'll have missed dinner.'

'I'm not hungry,' said the evidently preoccupied Lindsay.

'Well, I am,' he said.

I said, 'Me too.'

We stopped at a pizza place, not far from the hotel. They came in small, medium and ridiculous, so we got a ridiculous with everything and loaded it back into the cab.

It was only when we were on the road again that Lindsay picked up something at last. Her eyes widened. 'Excuse me, are you two holding hands?'

I felt Guy's suppressed chuckle through my own shoulder. 'Afraid so,' I said.

Her dumbfounded expression was a picture. 'Since when?'

Guy's thumb moved over the back of my hand in a gentle caress. 'It's been coming on for some time.'

She gave an incredulous little laugh. 'You cagey devils!'

'You can talk,' I said. 'What about Neil?'

'That's *diff*erent!' But she did laugh. 'Right, I'm going to sulk now.'

Back at the hotel, most of the party was in the open bar

329

next to reception, waiting for news. Guy and I got away after a few minutes and took the pizza back to my room. We found Robbie fast asleep and after I'd paid the babysitter we took the pizza and a couple of beers from the mini-bar on to the terrace.

Oddly enough, now that we were alone at last, there seemed to be no mad rush. I felt no need to fall instantly into his arms. It would be all the better for waiting, and besides, the pizza would be stone cold.

The air outside was warm and soft. The Tree Frog Singers were doing their usual stuff, backed by Wavelets On The Sand. I wished I could buy a CD of them to take home.

'You do realise,' I said, as we opened the 'ridiculous' pizza carton, 'that we haven't even got a knife to cut it with?'

'Fuck it,' he said. 'I'll tear it apart with my bare hands.'

We looked at each other and laughed.

But only for a moment.

Thirty-five

We came together like a couple of those magnets you learn about in physics, but there was no frantic, fast-food gobbling. There was another heart-stopping little starter, but this time we had the main course, too.

I know I'm prejudiced, but I defy any Michel Roux of kissery to come up with a better entrée. He knew exactly what to do with kissing equipment, and I think I demonstrated my own first-class training, too.

But there comes a point in a gourmet kiss like this when too much could make you uncomfortable, especially when you know there isn't going to be anything off the pudding trolley. The increasing quivering heat and tension in his body matched my own, but with Robbie sleeping only feet away we both knew anything more wasn't on just now.

'Don't take this the wrong way,' he said, as we finally drew apart, 'but if I could safely magic Robbie away for the next twenty-four hours . . .'

The warm, rough edge to his voice only doubled what I was already feeling. Just as I was keeping mine, I knew he was keeping his lovely inner rampant beast firmly on the leash. 'You think I wouldn't?'

Locking his arms around my waist, he looked down at me. 'So where could we magic him to?'

'Chessington. With a couple of minders to take him on all the rides.'

'Brilliant.' He dropped a little kiss on my forehead. 'Send me the bill.'

I laughed, and kissed him. 'Come on,' I said. 'Pizza.'

No matter how exquisite the food or fine the wines, I wouldn't have changed that meal for any other venue. Second course and liqueurs consisted of KitKats and a couple of cognacs from the mini-bar.

With our chairs pushed as close together as they'd go, we sat afterwards, hand in hand, talking lovely rubbish, drinking in each other and the shimmering sea. But eventually he turned to me with a slightly different tone to his voice. 'It was weird, you know. When I saw Lindsay a couple of weeks back I'd just been thinking about you. I'd been thinking about you a hell of a lot. And then she told me you were coming here.'

My heart turned over. 'I bet you say that to all the girls you pick up at weddings.'

He laughed softly, and his hand tightened on my own. 'Only then all the Neil business came out and it got complicated. She was in such a state about him, I couldn't say, "Sorry, you'll have to be a spare part anyway, I'm hoping to be otherwise engaged."'

I had to ask. 'What did you think when you got my very rude email?'

It was a moment before he answered. 'I thought: Well, that solves that one. Just get her out of your head. She was too far away anyway.' He paused. 'And whenever I had second thoughts later, I told myself it just wasn't on, I couldn't handle any more abuse from Little Ted.'

I swallowed a laugh. 'Sorry about that. He's getting very grumpy in his old age. Teds are like dogs, you know. One year of ours is worth seven of theirs.'

He glanced back at the curtained sliding doors. 'I hope he's not the jealous type.'

I took another sip of cognac. If I hadn't been warm inside already, it would have turned up the thermostat nicely. 'I didn't bring him.'

'Don't tell me you've left him Home Alone?'

'He's got Jeff. In any case, he doesn't like flying.' I remembered what he'd said before. 'Have you still got Jumbo?'

'No, he went to the tip when I was about fifteen.'

I didn't have to fake shock. 'Guy, how *could* you?'

'It wasn't me. My stepmother was having a clear-out. It wasn't her fault,' he added. 'I'd been pretending I was far too cool to give a toss, so she wasn't to know.'

'I don't care, it's still cruel.'

He laughed softly.

We sat out there until the small hours, talking. He told me about his father and stepmother moving to Dorset, and now spending half the year in Florida. He didn't see them often any more. I told him about when Dad had left for Tina, and how Andrew had heard Mum crying in the night, and crept into my room to tell me. He told me about a colossal row with his father after failing one of his A levels, how he'd refused to subsidise him any further, and how it had come as a hell of a shock to do retakes and earn his own money at the same time.

We talked about trivia, too. We talked about everything, until he finally checked his watch. 'If you don't tell me to clear off soon, you'll be fit for nothing in the morning.'

I hated to see him go, but he was right. I didn't want to be shattered for our last full day. 'Go on, then. Before I change my mind.'

His goodnight kiss was soft and tender: nothing to make it more difficult than it already would be for either of us to sleep peacefully. 'Call me the moment Robbie wakes you up, all right?'

'Even if it's six-thirty?'
'Even if it's six.'
I was out like a light.

After an early breakfast with the little devil, who was in a little-angel mood for a change, we went for a wander along the beach. On the way back we met Neil and Lindsay, and I have to say she wore that pleased-with-herself look that only comes from one thing.

'About time too,' Guy murmured, after they'd passed. 'I know it wasn't the greatest start in the world, but he doesn't strike me as a bad sort of bloke.'

Lindsay had called Fleur, who was going to tell her father. Lindsay went back to the hospital and found Kay fretful and uncomfortable. Lindsay had apologised for her remarks, blaming them entirely on a bad case of PMT and the fact that she rather fancied Lennox herself.

Her Rasta friend passed by the beach later, and she bought that necklace. I bought a shark's tooth on a leather thong for Robbie, who thought it the coolest thing since PlayStation. With a present for Mum in mind, he then chose a necklace of pink shells that might have looked all very well on a hula-hula girl in a grass skirt. I tried to steer him towards something that wouldn't look completely out of place in Sycamore Road, but his mind was made up. It was miles nicer than any of Mummy's other boring old necklaces – she'd love it.

I gave in. She'd love it anyway, just because he'd chosen it himself.

That night was our last. And much as we'd have liked to eat somewhere romantic, alone, there was David's mother, left spare now AK was in hospital. In the end nine of us ended up at that seafood place on the south coast, on a tiny bay lit with lights like a string of golden pearls.

Afterwards, Guy and I strolled the beach. Leaving our shoes in the soft sand, we walked where the wavelets just lapped our feet. I was trying to imprint the whole thing on my memory: the shimmering wedge of moonlight on the water, the squish of wet sand between my toes; the sounds of soft steel band coming from somewhere up the beach. The lamps hung high in the trees; the little crabs that scuttled across the wet sand. The fallen frangipani blossom Guy tucked behind my ear. And above all, the *shish* of the sea and the tree frogs, with our arms around each other.

In the middle of the secluded bay around the corner, we stopped. Here there was no light but moon and stars, nobody to see us but the crabs. Standing against the trunk of a casuarina tree, Guy held me with my back against him, his arms locked under my breasts. 'Skinny-dip Bay, I think,' he said, as we gazed at the water. 'If you want to give it a go, feel free to use my shirt for a towel.'

Now we were here, with his chest firm against my back, my arms folded over his own, and his warm, male scent whispering to me, I'd rather gone off it. 'I hate to be chicken – I know there aren't supposed to be any nasties here – but after all that Death By Jaws I'm not mad keen. That water looks black enough for anything to be lurking in it.'

He chuckled, nuzzling his lips against my hair. 'Thank God for that.'

'Have you got a *Jaws* thing, too?'

'No, but I do like to see where the coral is. It's not much fun scraping yourself to ribbons on – look! Did you see that?'

It was a shooting star, falling in a swift, bright arc. 'Well, that should be a cue for something,' he said.

I turned around. He drew me close, my arms slid around his neck, and with no one but the crabs to see us, the kiss that followed turned into rather more of a main course than the night before. As his fingers caressed the side curves of my breasts under the soft silk, it was like letting the brakes off. His own condition was increasingly obvious, and it only inflamed my own.

Eventually we came apart, trembly and with racing hearts. 'We could go to your room,' I whispered. 'The babysitter should be all right for another hour.'

'But you'd only have to go afterwards.' Drawing back, he brushed a wisp of hair from my face. 'Having waited this long, I'd like to wake up and find you still there in the morning.'

For a moment I couldn't utter. A lump came to my throat. 'That's the most romantic thing anyone's ever said to me.'

'Then I must be doing something right at last.'

We kissed again, and despite what he'd said, this got out of hand, too. In fact, it got to the stage when I began to think the gritty and over-rated business of doing it in the sand had a good deal to recommend it.

Just as I was starting to think I really couldn't take much more of this, he slipped a hand down the waist of my skirt. My heart almost stopped as he slid it down over my stomach, and into the filmy scrap of my thong.

He barely had to touch me. It was instant and explosive. I gasped and shuddered, holding tight to him as my thumping heartbeat died down.

He kissed the top of my hair. 'Just a little something to be going on with.'

But it wasn't fair. I didn't say it, but I moved my hand gently down.

'No,' he said, moving it equally gently away. 'It'll keep.'

Hang on to this one, said my inner wise woman. *You don't get too many of these to the kilo.*

I almost prayed for rain next morning. I'd have liked non-stop sheets of cats and tree frogs, so that it wouldn't be such a wrench to leave. It just wasn't the same, getting up in the knowledge that you wouldn't be here tomorrow morning; you wouldn't be there for the sunset and the Tree Frog Singers; you'd have to get off the beach by two, to throw sandy things into your case and get in a cab by three.

Far worse than all this was the thought of parting with Guy. His flight was a good two hours later. I couldn't bear to think of driving away; of feeling sick and bereft as I waved at him from the window; of queuing at check-in and sitting on that cramped, smelly plane without him. I dragged myself off the beach at the last possible moment, stood under the shower for two minutes, and threw the last wet, sandy items into my bag.

He strolled into reception while I was paying my bill.

'Ready to go?'

'*I* don't *want* to go,' grumped Robbie, dressed in his shark's tooth and Jolly Roger T-shirt. 'Why can't we stay a few more days?'

'Because we can't,' I snapped. 'So stop moaning, will you?'

The cab was already there. As I stuffed my credit card back into my purse, Guy picked my case up. 'Come on, then. No sense in hanging about.'

He dumped it on the forecourt for the driver, who loaded it in. 'Is that it, dear?'

'Yes,' I said.

'No,' said Guy. 'Hang on while I get mine . . .'

I gaped as he went off and came back with a leather

337

grip. 'You're not coming now? You'll have to hang around the airport for ages!'

'No, I won't.' He slipped an arm around my waist and kissed me. 'I changed my flight.'

'You *what*?'

But since Lindsay and the others had come to say goodbye, he didn't explain until we were on our way. Lindsay knew, of course. She wore that knowing little grin as she kissed me goodbye, and gave me a thumbs-up as we finally left. I waved until they were all out of sight.

In the back of the cab, Guy took my hand. 'I'm afraid I told you a little porkie the other day. I did go to the airport, but not because I was wait-listed.'

'This is extremely serious,' I said, deadpan. 'I'm not sure I can share a cab with a teller of porkies.'

'Oh, come on. It was a case of desperate measures. I was beginning to think the only way I was going to get more than two minutes alone with you was on a night flight. After a certain other little party crashes out.'

It was very funny how leaving suddenly didn't seem too bad at all. 'How devious can you get?'

His eyes held a wicked, delicious little glint. 'Yes, I thought it was pretty good myself.'

'I shall have to exact a very stiff penalty for this,' I said, kissing him. 'Just you wait.'

Robbie's nose was pressed up against the window. 'I'm glad Guy's coming with us, because it's really *bor*ing with just you. He'll be able to play Go Fishing with me all the way.'

They did play cards, but the little devil crashed out soon after dinner. There were some passable movies on the menu, but my headset and Guy's stayed in their wrappings. While most of the plane slept, we talked softly until I fell asleep with my head on his shoulder.

Arriving on a reasonably bright morning, we took a cab to Sycamore Road. As I had work the next morning I had to give Robbie back. I was supposed to be picking Mum up from Gatwick some time that evening, but as Jean had had the tickets and she didn't know precise flight details, she'd said she'd leave a message on the answerphone. The first thing I did was check.

Hello, I hope you've had a lovely time. Don't bother meeting me, you'll be far too tired after a night flight. I'll just get a taxi or something.

'Or *some*thing?' I echoed to Guy. 'Why didn't she say? She'll fag home on the train, I bet. She's just being awkward.'

'Come on, Miss Pot,' he said. 'That's no way to speak about your Kettle.'

I called flight enquiries anyway, but since I didn't know which airline or the arrival time within four hours, I didn't get very far.

After little sleep Guy and I were feeling slightly limp by then, but going to bed with Robbie let loose on electric sockets was not an option. Guy stayed with him while I showered. I came down in some old tracky bottoms and a sweatshirt I kept at Mum's, combing my wet hair. Guy and Robbie were watching *Finding Nemo*.

I urged Guy to go up and get his head down, but all he did was shower and shave. I made breakfast, unpacked Robbie's things and put some washing on. We took Robbie to kick a football in the park, and afterwards I lay on the sofa with my head in Guy's lap, while Robbie watched *Beyblades*.

The next thing I knew, Robbie was shaking my shoulder. 'Wake up! Mummy's here!'

Coming groggily out of a deep sleep, I found Guy had crashed out, too.

Robbie rushed to the door, still in the Jolly Roger T-shirt

he probably wouldn't change out of for a week. As the door opened, I heard his excited voice from the hall. 'Look what I got! We went on a pirate ship and walked the plank and everything!'

'Well, you lucky duck! Haven't you got a kiss for me?'

'OK.' There was a minute pause. 'Who's *he*?'

Thirty-six

'Oh, that's Alan, he's just bringing the bags . . .'

Staggering groggily to the window, I saw a strange man unloading bags from a strange car on the drive.

I then made my dopey way to the hall, where Mum wore a rosy tan and a smile. 'Goodness, aren't you brown! Did you have a lovely time? This is Alan, by the way.'

Strange Man had just deposited her suitcase in the hall. 'Alan *Rich*ardson,' she explained. 'Jean Richardson's brother. I knew him years ago, of course. Alan, this is Abby.'

Alan looked like an advertisement for early retirement while you're still vigorous enough to spend your children's inheritance on the good life. On golfing holidays in the Algarve and cases of wine from the *Telegraph* wine club. At the same time he also looked like an advertisement for the type of jolly, youngish grandfather who'd still take the kids on the Vampire Ride at Chessington.

He offered a hand and the heartier type of smile. 'Hello, Abby. I've heard all about you.'

'Er, how do you do? Lovely to meet you – I'm sorry, I'm afraid I'm a bit half asleep . . .'

'Guy's here, too,' Robbie informed Mum. 'I think he's sort of Abby's boyfriend now. I saw them kissing in the park. Have you got a present for me? I've got a *really* nice one for you.'

* * *

It was a while before I got Mum alone, in the kitchen. By then I'd woken up properly, and Robbie's shells had been fastened around her neck. There had been exclamations of, 'Ooh, how *lovely*!' in the hall mirror, and Robbie had gone all pink with gratification that she appreciated his excellent taste.

'I thought it was going to be just you and Jean!' I said. 'Why didn't you tell me there were going to be four of you?'

She was loading washing into the machine. 'Because I wasn't sure, was I? Jean did say she might get a couple of others along – as the chalet sleeps five it would have been a shame not to – but I didn't know until I got to the airport.'

I said, 'Well, he seems very nice.'

Busily stuffing laundry, she was trying to hide a slight flush, but I certainly wasn't going to comment.

'He is,' she said. 'Heavens, just look at the state of these shorts! I always did think he was rather nice, but he must have been seeing Barbara from when he was about sixteen. Jean said it hit him very hard when she died, poor man.'

'How long ago was that?'

'Four or five years now.'

At this point Pudding came through her cat-flap.

Mum went to greet her, but as usual when her slave had had the temerity to go away and leave her to be fed by the neighbours, Pudding wasn't having it. Turning a disdainful, quivery tail, she stalked off to her bed in the utility room.

'Oh, well.' Mum turned to me. 'But what's all this with you and Guy?'

'There isn't any "all this" – it's hardly started. Anyway, I've got some other news for you.'

I told her about Kay's accident, and Uncle James and the landscape gardener, with the caveat that I wasn't supposed to know, so if she let it out she was dead.

By then she was sufficiently dumbfounded to have sat at the kitchen table. 'Heaven help me. So who's with her now?'

'Rosemary's staying on.'

'Well, poor Kay. Not that I'm going to pretend I feel sorry for her over James – she always did take him for granted. The nice, devoted fixture who paid the bills and never even looked at anyone else. This might just open her eyes a bit. At least it might make her remember how quietly satisfied she felt when Daddy finally left me.'

'Oh, Mum. Can't you let all that under the bridge now?'

'It's all very well for you to say that, Abby. It felt as if her curse had come home to roost, after all.'

'*Curse?*' I gave an incredulous little laugh. 'Come on, even Kay can't do curses.'

'All right, but it felt like one at the time.' She went back to loading the washing machine – an operation she'd interrupted on hearing about Kay.

'You never told me!'

'No, because it wasn't very nice.' She closed the door and straightened up. 'Fetch me the non-bio, will you?'

I fetched. 'Well?'

She poured it into the drawer and switched on. 'It was shortly before the wedding. I hadn't seen her for weeks, but she came round to "wish me joy". There was nobody else there, so she didn't have to pretend.'

'*Well?*'

She hesitated only a moment. 'She positively screamed it, Abby. "I hope you never have a minute's peace with him! I hope he takes off with the first little tart who catches his eye!"'

I felt obliged to point out the obvious. 'You know perfectly well he'd have done it anyway. You're the one who's always said that even when he's ninety-six and in a geriatric home, he'll still be eyeing up the nurses.'

'I know, Abby, but it was horrible at the time. Still, I could have forgiven her that. What I couldn't forgive was when she dragged you into it.'

'*Me?*' I did laugh then. 'I wasn't even born!'

'That didn't stop her. She screamed, "And I hope you have a daughter one day, and someone does to her what you did to me! And I hope *I* have a daughter and she's the one who does it!'

This really was a turn-up. At the same time, I was somehow barely surprised. 'Why didn't you tell me before?'

'Because it's not very nice, is it?'

There was no arguing with that.

'I know it might sound ridiculous *now*,' she went on, 'but at the time it really did sound as if she were hurling curses over your unborn cradle. Almost like the Bad Fairy in Sleeping Beauty. It's not funny, Abby,' she added, seeing my face. 'When she sent that little teddy after you were born, even Daddy joked that she'd probably put the evil eye on it.'

'Little Ted?' This really gave me a jolt. 'Are you telling me she gave me Little Ted?'

'Well, yes, bless him, but it was hardly his fault.'

Guy and I left around six, taking a cab to my flat.

Draped in his usual position on the sofa, Jeff actually raised himself to the vertical when I said, 'Do you remember Guy?'

'Just about.' He grinned. 'Hi, how's it going?'

After they'd re-met I said, 'We're just going to drop the bags and change, and then we're going out to eat.'

'Oh, right,' he said. 'In that case, I might toddle off to the South Bank. I've got a feeling there's a Buñuel on.'

We ate at a little Italian that had recently opened half a mile away. It was a lovely evening, for Southfields, though even if it had been hailing and blowing a Force Ten I'd still have been walking on squashy pink air-soles.

It was a small, intimate Italian, with the kind of waiters who know better than to hover. I'd never heard of saffron risotto being the food of love, but that was what I chose. With a nice green salad its creamy delicacy was just right, when I didn't want to be too full later. Guy had linguine with clams, and we washed it all down with what was almost the most expensive white wine on the list.

I didn't tell him about the Sleeping Beauty bit. When I was in such a lovely mood I didn't want any sourness intruding. In flickering candlelight, with lots of lovely drowning eye language, we talked about Mum and Alan, and us, and Barbados.

'You hardly saw any of the island,' he said.

'Neither did you.'

'I saw the Atlantic side. Though with Lindsay in her best "let's bitch about everything" mode, I wasn't in the best frame of mind to enjoy it.'

'Poor Lindsay,' I teased. 'She was under stress.'

'Poor Lindsay my backside. Or rather, her backside. I was hard pressed not to apply a good hard slap and dump her at a bus stop.'

I bit my lips. 'Really, Guy. That's not very nice.'

'It would have felt pretty nice at the time. I kept thinking of someone else I'd much rather have had sitting beside me. Of course, she can be awkward as cuss at times, but I could have handled that.'

'She'd have been even worse,' I pointed out. 'She'd have had a little item of baggage in the back, saying, "How much *long*er?" and, "I'm *bored*!" non-stop.'

His mouth quivered most deliciously. 'There is that.'

'Still, she's minus her little baggage at the moment.'

'So she is.' In the flickering candlelight, his eyes had

warm liquid Later written all over them. 'Shall I get the bill?'

Jeff had not only taken himself off, he'd very considerately left a note saying, 'Back very late – don't wait up.'

I looked from this note to Guy. 'What a shame,' I said, as deadpan as I could, which wasn't saying much. 'Still, would you fancy a cup of tea or something?'

'Come here.' His voice was lovely and husky as he pulled me to him. 'And I'll give you a "something".'

I melted into sheer, glorious, wanton abandonment.

Give and take, though. Since he'd given and not taken on the beach the other night, I did my best to make it up to him. However, keeping each other on the edge for hours was never an option. His lovely rampant beast had been straining on the leash for far too long, and my own was only too happy to meet him.

As it was still barely ten o'clock we lay for ages afterwards, talking. In delicious, woozy, post-coital bliss, I had my head on his shoulder, my arm across his chest. His arm curled around me, his fingers laced in my hair. We talked about a hundred things, from the Italian way with clams, to Pudding's sulking. This led to a stray cat called Kipper that had attached itself to his mother, and that was when I felt able to ask. 'What happened?'

'Some idiot driver,' he said. 'She was crossing the road after doing some shopping. Never had a chance.'

My arm tightened around him. 'God. How awful.'

'Yes, it was. She'd dropped me off at school that morning.' There was a long pause, his fingers playing softly with my hair. 'I was sent to the Head just before chuck-out time. He said she'd had an accident, she was in the hospital. I wasn't to go home, I was to go to the Martins'.'

Lindsay and Rachel's.

'I wasn't particularly worried,' he went on. 'I was thinking broken legs, that sort of thing. I always liked going to Lindsay and Rachel's anyway. Rosemary used to do a fantastic chocolate cake now and then. And she'd done one. I remember thinking: Wow! She was more than usually nice to me, too. Said I could have anything I liked for tea. And when old Matthew came home, he was the same. Said how about a game of cricket on the lawn?'

I didn't say anything. With my own throat constricting, I thought it might sound too wobbly and shut him up.

'The old man couldn't bring himself to tell me,' he went on. 'He got my grandfather to do it. My mother's father. He was heavily into religion, that one. He kept saying, "She's with God. He knows best, and He's thought it best to take her."'

'Oh, Guy . . .'

'So that was the end of my good relations with the RE teacher at school,' he went on. 'I told him I thought atheism had a lot going for it – I was very proud of knowing that word – and when I grew up I was going to be Prime Minister and sling all the vicars and bishops into jail. And the poor old sod tried to explain that a Prime Minister couldn't do that, I'd have to be a dictator, like Mussolini. So that shut me up, because I didn't like to admit I hadn't a clue who Mussolini was. I just played the poor old sod up for ever more.' He gave a nostalgic little chuckle. '"Fielding! Are you going to pay attention?" "No, sir, I'm not."'

I could only laugh softly with him. I knew he wasn't going to dissolve, or 'let it all out', except like this. We talked of other things and I stayed awake till he'd fallen asleep in my arms.

* * *

The alarm went off at seven. I hit it with a sleepy hand, groaned, and cuddled up again. It went off again at ten past, because it was that sort of alarm clock. I'd bought it for the purpose. By the second hit you'd more or less come to terms with the fact that you had to get up.

'Hideous Monday morning,' I murmured, re-cuddling.

'Oh, I don't know.' His arm re-curled around me and he gave me a slow, sleepy smile. 'It's not looking too bad from where I'm lying.'

'I mean I've got to go to hideous *work*. And so have you, *and* you've got to go and pick up your car.' He'd left it in the long-term car park at Heathrow, and we'd flown into Gatwick.

'Stuff it.' He kissed my nose. 'Let's just go for a walk down the beach.'

'Don't!' It was torture, thinking of that. 'Why can't it be Sunday?'

'I know. Complete arse, isn't it?' His hand was moving lazily over the curve of my hip. 'Complete peachy little bottom, come to that.'

How was I supposed to get up with this going on, and his lips nuzzling my neck? 'I really must get up in five more minutes.'

'Make it twenty. There's a rather important exercise that won't wait.'

Funnily enough, signs of this were already pressing.

'Oh, yes?' I said. 'And what might that be?'

'Checking that all your little bits and pieces are present and correct,' he murmured into my cheek. 'I completely forgot my checklist last night.'

'Oh, dear.' Suddenly recalling Robbie's giggles back in Barbados, I bit back one of my own. 'I hope you weren't thinking of checking any really rude bits, like bosoms?'

From his stifled laughter, I knew he'd caught my Robbie-tack. 'I'm afraid so. Would that be too rude?'

I couldn't resist it. Turning to lie on my back, I clutched the duvet primly to my chest. 'Far too rude. I can't have *boys* looking at my bosoms, you know.'

Propped on an elbow, he gazed down at me with a delicious, lovely-kisser quiver. 'Oh, go on. I'll buy you a Mars bar.'

I'm afraid I was a little late for work that day.

Thirty-seven

I never made it to Mykonos with Lindsay. She flew to Singapore, instead, and from there she and Neil did Lombok. Her ticket was transferred to Guy and we did some island-hopping of our own, round the Cyclades in a little hired yacht called Kalypso. We moored in little bays you could only get to by boat, swam in water like liquid aquamarine glass. I took real and mental snapshots of Guy on the boat, in the sun, with the wind in his hair, the tang of the sea on his skin and on his lips when he kissed me. We sat in harbourside tavernas on warm evenings, watching the sun set over wine-dark sea. We agreed that the ancient Greeks must have had very weird-coloured wine, but that Homer had probably sunk a few when that particular simile came to him. By the end of that holiday Guy said he'd make 'competent crew' of me yet, and I'm pleased to say his water-skiing had come on no end, too.

It was only on our last evening, while we were finishing a bottle of wine at a rustic wooden table, eating fresh figs while bouzouki music wafted from inside, that he spoke to any extent about Fleur. I'd have felt disloyal bringing her up before, as if I were probing for details that should remain private. I forget how she came up, but it was during one of those conversations that drift from this to that on a whisper-warm breeze.

'It took me a while to realise how vulnerable she was,' he said. 'She covered it pretty well at first.'

I was glad he didn't say 'jealous' or 'neurotic'; hearing him denigrate her would have been the first blemish. 'Not that that was a problem in itself,' he went on. 'But it made things more difficult towards the end.'

He never actually said he'd been ready to finish it for some time, but I knew. He never said he'd hated the thought of hurting her, or that his friendship with Rachel and Lindsay would have made him feel even worse, but I read all this between the lines. I was only glad he didn't say anything I'd have hated her to overhear.

'I just wish she hadn't got back together with wretched Scott,' I said. 'I've got a horrible feeling he's one of those men who just have to prove to themselves that they can always worm their way back.'

'I'm not so sure he'd have had to do much worming,' he said. 'In hindsight, I think there was always an element of *boing boing* there.'

Rebound. If he'd never quite eclipsed Scott completely I could only be grateful, even if I privately thought Fleur was mad. 'Not at first there wasn't, or she'd never have got so wound up about the Flytrap.'

'The what?'

Eeek! I'd never let this out before. 'Just a little pet-name for Cara. As in Venus, and zips.'

He nearly choked on a mouthful of nice fresh fig.

Before I knew it we were into autumn again: Hallowe'en and Bonfire Night, and the magical run-up to Christmas. And just over a year after Andrew's wedding, we were at another. This was a much more low-key affair, as the bride didn't want a lot of fuss. In an oak-beamed function room at the Black Swan Hotel, not a million miles from Sycamore

Road, about forty guests were mingling. There was a Christmas tree in the corner, and because it had been a very chilly walk from the register office, mulled wine was on offer as well as champagne.

'Smile, Dad!' I said, as he wore a look of faintly wistful nostalgia. 'It was always on the cards that someone would snap her up eventually.'

He did sort his face out then. 'I did ask her if she'd like to give it another go,' he said. 'After Robbie was born.'

'And you know perfectly well why she turned you down. She said she'd always be on tenterhooks even if you were half an hour late back from the garden centre.'

'It's the genes,' said Midge, beside him. 'His father was just the same.'

I moved on to Fleur. Scott hadn't lasted more than a couple of months second time around. She'd told me she'd finally got him out of her system, and funnily enough it was that Tuscan holiday that had done it. He'd been boring, uninterested in virtually everything and rude to waiters. Currently very much in her system was Iain, a maxillo-facial surgeon she'd met through work.

I didn't feel funny any more on seeing her with Guy beside me, though I had at first. As I'd said to Guy, it was probably just as well we'd had those eight months in cold storage. I'd never told him, but it had occurred to me that Kay's heat-of-the-moment 'curse' might have come back to haunt her. She might have worried that it was going to backfire, that it would be the other way around. It would certainly explain why she'd been less than thrilled that Fleur and I were friends.

'I do think it's so lovely for Auntie Penny,' Fleur said, glancing at the bride. 'Alan seems so nice.'

'Apparently Robbie-proof, too.' He had grown-up children with children of their own, so young children held no horrors for him. Robbie had met his grandchildren more than once, and thank heaven they'd all got on. Mum had been in a terrible tizz about meeting Alan's own children: 'What if they resent me for taking their mother's place? Though heaven knows I'd never try to do *that*.' But it had all gone as well as these things ever can.

Eventually I got around to Kay. There were no lasting scars from her accident, or from earthy Joss. Uncle James had got on a plane within twenty-four hours of hearing that she was in hospital. ('Wouldn't you know it,' Mum had said.) And since none of us was aware of her little peccadillo (or so she thought) she hadn't lost any face. In any case, basking in the reflected glow of surgical Iain, who was evidently besotted with Fleur, she felt able to be gracious. 'Penny's looking very well,' she said.

'Yes, isn't she?' I'd like to be able to report here that there had been a tearful making-up between these two, but the estrangement had gone on too long. All I can say is that if relations still weren't precisely huggy-kissy, at least they were no longer Cold War.

'I suppose you'll be having Robbie while they're on their honeymoon?'

'Not this time.' I glanced at Robbie. He was in a posse with Alan's grandchildren. Wearing Christmas cracker paper hats, they were bustling about importantly with plates of nibbles. 'Dad and Will are taking turns.'

Her eyes went to my beloved, who was talking to Lindsay's folks. 'Has Guy put weight on? I do believe he's looking ever so slightly portly round the tummy.'

It was a comfort to know that she could still revert to her old form now and then. It made me feel better for the odd giggle over visions of her as Maleficent in Sleeping Beauty. Complete with scary, twin-pointed headdress and grey-green face, she was hurling curses over my unborn cradle. 'Oh, I don't think so,' I said, trying to keep a straight face as this vision popped up yet again. 'But even if he had, another pound or two to cuddle up to wouldn't bother me.'

'And it must be difficult when he's hardly round the corner. Distance was the main reason Fleur finished with him, you know.'

If she genuinely believed this, I could only be glad. More than once I'd thanked heaven that Guy had not seriously broken Fleur's heart. God alone knew what kind of 'curse' Kay would have come up with if he had. I'd probably be sprouting hairy green warts by now, and as for Guy, it didn't bear thinking about.

'Don't you find it a problem?' she went on.

'It's not perfect, but we manage. I might well move in the spring – there are stacks of English language schools on the south coast. I'm overdue for a change, not to mention a step up the career ladder.'

Having done my niecely bit, I went to join Guy. Now and then he'd crept into my Sleeping Beauty visions, too. After all, if you had a Maleficent you might as well chuck in a prince to sort her out. My Aurora wasn't quite the Disney version, though. She certainly didn't go around singing her head off in forests like a nutter. She'd be swimming in a crystal pool when her prince came upon her, thinking: Hey, that's not a bad idea, because he'd be all hot and sweaty from galloping his trusty steed o'er dale and forest. And of course they hadn't invented swimming costumes in those days. I'm not sure Mr Disney would have approved of the next bit, but there you go.

'I gather you two are off to New Zealand,' said Uncle Matthew.

'And Australia,' I said. 'On New Year's Eve.'

Guy slipped an arm around my waist. 'She was originally going on her own, but I talked her into taking me. I was afraid of her falling for some strapping Kiwi's bungy.'

I'd told him about Emma, but I swear I was not trying to put the wind up him.

Well, not much.

'But, Abby, weren't you going for ages?' asked Rosemary.

'Six months, but it's down to one now. Far more sensible, really, and by the time we get back at least miserable January'll be over.'

Later I got around to Lindsay, who was not with Neil. A couple of weeks after getting back from Singapore she'd met someone called Alex, who'd rather cast Neil into the shade. 'Typical,' she'd said. 'You wait all that time and then two come at once.'

She eyed Jeff, who was doing his dark-night-of-the-soul bit for a susceptible-looking niece of Alan's. He'd actually donned a suit for the occasion, and Mum had been heard to say that when he was all tidied up Jeff could really look quite presentable. 'I hope you'll make sure he can spell Hoover before you go away, or you'll come back to something out of *Life of Grime*.'

'I doubt it,' I said. 'He'll find some poor girl with a poetic soul and a pair of rubber gloves, and tell her his mind's on higher things.'

I moved her slightly out of the crush. 'I saw Cara the other week. We went to a do thrown by some old friend of Guy's, and she was there.'

'And?'

'Just the same. She said how was Rachel, she hadn't heard from her in ages, and I said, "Not surprising, is it?" OK, I didn't,' I added, seeing her face. 'I just said, "Fine." Guy was talking to someone else and I caught her eyes on him. And then she caught me catching her. She turned to me with that infuriating little smile and said, "Don't worry. I'm not going to invite myself for lunch with him."'

'You're kidding!'

'As if to imply that she only had to lift a finger,' I went on. '*Still!*'

'What did you say?'

'"Oh, feel free! He's been meaning to see you. He wants to introduce you to a friend of his who's doing a thesis on sad little compulsive predators."'

Lindsay nearly choked on her mulled wine.

'Actually, I didn't,' I confessed. 'I couldn't think of anything suitably crushing before she oozed off.'

'Did you tell Guy?'

'Of course.'

'What did he say?'

'Something satisfyingly rude. I think part of him still feels slightly sorry for her, though. He once said it's just the way she's made, she can't help it. Anyway, she's apparently going back to South Africa soon.'

'Not surprising,' said Lindsay. 'Considering the depths of winter's coming up. Flytraps need warm conditions, don't they? Their chlorophyll goes sluggish in the cold. It plays havoc with their sticky fronds.'

We collapsed into fits together.

Shortly before we left Guy and I were with Dad and Midge when David and Rachel came up. 'Aren't you the ones who got married in the summer?' Midge asked. 'On a beach somewhere?'

'It was more in the gardens,' explained Rachel. 'Though we did have a lot of lovely photos taken on the beach.'

'Dear me,' said Midge, who'd had a few by then. 'All these weddings – at my age I can't keep track.' She gave me a roguish little wink, a nudge and a whisper loud enough to carry to Banstead Downs. '*You'll be next!*'

It turned into a very protracted do. A dozen of us moved on to the Star of Siam once the Black Swan said sorry, they

356

had to kick us out, the Rotary Club was turning up in an hour.

'What is it about weddings,' said Guy, when we were eventually getting ready for bed, 'that makes elderly relatives tell every couple under eighty-five that they'll be next?'

'Tradition,' I said. 'Like the cake that hardly anybody eats. I wonder how they'd like it if we did it at funerals? Here, let me.' He was starting to remove his cufflinks, an exercise that always involved muttered cussing. 'Family weddings can be hideously embarrassing. I swear I'll never inflict another on you.'

'Hmm. Are you sure you should be making drastic promises like that?'

'Well, maybe not.' Dumping one set on the bedside table I tackled the other cuff of a Sea Island cotton shirt. I'd been known to pick up his discarded shirts and sniff them later. In fact, I'd sometimes kept one after he'd gone and used it as a sort of over-pillow. 'I suppose I'll have to stretch a point if Will ever gets hitched.'

'Or your old man. If hope continues to triumph over experience.'

'You never know.'

'Or in certain other, very specific circumstances?'

The link slipped out. I let go his wrist and looked up at him. It was rather a wobble-moment. 'There's no need to go all "specific" on me, just because I've taken your cufflinks out.'

His mouth gave that lovely, warm little quiver that still made me want to eat him. 'Are you going all shirty on me? Just because I'm getting "specific"?'

'Er, do you want a specific answer to that?'

Although he used no words, his answer was specifically clear.

IF YOU ENJOYED *MAKING MISCHIEF* WHY NOT TRY
FURTHER NOVELS BY LIZ YOUNG,
ALSO AVAILABLE IN ARROW

Asking for Trouble

It was only a little white lie . . .

Sophy's single and happy about it. She does, however,
have an imaginary boyfriend, Dominic, a little white lie
designed to keep Sophy's mother off her back.

Which is fine, until his presence is demanded at a family
wedding. So does Sophy admit Dominic is a fantasy?
Oh no. Sophy hires an escort.

But when the distinctly delicious Josh Carmichael arrives
on her doorstep, Sophy can tell things are going to get tricky.
And the wedding is only the beginning . . .

Fair Game

Let the best woman win . . .

Up to her eyes with her friends' dramas, Harriet Grey has no
time for her own. Let alone getting entangled with John
Mackenzie. He might be the most gorgeous man she's met for
ages. But he's entangled with someone else. Nina.

Glamorous Nina wasn't exactly Harriet's best friend at school,
but Harriet has principles. Still, surely one innocent little drink
to repay a favour wouldn't hurt? Her friends aren't so sure.

Harriet tries to be strict, but John Mackenzie won't stay out of
her life. When she finds herself alone at Christmas, she'd have
to be a saint to walk away. And halos never did suit Harriet . . .

arrow books

A Girl's Best Friend

'Dogs are better than men because . . .'

So says the poster on Izzy Palmer's fridge, and she's only half
joking. At a long-planned murder mystery party, Izzy has to
play scheming little tart Emerald without her boyfriend Leo,
who's let her down yet again. Cast in fiendish skulduggery
with local vet Noxious Nick, who would have been improved
by a spot of murder himself, Izzy can only grit her teeth and
play along. Not content with insulting her beloved mutt,
Henry, and telling her to hold her stomach in, Nick then has
the gall to turn halfway human just as Izzy's decided she
can't stand him.

Still, at least he provides the means of making Leo just a
little bit jealous at last, but that's all that can be said for
him. That is, until Izzy's life starts falling spectacularly apart.
Picking up the pieces on her own isn't much fun, but who
needs a rock to rely on? They only turn into hard places
when you're not looking . . .

arrow books

**Order further Liz Young titles
from your local bookshop, or have them delivered
direct to your door by Bookpost**

☐ **Asking for Trouble**	0 09 946337 7	£6.99
☐ **Fair Game**	0 09 946335 0	£6.99
☐ **A Girl's Best Friend**	0 09 946034 3	£6.99

Free post and packing

Overseas customers allow £2 per paperback

Phone: 01624 677237

Post: Random House Books
c/o Bookpost, PO Box 29, Douglas, Isle of Man IM99 1BQ

Fax: 01624 670923

email: bookshop@enterprise.net

Cheques (payable to Bookpost) and credit cards accepted

Prices and availability subject to change without notice.
Allow 28 days for delivery.
When placing your order, please state if you do not wish to receive any
additional information.

www.randomhouse.co.uk/arrowbooks

arrow books